KINGDOM

Anderson O'Donnell

Tiber City Press

The characters and events in this book are fictitious. Any similarity to real persons, living or dead, is coincidental and not intended by the author.

Tiber City Press
www.TiberCityNoir.com

Second Edition: July 2012

ISBN: 978-0615553184
Library of Congress Control Number: 2011940885
West Hartford, CT

Printed in the United States of America

For Whitney

Tiber City Calling
or
Bio-Punks on Zinc

By Jack O'Connell

Three weeks ago, I wrote the following introductory essay for Anderson O'Donnell's debut novel, *Kingdom*. This essay, I have just discovered, is now obsolete and misleading. I include it here as an illustrative comment regarding the writer and his work.

Not so long ago, I was sharing a drink with O'Donnell at the Vernon, way back in the ship room. We were tippling some Bushmills and talking, believe it or not, about Aquinas' theory of the soul and its ability to exist outside the body. Somehow, O'Donnell made an interesting connection between Aquinas and John Lydon. Or maybe it was Joe Strummer. I was about to ask for some clarification when his cell phone went off. My young friend held up a finger and disappeared into the men's room. A few minutes later he returned, shaking his head.

"There's a story about to break in Mexico," he said, sliding back into the booth. "Mutated soldier ants."

"Soldier ants," I repeated.

"Yeah," he said, nodding. "They protect the colonies. But these mutations are apparently man-made. Gigantic heads. Ridiculous strength. And get this, they can spray formic acid like their bullet-ant brethren."

"To science," I said, raising my glass.

"All about the *coulda*," he responded, quoting Patton Oswalt, "and never the *shoulda*!"

And thus, a typical night in Wormtown on the Blackstone.

Typical, in fact, of almost any night I happen to spend with the mysterious Mr. O'Donnell. Whether it be in New Orleans. Or Marseille. Or Berlin. For he is plugged-in deep. Hardwired to information sources of which most of us will never hear, let alone access. I have known the guy over 10 years now and I still have no idea where he gets the tidbits he casually lobs like plasma grenades across the saloon table. I don't even know which of the many rumors about him have any credibility.

For instance: I tend to believe that he *has* worked at a variety of weird-ass think tanks. But I doubt that any of them were located in Central America—his Spanish strikes me as classroom slick. I sometimes believe that, yes, okay, it is *possible*, however unlikely, that he once labored as a child audio engineer for Throbbing Gristle. But I reject the story that he is really the love child of Genesis P-Orridge and Lady Jane Breyer. Likewise, I have no evidence that he spent some time in a heretical Gnostic seminary somewhere in Japan. But, Jeez, the guy knows a lot about Gnosticism and where to get the best sushi in Kumamoto. (Supposedly, a place called AzumaZushi.)

What I have, like all his other acquaintances, are anecdotes both amusing and perplexing. I first met the guy at a rare reading by the late, great fantasist, Donal Zies, in the sadly defunct Roanoke Lounge down on Lafayette St. (It was a small crowd that night, but it included Patti Smith *and* F.G. "Froggy" MacIntyre and Sol Yurick.) At intermission, I went out into smokers' alley for some air. Three young punks were involved in some kind of transaction on the far side of a pink dumpster that smelled, I still recall, of burning sulfur. One of the transactees was wearing, I swear, a three-quarter-length chartreuse leather coat. Despite this fact, I tried to ignore them. Tried to dream up an opening line with which I could introduce myself to Yurick. But their haggling took an ugly turn into mother-based obscenities and some pushing and shoving. Soon, one of the trio was knocked to the ground. To this day, I don't know why I didn't just hightail it back inside or even back to the worst room I have ever had at the Chelsea. But this was the heyday of the Doc Martens steel-toe and the thought of a guy's cranium being bashed in by somebody in a chartreuse leather coat annoyed me for some reason. Also, one side of my family is loaded to bursting with cops and, I've found, in moments of stress I can give some passable cop-voice. So I turned in their direction and said something like, "Is everything alright over there?"

Realizing they had an audience, Chartreuse and his buddy took a moment to reach down and take something off the assualtee, and then strolled out of the alley. I walked over to the dumpster to give a hand to the guy on the ground but he was already upright by the time I arrived.

Seeing that I wasn't a cop, O'Donnell's first words to me were, "When did the fanboys turn vicious?"

"You okay?" I asked.

He was dressed, I'm pretty sure, in black jeans, a white t-shirt, and an old Dark Carnival tour jacket. He brushed himself down and said, "I'm just pissed. Fuckers took my rent money," then, looking up at me, added, "Are you Vinny? You here to score?"

That night I was more on the wagon than off, so I shook my head at him and turned to go back into the lounge.

"Hold on a second," he said from behind. I stopped, he came around in front of me and slapped a stained manila envelope into my chest.

"I'm not Vinny," I told him. "And I'm not here to score."

"Listen," he said, standing between me and the back door to Roanoke, "Screw Vinny, right? He's late and you're here."

"I have to get back inside," I said.

He nodded but kept the envelope pressed against my chest.

"That's fine," he said, "but I owe you. So keep this as a token."

Then he just walked away.

I never made it back into the Roanoke for the rest of Zies' reading. I never got to meet Yurick or MacIntyre or Smith. Overcome with curiosity, I made my way to that horrific Roanoke rest room and opened the envelope I'd been given. Inside was the weirdest manga I had ever encountered. You think *Uzumaki* and *Soma* are weird, kids? The stuff in O'Donnell's envelope makes them look like *The Family Circus*. The artwork was amazing and deeply unsettling. If I write, *It was like Giger on a barrel of DMT*, I would be criminally understating the case. I will admit that I am no connoisseur of the weird, but I know people who are and, when I've shown them the contents of that envelope, they react in ways that encompass aspects of both the violent and the swooning.

I left the Roanoke toilet on a mission to find the young man who'd given me this bizarre, brutal, gorgeous, epiphanous artwork: The envelope had a return address that brought me to the Gray's Papaya at 72nd and Broadway. I hung out there for three nights before I spotted the man from the alley. He did *not* seem surprised to see me. More like amused.

I introduced myself.

He surprised me by doing the same without any hesitation and, noting the similarity of our names, said, "We're bog-trotting cousins."

He bought us dogs, then took me to an afterhours club downtown, where we drank some strange hot chocolate before adjourning to the rooftop, which must have contained a half-dozen leather couches that had been ruined by the rain. There he explained that he was currently working as the North American broker for a pair of Japan-based brothers, known collectively as "Gaki."

"The online scuttlebutt,"—yes, he used that word—"says they're twins, but they're not."

One brother or the other had been trained as a pathologist. One brother or the other was severely schizophrenic. They lived, O'Donnell explained, "underground—both figuratively and literally. They come from a very wealthy family, which is utterly ashamed of them. And they're geniuses." The brothers were involved in a lifetime's project of producing an epic, serial narrative, which had no title, no captions, and no dialogue bubbles. Just images. Such as the ones I'd seen in the alley outside the Roanoke Lounge.

Though it's a great one, I won't go into the story of why and how O'Donnell eventually broke with Gaki. I will simply say that they were only one of many influences that inspired O'Donnell to leap into the world of biopunk. There are numerous others, some of which I know would surprise you. Some of which come from those subterranean information nodes, of which O'Donnell appears to have a psychic ability for locating and plundering.

The story you're about to read, *Kingdom*, is your introduction to a narrative as wild and large and exciting as anything those Japanese siblings dreamed up in their freaky little lair. The story gets bigger as you proceed. And Tiber City is just one pulsing gland inside the heaving new creature that O'Donnell has been constructing for the past decade. This is a gargantuan and complex transmedia beast, folks. And yet, you need to remember as you read that half of its DNA comes from the underground global news services into which O'Donnell is always jacked. So consider that warning your passport stamp. And hold on tight as this thrilling new writer takes you into tomorrow's territories at speeds that will rattle your spine.

Okay, now, listen: Two weeks ago, I met O'Donnell at the venerable Coney Island hot dog luncheonette here in Wormtown. I gave him the essay to read while I fetched us lunch. As usual, there was a long line and by the time I got back to our booth, O'Donnell had his head thrown back and was sort of giggling to himself.

I put his plate in front of him and asked, "What's wrong? You don't like it?"

He shook his head at me for a while and then said, "I forgot all about that shit."

I slid into my side of the booth and asked, "What shit?"

"All that stuff," he said, "About Gaki. And the crazy Japanese brothers. And their underground studio bunker."

"What are you talking about?" I asked.

"I thought you knew," he said. "I really thought that, by now, you knew."

"Knew what?" I asked, not sure I wanted to know.

"I made all that shit up."

In retrospect, I regret throwing my hot dog at him and storming out of the place. It was a juvenile and wasteful gesture. And it prevented me from asking where the original biopunk manga really came from. And, more importantly, how many of those "news stories" with which he'd bombarded me over the years he'd also invented. And, now that I think about it, who he was, and where he'd been, and why he so enjoyed blurring the lines between fiction and fact wherever he went.

Like I said, all I really know about the guy are some peculiar anecdotes. And I have no idea which ones, if any, contain some degree of veracity. For example, I wonder, today, if O'Donnell was kidding me when he told of his plans to get a bar-code tattoo, the scanning of which would allow instant download of his novel. (In fact, now that I think about it, I'm wondering if that fashion model wife and toddler son that I met last year are genuine …

or did the trickster rent some talented actors for the evening—just to mess with me?)

Of course, in the end, I suppose it doesn't much matter who Anderson O'Donnell is or what is and is not true in his personal history. What matters is this introductory visit to the ever-expanding world of Tiber City. Be careful as you walk its streets. Remain always alert. Don't take any candy from strangers. And guard your genetic material as if it were your life.

Come, make gods for us, who shall go before us; as for this Moses, the man who brought us up out of the land of Egypt, we do not know what has become of him.

–Exodus 32:1

All around the child, the land was dying.

From every corner of the burnt-out urban slum drifting past the car's bulletproof window, lights glared back at the girl. But these were empty lights that cast shadows everywhere, illuminating only the impossibly angular features of nameless faces staring down at her from the cracked screens of broken digital billboards.

This fading, pale light eclipsed all the stars the girl had once learned about in school; neon corporate logos were the new constellations by which lost men now sought direction. In this final century, there was no night and there was no day. Instead, an artificial twilight was perpetually draped over the city like a shroud. And it was through this twilight that the girl watched the slum burn.

The girl knew nothing of the slum's history; she knew nothing of the men who, years ago, came out of the desert, their black SUVs cleaving toward the edge of the continent in a blur of chrome and steel and exhaust, offering the people who lived in these forgotten slums free medical treatment, performing procedures and delivering vaccinations that would otherwise forever remain inaccessible, distant as the skyscrapers and towers twinkling on the horizon; she did not know that these strange men had demanded nothing in return, no pound of flesh—they offered only charity.

Or so the people of the shantytown had thought until tonight, when the same SUVs brought different men to the slums, men who carried machetes and guns and covered their faces. These men swept through the slum, bringing death and the oblivion of the desert with them.

The girl tried to turn away. She did not want to see the rows of men lined up, awaiting execution; she did not want to hear the screams as women and children were fed to the flame; she did not want to smell the roasting human flesh.

The girl looked across the car at her father. Why had he brought her to this place?

He only smiled.

As the car pulled away from the burning slum, the girl, with tears streaming down her face and the smell of charred flesh in her nostrils, watched as hunched figures appeared at the edge of the slums, and, moving through the darkness, began dragging several of the burnt bodies back into the desert.

Chapter 1

The American Southwest
Nov. 15, 1986
2 a.m.

The elevator raced past the research dormitories and the corporate soldiers' barracks, past the replica of Central Park and down into the earth. When it finally glided to a soundless halt, Jonathan Campbell stepped out into the seventh and final level of the Morrison Biotech arcology's research facilities.

It had been three years since Project Exodus had gone underground, since Campbell and Morrison had struck their bargain. It had been almost as long since Campbell had visited these lower laboratories that Morrison marked as his own. The two men labored separately, their results synchronized by the massive mainframe computers that linked every corner of the corporate arcology. Much of the work Morrison performed in these underground labs had been indispensable to the work Campbell performed aboveground. And so, for many months, Campbell did not question the origin of his former pupil's data: What did that matter when they were within a fingertip of curing so many of God's mistakes?

Yet the whispers had grown darker in the recent months: hushed rumors of trucks coming and going in the dead of night, urban jungles swallowing children whole, Mexican immigrants vanishing from the lands surrounding the arcology—the Chihuahuan desert. As a man who had devoted his life to science, Campbell could no longer bear the uncertainty.

Although the corridor outside the elevator was deserted, Campbell's presence would not go undetected. Security cameras craned their necks, silently transmitting a detailed bio-scan of Campbell to five different security control centers, and, inevitably, to Morrison himself. The hallway itself was little more than a tight white tunnel, funneling visitors toward a single steel doorway no more than 40 feet from the entrance to the elevator. All around Campbell the walls seemed alive with the sounds of industry: Unseen machinery hummed and whirred, greedily consuming the glut of megavoltage pumped daily into the building by thousands of miles of fiber-optic arteries. Yet as Campbell forced himself toward the door, the hallway went silent, as if the building itself was waiting for him to open the door.

Campbell punched in his security code, his fingers trembling as he entered the five digits. His code would work; he knew Morrison no longer considered him a threat. The keypad flashed red, then green and then, as he expected, the door to Morrison's research sector slid open with a barely audible hiss. Campbell stepped through the doorway, the closed circuit camera above him straining to follow his every movement. One by one, the overhead lights in the laboratory came to life, flooding the room with a harsh light. For a moment, Campbell was blinded. When the room came into focus, he screamed.

Vague approximations of human beings, sealed away in suspended animation chambers, lined the two opposite sides of the laboratory. Strange limbs protruded from the torsos of some of the creatures; others had two mouths and no eyes. Some seemed to be infected with diseases the Western world had not known for centuries. Yet, all were still alive, staring at Campbell, mute agony plastered across their faces.

Campbell stumbled deeper into the laboratory. All around him machines continued to record data on their subjects, running experiments throughout the night. Morrison had not attempted to conceal anything from Campbell: Morrison had won; there was no longer any need for secrecy between the two men. Campbell threw up twice, hard, the smell of vomit mingling with the antiseptic already in the air. All the while, Morrison's creatures continued to watch him.

When Campbell stopped retching, he noticed something he had not seen when he first entered the room: a row of incubators in the far right corner.

"No..." Campbell whispered.

Inside the incubators were four tiny babies, each one's accelerated skeletal system growth stretching the infant's skin until bones began to grind up through the flesh. Germline manipulation, accelerated growth experimentation: Campbell instantly realized that Morrison had taken Exodus beyond even his darkest fears. And staring into the incubator below him, Campbell knew he was responsible. So he ran; into the hallway and back up the elevator, lurching through the main lobby and out the front door, the ruined sky above the arcology pressing down upon him.

Chapter 2

Tiber City: Glimmer District
Aug. 26, 2015
1:15 a.m.

In a single, hard gesture, Dylan Fitzgerald leaned forward over the table and snorted a thick line of coke off its smooth black surface. The coke belonged to a guy with a greasy ponytail who was sitting across the table from Dylan, and who looked at least 15 years older than everyone else at the party that night. Dylan's old college roommates, Chase Kale and Mikey Divert, were also at the table, which was one of several arranged into a casual formation around the edges of a massive infinity pool on the rooftop of an overpriced apartment some 60-odd stories above the clogged streets of Tiber City's Glimmer district.

Dressed in a Savile Row suit that had once belonged to his father, Dylan was attending his 24th birthday party. He was not sure, however, of the name of the host, let alone the names of half the guests, and no one, except for ponytail guy, had offered him a "happy birthday." And ponytail guy had spent the last 30 minutes trying to recruit Dylan for an Internet reality show, which was not exactly the kind of birthday surprise he was hoping for.

Still, Dylan was trying to pay attention to the ponytail guy's spiel—he had promised Chase and Mikey he would listen, so he sat at the table, hoovering up the free blow and staring at the guy's ponytail as it bobbed up and down like a thick rat's tail. But guys like ponytail had been trying out their tired hustle on him for years and Dylan felt his attention wandering away from the table, over the side of the roof, and out across the city skyline.

Corporate insignias and digitalized billboards stared back at him, offering a barrage of focus group-approved advertisements and imagery. Dylan shifted in his chair and adjusted the Ray-Bans he was wearing; he was growing restless, an anxiousness that was partially the result of doing too much of the less-than-stellar blow heaped in front of him like frankincense and myrrh for the midnight messiah and partially because, as Dylan's glare strafed the skyline, there was no T. J. Eckleburg, no invitation to Disappear Here—nothing concrete upon which he could focus his discontent—only images exploding across the sides of skyscrapers before vanishing seconds later. Dylan struggled to concentrate on a single message, a single instruction, but found that impossible; the billboards and video monitors were changing too quickly, image replacing image replacing image. Immediate recall of specifics was impossible but later, when he was wandering the antiseptic aisles of a grocery store, some otherwise inaccessible alcove of his brain would awaken and drive him to purchase a new product he did not need, let alone even particularly like.

A hand pressed against his shoulder, causing Dylan to startle. He looked around the table and saw Chase, Mikey, and the ponytail looking at him, waiting for him to say something. Snippets of conversations from the party continued to drift out of the loft apartment and onto the rooftop: Two guys were both trying to explain to a girl the benefits of Sony's new 1620i resolution televisions, as though whoever provided the most coherent explanation of this important technological breakthrough would be inside her a few hours from now. For a moment Dylan was acutely aware that this was a possibility; that he was living in an age where the resolution of a man's television set and his ability to convey the importance of such resolution constituted natural selection.

"The naked eye can't even detect the difference," Dylan mumbled.

"What?"

Dylan looked around the table again and realized that wasn't the answer his friends wanted. He leaned back over the lines of cocaine the ponytail guy had laid out for him, took another massive bump and felt the world shimmer, tighten, and finally focus. In the distance, beyond the billboards and the blurred sea of brake lights, the moon hugged the horizon, too tired to finish its ascent over the massive skyscrapers vying for infinity.

"I meant, what did you say?"

"Tell me you caught at least some of that," Chase pleaded.

"I caught...some," Dylan said, the coke tickling the back of his throat. He swallowed hard.

"Bottom line here," the ponytail said, "is that it's a win-win. And it's going to be tasteful. In no way are we trying to exploit you or your family's... legacy."

Dylan felt his body tense.

"Family? What are we talking about here?"

"The Network has a few new Web reality shows debuting next month. Nothing too radical—most follow the traditional format that viewers seem to really respond to; basically we stick you and several other citizen-celebs in an enormous house, supply virtually unlimited amounts of drugs and alcohol, and turn you loose. There will be an objective of sorts, vaguely defined and open-ended—run a boutique non-profit, help poor kids, that kind of thing. We would like you to try to accomplish this goal, whatever it might be, but if that's not happening—and it's OK if it's not—all we ask is that if you choose to fuck up, fuck up spectacularly. And I'm not talking death here, although the download sales on that would be stratospheric."

"And this isn't exploitive?" Chase asked, glancing back to Dylan, trying to gauge his friend's reaction.

"Anything but, my man, anything but," ponytail insisted. "And it's not tacky. There might even be an opportunity to move beyond the established reality-programming paradigm here. Push socially conscious issues; introduce morally responsible product placement. And that's where we—you and the Network—could come together and really do something special."

To emphasize this point, ponytail brought his hands together at eye level, interlocking his fingers in a gesture that reminded Dylan of a game from childhood: here's the church, here's the steeple; open the door and see all the people.

"Come together to...?" Dylan asked, barely paying attention, focusing instead on the planes taking off on the horizon and on the idea of travel, of transcontinental flights, and how airports feel at 1 in the morning.

"Look man, I can see what you're thinking," he said. "But it's not about the money. Everyone has money. We're offering you genuine celebrity status.

Sure, people already know who you are because of your father; you've got that fallen prince thing going on, which is why, to be frank, I'm even talking to you in the first place. But we're offering you a chance to branch out and generate some celeb-currency on your own."

Ponytail offered the table a toothy, wired grin, but Dylan was already on his feet—it was time to go. The coke euphoria was fading fast and already he was feeling edgy and tense, his upper teeth hell-bent on grinding the lower set into dust. He began rifling through his pockets—iPhone, random pills, a pack of cigarettes. Pulling the Camels from his interior jacket pocket, Dylan mumbled goodbye to the table before lighting the cigarette on one of the tiki torches ringing the rooftop.

He felt guilty about leaving his friends. Chase and Mikey meant well; best friends since college, the three shared a bond that ran deep. Yet as more and more of their peers took steps in a definitive direction—marriage, law school, overdosing, Wall Street—a sense of unease had begun to descend on the trio's stage of nightclubs and narcotics. Half-baked schemes for opening bars, real estate speculation, and HBO pilots had led to increased contact with hustlers and entertainment industry bottom feeders, most of whom resembled the dude with the ponytail. But he had given the ponytail guy a chance and it turned out to be bullshit like everything else. Plus the guy mentioned his father and now, everything was fucked.

Chase and Mikey were calling for him to come back to the table, to discuss other options, other ways of making something happen. But there was no other way, no different way; it was always the same way: exploitation and degradation for cash and headlines. Dylan had experienced his fair share of all four and he was worn out, so he kept moving away from the table and around the perimeter of the unnaturally blue infinity pool. Two girls and a guy were in the pool, naked and sharing an enormous joint. The guy shouted out to Dylan, confusing him with some guy named Graham, encouraging him to get in the pool because apparently the water was fine, until one of the girls, a blonde with OK tits, giggled and whispered something in the guy's ear. He shrugged at Dylan, laughing before throwing his head back and declaring that he was fucking high, man. But whatever—Dylan was still welcome to join.

Dylan took a drag on his cigarette and considered the invitation for a moment before shaking his head. Tonight was supposed to be different, but as he pushed his way past the pool, beyond the rising stream and lights from the city reflecting off the surface of the water, everything felt the same. The girl with the decent tits giggled again, although this time the noise jumped an octave or three. Dylan winced but kept moving toward the sliding glass door that funneled revelers from the main party indoors to the pool to the balcony then back again.

Inside the enormous apartment, Dylan scanned the party, his eyes stopping on a striking, raven-haired woman lingering along the edges of the giant main room. He took a double take, wondering if the coke was cut with a hallucinogen, with something harder, because if he wasn't seeing things then standing across the room was the only woman he had ever loved: Meghan Morrison.

Dylan began to move toward her, shoving through the doorway before plunging forward into a sea of exposed midriffs and alcohol-fueled bravado, wolfish white teeth complimented by artificial tans and expensive watches. The room seemed huge, endless, and the woman he hoped was Meghan kept slipping out of view as he tried to traverse the crowd between them. A few times he thought he heard someone call out his name, but he didn't recognize the voice and simply nodded his head in return. The stereo was playing an ancient Velvet Underground tune and although Lou Reed was explaining that "there're even some evil mothers who are gonna tell you that everything is just dirt," no one was paying any attention.

Then the crowd shifted and she was gone, swallowed up by a wave of flesh. The guy who owned the place—some Russian wearing a gold coke spoon necklace; Dylan could never remember his name, let alone why he was hosting Dylan's party—came by talking a mile a minute, wishing Dylan a happy birthday and explaining in broken English how much he loved American bitches. Dylan started to ask him if he knew Meghan but before his Russian host could answer, the crowd heaved forward, knocking Dylan backward onto a minimalist leather couch. Then someone was screaming "fight" and the crowd heaved again, sending wall decorations and stacks of expensive electronic equipment crashing to the floor.

Dylan didn't see how the fight began, but that was irrelevant because he knew how it was going to end. Even before the guy with the shaved head smashed a tattooed forearm into the nose of the other guy—short, pudgy, vaguely Puerto Rican—the crowd, trained in the modern art of capturing violence, already had its phones raised and recording. Within the hour, the video would be forwarded around the globe, so some kid in Stockholm could see that kids in America bleed the same deep crimson. Whether the video caught the crunch that accompanied the pudgy Puerto Rican's septum being driven up into his brain would, of course, depend on the device performing the recording. Judging from the number of Rolexes and Tiffanys attached to the tan arms holding up the phones, Dylan had a strong suspicion that the kid in Stockholm would get that crunch in surround sound.

Later, when Dylan would think back to that night, it wasn't the sound he would remember, but the look of utter disbelief stenciled across the pudgy kid's face as he tumbled backward, an expression prompted by the realization that this moment was no longer a video game, that pressing the reset button was not an option. Seconds later the expression was gone, washed away by a tide of red as the plump Puerto Rican crashed through a glass dining room table.

An incoming plane roared overhead, bathing the loft in alternating patterns of red and white light while muting the massacre unfolding in front of Dylan. The psycho with the shaved head was screaming something, his mouth opening then snapping shut then opening again, spittle landing in front of him, his eyes bloodshot crazed. And then he was on top of his fallen adversary, oblivious to the shards of broken glass boring into his own skin, his hands moving like pistons on overdrive, pummeling flesh until that flesh gave way to bone.

As the beating intensified, bystanders jockeyed for position, each auteur trying to create the definitive narrative of the brawl, the footage that, regardless of its accuracy, would become the truth. Dylan considered this, watching the lawyers and brokers push each other aside as women pretended to look away. He was suddenly aware that he, too, was screaming, shouting, and another ringside reveler was shouting back, giving him a high-five even though Dylan couldn't remember putting his hand up.

And then he was moving, away from the brawl and back out to the rooftop, looking for Meghan, wondering if it even had been Meghan he saw and, if it had, why she had come to what was, in name anyway, Dylan's birthday party. But whatever the answers, the girl who looked like her was gone and a familiar sense of dread was beginning to descend across his psyche. He needed another bump but the ponytail guy had vanished, leaving in his wake only the faint residue of white lines on a black table like the vapor trails of the jets roaring overhead. The pool was empty too; the two girls and the guy must have split. Maybe they left because of the violence, or maybe they had just moved to a better vantage point.

Anything was possible and for a moment Dylan imagined he was falling forward into the pool; the water would be cold but cleansing and he could float down toward the light at the bottom, leading him away from demographics and downloads, mujahedeen and McDonald's, from Blu-ray and the blur of airplanes coming and going, people across the world waiting for the lives they had been promised to begin.

A hand clapped across Dylan's shoulder and there was Mikey, his mouth moving but his words muffled by the jet.

"What?"

"Cops, man. Some bitch called the cops. That's the last kind of drama you need tonight."

The Russian host appeared on Dylan's periphery, apologizing and cursing Puerto Ricans and white trash and promising more bitches and more coke— "we party all night my man," he insisted in his thick Eastern bloc accent. But the coke would be shitty and a sinister vibe, born of the violence, had settled across the party.

"We have anywhere else to go?" Dylan asked Mikey.

"The Graveyard kicked off about an hour ago. We know people there," Mikey answered, swiping his finger across his phone's touchscreen, scrolling through texts.

"We can do Abyss; End of the World party and best coke in the city," Chase chimed in, materializing at Dylan's side.

"Fuck that; Raul at No Exit gets top shit. Those psycho bikers run it in once a month—the Abominations or some shit like that."

"Red-eye to Vegas? I can call A.J. at Mirage, tell him we're coming in."

"Just got off the phone with Jose at Oblivion; VIP room reserved till 8 a.m."

Leaning forward against the railing overlooking the city, Dylan lit another cigarette as the voices continued to swirl around him. The clubs and the coke and the women were almost indistinguishable at this point but he would go anyway. It was, after all, his birthday. It was also an entirely different kind of anniversary.

Swallowing hard, trying to clear the coke dripping down the back of his throat, he exhaled, letting the smoke of the cigarette drift out into the blur of neon and skyscrapers and billboards and jets, and wondered if this was how his father felt when, on this exact night 10 years ago, he had stood alone in the presidential suite on the eighth floor of the Hotel Yorick, the world lain out before him, placed a single bullet in the chamber of a 9 mm Beretta, and blew his brains out over the balcony, raining them down along Chiba Street like confetti after a political convention.

"Fuck it," Dylan sighed, stubbing the cigarette out on the rail in front of him. "Call the limo."

Chapter 3

The American Southwest
The End of the 20th Century

After fleeing the arcology, Campbell wandered south along the shantytowns bordering the Chihuahuan, drifting through the forgotten landscapes of post-geographic America. Rock, no water, and a single sandy highway: These were the lands that had given birth to Morrison Biotechnology.

The landscape around Campbell was dying or already dead, soil and sky poisoned by the waste Morrison Biotech generated. Once there had been farmers in this land, men who coaxed life from the barren countryside. In the past decade, however, as the shadow of Morrison Biotechnology grew, these farmers had left, their crops failed. The traditions of farming passed down from father to son—practices that in past eras had withstood locust, drought, and depression—withered before this new enemy. So one by one, the caretakers of the Great American Southwest gathered up their families and departed, some pushing south into Mexico, others east toward Texas. And all the while, the arcology's towers continued to grow, piercing the sky with their crooked clusters of satellite transmitters.

While some men, like the Chihuahuan farmers, seek life wherever they can, others rush toward death; such were the men who entered these lands after the farmers left. The rogue scientists came first: Chemists set up meth-amphetamine laboratories in the basement of abandoned farmhouses while black-listed surgeons performed cut-rate surgeries across the street. Some even did both, everything the desperate and dying might need, all under one roof. And all for a small fee. There was, after all, always a small fee. And while in some parts of the globe Visa might enjoy a death grip on non-cash transactions, these outposts of the new American frontier only accepted two forms of payment: hard currency or soft flesh. Somehow, tourists always seemed to have at least one of the two on hand.

Most who made a pilgrimage to these Meth boomtowns ended up stay-ing and a new settlement sprang from the poisoned soil: liquor stores, truck stops, strip clubs, fast-food joints, and 24-hour 7-Elevens with the Sudafed sealed away behind bulletproof glass and glossy covered porno magazines promising girls who just turned 18 sucking and fucking on each and every page. It was impossible to tell where one settlement ended and the next began; at night the single sandy road leading farther into the desert was one harsh light fixture bleeding into the next

There was no point to Campbell's wandering, no particular destination he had in mind. There was no wife, no family, no children; he was killing time, waiting for one of Morrison's minions to materialize out of the shim-mering desert air and put a bullet through his skull. And yet, as the urban sprawl began to lessen, dying out under the unforgiving Chihuahuan sun, that bullet did not come.

The first few nights, Campbell crashed in hourly-rate fuck pads. However, as he continued down the solitary highway and the urban sprawl gave up more and more ground to the Chihuahuan, these motels grew increasingly infrequent. For miles, there was only the highway, framed by giant satellite towers jutting up on the horizon like crucifixes adorning the Appian Way. Now, as he contin-ued his exodus across the same lands where the Anasazi had once constructed their own culture built on cannibalism, darkness was again pressing down low and hard against the desert, suffocating the light and raising the dead.

Pushing forward, Campbell could hear packs of wild animals gathering on either side of the road, emissaries of the desert nothingness. With little humidity to trap the sun's warmth, at night the temperature in the Chihuahuan would plummet, tumbling well below freezing. These creatures had spent millennia adapting to the desert's wild range of temperature; man had yet to do so. He considered turning around and heading back toward the artificial glow on the northern horizon but the sun had already ceded most of its celestial territory to the night and Campbell knew he would freeze to death before he made it back to the settlements. A mile or so up the highway the road seemed to shift right and beyond that, there appeared to be something. And if there wasn't? Death wouldn't come from a bullet after all.

A little more than a half hour later, Campbell discovered there was something along the side of the highway after all. Rising from the cracked earth was the skeleton of an abandoned freight yard and although the entire yard was closed off from the main road by a steel fence crowned with barbed wire, the main gate, smashed in years ago, lay broken on the desert floor, its red warning signs covered by sand. The aluminum signs clanked as Campbell forced his body over them; whatever warning they offered applied to a different time. A few yards from the entranceway was a building Campbell presumed had once been the yardmaster tower, a rusty, rectangular two-story building with clapboard siding and a peaked roof that acted as the hub for all freight traffic. Tormented by the desert wind and heat, the tower's wooden exterior had begun to splinter and crack, the once proud yellow and blue color scheme reduced to variations of a washed out brown. Recently, someone had tagged the side of the building with white graffiti, spraying an asterisk in a circle over the decaying tower façade. As Campbell moved closer to the symbol, he was struck by two observations: The paint was still fresh and the job had been done in a hurry.

A fire escape ran up the back of the yard tower. Campbell trudged to the top of the ladder, then pulled himself onto the roof. From this new vantage point, the abandoned freight yard seemed to extend for miles in every direction, a sprawling industrial relic from a different America than the one he had just fled—dozens of different tracks converging upon the yard from every direction before melting into one massive primary track that ran into the building upon which Campbell now stood. Long dead signal lights constructed beside each track stared back at Campbell. Once upon a time, this freight yard helped subdue an entire continent. Now the continent was exacting its revenge.

Campbell found it difficult to imagine these tracks ever carrying freight trains. Yet, this yard had been a thriving commercial hub; the sheer amount of discarded freight was stunning. Burnt-out boxcars seemed to litter every track, some turned onto their sides, others merely left in the middle of the rails, their doors ajar. Other cars, which Campbell thought were called container cars, had been broken into, their steel bellies breached by some kind of welding tool, their cargo looted long ago.

The sun was now dropping below the horizon, lighting up the entire yard like a pinball machine, the dying sunlight bouncing off every half-buried piece of industrial treasure: steel, iron, and glass asserting their presence with unexpected majesty. As the wind whipped through the mechanical mass grave, it unleashed a mournful whistle. Looking down at his feet, Campbell noticed he was standing on top of another graffiti asterisk, also inside a circle and made with the same hurried strokes as the one grafted onto the side of the tower. A chill swept through Campbell and he wished the massacre he now surveyed was the result of a nuclear holocaust or some great plague; some brand of biblical disaster—real Book of Revelation shit. Instead, the dead eyed signal posts staring up at him were simply the result of neglect, of "number crunching" at some inaccessible corporate level, and of the blunt fact that the world was no longer what it had once been.

Not that Campbell had ever been a sucker for nostalgia: An Ivy League academic—Princeton for undergrad, Harvard for his Ph.D.—Campbell had long considered himself beyond any cheap addiction to cultural revisionism; every American neighborhood in the 1980s wasn't a fucking John Hughes movie. No time in the past was ever as good or pure as those living in the present recalled it to have been. He understood that change was not only inevitable, but the very means by which species bettered themselves. But despite his deep disdain for those who pined for some make-believe past, Campbell had been unable to shake a sneaking suspicion that here, at the end of the American century, something was going very wrong.

Accompanying this nebulous, nagging dread was a growing disillusionment with his self-styled role as a man of science. Campbell was brilliant and, for a long time, he had surrounded himself, perhaps subconsciously, perhaps not, with men who made sure he never forgot this fact. But as the years began to tumble away, acclaim bred arrogance. The partnership he had joined into with Morrison—that was designed to cure America. Now he wasn't so sure he didn't help poison her. Campbell suspected there was something necessary, something vital about the materials left to rot in this industrial depot; they had once formed the foundation of America and now, choosing to reinvent herself for the digital age, she apparently had decided she no longer required their services. This struck Campbell as an extremely dangerous proposition; he was just too exhausted to explain why. But perhaps that was best: He was growing weary of theory and wished he could somehow just reinvent himself like a pop star.

By now, the sun had dropped below the horizon, the last rays of light extinguished as dusk stole across the desert floor. Campbell snapped back to the immediacy of his situation, of the fact the temperature was dropping. He needed to find shelter.

After maneuvering his way back down the same fire escape-cum-exterior stairwell, Campbell cut around the side of the control tower and into the main freight yard. Traces of limestone and coal mingled with broken glass crunched under his feet as he pressed deeper into the yard, scanning the abandoned freight. The boxcars, the ones with the already half-open doors, would be the best bet for shelter, he reasoned.

The desert wind was intensifying, strafing Campbell's eyeballs with bursts of sand and debris as he struggled to make his way through the train yard. Before he could make it any further, however, his left foot snagged the inside of a train track, catching itself on the intersection of steel and wood. Seconds later, he was tumbling forward, the earth rising up to land a body blow. Campbell's shoulder took the brunt of the impact, but the unpleasant crash landing was nothing compared to the pain that exploded just above his right kneecap. Campbell screeched in agony. His hands shot down to his knee and when he pulled them away they were sticky with a warm liquid. He was cut. Badly.

As Campbell probed the wound, his fingers closed around something cool, metallic, and very sharp. He looked down: A large rail spike, twisted out of its natural place in the track and curled toward the sky, had helped to break Campbell's fall. Unfortunately, it had done so by driving itself through Campbell's calf. It was difficult to discern exactly how deep the wound was, although judging by the amount of blood, it sure as hell wasn't a paper cut. The pain was excruciating and he realized it was only a matter of moments before he would pass out. Summoning every last bit of will left in his body,

Campbell, digging his nails into the desert floor, dragged himself forward, sliding on his belly like a serpent. Pain laced through his leg and Campbell's consciousness began fading in and out like poor radio reception.

And then he was free of the spike, fresh, hot blood pouring out of the now-gaping wound, splashing out onto the earth as Campbell continued to crawl across the desert floor, gagging as the wind kicked the dust up past his cracked lips before mingling with the cold metallic taste rising in the back of his throat.

The last thing Jonathan Campbell remembered was wriggling toward one of the forgotten boxcars, its sliding side door slightly ajar. Another asterisk in a circle, barely discernable in the last seconds of dusk, was tattooed across its exterior. And then there was nothing but the howl of the wind.

The nightmares came hard and fast, accentuated by the fever-induced delirium gripping Campbell as darkness crashed across the land. Sprawled out on the boxcar floor, the desert winds rattling the freight's loose steel frame, Campbell spent the night in a haze, crying out as each of the creatures he encountered in Morrison's lab paraded through his dreamscapes. There were other visions as well; strange men and women creeping across the desert, moving in and out of Campbell's boxcar, working silently under a starless sky. His left leg was paralyzed with pain and, as a result, Campbell could only lie on the floor, covered in a blanket that may or may not have been in the freight last night, staring up at the side of the car, losing himself in the simplicity of the symbol tagged halfway between the floor and the ceiling. The sharp smell of spray paint permeated the boxcar, or at least Campbell thought it did, and while he recognized that this was probably an important detail, he no longer cared for such complexities and instead was content to slip back into a near-coma as darkness once again descended.

At first, Campbell thought he was having another nightmare. Lashed to an ancient gurney, he was being hustled down a bland adobe-walled corridor while strange men, their features obscured by green surgical masks and 300-watt headlamps, stared down at him. His head, like the rest of his body, was held in place by a thick leather strap so when Campbell screamed, the only ones paying attention were crude images of angels carved into the patchwork ceiling of dried earth and stone. From the corner of his eye, Campbell noticed a flicker of color; the adobe-induced monotony was shattered every few yards by a series of blurred frescos recounting the biblical punishment of Korah. The gurney, uttering terrible mechanical moans as the men in masks cajoled it across the rocky terrain, was held together by several pieces of dirty surgical tape slapped tightly around the essential load-bearing joints, and Campbell wondered if it was going to collapse, prayed it might collapse. The gurney men quickened their pace and everything around Campbell became a blur of light and pale surgical green. Nausea washed over him and just as the gurney slammed its way through a pair of plastic double doors, he lost consciousness again, slipping back into a darkness punctured by blurry images of Aaron swinging an incensor while the earth around him broke apart, swallowing men whole.

Campbell's eyes shot open, an involuntary response to the pain tearing through his entire lower left side. For a moment, the world was an explosion of hot light, the kind of light that illuminated dentists' offices and convenience stores at three in the morning. Still strapped to the gurney, Campbell could sense people moving around him, hands passing objects back and forth over his body. He tried to shout out, demanding an explanation for any of the questions racing through his mind, but his mouth felt like it was stuffed with mothballs and his speech dribbled out in a series of whimpers.

A single, massive light bulb dangled five feet above Campbell's head, engulfing the entire room with its relentless illumination. Two of the men who had pushed the gurney were now hovering over Campbell, one on either side. Seconds later, a third gurney man entered the room pushing a stainless-steel cart, its wheels squeaking as it made its way across the room and toward Campbell. Partitioned by three shelves, each level of the cart was a mess of gauze, syringes, and strange instruments that looked as though they might be useful under the hood of a car. On the top level of the cart was the biggest saw Campbell had ever seen.

"Oh God," moaned Campbell, sweat cascading down his brow as he thrashed about on top of the gurney like a fish with lungs full of oxygen. The gurney men paid scant attention to these wild movements; his body ravaged by fever, Campbell was no match for the leather bindings securing him to the gurney. Instead, the man closest to Campbell picked a syringe filled with murky brown liquid up off the cart and without warning slammed it into Campbell's left thigh. Loaded with morphine, the needle pierced a large blue-green vein traversing the length of Campbell's left leg, instantly flooding him with a twisted euphoria. Seconds later, entranced by the beautiful numbness blooming throughout his entire central nervous system, Campbell passed out.

"You won't feel a thing," commented the gurney man closest to Campbell.

And he was right; even when they re-broke the bones in his leg and began scraping away the destroyed ligaments, Campbell never felt a thing.

For several nights, Campbell lingered in chemical twilight, drifting in and out of consciousness. At some point in time, his naked body had been transferred from the gurney to an actual bed and this was where he now found himself, in a massive hall filled with other small beds. The beds were arranged in two rows facing one another with space cleared down the middle. A few gurney men moved about the room, tending to the occupants of each bed. Campbell cried out to them but they ignored him and continued to move back and forth between the various beds. He still had no idea where he was or why he was even still alive, but he was getting tired of other people making that decision for him. He could remember nothing about the past week; everything after the freight yard was a blur. And the people who might be capable of filling in the blanks were in no hurry to do so.

Inhaling sharply, Campbell ripped the IV from his bruised inner arm before swinging his lower half over the edge of the tiny, sweat-soaked mattress. Pressing his right leg down on the cool concrete floor, he pushed his body forward, transferring his weight from right to left as his muscles, dulled by inaction and morphine, returned to life with a series of spasms. And then Campbell was tumbling forward toward another bed, his body refusing to aid him in his escape plan. Throwing his arms out over his face, Campbell braced for the impact, which arrived a half a second later as he landed on top of another patient, bone meeting bone with a sickening crunch. Campbell, the bed's occupant, and the bed itself all crashed to the floor, an IV stand chasing after them. The other patient was thrashing about under the sheets, screeching incomprehensibly. Campbell tried to put his hand over the other patient's face but the man would not stop screaming and now there was movement rippling across the room as other guests of the gurney men, roused by the commotion, began stirring.

Realizing that the already narrow window for escape was about to get a whole lot smaller, but before he could drag himself to his feet, Campbell found himself beneath the other patient, gagging as breath, ragged and rank, exploded in bursts, centimeters from his face. But it wasn't a man that was on top of Campbell. It was something else, a creature with thick, hairy teeth protruding from where its eyes should have been and a half-developed, puss-caked appendage protruding from the side of its neck. The creature seized Campbell with swollen, six fingered hands, pinning him to the earth as it tried to force speech from its ruined vocal chords.

"Kill...Kill me. Now. Kill. Me. Now. Kill me now," the creature wheezed.

Screaming, Campbell heaved the monstrosity to the ground and began scrambling backward on his hands. The gurney men were moving toward Campbell, syringes at the ready. Prepared to make a final stand, Campbell attempted once again to pull himself to his feet. It was at this moment, however, when Campbell realized the lower portion of his left leg was covered in blood-soaked gauze. He stopped screaming and just collapsed.

A needle pricked the back of Campbell's neck but he barely felt it. The creature was still crying out to Campbell as the gurney men dragged it away because it knew, just as he knew, that they were kin. Campbell was the father, and the creature, the creature was the son; two members of the same terrible brood born deep below Morrison Biotechnology.

Chapter 4

The American Southwest
The End of the 20th Century

For the rest of his life, Campbell would bear the mark of the gurney men, the men he now knew as members of the Order of Neshamah.

He had remained in their custody for weeks after his encounter with the creature, convalescing alongside those he had helped ruin. And then, one morning, he woke up in a nameless motel near the Texas-New Mexico border, naked with only a single pair of pants left atop a rickety dresser, along with his ID and credit cards. His leg ached and at that moment he would have performed any number of reprehensible acts for a few opiates and a shot of Jameson. There was, however, no scar; only a deep, consuming pain that expanded then exploded when he swung his legs over the side of the bed and onto the floor. Gritting his teeth, he managed to weave his way to the shower.

Stepping under the piss warm water dribbling from the motel showerhead, Campbell felt a new pain, one that dwarfed the discomfort in his leg and drove him to his knees. Staring down into the drain, he noticed the water collecting around a hairball missed by the maid was pink. A cold panic washed over him, twisting his stomach into knots, and he began running his hands over his arms, his legs, his torso, searching for the source of the blood:

nothing. The panic mushroomed and he saw stars, little explosions of light dancing across his field of vision as he tried to retain consciousness.

Campbell managed to stumble out of the shower before collapsing, bits of broken tile piecing his skin as he hit the floor. That's when he saw it: Reflected back from the cracked mirror fixed to the ceiling, running the length of his back, was an enormous tattoo—still fresh, the skin still raw—of an asterisk in a circle. He had been marked.

In the following years, Campbell would court oblivion, trying to escape the things he had done and the things that had been done to him. And yet, no matter how deep into the American night he sank, the mark remained, both a reminder and a warning. Yet Campbell believed the mark was also a promise that, one day, he might be forgiven.

Until that day arrived, he would remain a shadow, a former colossus consigned to the fringes of the fading century. Specific details from his days in exile were impossible to recall; his memories were a blur of biker bars, methamphetamines, and cocktail waitresses. Eventually, Campbell had found himself on the edge of the Vegas Strip. He overdosed once, twice, but even the third time wasn't the charm. He bought a gun and on more than one occasion, wrapped his lips around the barrel. One night, however, stood out from the rest.

He had been at some strip club on the outskirts of Vegas and it was the pre-dawn crowd, with the pre-dawn dancers presenting their decidedly pre-dawn wares next to a picked-over buffet table. Motorhead's "Ace of Spades" pumped from a decade-old sound system while junkies and single mothers flashed tit on stage, feigning arousal at 4 o'clock in the morning to a crowd of exhausted second shifters, bikers, and ageless drunks sulking in the shadows. Campbell was in the corner, chasing Benzedrine with bourbon, and then bourbon with Benzedrine, just trying to build up the courage to die, when he saw it: Mounted over the bar was an ancient CRT television monitor, the only one not tuned to a horse race or ballgame—or maybe it had been and the news feed had interrupted the broadcast. Regardless, there it was: The press conference of his old pupil, Michael Morrison, announcing that Morrison Biotechnology would break from its long-standing tradition of political neutrality and endorse a candidate for the U.S. Senate.

It wasn't seeing Morrison grinning through the flickering satellite feed that sent Campbell stumbling back to his motel room to finally pull the trigger; it was the young congressman—a Robert Fitzgerald, the screen informed him—standing next to Morrison at the press conference. Campbell had seen this man before, only he hadn't looked quite so dapper. But, considered Campbell, it's hard to pull off dapper when you're half-formed and floating in a vat miles beneath the Chihuahuan desert. Even now, Campbell could remember laughing hysterically at that notion, laughing and crying until a bouncer dragged him off his bar stool and cast him out into the moonless night; the radioactive glow of neon from the crumbling core of Vegas was Campbell's only guide as he weaved back toward his motel and the single bullet that would allow him to fade into the blackness he so desperately sought.

When he returned to his motel room, there had been a letter waiting for him, a note bearing the same symbol that was tattooed across his back, a rosary, and an address: 321 Easton Ave., Tiber City. Campbell put the gun away, but kept a bullet in the chamber.

All night, the pay phones lining the back wall in the Greyhound bus station rang.

At first, Campbell answered, picking up the sticky metallic handset on the third or fourth ring. Each time, however, the line was dead. Giving up, Campbell retreated to a corner of the station with a bottle of whiskey, the onset of Benzedrine withdrawal gnawing at the edges of his frayed nervous system.

Located on the western edge of the desert, the bus station was too far away from the Strip to attract tourists. Instead it hosted a collection of the souls Vegas had broken: not the businessman flying home to the little woman with a substantially smaller bank account, but the showgirl, the real estate hustler, the valet, the handicapper who caught a hot streak five years ago and decided to stay; the people who couldn't leave until Vegas cycled them through the system, using them until they broke before discarding them on the edge of the desert. Cities like Vegas were machines; human flesh and blood were the gasoline. The phones continued to ring; sudden, strident cries with no discernable pattern or purpose. For a moment, Campbell wondered if he was hallucinating; it had, after all, been a fucking long night. He scanned the station, searching for an indication he was not the only one who heard the phones, but the bus station was empty except for two homeless black men and a plump teenage girl in fishnets who was crying, her mascara running down her cheeks as she sniffled. There was also, Campbell noticed, a trannie leaning back against a pinball machine on the other side of the station, leopard skin skirt hiked up past bruised thighs, legs spread with mutilated genitalia visible whenever the screen mounted above the game cycled through the high scores.

While the girl and the trannie were oblivious to the phones, the homeless men were visibly panicked, their bloodshot eyes darting from the phones to Campbell, back to the exits, and finally, back to the phones. It made Campbell dizzy and the whiskey wasn't sitting well; nausea began to rise in his throat. Then he was on his feet, rushing past the homeless men. Campbell's sudden charge toward the bathroom was the last straw; the two homeless men took off, shuffling back into the night.

Seconds later he was alone in the unisex bathroom, the mosaic of reds and browns lining the inside of the toilet bowl fueling his nausea, the smell of regurgitated whiskey sealing the deal.

After staring into the mirror for five—or was it 15—minutes, Campbell wiped his mouth on the sleeve of his Salvation Army jacket and headed back out into the station's waiting room just in time to see the chubby girl board a bus to L.A. She was no longer crying, just the occasional sniffle, although the mascara had left two long black streaks connecting the bags under her eyes to the cold sores above her lips. She was heading toward one end of America, leaving Campbell alone—save for the comatose transvestite—waiting for his ride to the other.

A strong, hot wind had kicked up and the station's foundation groaned while the palm trees outside the grimy glass door pitched so far forward Campbell was convinced they would snap in two, crashing through the roof and rendering everything that had happened to him irrelevant. Occasionally, the wind would blow so hard the door would pop open, wind and debris rushing into the breach.

Campbell struggled to stay awake as his eyes began to shut involuntarily; he suspected that his odds of escaping Vegas alive would decrease dramatically if he fell asleep. Funny, he considered, only a few hours after almost committing suicide, staying alive was suddenly his priority.

Eventually, Campbell's bus arrived and as he moved to the boarding area he noticed that one of the phones—the very last one in the row—was off the hook, dangling from its armored cord inches off the floor. Campbell shut his eyes tight and tried to remember whether the phone had been like that the

entire night. For a moment, he was convinced the last phone had been hanging there for all eternity as the voice on the other end continued to speak
without a response, insistent and determined to communicate the incom-
municable.

Suddenly all the other phones began to ring at once, jarring, mechanical
cries that rose up in concert, breaking the wind's dull roar. Campbell was
filled with a sense of dread and he began to jog toward the exit. He pushed
open the glass doors, moving past the tattered missing-children posters taped
to the glass and out into the depot, the phones still calling to him. He was
running now, careening toward the idling bus, the entire depot awash in a
sick, soft florescent glow.

Taking the steps two at a time, Campbell bounded aboard the bus, his
hands trembling as he looked down at his ticket before handing it over to
the driver:

Tiber City, One Way.

For days, Campbell's bus crawled across the American landscape
as he drifted in and out of slumber; it seemed that every time Campbell
approached something resembling a genuine REM cycle, the bus arrived at
another station in another town ripped from Americana mythology, garish
lighting and muffled announcements over the intercom jarring him awake.
Sioux City, Des Moines, Allentown; Burger King, McDonald's, Arby's: each
new stop indistinguishable from the last, a blur of downsizing and outsourcing and stadium naming rights. SUVs and minivans rocketed past the bus
and Campbell tried to remember when the backseat of cars turned into de
facto movie theaters; every car that shot past him sported two or three miniature LCD monitors extending from the ceiling, giving off an artificial flicker
as jump cuts destroyed the attention spans of a generation. Once upon a time,
Campbell considered, backseats were reserved for an awkward fuck on a Sat-
urday night; now they belonged to computer-generated Disney characters.

These were the things Campbell thought about as night bled into day
and back into night and then the voice over the intercom was calling out
"next stop Tiber City." There was no iconic entryway to Tiber City, no massive bridge to traverse, no mountain range to subdue: The highway ended and
the city began and only the massive skyscrapers looming in the distance gave
any visual evidence of the city's size. Campbell wondered how long the trip

had taken. Days? Weeks? Hours? Even the date was uncertain; newspapers scattered on the floor of the bus each offered differing opinions. It was the end of the American century and Campbell was limping out of a bus station in Tiber City in search of an address scrawled at the bottom of an anonymous letter: At the moment, he could be sure of nothing else.

The moon was nowhere to be found when Campbell stumbled out of the station and into the street but the downtown financial district threw enough light over the horizon that the slums ringing the city were bathed in a perpetual twilight. Campbell's legs were stiff and unresponsive and the world was swimming as he tried to ward off chemical withdrawal. The Benzedrine ran out somewhere in Ohio but that was only part of his problem: There were chemicals he had shot into his system when he was with Morrison, chemicals that helped his body defy the aging process, complex compounds that he could approximate through black market connections; he would often do a little work in return for the materials he needed. At best though, his supply was inconsistent; in Tiber City it was nonexistent.

A steady rain sizzled down against the pavement as hustlers descended upon Campbell, watches, wallets, and phone sex advertisements waved in front of his eyes, sales pitches and sob stories delivered in a dozen different dialects as the rain continued to bounce off the roofs of cars and broken neon signs. In the distance Campbell could see two spotlights strafing the sky and then he was moving away from the masses mobbing the bus station and into a cab, rumbling through the broken streets of Tiber City.

Campbell didn't remember telling the driver where he was going but before he could say anything the cab door opened and the driver was already explaining to him in broken English how much he owed. Unable to understand the exact amount requested by the driver, Campbell thrust a fistful of crumbled bills at the driver, who took them but not without admonishing, or was it warning, Campbell about…What? His accent was too thick and it was possible the man—older than Campbell originally assumed, with strong body odor and several missing teeth—was not even speaking English but another ancient language that whispered of ritual, custom, and gods long dead. What was the man trying to convey? It didn't matter because the next minute the door slammed shut, water splashing up against his jacket as the cab sped away from the curb and into the night.

Campbell could hear cars in the distance—the familiar sound of automobiles coasting through the enormous puddles; that rolling, elongated whoosh as rubber meets rain—but the streets in front of him were deserted. He tried to read the sign hanging off an overpass several dozen feet down the road but it was too far, the night too dark.

There was movement behind him. He spun around, noticing—for the first time—that amidst the abandoned row houses and dead neon was a bar. A man shuffled out of the front door, his eyes tracking the pavement as he drifted into the night. Muffled noises carried out from the inside and a tiny crack of light spilled out of the darkness, just enough to illuminate the name and address scratched over the doorway: Lazarus. And, below that: 321 Easton Ave.

Campbell felt his heart leap and he took one step toward the building's entrance and then another and he was moving, pushing his way past the steel door into the bar. He was greeted by a wall of warm, stale air and the sound of a cue ball breaking rack.

He stood in the entrance for a moment, scanning the room, looking for something, anything that could help explain the nightmare his life had become. Yet, whatever he had expected to find, he was pretty sure this wasn't it.

Weaving his way across the room, Campbell stepped unsteadily over puddles of spilled beer, crushed cigarettes, and a discarded condom, which may or may not have been used. There seemed to be blood streaked across the wood paneled walls but it was too dark to tell for sure. He managed to pour himself onto one of the stools lining the bar, signaling to the monster tending bar for a drink as he struggled to maintain consciousness. How long had it been since he had last eaten? Hell, when was the last time anything other than whiskey or speed passed between his lips? Catching his reflection in the mirror behind the bottles lining the back wall of the bar, Campbell was struck by how quickly he had aged and suddenly the fact that he had fled the desert, that he had fled Vegas, that he hadn't deep-throated the desert eagle tucked away in his bag and pulled the trigger seemed ludicrous. The image reflected back at Campbell was that of a dead man: Why drag out the inevitable?

But sitting there in a tiny bar somewhere in the slums ringing Tiber City, listening to the rain pound the tin roof overhead, his joints on fire, Campbell knew he couldn't walk away.

And then the bartender—a giant in jeans and a faded white oxford shirt rolled up at the elbows to reveal thick hairy wrists and a mosaic of tattoos—

was pouring two shots of Jameson: one placed in front of Campbell, the other for himself.

"Welcome to Tiber City," he said, raising his shot glass toward Campbell as an old jukebox kicked back to life and three seconds of vinyl scratch introduced "Highway to Hell" with Bon Scott assuring the darkened bar that he was still on his way to the promised land.

Campbell raised his shot as well, tapping the rim of his glass against the bartender's. He opened his mouth to return the greeting but as the bartender finished his shot and raised his hand to wipe his mouth, Campbell saw it: Tattooed just above the man's right wrist was a circle with an asterisk in the center.

Campbell's arms and legs went numb as the shot glass crashed to the floor. He tried to get off the stool but his body was done and the world went fuzzy, disintegrating as if it were a movie shot by a student filmmaker who just discovered the soft focus lens. And then he was falling and the last thing he remembered was waiting to hit the floor. But he never did.

Chapter 5

New Mexico
Aug. 25, 2015
11:22 p.m.

The Morrison Biotech arcology pierced the rust-colored sky high above the New Mexico desert, a twisted mass of satellite receivers and helicopter landing pads, all designed to extend man's influence beyond its natural boundaries. Strange purple and orange hues danced around these upper levels of the arcology, stratospheric symptoms of a poisoned atmosphere that pressed low against the desert, choking out whatever sparse life still remained. Toxins drifting downwind from Los Angeles, smoke from the border riots, meth labs littering the Chihuahuan desert; all these contributed to the pollution that hung like a rotting crown around the headquarters of one of the world's most powerful corporations. The never-ending surge of Mexican immigrants had rendered traditional geo-political boundaries irrelevant and whether Morrison Biotech was bound by the laws of the United States or Mexico was a matter of open dispute. However, as long as the corporation stuffed cash into the pocket of politicians from both sides of the Rio Grande, there was no rush toward resolution. Mexico was a failed state run by narco-terrorists and the United States was especially fond of Morrison Biotech's shadowy existence—the company's private security forces filled these power vacuums nicely, providing a buffer between the interior United States and the chaos along her borders. Subsequently, for CEO Michael Morrison, acid-tinged rain and a strange sulfuric smell were a small price to pay for the pleasure of doing business in the Chihuahuan.

On most nights, Morrison spent long hours alone in his office on the 21st, and final, floor of the biotech arcology—the sprawling, self-sustained research facility where Morrison's most skilled scientists both worked *and* lived—staring into the nothingness of the New Mexico night. Sixty-five years old, Morrison had twisted science, achieving an ageless appearance. He was neither young nor old but reaped the benefits of both; Morrison's physiology was the flesh and bone equivalent of a masterfully tuned sports car. While forced to temper his epidermal alternations—only so much could be attributed to plastic surgery—the nine systems scattered throughout Morrison's anatomy could now only vaguely be called human.

Yet, tonight, Morrison turned away from the desert he had created. Clenched in his right hand were the latest results from the labyrinth of labs buried so deep under the arcology that a direct nuclear blast would only rattle a few test beakers; his scientists again failed to replicate the Omega gene—that was the name his company had given to the final gene in the human genome whose function remained a mystery.

Morrison had read the report twice, absorbing the graphs and numbers with preternatural speed, before feeding it into the cold blue flames dancing in the open hearth fireplace that was the center of the office. The time for his scientists, considered Morrison as he watched the flames devour the report, had passed.

From the darkness swirling below Morrison's window came a sudden explosion of light noise—steel scraping steel, followed seconds later by the unmistakable short bursts of automatic weapon fire. Morrison moved back toward the window, watching with vague interest as tracer rounds lit up the desert night. This was not the first time his private militia would have to repel an armed assault against the facility; speed freaks never seemed to learn. Every few months, another group of outgunned meth addicts, roaming the desert like nomads, borne by Harleys instead of dromedaries and looking for the cheapest way to stay high, assailed the outer perimeter, attempting to break into the laboratories Morrison had spent a lifetime creating as if they were no more than an upscale Rite Aid flush with pseudoephedrine. And despite the fact that the facility's integrated defense systems rivaled that of some smaller European nations, still the border tribes came, flinging them-selves upon Morrison's corporate fortress, frothing like mad dogs.

Usually these assaults lasted less than 30 seconds; tonight's was no dif-ferent: By the time the Benzedrine-fueled Bedouins had reached the perim-eter of the arcology, the Electro-Optical High Energy Laser Systems were already online, strafing the sand and stone, cold blue light lashing out from the omnipotent eyes of Morrison Biotech's defense systems turning flesh into ash until there was nothing but silence washing across the dunes. Frequently, Morrison's Predator drones would be waiting in the poisoned atmosphere high above the Chihuahuan, beryllium birds of prey circling the landscape with infinite patience. On such nights, the desert junkies never even got close enough for their CCTV close-up; the only notice of their execution was a twinkle in the heavens. Morrison imagined women and children packed into one of the overcrowded refugee camps along the Rio Grande mistaking the deployment of a Predator missile for a shooting star, making a wish as a $40 million toy dealt death from impossible heights.

Morrison's defense systems fell silent and a stillness collapsed across the desert as the landscape settled back into itself, ancient sands digesting the still smoldering corpses. It was an almost holy rite, considered Morrison, the way in which the desert sand and wind could wipe away evidence of a civili-zation's triumph as well as its failure, cleansing the path for the next rise and inevitable collapse. In the beginning, there was the nothingness of the desert. And in the end, there would be the nothingness of the desert.

Two hours later Morrison was aboard his private jet, thundering away from the desert and toward the East Coast. He sat silently in the darkened coach as his plane cut across the sky, miles above the cities that sprawled infi-nite in every direction, a never-ending sea of blinking light patterns that cre-ated an artificial twilight as constant and tranquil as the tide. Staring down from 25,000 feet, Morrison observed as these light patterns danced across the land, consuming the fruited plan. Eventually, he knew, any remnants of America's majestic solitude would vanish completely, leaving a single mas-sive post-geographic network of light and information. No one would ever be alone and yet, everyone would be alone: So would be Morrison's kingdom.

However, before these things could come to pass, Michael Morrison needed to pay a visit to an old friend.

Project Exodus Memorandum #25-98541-B
Re: The Order of Neshamah

Although little is known publicly about the Order of Neshamah ("Order"), Morrison Biotechnology operatives have been able to engage several purported members; the information contained in this report is the result of these engagements.

Background

The Order was originally founded by a group of 19th-century monks devoted to the cultivation of the human soul. But what made these monks so different, what distinguished them from other monastic organizations, was their quest to understand the soul's function from a biological, scientific standpoint. The moniker "Neshamah" is a reference to the Hebrew word for the "soul" as the thing that allows for the awareness of the existence and presence of God. In its earliest incarnations, the Order's search for the soul focused primarily on rudimentary mapping of the brain—neuroanatomy— as well observing and recording the phenomena of religious experiences. Much of this primitive neuroanatomy involved comparing the various sections of the human brain with those of other monks and holy men—priests, rabbis, shamans—trying to find some genetic distinction that would explain why some men are so readily able to experience the mystical, to commune with a dynamic external presence so often referred to as "God."

The Order maintains at least three separate "camps" in the United States. The purpose of these camps reflects the two-fold mission of the Order: to identify and cultivate the human soul. Advances in medical technology—brain scanning tools in particular— allowed the Order to make steady progress toward isolating the section of the brain responsible for producing the responses documented during religious experiences. While the brain scanning continues in these camps, the monks also serve as doctors to the legions of illegal immigrants and uninsured slum dwellers that make up the urban core of many American cities. By serving the suffering and dying, the members of the Order seek to submerge the self, thereby increasing their sensitivity to the divine. While the veracity of these fantastic claims is impossible to verify, the intelligence methods used to gather this information strongly suggest that our sources at least believe such "service" has a direct impact on the ability to experience religious or supernatural phenomena.

Ties to Jonathan Campbell

Campbell has been in contact with the Order for the past several years. As previously discussed, he was recovered by the Order from an abandoned freight yard several miles away from the arcology. Since that time, Campbell has remained associated with, although not a member of, the Order. Through the Order's not-inconsiderable "underground" associations, the monks were able to supply Campbell with an anti-aging serum, a crude approximation of the Treatment that has nevertheless proven to be effective enough. Despite his advanced age, Campbell remains in outstanding physical condition and has retained all of his considerable intellect. While it is unlikely that these injections will sustain his condition for any extended length of time, for now they have allowed Campbell to remain an active, albeit informal, member of the Order.

Campbell's exact role in the Order remains unclear: He works in the "field hospital" sections of the camps, tending to the sick and dying; his motivations for doing so, however, are difficult to discern. Some of those braced by our operatives believe Campbell to be little more than a mercenary, working to ensure himself continued access to black market medical materials. Others speculate that Campbell is providing Neshamah with assistance in its search for the biological soul, which, given his background in genetics, seems plausible.

Conclusion
Presently, the Order of Neshamah presents little, if any, threat to Morrison Biotechnology. Jonathan Campbell's association with the Order will, however, continue to be monitored.

Chapter 6

Tiber City: Glimmer District
Aug. 27, 2015
1:18 a.m.

As the limo drifted through the streets of Tiber City's Glimmer district, Dylan stared out the window, watching as an abandoned Ferris wheel churned against the horizon. One of the passenger buckets was on fire, a solitary flame pressing against the blackened sky like a signal flare from a dying land, an SOS that would never be answered.

Dylan tried to remember if he had ever ridden the Ferris wheel as a child—or any Ferris wheel for that matter—but when he shut his eyes there were no original memories, just a series of images from popular culture, the collective understanding of childhood replacing his own.

A panic washed over him and he opened his eyes and the Ferris wheel was still rotating but the flaming bucket had dipped back below the horizon and before it could resurface, the limo turned a corner and the landscape shifted: Skyscrapers rose out of the concrete like weeds made of steel and glass, some adorned with names Dylan knew in that dull, impassive way most recognize the public monikers of nebulous financial groups, subsidiaries, and international holding companies. Other towers went nameless, barely visible street numbers stenciled over the entrance the only means of differentiation.

The limo turned another corner, past the hordes of glitterati, those Gucci-clad vampires ready to devour each other whole, held at bay only by the modern-day talismanic magic of the red velvet rope, then another, before turning onto Chiba Street: playground of Tiber City's mega-elite, ground zero of which was the infamous Hotel Yorick—the same hotel in which his old man ate a bullet years ago.

The limo was not supposed to take this route; there were other ways to go, other paths through the Glimmer district that could take the revelers to whatever destination they desired—any way but past the Yorick.

And then Dylan saw it: Illuminated against the glow of the city, his father stared back at him from the side of one of the anonymous skyscrapers, the man's face blown up and expanded to cover several stories, framed by reds and blues and whites, vague hints of Soviet-era realism and a single word spelled out underneath his face in bold lettering—**PROGRESS**. As the building drew closer, the face's similarities to Dylan's father blurred and then, as the limo sailed past, faded—except for the eyes: Those were his father's eyes. Dylan swallowed hard and considered demanding the limo halt its march through the city, then ordering everyone to inspect the massive ad—was it for a movie? A band? A brand? Was it a misguided attempt at art? Was it some sort of, oh fuck, *a statement* for Christ's sake?—and assure him that the man staring out across the horizon, staring in the direction of the Ferris wheel on fire, past the Hotel Yorick, was not his father, that the confusion, or was it a hallucination, was simply the result of having done too much coke and because tonight, after all, was not only his birthday but the anniversary of his father's death although, depending on the exact time, the exact anniversary of those events—of Dylan's birth and his father's death— may have been yesterday but what the fuck was the difference? Ever since his old man had shoved the barrel of a Beretta into his mouth and pulled the trigger, Dylan's birthday had nothing to do with celebration: only oblivion.

The PROGRESS ad was receding into the distance and when Dylan turned his attention back to the limo, it was clear that no one had noticed. The limo turned off Chiba Street, heading down a poorly lit alleyway, and the Hotel Yorick vanished, obscured by the neon and the looming, terrible skyscrapers. He was still sweating though, his heart slamming into his rib cage with a frightening ferocity, and then he was trying to ask which club they had settled on—Void or Absolution—because he needed to say something, anything.

His mouth—dry and numb, a bitterness lingering in the back of his throat, under his swollen, fat tongue—was moving and he was saying something, asking about where the limo was going but no one seemed to know; he mentioned something about the fight, trying to distance himself from the PROGRESS ad, from the Hotel Yorick sighting, but people were shaking their heads: What fight? It dawned on him he had no idea who he was speaking to: Chase and Mikey were on the other side of the cavernous car, miles of leather and mirrored glass slapped over wet bars illuminated by dozens of weak white lights separated them from Dylan, and there were other people in the car, people he had never met or maybe he had and their names were already forgotten and then a girl—blonde, beautiful in that way only American girls can be beautiful but wearing too much makeup, too much leather, too much silver—was whispering in his ear, asking if he had any more coke before confiding in him that she was afraid because she heard that in London the government was considering stacking corpses in graves because they were running out of space but that the whole situation might be OK because only abandoned graves dating back more than 100 years would be disturbed.

Her hand was on his thigh as she was telling him this, her fingers— immaculately manicured, her nails adorned with a garish red—crawling toward his crotch but then the limo was stopping and people were getting out and the girl was trying to pull Dylan toward the door but he resisted, hanging back until the last possible second, until the point where if he waited any longer there would be concerned inquires, knowing looks exchanged followed by encouragement to bump another line because like, after all, everyone's waiting.

Not that another bump was a bad idea: He couldn't shake the memory of the PROGRESS poster, of the man's eyes boring a hole in the horizon, eyes that reminded him so much of his father. Reaching into the breast pocket of his suit jacket he produced a small glass vile half-filled with white powder, a little bit of which he proceeded to dump out on the faux granite surrounding the wet bar. He used a credit card to divide the coke into two fat lines, one for each nostril. Seconds later both lines were gone and the memories of those eyes staring back at him from that monstrous skyscraper? Fucking irrelevant.

Laughing at nothing, his world suddenly very bright, tight, and shiny, Dylan kicked open the car door and launched himself into the street. A crowd had gathered outside the entrance to the club—there was no name anywhere on the building's exterior, not even a symbol ripping off some long-forgotten culture, some kind of ancient totem turned marketing gimmick. There were velvet ropes running in every direction but each time Dylan approached one a voice crackled over a headset and an instant later a hand appeared from nowhere, removing the rope, allowing Dylan to continue past the crowds, past the voices shouting—he heard Spanish, English, Russian, Arabic—the different languages all conveying a single frenzied emotion: want. Several flashes went off, prompting Dylan to turn in the direction of the light. Someone was shouting his name and he was smiling at no one, at everyone, his jaw clenched tight from the coke.

Dylan pushed forward into the club, confused, the coke racing through his nervous system. And then someone was welcoming him—not to any specific destination, simply "welcome"—offering to take the coat he wasn't wearing before ushering him through the doorway and propelling him into a shadowy hallway, the only light coming from a chandelier hanging over-heard, a security camera nestled between the fake candles. The hall was empty, serving only to funnel customers toward a staircase 30 or 40 feet beyond the entrance. Dylan proceeded down the hallway, one hand on the wall, tracing the bumps of plaster under the yellowed, peeling wallpaper—pre-aged for effect by an interior design company—imagining they were a new form of Braille, a secret language capable of providing an answer, some wisdom or guidance, if one knew how to interpret the patterns hidden behind the paper. But such divination was beyond Dylan and he began to climb the stairs, nodding at another bouncer stationed at the top of the flight.

The main room of the club reminded Dylan of every other bar in Tiber City's Glimmer district: dance floor in the middle of the room, with several tables and three bars framing the perimeter. On the far end of the dance floor, three or four steps off the floor, was the VIP area. The aesthetic was a schizophrenic mess, a victim of several ownership changes and desperate attempts to graft edginess and authenticity onto an otherwise nondescript building. Genuine was not a necessary trait however; illusion was the only requirement. Allow the 20-somethings, or even the Peter Pans pushing 40, to believe they were somewhere happening, somewhere hip: That was the goal. So, vague concepts were slapped together to procure capital and then half-heartedly implemented, the illusion of exclusivity manufactured, and—voila—you have Void or Absolution or No Exit or wherever the fuck Dylan now was.

The current décor was Victorian mansion: low lighting with lots of plush, over-stuffed chairs and couches, chandeliers with electric candles, a fireplace, velvet drapes, several ancient London newspapers with giant headlines—Jack the Ripper had struck again; the dance area was smaller than usual, in order to make room for the couches. Ambient trance washed across the room as Dylan cut across the dance floor toward the VIP area, sliding between couples and groups of single women as he continued toward the back of the room. Someone was screaming "happy birthday" and then Dylan was doing a shot—piss-poor tequila that went down rough—but he was saying thank you anyway, nodding to someone he had never seen before in his life, smiling at beautiful girls writhing on the dance floor who were watching themselves in the mirrors over the bar, and then Chase and Mikey were there, asking where the fuck he had been, and for fuck's sake guy—smile: It's your birthday.

The VIP section consisted of a dozen canopy beds stacked with pillows and serving trays: Some of the canopies' dark silk covers were up; others were down, rendering the beds' occupants mere shadows. Waiters buzzed from bed to bed, delivering orders to the open canopies, tactfully ignoring the moans and sniffling noises emanating from the others. In the far corner of this VIP wonderland a girl was crying hysterically, rolling around on one of the beds, gnawing on a pillow while everyone looked in another direction.

Although he didn't recall making a reservation, four beds had been set aside in Dylan's name. The beds were arranged in a square, with two or three feet separating each bed, and though Dylan wasn't even sure he wanted to spend the rest of the night sitting on a bed he didn't really have any alternative to suggest so he grabbed two of the girls from the limo—the one with the red nails and brunette he assumed was her friend—and jumped onto the bed furthest from the entrance. Chase and Mikey and a girl they grabbed off the dance floor took up residence in the bed across from his.

Dylan slumped back into the pillows stacked against the headboard, the two girls sitting a bit further down on the bed, one on either side of him, handbags, iPhones, and packs of cigarettes occupying every available section of the bed. The brunette leaned over and, placing her hand behind his head, began kissing him, her tongue flicking in and out of his mouth, her lips a combo of cherry and cigarette.

"Happy Birthday," she said when she pulled away.

"Yes! Happy Birthday," the other girl said.

"Thanks," Dylan mumbled, distracted, looking for one of the trays he had seen on the other beds, spying one on the floor next to the bed. He leaned over the side to retrieve it and when he pulled himself back up two bottles of champagne—uncorked and set into ice buckets arranged between his bed and his friends' bed—had appeared, and everyone had a glass. One of the girls in the bed—the one he hadn't met yet—handed him a flute filled to the brim and simultaneously everyone screamed "Happy Birthday!"

Mildly embarrassed, Dylan just smiled and drained his glass in a single gulp. He noticed the two other beds adjacent to his were full: a mix of girls, guys, and even a dog—he thought he was hallucinating but someone had not only brought a small dog to the club but had actually been allowed to enter with said small dog—all of whom he had never seen before in his life. Still, he considered, it could be worse: Chase and Mikey could have brought the ponytail guy from the last party.

Dylan placed the tray—the kind on which his mother used to bring him saltines and flat ginger ale when, as a child, he was home sick from school— at the bottom of the bed before again reaching into his pocket, taking out the vial and snorting a massive line of blow.

The music in the bar was changing, an aggressiveness creeping into the lounge beats, and Dylan dumped more white powder onto the tray, again chopping it up into several lines but this time he turned back to the two girls who were eyeing the coke like starving orphans from a Dickens novel.

"I'm sorry," Dylan said, as he gestured to the coke, "I'm being a terrible host. Please."

The blonde from the limo, the one with the red nails, swooped in, one hand holding back her hair, the other pressing her right nostril as the left hovered up two lines. She tilted her head back, her eyes shut, and a smile slowly crept across her face.

"Wow," she said. "Just...Wow. That is killer coke. I'm Sarah by the way."

"And I'm Brandi," said her friend, who had better tits but a less pretty face. "Is it cool if we hang out and party?"

"Yeah, it's cool. How did you guys wind up in the limo?"

"Um, that guy," Sarah replied, pointing across toward the other bed at Chase.

Chase waved, giving Dylan the thumbs-up before snorting a line off his own tray.

"Cool. Are you guys...models?"

"Yes!" they shrieked in unison.

"Oh my God," Sarah said, "You are like, so perceptive. I mean, a lot of people eventually figure out that we're models. I mean—hello, right? Look at this bod!" She reached over and squeezed Brandi's right tit, smiling at the other girl and sniffling once, twice, before continuing.

"But not right away and they're usually just guessing by that point. And yeah it's not like either of us are doing Fashion Week or anything like that and success doesn't just come overnight but Brandi knows this guy who has a lot of connections in the industry and he thinks we both could be stars, easily. By the way, this is killer coke. Did I already say that? Sorry if I did but baby this shit is to die for."

Sarah leaned back over the tray, did another massive line, a line Dylan had cut for himself because the situation was deteriorating quickly. He glanced over at Chase and Mikey's bed: Mikey was rolling an enormous joint while Chase and the slightly overweight girl they picked up did bump after bump after bump, any sort of discretion abandoned, his hand creeping up her thigh, moving under her leather mini skirt.

"So, are you famous or something?" Brandi asked, not even waiting for Dylan's answer before diving forward and taking another bump.

"No," Dylan replied, "Not famous. Not famous at all."

"Are you sure? I think you're lying..."

Sarah leaned over to Brandi and whispered something in her ear. Brandi's eyes got big and she leaned forward, her mouth open, her lips glistening.

"I'm usually not very political or anything. But your dad," she said slowly, "was sexy."

"You do realize that it was exactly 10 years ago that my father blew his brains out?"

"Brains—yeah smart guys can definitely be hot too," Brandi continued, raising her voice over the music. "That new guy—what's his name? The one on all the ads..."

"Heffernan," Sarah added.

"Yes, Heffernan. He reminds me of your dad. You see all those giant posters downtown? God who knew politicians could be so fucking gorgeous? Those eyes..." Brandi said, finishing her martini that Dylan didn't remember her ordering, a martini that might as well have materialized out of the smoke drifting up from every corner of the club—tobacco, cloves, weed, and meth.

"You know, the eyes are a window to the soul," Sarah was whispering in his ear, confiding in him information she apparently felt too important to say any louder, before slumping back against the bed, as if the effort to make such a profound statement had consumed every last ounce of physical strength she had left. She lit a cigarette and took a drag, exhaling as she stared at the ceiling, through the ceiling, toward nothing.

"I gotta hit the head," Dylan shouted over the music, swinging his legs over the side of the giant bed. This was true; he really did have to take a piss. But he was also so restless he just couldn't sit there on the bed, making small talk, killing time until he could bring one of the girls back to his apartment and fuck her. That was the game: You bring me to the VIP lounge at an exclusive club and provide the coke, I'll let you fuck me any way you want. And so many nights, that was just how it happened. But right now Dylan had to move—his mind was a mess of memories and emotions he wanted to keep at bay but suppression through chemicals and flesh was extracting a heavy price; he just needed to move and so he was off the bed and heading down the stairs from the VIP area back toward the main dance floor. There was probably a private bathroom somewhere but he really couldn't give a fuck so he just keep moving, circumventing the dance floor, watching impossibly young kids grind up against one another, the earlier lounge vibe dead, the sound system now blasting out angry rappers spitting verse after verse after verse over cold impersonal beats, clusters of young women—early to mid-20s, bachelorette party perhaps—raising their glasses, sing–screaming along with the words of the song: "Fuck a bitch/they ain't shit/lick on these nuts and suck the dick," laughing, bracing themselves against the bar, against their friends, against strangers, their drinks spilling all over the floor but no worries someone would clean it up later because hey—life takes Visa.

And then the dance floor was behind him, falling away as Dylan kept moving, down a flight of stairs and into the area of the club where suddenly every attempt at ambiance or vibe or décor was abandoned and the place was just another club in another city: dim lights with empty kegs stacked in the corner, Mexican busboys running in and out of the kitchen, hauling large crates filled with clean glasses as girls lined up to use the bathroom. A couple of dealers were hanging around, and Dylan nodded to the ones he knew, or at least thought he recognized, before pushing the door to the men's room open.

This particular bathroom smelled like only the bathrooms of clubs just before last call are capable of smelling: a mixture of piss, vomit, and stale

beer, with a hint of industrial strength antiseptic which, rather than conceal-
ing the smell, just made everything worse.

The floor was slippery, the cracks between the individual tiles transformed into miniature canals of gray water. Dylan navigated the empty bathroom carefully, stepping over pools of liquids he couldn't identify as he made
his way to a urinal. As he began to piss, he stared straight ahead, a series of
advertisements rotating across three 9-inch-by-9-inch digital screens positioned at eye level on the three walls ringing the urinal. Dylan tried to look
down into the urinal but there were pubic hairs and loogies and pink chunks
of something unidentifiable ringing the pale blue urinal cake, which looked
as though someone had taken a bite out of it. A wave of nausea passed over
him and he tried shutting his eyes but that only made the feeling worse, so
he stared straight ahead at the advertisements, which seemed to change every
few seconds until everything was a single blur of color, light, pixels, products.

Stepping away from the urinal as he zipped his fly, he heard giggling in
the hallway outside the bathroom and then the door was opening and Sarah
and Brandi slipped inside. Dylan opened his mouth but before he could say
anything, Sarah was kissing him, pushing him up against the end stall as
Brandi giggled before adding, "It is your birthday after all, right?"

For a second Dylan flashed back to the party, to the possibility that Meghan Morrison had been there but then he remembered how he had blown the
whole thing years ago and it probably wasn't even her anyway and besides,
Sarah was smiling as Brandi closed the door behind them and then Sarah
and Brandi were kissing, Sarah's hands climbing underneath Brandi's skirt as
Brandi leaned against the wall. Dylan was sitting on the toilet, watching, his
cock growing harder as Sarah slid Brandi's panties down her smooth, toned
thighs, calves, finally over the four-inch black heels. She tossed the panties
at Dylan, lifting up the skirt as Brandi urged her on, imploring her to *eat
my pussy*, which Sarah did as Dylan watched, a grin plastered across his face,
wondering when he should join in. Sarah answered that question for him
when seconds later her head was out of Brandi's lap and she was kneeling
in front of him, unzipping his fly and pulling his cock free. Brandi was still
moaning, trying to finish with her hand what Sarah started. Dylan stared at
Brandi as Sarah took his cock into her mouth, sucking the head then moving
down his shaft, taking his balls into her mouth, sucking hard on one, then
the other, before letting go and pulling her head back, taking a breath before
deep throating the whole thing.

Now Brandi was moving toward him, her face flushed, the skin on her breastbone glowing red. Sarah took her mouth off his cock, spitting on it before Brandi, facing Sarah and the door but turned away from Dylan, her thighs slick with her own juices, eased herself onto him, grunting softly as he pushed inside of her. Sarah was still on her knees, licking Dylan's balls and Brandi's pussy, pausing only to take a breath or urge Dylan to fuck Brandi harder, her hand between her own legs, fingering her pussy, her asshole, frantically trying to get herself off.

The bathroom door swung open, the music from the club spilling into the bathroom before fading back to a muffled pulse as the door closed. Someone was in the bathroom but Dylan didn't give a damn; he could feel his own orgasm starting to build up from the base of his cock, and he began fucking Brandi even harder, the smell of her hair—cigarettes and perfume and sex—driving him crazy, the sound of skin slapping skin echoing off the concrete walls.

With another burst of music and noise and voices the door opened again then shut and Brandi was leaning forward now, forcing Dylan deeper into her, grinding her clit against Sarah's mouth, her hands pressed up against the stall door, her nails digging into the stickers advertising defunct bands and live-sex websites slapped haphazardly across the metal.

"Oh my God I'm coming," Brandi announced, moaning, her hips bucking uncontrollably—that pushed Dylan over the edge and he pulled out of her, exploding all over the word tattooed across her lower back: FEAR.

"Jesus Christ," Dylan gasped as Brandi stood up, smiling, helping Sarah to her feet, both girls pulling their clothes back into place. "Jesus Fucking Christ. That's the best birthday present I've ever had."

"We thought you might like it," said Sarah, smiling over her shoulder as she pushed open the stall door and began straightening her clothes in the grimy men's room mirror.

"Like it? That's an understatement," said Dylan. "Nice tattoo too...But why 'FEAR'?"

Brandi turned around, a blank look plastered across her face, her eyes looking at him, through him.

"Aren't you afraid?" she asked.

The room was suddenly very quiet and all Dylan could hear was muffled bass rumbling behind the door, vibrating off the walls, and the buzz of dying florescent lights.

"Let's do another line," said Sarah, breaking the silence.

Chapter 7

I n the abandoned warehouse deep within Tiber City's Jungle district, Campbell tended to the dying child.

Campbell was amazed the child was still drawing breath. The boy had been brought to the warehouse-turned-field hospital, known as Camp Ramoth, less than five hours ago, his body ravaged by disease, his skin glowing, radioactive with fever, transforming the frail, prepubescent frame into a furnace of flesh and bone. A puss-caked lesion running the length of the child's stomach quivered with infection.

Despite the introduction of antibiotics, the fever persisted and the boy was writhing on top of the tiny cot that had been prepared for him, crying out in agony, his little hand reaching into the air for his mother, his father, for some reassurance that the pain would end and everything would be OK. But there was no mother, no father, only Campbell, and while the doctor knew the pain would end, he also knew that everything would not be OK.

Taking the child into his arms, Campbell raised the boy off the sweat-soaked cot, whispering reassurances before gently lowering the tiny, shivering frame into a small tub of lukewarm water. The child moaned, his skin trembling as the water rose around him. He placed one hand behind the boy's head, creating a fleshy buffer between the hard ceramic of the tub and the child's skull. With his other hand, Campbell picked up a sponge and began to clean the lesion. A thick layer of crust covered the disease, although when the sponge began to move across the infected area, fresh puss—yellow with the consistency and smell of mayonnaise left to bake in the sun—began oozing from the deformity. The child moaned, delirious, as Campbell continued cleaning the lesion, the boy's body shaking as fever and bacteria revolted against the soapy green-gray water. Gradually the crust sealing the infection broke away, bits of scab crumbling into the tub, floating across the top of the water like bath toys.

The boy was crying now, tears streaming down his scarred face as his mouth tried to form words but none would come because this child did not know language, only sound, but even in anguished wails his question was still clear: *Why?*

There was no way Campbell could answer the child, no response that would provide a sufficient explanation as to why this child had been chosen to suffer. Instead, he knelt by the side of the bathtub, continuing to bathe the boy as the infection cleared, squeezing the lukewarm water over the child's bald and bruised head, and in that moment, the rest of the warehouse-turned-makeshift hospice seemed to melt away and there was only Campbell and the boy, and he began speaking to the child in low, soft tones, telling him of places far away from Tiber City, of lands filled with good men who performed good deeds, ancient tales in which *hero* was not a word that triggered snickering and the rolling of eyes, stories that, above all, were an attempt to convey to this dying child that the world had not always been like this.

As if to reject this suggestion, the boy began to convulse, and Campbell dropped the sponge, placing his hand on the child's head, cursing softly as the fever refused to break.

Lifting the boy back out of the tub, Campbell held him in his arms, water soaking his shirt as he wrapped the boy in towels, calling out for assistance; he needed to pack ice in towels and wrap them around the boy to have any chance of breaking the fever. There was no intercom, no call button in Camp Ramoth, just Campbell's voice booming off stone and exposed piping.

Seconds later the gurney men arrived. They moved silently into the warehouse, entering from a side hallway two by two by one: five total. There was

no particular urgency to their movements yet there was purpose and precision and within seconds they were gathered around the child's cot, laboring
in silence as Campbell, exhausted, took a few steps backward before slumping against a crumbling wall. He exhaled sharply, watching as the gurney
men began wrapping ice in tattered, stained towels, a terrifying helplessness
washing over him as he saw the sheer horror reflected in the child's eyes.
There was so much he wanted to try to explain to the boy but there was just
not enough time: This child would die like the others.

But until that moment came, Campbell would do everything in his
power to alleviate this child's suffering. For the past decade Campbell had
been a servant of the gurney men, tending to Tiber City's sick and dying:
those forgotten as the rest of the city, the country, the world drifted deeper
into the future.

There had been a resurgence of diseases forgotten by the Western world:
leprosy, bubonic plague, smallpox, and Ebola had begun to make sporadic
appearances throughout Tiber City's Jungle district. There were hospitals, of
course, but the emergency response services no longer ran to all parts of the
city. The numbers of uninsured had skyrocketed over the past few years, as
had the number of illegal immigrants cramming into the already-swollen
Tiber City slums. As conditions deteriorated, a wave of disease swept across
the city; some families chose to simply abandon their terminally-ill children,
moving into another slum without their young: Finding sick children left to
die in squatter pads or shooting galleries was no longer an unusual occur-
rence. Yet, in the time it would take to move these children into some sort
of government home, they'd most likely be dead, forced to spend their final
days on earth bound in red tape. And so Campbell worked in this subterranean camp, a witness to human suffering in its most absolute form, doing
what he could to alleviate misery.

Watching the gurney men work—packing the wrapped ice around the
boy before hooking him up to an ancient IV and heart monitor, administer-
ing antibiotics, all in a vain attempt to contain the fever ravaging the child's
fragile frame—Campbell's mind began to race, conjuring up images of the
life this boy might have led—that pastoral American existence. Instead, this
boy, nor any other of the dying children hidden away in Camp Ramoth,
would never go to school, fall in love, fight, fuck, or have children of their
own; they would know only shadow, pain, and loss. As the gurney men began
spreading an ointment over the puss-caked lesion, Campbell's legs buckled

and he slid down the cracked and crumbling concrete wall until his ass met the floor. Squeezing his eyes shut, Campbell focused on the bleat from the rusty monitor, tears beginning to tumble down his cheeks as the EKG again spiked, the beeping quickening in response. In that instant, Campbell's entire universe was that robotic blip and the attendant reminder that no matter how many times he did this, each death was his own personalized trip to hell.

The noise coming from the monitor reached its crescendo, that split second stretched out for an eternity where it might break in either direction: flatlining or easing back toward a stable rhythm. In that moment the child cried out—no words, only a single wail that expressed more than any language ever could—and Campbell gritted his teeth, waiting for the monitor to emit that drawn-out insistent drone that generations of Americans since the advent of television recognized as an EKG flatline, the modern equivalent of the passing bell. Yet, seconds later, the monitor's moan was slowing, falling back into a steady beat and Campbell opened his eyes, disbelief dragging him off the floor and onto his feet and for an instant the gurney men parted, moving to either side of the child in order to give him a clear view of the boy who was not dead but asleep, the lesion dressed in a clean bandage.

The gurney men moved away from the cot, filing back down the corridor. There was no need for words; there was nothing to say. Campbell took a deep breath and, leaning over the child's cot, tucked in the edges of the blankets.

Taking a final look at the boy, at the monitor beeping softly and consistently, Campbell turned and began walking across the room toward the exit, trying to ignore the empty cots lining the walls on both sides of the room. Those cots, he remembered, had not always been empty.

Campbell drifted through the rest of the camp, his mind slipping back to when he first arrived in Tiber City. Ten years ago, after stumbling off that cross-country bus and into the Lazarus bar, Campbell had slept in a room above the bar for a week straight. When he woke up, he wandered downstairs, where the bartender, a guy named Sweeney, already had a couple of burgers waiting. As he began devouring the burgers, Sweeney poured two double shots of Jameson and began telling him about things that, only a few weeks earlier, he would have dismissed as absolute bullshit. The way Sweeney told it, the men in the surgical masks—the ones Campbell referred to as the gurney men—had another name: The Order of Neshamah.

According to Sweeney, the Order was founded by a group of renegade scientist-monks. Most were disillusioned scientists—men uncomfortable with the divide between spirituality and science. A few other founding members had been theologians in search of a new theology. There was no specific religion driving these men, Sweeney had explained. Just a single common quest: to better understand the nature of the human soul. That's where the name came from—

Neshamah was an Old Testament word meaning "breath of life." Sweeney had whipped out an old Bible, weather-beaten with a black, cracked cover; the following verse in Genesis was highlighted:

> Yahweh God formed man from the dust of the ground, and breathed into his nostrils the breath of life; and man became a living soul.

It was this breath of life, this *Neshamah,* that gave man a full and connected life, an existence separate from the dust and the void. In short, it gave man a soul.

Campbell had tossed back the shot and immediately asked for a refill; Sweeney's story sounded like complete and utter bullshit. Once upon a time, Campbell had been perhaps *the* preeminent geneticist of a generation and old habits were hard to shake; the scientist in him recoiled from Sweeney's tale. But at that moment in time, he had few precious options left. Besides, the Order had saved his ass back in the desert and, despite the fact he had been forever marked with the tattoo on his back, he figured he still owed the gurney men a few favors. And, to be honest, Campbell was pretty curious why they even bothered to drag him out of the desert in the first place.

In the months following his arrival in Tiber City, Campbell spent most of his time trying to answer that question, wandering the underground tunnels that led in, out, and through Camp Ramoth. He took instructions from Sweeney and a woman named Jael who was head of security at Ramoth—the gurney men never said a word to him. Sweeney wasn't technically a member of the Order, but he was privy to many of its secrets and, in addition to running Lazarus, he served as the group's liaison to the Tiber City underworld. It was Sweeney who provided day-to-day instructions to Campbell, Sweeney who gave him a room above Lazarus to call his own. And it was Sweeney who finally explained to him why he had been brought to Ramoth: to serve.

And Campbell had served—he had spent much of the past decade tending to the sick and dying housed in Ramoth. Yet, the Order did not exist merely to serve. There were other rooms constructed in the back of the camp and filled with various pieces of aging yet still functional pieces of medical equipment, mostly diagnostic tools such as PET scanners. Despite his relative familiarity with the equipment, Campbell had no desire to explore these rooms. Not only was his job to tend to the residents of Ramoth, but, on the few occasions he had ventured into these posterior chambers, he had seen things for which he had no answer: members of the Order in deep meditation, some surrounded by religious icons, others sitting motionless on the stone floor of empty rooms. Each member's head was shaved and sported the asterisk tattoo, and each had a dozen or so wires attached to their bald heads, wires that were attached to the large gray blocks of medical equipment.

Campbell asked Sweeney about the meditation sessions, the wires, and the strange symbol that marked each of the members but Sweeney just shook his head, slow and sad, and smiled.

"Remember what I told you about the soul?" asked Sweeney. "The asterisk in the circle, well, that's meant to be representative of the divine spark within every man; that spark, that connection to the divine, it's made possible by the soul. The mark is just a reminder because man, let me tell you: It's easy to forget. As for the machines and the meditation, well, that's how they look for the soul."

Campbell raised an eyebrow. "Yeah and how's that going?" he asked, the skepticism in his voice unmistakable. "They find anything?"

Sweeney only offered that same slow smile. "Maybe someday you'll find out. First, you gotta be ready. And let me tell you, you ain't ready yet. But the Order is patient. So if I were you, I'd just do what you've been asked to do."

"Serve," Campbell said.

"Serve," Sweeney nodded. "And wait."

Initially, he bristled at the idea of being kept in the dark—Morrison's treachery was seared in his memory forever. But Campbell was granted entrance to every inch of Camp Ramoth; he just wasn't cleared to review the data compiled by the Order. And so Campbell learned to wait. And to serve.

In many ways, this place, Camp Ramoth, was identical to the room in which he had awoken almost 20 years ago after the gurney men found him left for dead in that abandoned freight yard. Serving as a hospital but more closely resembling a subterranean refugee camp, the room he just exited was located in the slums of Tiber City, in an area known only as "the Jungle." The original camp—Camp Golan—had been constructed in the basement of an abandoned Church in the Chihuahuan desert. Golan was where Campbell had first encountered the gurney men, where they had saved him from the nothingness of the desert. It was also where Campbell came face to face with the ruined creatures he helped create, the creatures produced by Project Exodus and recovered by the Order. But those creatures had long since died, and Golan, along with another camp—Bosor—became just another place of refuge, a place where the Order might continue its search for the soul. Ramoth, established in Tiber City, became the third. Why Tiber City, Campbell had asked Sweeney once. The surge of sickness and disease in Tiber City, Sweeney had explained: It's not just physical.

As Campbell stepped into the stairwell, a familiar atonal beep echoed off concrete, alerting the camp that someone was exiting or entering the facilities. This was the extent of Ramoth's security system: a single, annoying electronic blast. *Did it even matter?* Campbell wondered. There were no police, no corporate cavalry riding to the rescue if someone did manage to stumble across Ramoth and shit went sideways.

Campbell trudged up two flights of stairs that led from the basement of the warehouse, toward the front of the building, and out into the Tiber City night. There were other ways out, emergency exits that led into the maze of alleyways behind the building, but, so far, those had gone unused.

Reaching the exit, Campbell pulled open the steel door that marked the camp's main entrance. Like much of Tiber City, the old warehouse—the basement levels of which held Camp Ramoth—had been hastily constructed to satisfy an immediate need and then forgotten, money, politics, and power always pushing forward, need begetting need begetting ever more need. Consequently, rather than taking the time and the money to tear buildings down, these structures were buried alive, fresh concrete and steel poured over the still-viable structures. When the money dried up, these new buildings—little more than heaps of cheap material slapped together atop uneven foundations by strangers, by men who were not from these neighborhoods, by men who couldn't care less—began to crumble. And when they did, no one gave a shit because the goal had never been sustainability; turn a profit and move on was the fundamental philosophy. Structure began cannibalizing structure, and as the foundations of the newest buildings collapsed, older, forgotten buildings were unearthed. As a result, the Jungle's geography was forever changing as the slums rose up to reclaim the land, prefab material no match for the infinite patience of time.

The warehouse that became Camp Ramoth was one of these older buildings: The main entrance was still obscured by a partially collapsed wall but a tunnel led from the alley behind the building into the warehouse. After that, a single flight of stairs funneled visitors onto the first floor of a viable commercial warehouse: Electricity, plumbing, even heat were all still available; someone had simply forgotten to turn off the utilities. Advertisements covered the entire side of the warehouse, tattered and torn flyers pasted one on top of the other: Promo posters announcing the opening of a new club competed with notices of foreclosure auctions and shaky, handwritten phone numbers scrawled under messages promising transsexuals versatile enough to satisfy every taste.

Individually, these flyers were a schizophrenic mess of human desire and weakness; when considered in their entirety, they offered a crash course in the history of the neighborhood. Peeling back the yellow dog-eared edges of the current batch of flyers was like embarking on an archeological excavation: Dead rap stars still hyping their newest album gave way to ads for a mayoral candidate whose predilections for underage black pussy only resulted in single-digit defeat, an opportunity to make BIG $$$$$$$ (and lose weight!) while working from home, and finally warnings about a flu strain that, according to some, was responsible for thousands of deaths somewhere outside Mexico City while others maintained the only damage done was the insignificant death of several elderly residents in a nursing home in Boise.

The floor between the subterranean warehouse-turned-refugee camp and the street level had once served as a sales team bullpen and administrative area—the purgatory of the corporate theology. The place had been deserted for most of the past decade: windows boarded up, adorned with graffiti and posters of missing children. Inside, the maze of cubicles constituting the sales bullpen had been left behind, the cheap wood rotting and warped, the water cooler in the corner half full with stale brown liquid. Impossibly large rats dodged in and out of the various cubicles and stacks of office supplies, splashing through puddles created by a rusted and corroded piping system running the length of the ceiling leaking toxic water that had eaten through the cheap, prefab walls long ago. Motivational posters, still clinging to the walls of some of the cubes, edges curled and tattered, challenged the rodents and rust to *Dare to Soar*, because, after all, *Your Attitude Almost Always Determines Your Altitude In Life.*

The office had been thrown together on top of the warehouse in a desperate attempt to chase some new business trend, from an idea prompted by positive-thinking seminars filled with obese women and men with ballooning alimony bills networking in Omaha, in Orlando, in Phoenix, always in some Holiday Inn, forever earning miles or points or some other nebulous reward. But the world moved so fast that after the idea was sold, forces so far beyond the control of these Holiday Inn heroes shifted the economic landscape, sometimes in imperceptible ways—imperceptible, of course, until the markets began to react and the "can't miss" economic trend of the year became a footnote and new seminars and conferences were thrown together to take advantage of these new opportunities. So by the time the bullpen had been filled and calls were being routed from the U.S. to New Delhi, to Baghdad, to Singapore, the original vision that had prompted the creation of this office space was in tatters, leaving unfortunate would-be entrepreneurs to choose between picking the bones of the carcass or chasing the latest new dream. Either way, the results were the same: empty, abandoned office space. But in Tiber City, temporary so often became permanent. Men appeared and then disappeared seemingly overnight, and their businesses rose and fell so quickly that eventually people stopped paying much attention: Buildings might sit abandoned for months, years, decades.

Fuck it, Campbell thought, as he moved out into the warm Tiber City drizzle, squinting against the inescapable neon; whatever the story, all that mattered was that, so far, no one had noticed them.

"God damn lucky," Campbell muttered, squinting against the neon.

"Luck's got nothing to do with it, Campbell." The voice—female and low—drifted out of the shadows. Campbell grinned in spite of everything and ducked under an adjacent fire escape, lighting a cigarette.

"I didn't know you were around tonight," Campbell called into the darkness.

"Yeah, well, I heard they brought a new one in, so here I am."

Striding out of the shadows and into the neon twilight, Jael moved with purpose, studying Campbell's face before pulling the cigarette from between his lips and taking a drag. Her olive skin was accented by deep, intense eyes and full lips. She had scars but flaunted them like other women wore diamonds; Campbell was half-convinced she wore her hair back so everyone could see exactly how far the gash along the right side of her cheek went. She wore dark jeans, boots, and a knee-length leather coat, but Campbell knew that was all bullshit; underneath her street clothes was a network of ultra-high molecular-weight polyethylene.

"Pretty bad, huh?" It wasn't so much a question as a statement.

"Actually the kid was having a blast," Campbell replied. "Gurgling up blood—what kid wouldn't want an extended stay in Ramoth? It's like Disneyland. Next thing you know, the Order are gonna be running around in fucking mouse suits."

"Funny. I'm surprised they don't let you do stand-up down there," Jael said. "But I'll take that as a yes, because anytime your hard-ass act goes into overdrive, it's bad."

"When is it good?" Campbell asked, his breath hanging in the air, his words more accusation than question.

Jael turned away, taking another drag off the cigarette.

"You tell me," she shot back. "You're the one who decided to re-invent mankind; the one who decided the original model wasn't any good."

Campbell opened his mouth to reply but she was already moving away, flicking the cigarette into the air. Before she melted back into the alleyway she stopped, turning back toward him.

"Oh yeah. I almost forgot…" she said, reaching into her coat, seconds later producing a small leather carrying case—the kind Campbell had seen chefs on television use to store knifes. Catching the bag, his hands closing around the worn, cracked leather, he knew that, whatever its original purpose, it no longer carried knives; there was something else inside.

He stared at the bag for a moment before looking back toward Jael but she was gone. The red glow from the discarded cigarette burned for another few seconds but then the fire died and there was only the rain.

After tucking the carrier under his arm, Campbell stood there for a moment, watching two massive spotlights strafe the starless sky, wheeling back and forth, motion for motion's sake, purposeless and frenzied. The rain began falling harder and Campbell closed his eyes, tilting his face toward the sky, imagining for a moment that the water pelting his face was clean and pure and cleansing. But the smell was too strong: sulfur and garbage. And then he was moving, away from the entrance to Ramoth and deeper into the Jungle district, the taste of the rain rancid in his mouth.

The Journal of Senator Robert Fitzgerald
Excerpt # 1

To Dylan,

I had intended this journal to be a gift. I had visions of drafting a series of letters in this journal that, collectively, might guide you as you grew older. They would compensate, to whatever extent possible, for all the time our family was apart. Or, perhaps more accurately, for all the time I was apart from our family.

And yet, what you are holding is no gift. It is a confession, written by a scared, broken man. I do not seek absolution: such a luxury is well beyond my grasp.

I seek only to explain—to the extent that I can do so.

And to ask your forgiveness.

Love,
Your Father

Chapter 8

Tiber City
Aug. 27, 2015
Noon

Gripping one end of the red rubber tourniquet between his teeth, Campbell twisted his neck, tightening the other end's grip on his upper forearm, just below the elbow. Instantly, several veins rose to the surface of his skin; hungry, expectant. He ran his finger along the fat purple vein, the thickest of the group, slapping it until it strained against his flesh, the valve easily recognizable.

With his free hand, he picked a syringe out of the leather carrying case Jael had procured, which was now unrolled and stretched across the cot where Campbell was sitting. Including the syringe in his hand, Campbell counted three dozen doses, enough to last him six months, give or take a few weeks. But that was just an approximation: His battle against his own DNA was growing increasingly fierce and unpredictable.

Holding the syringe upright, the smell of wet leather heavy in the air, Campbell pressed down on the plunger, forcing himself to watch as the needle punctured the skin and pricked the vein. The effect was immediate: a huge mushroom cloud of warmth rising up through his chest before blowing out into his legs, arms, brain, white heat devouring his nervous system.

His jaw seized up and the rubber tubing tumbled from his arm. Campbell dropped the syringe as blood began to trickle out of the hole in his arm: This was the point at which most junkies would nod off, collapsing back onto some pile of filth in whatever abandoned building-turned-shooting gallery they scored in. Campbell, however, was not like most junkies; he was a special kind of junkie. Not exactly like the William Burroughs-Johnny Thunders brand of addict, but not exactly unlike them either. The tools of the trade were the same: rubber dinosaur tied tight around the crevice where forearm met elbow and a syringe full of shit churned out in a laboratory. Yet when he pushed down the plunger, Campbell had shot his body full of a different kind of junk, a chemical cocktail Project Exodus had dubbed "the Treatment": a series of designer enzymes created to keep the ends of certain specific chromosomes from degenerating, which, in turn, slowed man's aging process to an imperceptible crawl.

Campbell's head was pounding now as the chemicals he injected assailed his system, his brain an overloaded power grid flickering in and out of consciousness as it tried to keep up with his body's demand. He sank backward onto the cot, gritting his teeth, his eyes struggling to focus on his surroundings, on something—anything—other than the pain. When Campbell first left Exodus, he could go years without an injection. Now, he could go a month, tops. And he didn't even have the real thing; just a synthetic approximation that simply warded off total physical collapse. Jael and the Order helped him come up with the chemicals he needed to make an approximation of the Treatment and while it wasn't as good as the original, it beat the black market garbage he used to score in the first few years after he left Project Exodus.

Project Exodus. The words echoed through Campbell's brain, reverberating from synapse to synapse as he squeezed his eyes shut, his mind flashing back to the desert as he felt the Treatment bearing down on his body.

Project Exodus was originally a product of the Cold War. In the years leading up to Exodus, America had grown obsessed with gaps: The space gap, the first-strike missile gap, the education gap, the bomber gap; the concept of a gap between the United States and the USSR was the new national nightmare, complete with the specter of Khrushchev slamming his shoe on the table, promising to bury all the Orange County kids in their subdivided backyards. The government was spooked and began taking

action to address these "gaps." One such emerging gap was the "leader gap." Although information on Soviet party leadership was shadowy at best during much of the Cold War, by the time Watergate rolled around, there were some very powerful men in the government growing tired of defending the health of the republic from human frailty.

This was where Campbell entered the picture. By the mid-'70s, Jonathan Campbell had already established himself as the preeminent geneticist of his generation. The youngest faculty member ever granted tenure by Harvard, Campbell had talent that was matched only by his desire to use genetics to end the suffering of mankind: to not only eradicate genetic diseases but to actually learn how to reprogram human DNA to resist various viruses and influenzas. Campbell's focus wasn't just on the West, but the entire world—India, Africa, all the third world hellholes where the flu was still a death sentence.

Believing the Cold War would last indefinitely, the government approached Campbell about the possibilities of using genetics to close this "leader gap." As far as Campbell had been concerned, the proposal was ludicrous. But still, he accepted the government's challenge: How could he not? As human beings, America's leaders had failings that had been naturally hardwired into their DNA. If the alleged gap was to be corrected, Campbell would need to somehow reprogram the DNA of future presidents; that kind of program would grant him access not only to technology and resources the private sector couldn't match, but the freedom to pursue his true goals outside the established legal framework regulating the biotechnology industry. For those kinds of perks, he could deal with the occasional hysterical lecture from a cold warrior. So Campbell compromised; the first of many concessions that would haunt him for the rest of his life.

The operation, which began in 1976, was code-named Project Exodus: a reflection of the idea that the American people had been abandoned by their leaders, left to wander in the Cold War desert. The goal of the Project was simple yet audacious: Stem any potential for a "leader gap" by isolating the genes responsible for certain human failings that undermined American executives' ability to lead effectively. Eventually, the goal was to expand the Project to include the military and intelligence agencies—Wall Street was mentioned as well—but the executive branch was the primary concern.

To assist him in overseeing Project Exodus, Campbell recruited the only other scientist able to rival his talent and ego, a Harvard graduate student named Michael Morrison. Campbell had been Morrison's mentor at Harvard. While ostensibly working toward what he considered the government's rather delusional goals, Campbell dreamed of locating and isolating those poisonous genes transmitting conditions such as

Tay-Sachs and Alzheimer's: God's mistakes would now be corrected by Campbell and Morrison. At the time, Campbell believed he and Morrison shared the same ideals, the same belief in science's ability to liberate, to heal, to transcend. If that meant playing ball with paranoid cold warriors, so be it. Were he not consumed with his own crusade perhaps Campbell would have detected the subtle signs of treason earlier.

In order to placate their government sponsors, the pair sought to correct the genetic components of traits deemed "undesirable" in future leaders of the free world. The idea was to be able to cure certain genetic conditions that might hobble an otherwise effective leader: manic-depression, alcoholism, sex-addiction, Alzheimer's.

Almost all of these afflictions were the result of mutations that would cause the protein encoded by a specific gene to malfunction. When a protein malfunctions, cells that rely on that protein's function can't behave normally, which in turn causes so many of the conditions Exodus sought to eradicate. While medical treatment was available for some of these mutations, others remained untreatable. So, rather than merely wrapping a very expensive bandage around these problems, Campbell and Morrison committed themselves to pushing Exodus to the next level, to correct the source of the mutations, replacing faulty genes with healthy, fully functioning ones through a then-revolutionary technique known as somatic gene therapy.

After manufacturing a healthy copy of the mutated gene in the laboratory, the Exodus team placed the new, therapeutic gene into a transmissions device known as a vector. This vector was delivered to the patient through a series of injections into a specific tissue, and the new gene was carried into a subject's defective cells.

Determined to expand these somatic gene experiments beyond the government's desired scope, Campbell and Morrison soon began introducing genes into the blood cells of the patients with hemophilia and the brain tissue of Alzheimer's patients. There was some success: On a few occasions, Project Exodus research reversed the effects of some of mankind's most feared afflictions. There were also, however, some stunning failures: More than one "volunteer" from Attica's death row spent his final moments hemorrhaging to death in the Exodus laboratories. Campbell's resolve wavered after each death, but each time Morrison convinced him to stay with the Project.

Think of man's greatest achievements, Campbell recalled Morrison urging him around that time. The Great Pyramids, the Hoover Dam, and the atomic bomb: None could have been accomplished without some loss of life. It was the lives improved by these great works that justified such loss. So a few kiddie-rapists and serial killers died, so what? Morrison had asked. Campbell agreed.

Despite some early breakthroughs employing gene therapy techniques, both men realized their few early victories owed more to luck than skill. Two massive hurdles to *genuinely effective gene therapy remained: complete understanding of gene function and the development of a reliable vector. Without a complete understanding of gene function, the two-man Exodus team was shooting in the dark, never certain if the gene they repaired was the exact gene that caused the genetic defect. Furthermore, the delivery vectors were unstable at best.*

Despite these potential setbacks, the Exodus team pushed forward, spending the next five years attempting to complete the human genome sequence. The final secrets held by the human genome yielded to Campbell and Morrison in the dead of winter, 1981. While the rest of the world was just beginning to investigate the possibilities of mapping the human genome, Morrison and Campbell had already done it. They did not, however, go public with their discoveries. Campbell had wanted to share the data with the world, offering an open-source template that would fast-forward all genetic research by 20 years. Morrison persuaded him not to. There was, after all, still work to be done. The Cold War was again heating up, and when the few individuals in the government hip to Exodus learned of the breakthroughs being made out in the desert, money rained down onto the Project.

Although the Human Genome Project was a stunning scientific achievement, it was but a single piece in the Exodus puzzle. In fact, as Campbell and Morrison had repeatedly explained to their government contacts, the Human Genome Project was only the first step in understanding humans at the molecular level. While the sequencing phase of the HGP was complete, many questions remained unanswered: most important, the function of almost all of the estimated 30,000 to 35,000 human genes. The Exodus researchers did not know the role of SNPs—single amino acid changes within the genome—or the role of noncoding regions and repeats in the genome: two processes critical to the Project's final goal of creating a new man to lead the American people into the new century. But before that could happen, Project Exodus needed to understand not only the identity of every single gene, but the function of each gene and how that function affected human illness and suffering—both mental and physical.

Although their work thus far had revealed the order in which the 46 coiled strands of DNA found in every human cell are arranged on man's chromosomes, the chemicals located on those DNA strands, the ones which contained the instructions for making the proteins that comprise the human body, remained beyond their grasp. Until Exodus was able to identify these letters, any attempts to neutralize undesirable traits, in either political leaders or infants, would remain a high-tech game of pin the tail on the donkey. Even if, by some stroke of luck, Exodus managed to nail down one or two genes that caused defects, until the entire molecular picture was complete, it was impossible to know whether removing that particular gene would affect how another gene worked.

Even as the Project's successes grew, it became apparent that realizing the goals of Exodus was going to take a lifetime—most likely, longer. It would be a great injustice to the human race, Morrison argued, if the two men did not see Exodus through to its conclusion. Even if they lived long enough to solve all the mysteries of the human genetic code, Exodus would be devoured by young Turks clad for battle in white lab coats, and the two would be resigned to advisory councils and the lecture circuit, a.k.a. where old scientists went to die. There had to be a way, insisted Morrison, to use what Exodus had learned about human DNA to prevent this from happening. Morrison's reasoning had seemed to make sense: The Treatment would allow them to stay strong and sharp, retaining the mental and physical abilities Exodus would demand. Why come so close, only to be pushed aside by younger, stronger men; men who might not share their same vision? It was in response to this need that the Treatment was born.

Campbell came to an hour or so later, staring up from his bed at the room's only source of light: a single bulb hanging from a thin strand of wire, transforming raw electricity into the meager wattage that struggled to light the entire room. Any additional illumination spread out from a series of candles scattered around the room, pools of wax forming as Campbell's sleepless nights mutated into cold gray dawns. A makeshift desk—an unfinished wood door laid across two paint-splattered sawhorses—and a musty old cot were the only pieces of furniture in the room. Both had been there when Campbell first arrived; he never got around to moving the desk and the ascetic nature of the cot had appealed to him.

There were no decorations, just brown accordion-style files stacked next to a beat-up laptop resting on top of the desk. The crumbling brick walls were adorned with a collage of newspaper clippings and printed articles. When he wasn't working with the Order or drinking at the bar downstairs, this is how Campbell passed the time in Tiber City: scanning the Web or even occasionally rifling through newspapers—the ones that were still in print publication, anyways—looking for stories about Morrison Biotechnology, about bodies turning up in the New Mexican desert, about the sudden resurgence of ancient diseases, and about Jack Heffernan. Campbell had hung the most recent clipping the other night, the fresh black inkjet clashing with the yellowed headlines and curled paper from the past decade. "Jack Heffernan: Zeroing in on Presidential Primary Victory"—that was the headline staring out at the tiny room where Jonathan Campbell spent most of his time.

"Me personally?" came a voice from the doorway. "I'd say he's a lock."

Campbell shot up from the cot, the pain fading but still present, his head swimming as he turned in the direction of the voice that, no matter how much time passed, he could never forget.

In the narrow doorway loomed Michael Morrison, his 6-foot-4 frame complimented by a two-button Brooks Brothers suit, white French-cuff dress shirt, and onyx cuff links.

On his feet now, Campbell staggered sideways, away from the cot and toward the desk on the far side of the room, his chest tightening as he struggled to breathe.

"I don't blame you for looking so surprised Jonathan. It's been quite some time—almost two decades now? But I want you to understand our—let's call it a separation—has been difficult for me as well. After all, you left New Mexico without even saying goodbye," Morrison added with a wink as he walked through the doorway and into the room, strolling toward the series of articles stuck to the wall in front of the desk, a bemused grin spreading across his clean, hard visage.

"My God, he's impressive," Morrison said, studying the clips. "Must have some outstanding genes."

The initial shock fading, Campbell's world collapsed into a blur of fury, heat, and pain. He charged Morrison, his left arm arcing toward the man's jaw. But Morrison sidestepped the punch, allowing Campbell to stumble forward before slamming into the wall, the impact sending several of the newspaper clippings floating toward the floor.

"That answers one of my questions," Morrison said, picking the empty syringe off the desk, studying it as he spoke. "Whatever you've been using, well, let's just say nothing beats the real thing.

"But don't get me wrong, Jonathan," Morrison continued, tossing the syringe back onto the desk. "You look good. Damn good. But you just missed me by a mile. I should have at least felt a little breeze."

Campbell wheeled back around toward the cot, a flash of steel visible as he pulled a .357 Magnum from under his pillow before aiming it at Morrison's chest.

"Still want to feel a little breeze, Michael?" Campbell snarled, stepping toward his former pupil, an audible click echoing across the room as he released the safety.

"I have no idea why after 20 years, you've decided to drop by," he continued. "But things are different now."

"So it would seem," Morrison replied, adjusting his cuff link as he watched Campbell move toward him.

"Then why don't you just turn around and head back through that door to whatever private jet is waiting to take you to Bretton Woods or Davos or wherever you're scheduled to be lauded next and leave me the fuck alone."

"Given your apparent interest in Jack Heffernan," Morrison said, gesturing toward the clippings on Campbell's wall, "you're not even the least bit curious as to why I'm here?"

"Whatever you've done, Michael," Campbell said, "you've done. I don't want any part of it. I've got a different life now."

"I certainly can't argue with that point," Morrison said, a smile creeping back across his face. "I'm going to reach into my coat now but don't be alarmed—there is something I need to show you, and then, if you still want, I'll leave. And please take your finger off that trigger: Your hand is shaking."

Campbell looked down at his trembling hand and smiled.

"You're going to have to give me a better reason than that Michael."

Morrison nodded, pulling an ordinary manila envelope—the kind used in a million offices thousands of times every day—out of his overcoat, extending it toward Campbell.

"I think this should suffice," Morrison said.

After hesitating for a moment, Campbell—the gun still trained on Morrison, the trembling in his fingers intensifying—took the envelope, some part of him still needing to know what Morrison had done because, whatever was inside that envelope, Campbell knew there was a damn good possibility his own research had made it possible.

Placing the gun on the desk, Campbell unsealed the envelope and reached inside. His index finger and thumb closed around several documents, which, after a deep breath, he pulled into the light, the envelope floating to the floor.

At first glance, Campbell failed to note anything unusual. The papers were lab reports documenting a human karyotype: the complete set of chromosomes in the cells of an organism, easily obtained by staining a cell and then taking a picture of it just before cell division; mildly retarded kids in high school chemistry classes were capable of producing similar reports.

"Cut the bullshit, Michael. After everything that's gone down between us I know you didn't come all this way to show me a karyotype report."

"Actually Jonathan, that's exactly what I did. But as was so often the case when we worked together, you're just not seeing the big picture. Look a little closer."

Holding the report up in the direction of the bare bulb dangling from the ceiling, Campbell studied the document, searching each chromosome for any distinguishing characteristic, any marking that would explain Morrison's appearance.

Then he saw it. Despite the dull ache radiating from his joints, from behind his eyes, Campbell laughed, a sound like steel scraping across steel limping out from the back of his throat.

"Twenty-four," Campbell said. "You're showing me a karyotype report with 24 pairs of chromosomes."

What Campbell didn't need to say, what both men knew, was that the number of chromosomes the report showed was impossible: Human karyotypes are comprised of 23 pairs of chromosomes, allowing for 46 chromosomes total. The adult male, for example, had the same 22 pairs of non-sex chromosomes along with one X chromosome and one Y chromosome. Swap out the Y chromosome for another X, you've got a female. Although occasional genetic mutations resulted in 47 total chromosomes, a human being with 48 was simply not possible.

"You expect me to believe this bullshit?" Campbell spat, crumbling the report and tossing it at Morrison. "I don't know what your end game here is, but you and I both know how easy it is to forge a report like this. Just tell me why you're here. It's been two fucking decades, Michael. Why now?"

"Trust me, friend," Morrison said, a hint of menace creeping into his voice, "these reports are no forgery. In fact, they are the very reason I never ordered my men to hunt you down like a dog. It would have been so easy, whereas letting you live—that is, if you call this living—was a risk," Morrison continued gesturing at the water-stained ceiling, the crumbling brick walls, "but I knew this day would come."

"And what day is that?" Campbell said.

"The day when you return with me to Morrison Biotech, to the desert. The day that you and I, together, take the final step toward realizing Project Exodus' full potential."

Exodus. Campbell's world wobbled, but held steady.

"That's right, Jonathan. Exodus is alive and well. But it's not like I'm telling you anything you didn't at least suspect," Morrison continued, pointing at the clippings on the wall.

Campbell leaned against the desk and exhaled, his eyes locked on Morrison.

"Not a chance in hell I'll ever come back. You can send your men—there's no need to hunt, you know exactly where I am," Campbell said, his eyes turning back toward the gun.

"You and I both know it won't come to that," Morrison replied. "Look at this black market garbage you've been relying on: You've made a mockery of the Treatment. You're not going to last much longer and when the end comes, the agony will be unforgiving. And you'll die in this hellhole, with no legacy, working as an errand boy for these monks…this Order. The only redemption you'll ever find is waiting back in the desert, back in the Exodus laboratories."

Campbell felt his heart skip a beat; of course Morrison knew about the Order—Campbell never doubted that. But there was a part of Campbell that hoped that somehow, Morrison would ignore the Order; that they would somehow slide under his radar.

"So why now, Michael? If I'm so fucked, why not just let me go?"

"Because there is a flaw in the final Exodus design. Fortunately for you," Morrison continued, "you—or any of this—probably wouldn't be around if my version of Exodus was perfect. In fact, I can guarantee that. Unfortunately for me, here you are."

"What kind of flaw Michael? What have you done?"

"What I'm saying," Morrison said, ignoring the question as he moved closer to Campbell, "is 24 pairs of chromosomes. Think of the possibilities. I'm here to offer you redemption. To erase the last 20 years. To bring you home to finish what we started." He paused. "What you started."

Campbell lunged for the gun on the desk but Morrison was too quick, slamming his fist into Campbell's chest. The blow drove Campbell to his knees, and left him struggling for breath.

"What I started," Campbell gasped, looking up at Morrison, his voice little more than a low growl. "And whatever it is you're trying to finish... those two things have never been the same. And if I see you again, I swear I'll kill you."

"The father of Project Exodus deserves better than this," Morrison said evenly, gesturing to the warped wooden walls and tattered bed sheets before turning and slipping out through the doorway, leaving Campbell alone with the demons from his past.

Campbell watched as Sweeney ran his damp rag over the chipped surface of the half- century-old bar a few more times than normally necessary, his fat pale fingers, very much resembling uncooked sausages, working from behind the bar to extricate a particularly tenacious piece of grime trapped in an knifed carving. The engraving was just one of many littering the old oak: The entire history of Sweeney's joint could be traced by reading the various messages tattooed onto the top of the bar. Drunken, mad prophets and end of the line Romeo and Juliets—the ones who couldn't quite pony up enough for 30–second television spots or high-traffic Web banners—used the surface as their easels, scratching out their midnight messages—desperate attempts to connect to someone, something, anything—when they thought the bartender's back was turned.

"So Morrison finally paid you a visit," Sweeney asked, finally looking up from the bar.

Campbell nodded, his fingers wrapped tight around the glass sitting in front of him. The crumbled report Morrison had left with him was on the bar stool next to him; he couldn't bring himself to read the rest of it, not yet.

Sweeney laughed and reached behind the bar for a bottle of Jameson, which he used to refill Campbell's glass, the ice cubes cracking in response to the splash of brown liquor.

"Been a long time," Sweeney said as he put the bottle away. "A very long time. Safe to assume this wasn't just a friendly visit."

"He wants me to come back to Exodus," Campbell said, shaking his head in disbelief. "And he knows about the Order."

Sweeney raised an eyebrow. "Can't say I'm surprised about either. He gonna be back? Maybe next time, we have a little surprise waiting for him."

Campbell picked the report off the stool and laid it down on the bar. He took a gulp of the whiskey, squinting his eyes against the burn of the booze. He could still feel the Treatment grinding its way through his system, although the booze helped with some of the pain. He shook his head at the bartender.

"I don't know Sweeney. I just don't know."

But staring down into the murky liquor melting the ice cubs, Campbell knew that was bullshit. Morrison would be back—whether he intended on letting Campbell live was the only question left.

Chapter 9

Tiber City
Aug. 27, 2015
3:43 p.m.

Dylan was dreaming of giant reptiles—dinosaurs whose names as a child he could rattle off on command, names he had now forgotten—attacking great cities of the West, a blur of leathery wings, scales, and fire, atonal screeching ricocheting off steel skyscrapers as terrible Behemoths descended out of the nothingness, plunging toward the hearts of these cities, rendering cathedrals and skyscrapers an indistinguishable rubble. The nightmare was unfolding in an alineal clusterfuck: images bombarding Dylan's subconscious without bothering to assemble any sort of cohesive narrative. There was only confusion—men and women abandoning their children as monsters swooped down on rotting cities, cars left in the streets, infants strapped in car seats as their parents fled into the flame. A plasma television in a storefront window broadcast the carnage in real time to the empty, blood-soaked streets, the eyes plastered across the PROGRESS poster the only witness to these terrible events.

The images grew disjointed, dissolving into a series of catastrophes—volcanoes, jungles, mountaintops, vast deserts—until a great earthquake rendered the surface of the earth, and man, building, and beast alike tumbled into the abyss.

Dylan awoke, seconds later, the toneless cry of long-extinct monsters still ringing in his ears.

Soaked in sweat, he checked the time on his cell phone: 3:43 in the afternoon. Groaning, Dylan swung his legs over the bed and onto the hardwood floor. The room was dark, courtesy of the blackout shades pulled tight over the three eight-foot windows lining his bedroom wall. When the shades were up, Dylan had a stunning view of Capital Bank Park, which had been known as Garden Park but, as a result of the city going bankrupt several times in the last decade, was now under corporate sponsorship; "product information booths" competed with century-old statues and botanical gardens for visitors' attention. On rare occasions the shroud of smog covering the city lifted and Dylan could see beyond the Jungle district and out toward the lights of oil tankers twinkling on the ocean. Most of the time, however, the sprawl of the Jungle seemed endless, pressing up into the horizon until the two were indistinguishable.

But right now the heavy window shades eclipsed everything, leaving only tiny slivers of sunlight spilling between the side of the shade and the edge of the window, tiny spaces that, no matter how hard Dylan tried to block them out, persisted. Short of nailing the shade to the wall, he had long since accepted that some small amount of light would spill through the cracks, disturbing the darkness he coveted.

Just because he accepted this fact didn't mean that he was happy about it, especially on days such as this—when he woke up hung over, his nose, throat, body wracked with pain, tidal wave after tidal wave of anxiety washing over him, threatening to drown him as he ground his teeth and involuntarily dug his toes into one another until the big one began to bleed, when he couldn't stand being awake, his mind spinning and spinning and spinning but he was so terrified of his own subconscious that he didn't want to fall back asleep.

Dylan was naked and alone, the black 600-thread-count sheets rolled up in a sweat-soaked ball on the other side of the California king. The balled up sheets weren't a surprise—his nightmares were getting worse—but the alone part was a little confusing. He remembered the girls from the club, from the bathroom; he could still smell one or maybe both of them on his face, his fingers. He was grateful neither of them were in bed next to him but he was confused because he didn't remember how the night had ended, how much coke had been done, who decided when it was time to go home, if everyone had a good time, if anyone's feelings had been hurt, if anyone fell in love: Any time he closed his eyes, all he could see was those eyes from the PROGRESS poster watching as a city slowly consumed itself.

He checked his phone again, hoping that maybe he had been mistaken but the digital numbers confirmed that it was indeed almost 4 in the afternoon—which was a problem because he had somewhere important he needed to be. With trembling fingers, he began groping the metal nightstand next to his bed, knocking over a glass of water before his fingers closed around a bottle of pills. Screwing off the lid, Dylan dumped the contents of the bottle into his mouth—two, three, four, eventually five 15-milligram pills of Ativan tumbled over the sickly orange plastic and down his throat. Once upon a time, that was enough to knock him out until well after sunset. Now, it was the bare minimum required to ward off the worst of the nightmares and subsequent crippling anxiety that gripped him in those hours after the party was over, when everyone had gone home and his kidneys began flushing the alcohol from his system, the narcotics relinquishing their grip on his brain stem but not without first leaving him the lovely parting gift of ravaged serotonin levels and a nameless, nebulous dread.

Rolling out of bed, his entire body was in a state of revolt, the chill from the air conditioner doing little to stem the tide of sweat pouring from his arms, legs, back, forehead. He trudged forward with his head down, using the consistency of the hardwood floor to fight the nausea as he stumbled, still nude, from the bedroom to the bathroom down the hall. He had forgotten to close the blinds in the bathroom and light was streaming in, sending sharp jolts of pain through his skull. Dylan moved to pull the shade shut but before he could he caught a glimpse of the city skyline and for a moment the panic he felt so acutely in his dream returned and he swore he could see those terrible beasts gathering along the horizon, their scales a mosaic of metallic gray. He closed his eyes for a moment, the low hum of the AC the only sound in the world, and when he opened them his vision had cleared and there was nothing but a solitary jetliner cutting across a static pre-dusk sky.

He turned away from the window, pulling down the shade before sliding open the glass shower door and twisting the faucet. Hot water blasted out of the nozzle as Dylan took a step back and turned around, his head still pounding as he flipped open the mirrored medicine cabinet mounted above

a marble sink on the opposite wall. A dozen or so different off-yellow pre-
scriptions lined the tiny shelves but the Ativan was already working its way
through Dylan's system, some of the post-coke binge edge dissolving, and
now he just needed something for the throbbing pain in his head. After considering a plastic bag filled with Vicodin, he grabbed a bottle of some over-
the-counter painkillers, twisting off the cap and dumping two, three, five in
his palm then catapulting the green and white capsules down his throat. His
throat was too dry, however, and he started to gag but before he could throw
everything up he managed to stick his mouth under the sink's faucet, water
rushing past his lips, pushing the painkillers into his system.

Dylan swallowed hard, pulling his head away from the sink and, after
closing the door to the medicine cabinet, found himself staring at this reflection in the mirror: three days worth of stubble framed by longish-brown hair,
strong jaw line and normally bright blue eyes that were, at this moment, dull
and bloodshot. He stood in front of the mirror for a moment, inspecting his
body, the shower still running, hot water pounding the glass enclosure, filling the room with steam. The reflection staring back at Dylan began to dissolve, eclipsed by the condensation clouding the mirror. Suddenly very cold,
he turned away from the mirror and stepped into the shower, the hot water
burning his skin, reassuring him he was still there.

Stepping out of the shower, Dylan dried himself, slapped on some deo-
dorant, and dressed quickly—jeans, T-shirt, and a pair of old Chucks. His
apartment was a mess and someone was sleeping on one of the couches that
formed a perimeter around the massive television hung against the exposed
brick wall—bottles and cut straws and DVDs were scattered all over the
floor and the bundle of blankets piled on the couch in the shape of a human
began to groan.

"Chase, that you, man?" Dylan asked.

There was a muffled response, some incoherent grumblings, cursing, and
an admonition not to be a dick and turn off the lights, even though the television was still on, the sound muted—it was Chase.

Dylan grabbed a half-empty capped bottle off the floor filled with what
might have been lime-green Gatorade but just as easily could have been piss
and flung it in the direction of the pile of blankets, smiling in spite of his

splitting headache at the sound of the plastic hitting the sliver of exposed scalp peaking out.

"The fuck man," Chase called out from under the blankets. "I'm trying to get some sleep. Why are you awake so early? We didn't get in until what? Like 6? Go back to bed."

"It's like, almost 5 in the afternoon," Dylan said.

"Like I said, why so early?"

"I got some shit I gotta take care of."

"More coke," came the voice, this time with increased hope.

"Not exactly, dude. It's just some shit I gotta do."

"Fine man. Get all secretive on me. Just text me whenever you're done doing whatever. We'll grab a bite."

"Might not be back till late man."

"No worries—I'm good. These couches are comfortable as all fuck. Besides, isn't that *Godfather* box set around here somewhere? I might just chill, watch part one and two, probably avoid three…I think I got some oxy last night, too…Need to check my pockets."

That's when Dylan saw it: Staring back at him from the television was the same face, the same eyes he saw on the building last night. Dylan felt his stomach flip and the world went wobbly.

The look on his face must have been worse than he felt, because Chase was actually up, moving off the couch, asking Dylan if he was OK. Dylan could only point to the television in response; the close-up of the face had ended, segueing into a political ad for the man to whom those eyes belonged: Jack Heffernan. Strong, warm colors flooded the screen and Heffernan was shaking hands as he moved through crowds, as he toured construction sites, as he met with members of the United States military.

"Those eyes…" Dylan half-whispered, his throat dry.

"Yeah, man," Chase said, looking uncertain as he nodded toward the screen. "Kind of reminds me of your pop's. In a good way. I mean, everyone thinks so…Just no one really wants to bring it up around you, dude…You can't tell me this is the first time you're seeing this guy? He's everywhere…I might even register to vote. I mean, probably not but I'm considering it, you know?"

Dylan was shaking his head, no longer certain. Had he seen Jack Heffernan before? It was impossible to say; he just couldn't remember. The past few months had just been a blur, one continuous attempt to escape from fear and anxiety and memories—nothing was certain.

The ad ended and Dylan felt his pulse slow, his world steady. He glanced at his phone.

"It's all pretty intense dude," he assured Chase, trying to forget about the ad, trying to focus on what he had to do next. "Look, I gotta jet. We'll meet up later."

"Later," Chase agreed as he turned and headed back toward the couch but Dylan was already out the door, keys, lighter, and iPhone shoved in the front pockets of his jeans, wallet in the back left, sunglasses in the back right.

Dylan's loft apartment was on the 15th floor of a 20-story apartment building located in Tiber City's Glimmer district, a neighborhood populated by the young and wealthy who had chosen not to flee for the relative safety of the suburbs. The hallway of the building was bright and wide—too bright— and his headache mushroomed, his hangover serving notice it wasn't going away without a fight. Wincing, Dylan pulled the sunglasses—black-tinted aviators—out of his pocket and put them on, exhaling as the world dimmed. He continued down the rest of the hall, running his hand along the wall as he moved toward the elevators, where the doors opened on their own.

He stepped into the elevator, pressed the button for the lobby, and leaned back against the cool metal wall. A Muzak version of an old Doors song— "People Are Strange"—was playing and Dylan found himself humming along, the painkillers kicking in as the elevator crept down toward the earth before rumbling to a halt, the white button on the side of the wall marked "L" lighting up as the doors slid open.

Dylan walked out of the lobby of his building, which at one time may have been a factory but now was a series of absurdly expensive, minimalist lofts teeming with wealthy junkies and trust fund artists. A security desk was positioned between the elevators and the entrance, a dozen different CCTV feeds from all over the building displayed across a row of tiny moni- tors positioned under the elevated countertop where guests signed in and packages were left. But the desk was deserted, the monitors broadcasting to an empty seatback, and Dylan kept moving, pushing through the lobby's revolving door and into the street.

It was raining again—a warm drizzle that smelled like rotting hot dogs, which smelled like the city—so Dylan picked up his pace, cutting across the street that, even though it was still only the late afternoon, was jammed with taxis, with people trying to flag them down, with people shuffling in and out of the cabs, all the while vendors jockeyed for position along the packed sidewalks, each one of them crying out, a sense of urgency infecting the crowd as the sun began to fall behind the tops of skyscrapers.

On the other side of the street now, Dylan pressed ahead, the rain coming stronger, some people opening umbrellas, only adding to the chaos. The pills were kicking in, cascading nicely over the effects of the Ativan. Still, he wished he had taken something stronger but there was too much happening right now; too much he needed to do.

The current block ended and Dylan was crossing the street, moving onto the next block, the storefronts indistinguishable, overdressed black children trying to shake his hand, to introduce themselves and establish some sort of connection whereby Dylan would feel obligated to take their flyer, to listen to a story, to buy candy. But he looked past them, brushing them aside although even as he did he wished it could be different, wished there was no need to be on guard against a child, but this was America in the 21st century and there was no going back. And so Dylan marched ahead, pulling his collar up against the rain, his sunglasses now on his forehead, holding back his long wet hair, his eyes locked on his destination: In the middle of the block, a gap appeared between the row of storefronts and restaurants, revealing the top of a series of downhill escalators framed on each side by stone obelisks that meant something once but were now simply in the way, inconveniences around which harried commuters had to navigate on their way into the subway.

Dylan took the escalator down into the earth, past a toothless troubadour holding—not playing—a beat-up guitar, whispering lyrics to an old Doors song—the same one that had been playing in the elevator earlier that day— reminding Dylan and everyone else who passed that *people are strange* and as the moving steel stairs carried him away from the surface, Dylan turned and watched the old man, the rain intensifying, the busker just standing there, repeating the same phrase over and over, the other lyrics forgotten or irrelevant or both, the cracked case at his feet empty save for a few coins, a cigarette butt, and a HEFFERNAN FOR PRESIDENT button.

The escalator continued to pull Dylan deeper underground until the surface disappeared and for a moment Dylan could see neither where he started out nor where he would end up: His world was a large concrete tunnel—almost 30 yards across, hundreds of feet from top to bottom—sliced into thirds by steel escalators that bore diagonally into the earth. The escalator moved slowly, ferrying Dylan into the earth while an asexual voice coming from somewhere repeated the same series of instructions again and again—passengers should alert transit authority representatives of any suspicious activity and not be afraid to ask fellow commuters "Is that your bag?"—the message interspersed with a reminder that low-interest lines of credit were now available, followed by a website address travelers could visit for more information—subject to certain restrictions, terms, and agreements of course.

The concrete walls on either side of the tunnel were plastered with colorful advertisements, lit from below by a series of lights running through the small gap between the wall and the escalator. The advertisements on the walls framing the escalators were apolitical: One featured a non-threatening, healthy-looking heterosexual couple doing something vaguely athletic—there were hiking boots, paddles, a mid-sized SUV, a white Labrador—the scene constructed in order to explain that a popular herpes medication was now available without a prescription, while another—an image of an assault rifle resting across the top of a gas mask, the entire ad cast in washed-out green and gray—was promoting the release of a new video game set in a post-apocalyptic nuclear wasteland that, judging from the images etched behind the mask, bore a disturbing resemblance to Tiber City.

Several toxin-neutralizers were fixed above these ads. Visitors to Tiber City often mistook these devices for intercoms but, in the case of a chemical attack on the subway, they would deliver a life-saving blast of nanopowder. Or something like that—there had been an attack a year ago and very little toxin neutralizing had occurred or at least that was the impression left by the 50 or so dead bodies. In the aftermath, there was the requisite congressional inquiries, press conferences, and class action lawsuits but somehow the devices remained—version 2.0—and were now adorned with the insignias of corporate sponsors. Your defense against chemical warfare brought to you by your friends at Shibuya Industries East.

Placing his hand on the escalator's rubber rail, Dylan tried to focus on nothing, his eyes wandering down from the advertisements and toward the line of lights running underneath them. There was a consistency, an order to their arrangement that for a moment was somehow comforting but as the ground floor drew closer he noticed something else: In that tiny gap, interrupting the row of ordered lights, was a tattered sleeping bag surrounded by a mountain of clothes, dirty diapers, shards of glass, and a stroller laying twisted and broken on its side.

But then the escalator reached bottom and Dylan stepped off, pushing through the turnstile and onto the platform that, flanked on each side by tracks, cut the concrete subterranean chamber in half. Monday through Friday, this station was jammed with young executives, jostling, attaché cases transformed into shields, umbrellas wielded with more than a hint of malice as vigorous men shouldered women and old people aside in order to squeeze into a subway car already filled to capacity, chivalry forsaken even though the digital screen hanging from the ceiling noted that another train would be arriving in less than two minutes.

Late on a Sunday afternoon, however, the place was deserted. Dylan moved toward the far end of the tunnel, past a series of stone benches, his footsteps echoing off the floor, the walls, the ceiling. When he reached the last bench—the back of which was tagged in graffiti, in symbols and words that meant nothing, something, everything—he sat down, his hangover finally beginning to recede, his chest loosening, his breathing more relaxed as the Ativan continued to carve away the anxiety.

Staring at the empty tracks in front of him as he lit a cigarette, Dylan noticed a hole—or was it a crack—in the wall above the tracks. Water trickled through this break in the concrete, running down onto the tracks and forming a brown pool between the rails. Around this pool, which was filled with empty cartons of cigarettes, old newspapers and magazines—the paper disintegrating, the ink faded beyond recognition—a red plastic bag, and what looked like a pair of panties but Dylan couldn't be sure, clusters of vegetation were visible, tiny sprouts of green coaxed out of the earth by stale water and artificial light, only to choke on the recycled air and blasts of burning rubber before being cut down by the rush hour express. This process would repeat itself endlessly: Whatever plant life existed before the subway was built forever attempting to reclaim the land, heeding only instinct, striving to fulfill its sole purpose.

Dylan could hear the train rumbling in the distance, getting closer, dull red lights lining the edge of the platform beginning to flash in anticipation, in warning. Seconds later the train burst out of the darkness at the far end of the tunnel, brakes screeching as the giant metal worm ground to a halt, near-empty, poorly-lit cars flashing past the platform. Finally it stopped and the doors slid open with a hiss, the kind of noise that seemed to characterize even the most advanced commuter technology—like some kind of reminder that the thing was not fucking magic, that it was, at the end of the day, still a collection of steel and wire and electricity put together by human beings.

And then the automatic door was sliding shut, another computerized voice, this time vaguely feminine, cautioning Dylan to move all arms and legs away from the door because it was about to close. There was a sign on the wall of the subway car informing him that, in the event of an above-ground emergency, riders could opt to receive special alerts via their mobile devices, thereby ensuring that, even as the city dissolved in a mushroom cloud, nothing would inhibit the flow of information. Dylan imagined the subway continuing in a post-apocalyptic loop, the riders long dead, mobile devices still buzzing with alerts informing the corpses that the world had ended. He felt an urge to run out of the car, sprint through the city until he was back in his bed, but before he could move the car was gliding away from the platform and into the dark tunnel ahead, steel screeching as the train picked up speed, and Dylan was thinking about the fact that the earth was once ruled by giant reptiles—about dinosaurs, about extinction, about his father.

The Journal of Senator Robert Fitzgerald
Excerpt # 2

To Dylan,

Things have begun to unravel. For as long as I can remember, even before you were born, I have felt a disconnection, a sense of separateness from not only my fellow man, but from the very world itself. What about your mother, you might ask? The answer is as simple as it is terrifying: I married her because when she and I were together, that fundamental separation seemed furthest and I imagined that, with enough time, she would be the way through which I would dissolve these boundaries. I was wrong. Elizabeth has been everything I could have hoped for in a woman, in a wife. But the things I feel, the deep alienation from my fellow man, are not mere loneliness or alienation: I sense—I know—they are something far more systemic; the products of a fundamental flaw deep within me.

By the time you were born, I already knew Elizabeth couldn't save me. I didn't want kids; I knew I wouldn't be a very good father. Guess I was right. But the night we took you home from the hospital—that may have been the closest I ever came to escaping my demons. Holding you against my chest, I spent most of that first night walking around the house, whispering to you, telling you only the good things about the land into which you were born. The world was still and quiet and I felt that if only I could somehow freeze that moment in time things could be OK.

But I had to be in New York for a fundraiser the next afternoon and I remember sitting on the plane, watching the world fall away, wondering if it would be better for you if I never came back.

Love,
Your Father

Chapter 10

Tiber City
Aug. 28, 2015
3:05 p.m.

The helicopter moved over the city like a terrible angel, its rotor blades slicing through the thick smog pressing down on Tiber City. Earlier that morning, there had been a moment when the chaos of the city paused and, as a light breeze blew in from the Leth River, the natural world seemed to exhale, lending the entire landscape an unusual sense of calm. Yet by the time Michael Morrison's private chopper began its descent to the roof of IDD Energy stadium, the city was once again riddled with anxiety and expectation and as the sun—looking like a planet on fire—ascended higher in the sky, the breeze vanished, sending the temperature soaring.

As the city whipped past the window in a blur of steel and glass and concrete, Morrison scrolled through the messages on his phone, barely paying attention as one line of text merged into the next. Campbell's refusal to rejoin Exodus, while not entirely unexpected, was infuriating and as the chopper swung around the stadium, Morrison seethed. Were it not for a single gene—the Omega gene—he would have wiped Campbell off the face of the earth a long time ago. Instead, because the Exodus team could not divine the function of this single gene, Campbell was not only still alive and toiling in some refugee camp, he was now openly defying Morrison.

One gene, Morrison thought. It was incredible. There had been no problem identifying this gene and Morrison and his team were even able to reproduce this rogue molecular puzzle piece that, ostensibly, served no biological function. But when the Omega gene was dismissed as vestigial, a mere piece of evolutionary trash, and therefore excluded from the original Exodus prototypes, the results had been the things of nightmares: As the only explanation for these continued biological horrors remained the Omega gene, Morrison demanded the gene be included in all future prototypes. At first the transfer seemed to hold, and the mutations that plagued the early Exodus prototypes didn't surface. And so the first complete product rolled off the Exodus assembly line and into American political life.

The chopper set down on the roof of the stadium, bouncing once before settling on the giant "H" marking the center of the concrete landing pad. Morrison snapped back to the present, sliding the helicopter's door open, pushing past the two men holding semiautomatic rifles, ignoring their pleas to allow for a perimeter sweep as he strode out across the rooftop, barking orders into the tiny microphone attached to his collar, his voice carrying over the roar of the rotors. Seconds later, fireworks exploded overhead, confirming the information that had just been relayed to Morrison: Jack Heffernan was ready to take the stage.

The people gathered throughout the stadium were chanting Heffernan's name, and those seated on the field rushed toward the stage, a massive, faceless beast. Back and forth the beast swayed, agitated by the unusual heat, and this beast would surge forward before falling backward, only to surge forward again moments later. There were too many people in the stadium and the smell of sweat and body odor and fried food permeated everything and there was a tension building, a tension that Morrison and his public relations wizards had spent years cultivating, a tension that would continue throughout Heffernan's stump speech before the inevitable climax that would leave the collective beast delirious.

But the restlessness ripping through the crowd was just foreplay and a minute or two later, a beautiful young blonde woman, wearing a sharp but conservative black suit adorned with an American flag pin on one lapel and the red-and-black Progress Party ribbon on the other, stepped out onto the stage and, waving to the crowd, walked to the microphone.

"Hi Tiber City! How are you today?" she asked.

The crowd roared its approval, again surging toward the stage, sending bodies tumbling over the barricade as security scrambled to prevent anyone from getting too close to the woman who, still smiling, had raised her right hand over her heart.

And then she was reciting the Pledge of Allegiance, her eyes locked on the only U.S. flag in the stadium, which was attached to the roof and, as part of the ownership group's attempts to squeeze every possible cent out of the stadium, was sponsored by First Bank—the pole was an alternating white and deep blue, First Bank's corporate color scheme; changing the color of the stars hadn't polled very well.

But the color of the pole didn't even matter because each of the five dozen video monitors in the stadium were displaying the image of a waving U.S. flag, while the words to the pledge scrolled underneath and then the woman was waving goodbye and the opening chords of The Rolling Stones' "Street Fighting Man" began blaring through the stadium. Seconds later two fighter jets blasted over the stadium—they weren't actual fighter jets, just regular planes that Morrison had customized to look the part—and then the stage was opening and Jack Heffernan was rising on a platform, waving to the frenzied crowd, pumping his fist and giving the thumbs-up signal, even pantomiming a little air guitar as he stepped onto the stage.

LED flashes burst out from every corner of the stadium—digital cameras and cell phones and smart phones thrust toward the stage—and Heffernan was looking out over the crowd, his hand pressed over his brow as he surveyed the stadium, pointing at random people in the crowd and flashing his golden smile, an image enhanced in real time in a control booth under the stage before being projected to every end of the stadium by two massive video monitors hung on either side of the stage, which were broadcasting the rally in cleaned-up high definition, offering a hyper-realistic version of events that, for the assembled mass, was the genuine narrative: The unprocessed life unfolding on stage was secondary. Finally, the crowd settled down and Heffernan, holding the wireless microphone in one hand and standing at the front of the stage, launched into his stump speech.

For a delirious 30 minutes, Jack Heffernan prowled the stage constructed in the middle of the field, his sleeves rolled to the elbows as he spoke to the crowd, smashing the disconnect of modern life in the way no man had done since Robert Fitzgerald back in 2000. The video monitors cut back and forth from shots of Heffernan on stage to images of the faithful gathered in the crowd—men with tears glistening in their eyes; women with their arms stretched out toward the stage; everyone shouting and pressing smart phones toward the stage like relics to be blessed. It wasn't just the masterful stage-craft that had whipped the crowd into such a frenzy; nor was it the words or the pledges and promises; it was something else, something devised in the desert, in the vats of Exodus, a genetic code optimized to appeal to the larg-est number of people, based on criteria that had been run through thousands of focus groups; even Jack Heffernan's voice had been reworked over and over again, until the Exodus team was able to find the perfect combination of cadence and pitch and timbre to create and sustain the illusion that the indi-viduals in the crowd were no longer alone because Jack Heffernan understood them; that Jack Heffernan would save them.

And then something went wrong.

The light in Heffernan's eyes began to flicker, and the brilliant blue began to gray.

His voice grew hoarse; his limbs were shaking. He was opening his mouth, trying to deliver the lines that had left so many audiences spellbound but the words wouldn't come. Instead, garbled nonsense tumbled from his lips, guttural and frenzied, and a woman in the audience declared Heffernan to be speaking in tongues and people were shouting and pushing.

A sudden shift by the crowd knocked over a lighting rig in the corner of the field and screams were now mixing in with the cheers. Heffernan's micro-phone had been cut but his lips were still moving as he stared past the crowd, out to some point on the horizon or beyond; maybe toward the heavens or maybe just in the direction of Michael Morrison's luxury box and even though he was still smiling his eyes spoke of fear and helplessness and confusion and by now the audience began to grow restless, confused by the sudden change.

Heffernan had been their connection to a world in which they felt alien-ated and powerless; at the rally, bombarded by the multimedia product that was Jack Heffernan, this separateness—that nominal entry fee for the human experience—dissolved into an Edenic daydream. Heffernan's bizarre meltdown had torn that feeling away from them, and, in its place, a dangerous tension began fermenting among the tens of thousands gathered in the stadium.

Watching the rally from his private box at the top of the stadium, Morrison could feel his anger building. This was the moment he had hoped would never come to pass. Despite the setbacks of the past few months, Morrison still believed Heffernan would hold up, that Morrison and his team had stabilized the creature's genetic code to the point where Heffernan could still win the presidency and last four, hell, maybe even eight, years in the Oval Office. Long enough, anyway, to make Morrison the most powerful man in the world. And Heffernan, he was only the beginning. Eventually, Morrison would use the breakthroughs made possible by Exodus to bring genetic modification to the masses; a wildly popular President Jack Heffernan would serve as the ultimate product placement.

However, staring down at the field, watching his candidate come apart at the seams, the prospect of a Jack Heffernan presidency was growing dim. And those prospects would be nonexistent, Morrison knew, if he allowed a full-on meltdown to take place on stage that morning.

Reaching into the pocket of his suit, Morrison pulled out his phone and after typing a single word pressed send. Aware of the potential need for a diversion, Morrison's men had recruited several members of Tiber City's ever-swelling homeless population to pose as protestors who would, if necessary, disrupt the rally. If questioned by any members of the media, these "volunteers" would admit to being supporters of a rival candidate. Morrison's people had assured these homeless men and women there would be no violence. Morrison's people had lied.

Less than a minute later, to the left of the stage, a cluster of protestors appeared, carrying signs with slogans countering Heffernan's vocal support for genetic engineering: "Man Cannot Make Man" and "God Created Man in His Own Image."

Several of these protestors pushed their way forward, steamrolling the crowd, moving closer to the stage. This sudden surge sent several Heffernan supporters sprawling to the ground, prompting the crowd to push back, angry barbs flying between the opposing groups. All of a sudden, two protestors leapt up from the snarling mass of flesh roiling in front of Jack Heffernan and onto the stage, screaming and shouting snippets of rehearsed catchphrases and shop-worn rhetoric. Police—plainclothes and uniformed—along with Secret Service and Morrison's private security detail swarmed toward the two protestors. Seconds later, a cop took out one of them, tackling him from behind; it was one of those strange occasions when, during a moment of chaos, for the briefest of seconds, life seems to freeze, everything goes silent, and even the most insignificant sound is amplified, so as the two men crashed to the earth, the sickening snap of broken ribs reverberated across the arena. Then, all hell broke loose.

Just about the time several of his accomplice's broken ribs were puncturing his spleen, the other protestor who stormed the stage turned and leapt back into the crowd, knocking over Jack Heffernan's podium in the process. Several officers dove in after him, their fat faces bright red and swollen as they plowed into the crowd. Heffernan, standing where his podium used to be, his lips moving but his microphone long since cut, was still attempting to deliver his speech. And then he was gone, hustled away by Morrison's men as the initial clash between police and protestors escalated into a full-blown riot. Seconds later, a series of small explosions shook the earth and smoke began snaking out across the arena.

Watching the smoke curl up toward his private box, Michael Morrison was suddenly aware he was no longer alone in the booth. Without turning his gaze away from the chaos consuming the field below, Morrison spoke:

"Welcome, lieutenant."

"A pleasure as always sir," the voice behind him said, a voice Morrison knew belonged to Malachi al-Salaam, his head of security and a former special operations agent that one of Morrison's government connections found dying in the atomic wastelands ringing the Persian desert. The enemy had tortured the man, then bound his hands and feet and left him to be picked apart by the beasts foraging through the fallout zone. Any other man would have allowed himself to die: Anger—a festering, all-consuming rage at those who left him behind, those in whose name he had committed unspeakable atrocities—kept this particular man alive.

Morrison augmented al-Salaam's genetic makeup through the same somatic treatment by which he stalled his own aging process. Rather than preventing him from aging, however, Morrison enhanced all the physical and mental attributes that had made the man one of the finest mercenaries in the Middle East wars of the early 21st century.

Al-Salaam was more than just Morrison's first lieutenant: He was Morrison's death-dealer, the physical instrument through which the CEO advanced his vision of the world. From the moment he laid eyes on al-Salaam, even before the augmentations, Morrison knew he was perfect; it was something in al-Salaam's face, something in his eyes and his expressions—an emptiness reflected, a glare so devoid of feeling or empathy most men couldn't bear to sustain eye contract—absolute oblivion, Morrison's kingdom come.

"Lieutenant," Morrison began, his gaze still locked on the chaos below, "things seem to be progressing a little quicker than I expected. We will respond in kind. Send one of your men to retrieve Campbell—that won't be difficult; it's unlikely he'll be conscious, let alone sober."

"Let me go, Sir," al-Salaam replied, cool and detached, his accent gone, replaced by a geographically neutral, timeless whisper. "The Jungle is an unpredictable place, and Campbell has friends…"

"Under other circumstances, I would agree. But I have another task for you, one that requires your…personal touch."

"What would you have me do?" al-Salaam asked.

Smiling, Morrison began to explain.

Chapter 11

Tiber City: Jungle District
Aug. 27, 2015
4:49 p.m.

One of Dylan's earliest memories was of traveling with his father's campaign. They were somewhere in the Midwest—maybe Kansas City, maybe Tulsa, but it could have been anywhere—and the entire campaign was staying in some chain hotel that gave coupons for breakfast, left individually wrapped multicolored mints—the kind that tasted the same no matter what unnaturally bright color you selected for consumption—and pamphlets for local attractions next to the entrance. They boasted conference rooms with tan buckets full of melting ice and lukewarm soda, the aluminum cans slick with sludge from the ice and the dirt off the hands of everyone else who reached into the bucket before you; and, covering folding tables, tablecloths that inevitably bunched up or slid off the side of the table, revealing splintered wood and tarnished metal.

Everyone would always be awake before dawn, scurrying back and forth in those last few moments of darkness, the moments when electric light felt inappropriate, as if the night was offended that you were rushing the entire process, and the hallways seemed to shimmer and pulse with a surrealism that left man feeling like an unwelcome guest, acutely aware of the wind and the cold and the fact that the sky stretched eternal. In those few minutes before the sun broke over the horizon, Dylan always found it impossible to believe that there were people on the other side of the planet, stockbrokers and waiters and teachers—that there was life anywhere other than in this anonymous chain hotel with its breakfast coupons and brochures for local attractions and the rumble of eighteen-wheelers blasting out across the plains.

These moments always filled Dylan with a sense of dread and he would burrow in the hotel's Technicolor comforter and wait until his mother—who usually accompanied her husband on these trips—came to wake him. But on this particular morning, his mother wasn't out on the campaign trail—it was just him and his father and the legions of staffers. There was a pale light leaking from the bathroom out into the darkness; the light barely made it five feet beyond the cheap tile threshold before the night caught up and swallowed it whole. He could hear his father getting ready; the man's heavy sighs competing with the halfhearted spray of the shower and faux energy-efficient faucets and ceiling fan.

From underneath his comforter Dylan watched his father putting on his suit and for a moment there was no dread, no sense that the day was already over before it even began, just a son with his father, who, in his Savile Row suit looked like he belonged atop Olympus rather than struggling with a jammed armoire in the last days of the American century.

Dylan's father noticed him and, smiling, came over and sat down on the bed next to his son. Dylan shut his eyes tight and pretended to sleep, not because he wanted to deceive his father but because he did not want this moment to end. Yet this moment was, as all such moments are by their very nature, unsustainable. And peering out at his father from the scrum of blankets, he noticed that there was something on his father's tie.

"Dad," he had said. "Dad, there's something on your tie."

He father looked down at his tie, at the streak of crimson, and smiled, in a sad and soft way to which Dylan was unaccustomed.

"Guess I flossed a little too hard this morning," his father had told him.

And then the train was screeching to a halt, jarring Dylan back to the present. A mechanical voice was bleating out from somewhere, reminding passengers that this stop was the end of the line. Dylan opened his eyes, wincing, the lights lining the side of the subway car a reminder that he was still hung-over. Even though the voice continued to inform Dylan that he had reached the end of the line, the doors remained shut, the memories fading but not fast enough—he could still picture his father in that hotel room, trying to explain to his son why he was bleeding. Then saw it: The side of his own hand was streaked with crimson but there was no cut, no visible source of the blood, but his nose was tender and there was a good chance he had done some damage last night.

With a hiss, the doors pulled apart and Dylan was on his feet, moving out of the car and into the above-ground station at 98th and Hazor—the only subway stop in Tiber City's notorious Jungle district. The rain had stopped, but the humidity persisted and, before Dylan had even gone a dozen feet, he was sweating. The sounds of the Jungle were suddenly audible: the electric hiss of neon struggling to come to life; a man and a woman arguing in a language Dylan couldn't recognize, the words ancient and sharp, alien to the soft cadence of the Western tongue, their words cutting downwind from the immigrant slums scattered like buckshot throughout the Jungle. These sounds fueled the desperation pressing down across the shattered landscape and every time long-haul truckers—one of those jacked-up knights of American highway mythology, jaw clenched from too much speed and too little sleep—hit a pothole while barreling down one of the distant freeways that framed the Jungle like a quarantine zone, the entire district seemed to shudder.

Although many of Tiber City's denizens regarded the Jungle district as a single monolithic slum, Dylan had come to appreciate the area's geographic subtleties—an appreciation that kept him alive. The south end—which included the subway stop at 98th and Hazor—wasn't always part of the Jungle. Over the last decade, a reverse gentrification had been underway, the Jungle's aggressive sprawl devouring the failed industries and abandoned homes along its border. Neon sprung up seemingly overnight and the junkies, hookers, pimps, and street preachers followed like moths to the flame, driving away any square holdouts: the hipster couple with Ivy League degrees hunting for *authenticity* (and a bargain-basement mortgage), the businessman who was *convinced* that this time the area was going to realize its potential and wanted in on it. Generally, those folks learned quickly that the Jungle offered a lot more local color than they bargained for.

Not that the Jungle's south end was completely off-limits to the rest of Tiber City; there were enough dive bars, live sex shows, and hourly rate motels catering to bankers, lawyers, doctors, and politicians that the mobsters who took a piece of all the action knew too many headlines were bad for business. So the odds you might get jacked stepping off the subway were only about 50-50 and considering how fucked the rest of the world was—not to mention how boring the burbs could get—those odds weren't so terrible. Too bad Dylan wasn't staying in the south end.

Turning north, Dylan began moving through the dying light of the late August sun. Unlike the rest of Tiber City, there were no skyscrapers in the Jungle. Yet even as night crept over the horizon the temperature lingered in the mid-90s. Empty newspaper dispensers lined the side of the street, serving as a canvas for aspiring taggers, a toilet for bums, or both and as Dylan moved past them he noticed several fresh pieces of graffiti—territorial markers indicating a new king had been crowned.

Not that it mattered; Dylan had made this run enough times that he was familiar with some of the local players and he knew which blocks to avoid, which streets to take as he hit the sidewalk, striding north, deeper into the Jungle.

His hangover was almost gone by this point, the over-the-counter shit curbing the pain just enough to keep him functional but the image of his father, the old man's tie stained crimson, stayed with him as he pressed forward, eyes locked on the horizon, on the black clouds attacking the sun. Dylan could sense the expectant energy building around him; like vampires, the junkies would soon rise from their chemically induced comas and hit the streets to score. Even the speed freaks, the meth heads who had been up all night, were coming down—and the crash was never pleasant, which meant more meth was needed to avoid the crash. The doors to some of the shanty houses cracked open; bloodshot eyes peered from behind the blinds hanging in front of broken windows: The Jungle had begun to stir.

Dylan picked up his pace, but kept his movements casual. When he hit 104th and Hazor he took a deep breath: Six blocks down, six to go, but the neighborhood was getting worse. Even the ballsiest suburban tourist—the father of four hot for an anonymous glory hole, the guy with the most to lose and therefore the need to absolutely not run into anyone he might know— would be hesitant to come this far above the 100 block. Strange things happened north of 100th and Hazor: the Web was always buzzing with rumors of vampire cults, voodoo congregations practicing animal sacrifice, and desperate digital alchemists forever seeking spiritual enlightenment from binary code, trying to extract the true nature of matter from the 0s and 1s swirling above the city. Dylan wasn't sure about any of that—any time he ventured above 100th he was generally too busy avoiding the dangers he was familiar with: the junkies, psychos, and religious nuts that swarmed like piranha across the avenues and alleyways of the Jungle district. And so today he was being extra cautious.

But as far as Dylan was concerned, that kind of danger was just the cost of doing business; the way he looked at it, it was like driving a car: If you wanted to get where you needed to go, do what you needed to do, then you had to roll the dice and accept the possibility some fuckhead would have 10 too many, get behind the wheel, and T-bone you in the middle of an intersection. Generally, the only people who got picked off by the Jungle district's resident speed freaks were the ones who either looked like they just stepped off of the country club patio or who decided to take a detour into one of the dozens of abandoned buildings that now served as meth labs, shooting galleries, or both. Fortunately, Dylan didn't fit into either category so he just kept his head down, moving quickly but not too quickly, trying to focus on his destination and shake the images of his father, that hotel room before dawn.

Taking advantage of the sudden break in the rain, vendors hawking all kinds of wares were scurrying back out on to the street corners—offers for porn, sunglasses, fake designer bags filling the empty streets in a chorus that was about a quarter English, the rest something else: Chinese, Spanish, Russian, even Arabic. Dylan was hardly surprised by the Arabic; it had been a long time coming: Iraq had dissolved a few years ago, the country's artificial boundaries torn apart as the new iron curtain of Sharia law descended across the Middle East. Following a three-year regional struggle that culminated in a low-yield nuclear exchange between Israel, Turkey, and Iran, a new state known as Neo-Persia rose from the shattered borders and radioactive sand dunes of the Iranian desert. Civil war and genocide followed, ripping nations apart and forcing thousands of Iraqi, Turkish, and Syrian Christians to flee into the West—or face life under the hard-line Mullahs who had seized power. Many of these refugees were repatriated across Europe, but a few thousand wound up in tiny enclaves scattered throughout North America. One such enclave stretched across several blocks of Tiber City's Jungle district.

Didn't take them very long to adjust to life in the Jungle, Dylan considered, as a man with a thick Middle-Eastern accent thrust a DVD in front of his face, the cover showing a girl with a red ball gag in her mouth and genuine terror in her eyes.

"Hot shit," the man kept repeating, followed by a stream of Arabic. "Hot my main man. Very hot."

But Dylan waved him away, moving north along 104th, watching the heat shimmer over the top of the road as he passed a street preacher standing on top of a porta-potty laid horizontal on the sidewalk, an artifact from a construction project abandoned sometime last century. Crude oil paintings depicting apocalyptic imagery—locusts with human heads, the battle of Armageddon, the latest tween pop sensation lashed to a spit and apparently being disemboweled, or maybe sodomized, or possibility even a combination of the two in what Dylan assumed was hell—surrounded the preacher's makeshift pulpit, propped up on easels that were little more than pieces of rotting wood bound together by barbwire.

Dressed in a tattered, old patchwork suit and bowler hat with a chunk ripped out of the side, the guy must have been out there for a while—he was soaked from the earlier rainstorm—but his sermon was still going strong: Woe to the merchants of the earth for a great famine was coming. Usually these street prophets had three or four acolytes passing out pamphlets, shaking pedestrians down for donations, but this guy was alone, standing on his makeshift pulpit in front of a crumbling old hotel—the kind with the neon lettering running vertically down the side, but this place had been shuttered for years and only the letter "T" was still intact—preaching the apocalypse to the shadows heralding the sun's departure from the earth.

"You," the man cried, extending a long arm toward Dylan, the tattered sleeve of a too-small jacket sliding up to expose a bony forearm rotten with collapsed veins. "I know you. I've seen you before."

Dylan kept walking, careful not to make eye contact—this was attention he didn't need, and sure as hell didn't want. He should have taken an alternate route—ducked down one of the alleyways lining the main strip—but then again, such a deviation could have been equally dangerous: The back alleys of the Jungle were always changing; routes and pathways opening and then vanishing as new syndicates and subcultures rose and fell and rose again.

"This man is dead; yet he walks among us," the preacher continued, his voice echoing off the steel and concrete, rising hysterical above the din of the vendors and hustlers. "Look at his eyes, look at them. Those are the eyes of a dead man!"

Stepping off his stained, filth-caked pulpit, the street prophet swiped at Dylan, his gnawed, jagged nails raking the back of Dylan's jacket. Dylan spun away from the man's grasp, but several of the vendors and dealers had already paused in mid-hustle, their interest in the situation growing.

"I know this man," the preacher howled, shuffling back and forth atop his plastic pulpit. "We all know him. We have seen him staring down upon our city, upon this tomb of steel and titanium and cracked concrete. Look upon the dead man and know him!"

It was funny, Dylan thought, because of all the dangers inherent to an excursion through the Jungle, the street seers were at the bottom of the list. And yet this one was about to create a huge problem because whether the guy recognized him or whether he was just waxing very-fucking-crazy, the end result would be the same: Someone would notice him and start asking why Dylan Fitzgerald, son of Senator Robert Fitzgerald, was strolling through the Jungle district. And that would mean a lot more than some bad press coverage.

Dylan knew he had to make a decision and make it soon: He could feel the Jungle's collective attention shifting toward him. But then something happened that yanked that attention in another direction entirely.

Watching over the preacher's shoulder as he continued to step backward, Dylan saw another homeless guy surge out of a darkened alley, foaming at the mouth and screaming. The homeless guy—his face a mess of sores and boils—charged the porta-potty-cum-pulpit, knocking the thing over and sending the old man careening into one of the dealers who had drifted over during the commotion. The collision caught the dealer off-guard, knocking the White Owl blunt out of his mouth, and the preacher was trying to turn away, his attention still fixed on his desecrated altar, but it was too late: The dealer grabbed him by the shoulder, spinning the old man around before driving a fat, tattooed fist into the preacher's face. The punch connected and the preacher went down in a blur of crimson, his final remaining teeth skittering across the concrete and puddles of sewage leaking out of the porta-potty.

The Jungle's attention diverted, Dylan slipped away from the commotion, moving back up the street, the preacher's words *dead man* still bouncing around inside his skull. One block later, he turned down 106th and broke into a jog. By the time he reached his destination—a dive bar off Hazor—night had begun to fall.

The sign above the entrance to the bar said *Lazarus*, which, all things considered, struck Dylan as pretty fucking ironic; it was the last place his father went before committing suicide. And so, once a year, on the anniversary of his old man's death, Dylan sat at the bar, drinking Jameson and thinking about his father.

He picked the bar because he wasn't interested in mourning; that was what cemeteries were for. Instead, each year he went down to Lazarus to perform a resurrection, to drag his father's ghost out of the shadows and hammer it with questions that never got answered.

The first shot finished off the hangover from the previous evening; the second one was for his old man—it slithered through Dylan's system, warm and familiar and sad, and Dylan was aware of how much he missed his father, of how little he understood the world around him.

Dylan signaled to the bartender for shot number three; it was the same guy every year—probably late 40s but thick with sleeves rolled up to reveal a bunch of tattoos, the most prominent of which looked like an asterisk in a circle. Somewhere in the background Johnny Cash played on an old jukebox, the sound ancient and unsettling.

"Next one is on her," the bartender said, tilting his head toward the end of the bar.

Dylan looked up and almost fell off his stool: Meghan Morrison was walking toward him, a beer in her right hand.

Meghan raised her bottle and tapped the side of Dylan's shot glass, taking a long swig from the bottle as Dylan did the only thing he could think to do: throw back shot number three; the sound of pool balls cracking together and Cash singing about atomic skies and capitals of tin were the only noise in the bar.

"I know tonight's not the best night," she began, breaking the silence. "But I've been trying to get in touch. I even came by your party the other night, had to practically beg that scumbag Russian to let me in."

"I thought that was you," Dylan replied. "I was trying to come over, trying to reach you…But then all that shit went down and frankly, I was so fucked up I started to doubt whether I had really seen you or was just… hallucinating."

Dylan just shook his head, embarrassed, but Meghan moved closer to him, the smell of her perfume—subtle but unmistakable—cutting through the stench of stale beer and vomit and cigarette smoke, reminding him of the last time he felt something—anything—that wasn't selfish or chemically induced; of a time when things had been less complicated; of the summer he fell in love with Meghan Morrison.

They first met at a fundraiser for his father. He did boarding school in New England; she had spent the year in Switzerland.

She drank champagne straight from the bottle and smoked Winston 100s.

Who the fuck smokes Winston 100s, Dylan asked later that first night.

She just smiled at him and finished her drink.

I do, she said.

He fell in lust. He fell in love. They were 16. Life was good. Or as good as life would ever get. It was the beginning of summer, 2008.

Some nights, when there were no parties or maybe there were parties but the city was hot—too hot—and the buildings and neighborhoods seemed too narrow—seemed to press inward—those were the nights they would leave Tiber. She would climb on the back of his motorcycle and they would hit the highway and just go; blasting through the darkness and leaving everything behind, gobbling speed when they started to fade, then driving some more until they hit the coast and picked a random motel, making love until dawn before crashing in each other's arms, the comedown from the speed warded off by the smell of her skin, by the steadiness of his hand on her back.

In the morning, he'd slip out while she was still sleeping, returning an hour later with breakfast—the most unhealthy, delicious stuff he could find: pastries and pancakes and mountains of French toast from whatever diner was nearest to the motel. He'd bring flowers, coffee, and a fresh pack of cigarettes and they'd sit on the floor of the motel, half-dressed, picking at the breakfast spread out in front of them, no cell phones, no laptops, just an old map or two, and talk about places in the world they wanted to go, about the different places they wanted to see. Dylan always argued for Tokyo; Meghan pushed for Jerusalem. Everything and anything seemed possible and sitting there on the beat-up carpet, they talked about the future—running a dive bar in Tangier, teaching private school in Wellington, skydiving in Ghent. The fantasies were indulgent and wild and naïve but they were 16 and in love and did anything else matter?

Most afternoons were spent walking up and down the empty beaches, staring out into the gray-blue nothing, somehow relieved that they couldn't go any further, both taking quiet comfort in the limitations imposed by the natural world. They would sit side by side in the sand, drinking from his flask, a massive blanket draped across their shoulders, and stare at the ocean for hours, pressed tight together against the wind, watching solitary freighters crawl across the gray horizon.

She had a beat-up cassette with a bunch of old punk songs on it and in one of those beach towns, at a pawnshop, she found a boombox—bulky and gray and covered in stickers from forgotten causes—and some nights they would blast the tape until dawn, rewinding it over and over as they sat in front of the small fire Dylan would make on the beach, drinking and talking about bands that had long since broken up, bands they would never see live, bands whose surviving members still went on tour but Meghan swore she'd never go see them.

That summer he made love to her on the beach a few times, a blanket underneath them, protecting them from the damp, shifting sand; another blanket draped over Meghan's shoulders, blocking out the cool night air as she moved on top of him. And although beach sex was never what the movies promised—they never told you how much sand Deborah Kerr got stuck in her ass—afterward, lying side by side on the sand, watching the night sky, was paradise. They were far enough away from Tiber City that the sky was clear and bright and Dylan could see all the constellations and even though he had forgotten the names of the stars and their stories, he and Meghan made up new ones, tracing warriors and animals and gods in the sky, imagining new mythologies.

The world seemed to melt away with a totality that eclipsed any drug Dylan had ever used; when she whispered *I love you* in the dark his heart sang and any feelings of separation and boundary vanished. The universe felt electric and new and the boombox blasted all night long, Iggy Pop and Joe Strummer and Patti Smith shouting down eternity until the tape wore out. They buried it at sea before ingesting more speed, hitting the highway just as the sun poked over the horizon, the land glowing and alive.

There was an old amusement park on the coast and toward the end of that summer Meghan finally convinced Dylan to go.

But I hate amusement parks, he protested.

But this one is different, she assured him.

And she was right; it was nothing like the colossal theme parks littering the East Coast. There were no superheroes, no movie tie-ins, no rides named after aging rock stars—just an old wooden roller coaster, a Ferris wheel, and a few other "vintage" rides, most of which were broken-down and roped off from the public. They went at night, after the families were gone and the park was almost empty—there were some homeless guys and chubby Puerto Rican girls but no one hassled anyone—and there were no lines and even though the rides were older and simpler and looked like shit, they were happy.

They snuck in a bottle of wine and wandered the main concourse, stealing sips and playing the rigged carnival games—ring toss, water gun air, whac-a-mole, skee ball—laughing as they lost in impossible ways. When the attendant wasn't looking, Dylan snatched a giant stuffed whale off the prize rack and, on bended knee, presented it to Meghan. They made out for a while behind the bandstand—just kissing and groping—and the night was electric and then some old woman was yelling at them, telling them to get a room, and Meghan's mouth tasted like cheap red wine and gum and lip gloss and then they were running back through the park, toward the Blue Comet roller coaster—a rickety beast of wood and steel, one of the last of its kind in America.

And then they were aboard the roller coaster, her hand on his thigh, as the cars began to climb the wooden track, their ascent heralded by a series of mechanical creaks and groans, and as they rose higher and higher he could see the lights of Tiber glowing in the distance; he could see the stars overheard. A gentle breeze blew across the car as, having reached the top of the loop, the ride slowed to a crawl.

What if I asked you to marry me right now?

Well that depends, she answered. *Are you asking me to marry you?*

But before he could answer the roller coaster kicked back to life, plunging down the backside of the track, and she had her hands up, laughing and screaming as the ride whipped around the track at breakneck speed. The rest of that night was a blur of wine and cigarettes and when he woke up in the morning, she was already awake, sitting up in the bed, watching him.

You know, she whispered, *I would have said yes.*

But in the end, the strain of his father's suicide had been too great, pulling their relationship down like a weight around the leg of a drowning man, and things had fallen apart, like they always did.

~♥)

"You know," Dylan said, "you're the only person I ever told about tonight, about how I come down here."

"Look," Meghan started, leaning up against the side of the bar. "Say the word and I'm out the door. I just wanted to talk to you, make sure you're OK."

"What?" Dylan asked. "Why wouldn't I be OK? What are you talking about?"

"People are talking. A friend of mine said she ran into you last week at Ruin; said you were in really bad shape. And I saw those pictures in the Post; you looked awful. Your eyes were so…off. It scared me."

"That's pretty vague," Dylan shot back, the effects of three rapid-fire whiskey shots starting to take hold.

"It is," Meghan agreed, nodding, "But I don't know. I was surprised how concerned I was, actually. I can't really explain it."

"Fair enough," Dylan replied, first looking into her eyes, and then away, across the room, at an old cigarette vending machine stocked with brands discontinued last decade.

"Well, here I am," Dylan said. "Now what?"

Shaking her head, Meghan smiled sadly.

"I'll go," she said. "I guess maybe you are OK. I just needed to find out. I hope I didn't ruin tonight—I just didn't know how else to get in touch."

Dylan was suddenly aware that he and Meghan were the only two patrons in the bar. The television above the bar, which had been off when they arrived, was now on, displaying images from a riot that had broken out downtown at IDD Energy Stadium. The sound was turned down—Johnny Cash was still playing in the background, letting everyone know what happens when the man comes around—but the news crawl at the bottom of the screen added details to the images of riot police, of protesters with bandanas wrapped around their noses and mouths, of a young woman lying unconscious on the concrete, of Heffernan's people spinning the day's events, all while the stadium burned in the background.

"No," Dylan said, signaling to the bartender, "I want you to stay. Let's see if I have any stories about my old man you haven't already heard."

The Journal of Senator Robert Fitzgerald
Excerpt # 3

To Dylan,

When Michael Morrison approached me to run under the Progress Party banner, I thought it might be an opportunity to vanquish my feeling of alienation—to connect with my fellow man. Instead, my alienation has been amplified. Newspapers in Tiber City are heralding a new "political awakening" driven by an "unprecedented connection" between candidate and citizenry. If only they knew the darker truth: that the connection is completely one-sided. My life is a blur of legislative sessions, fundraisers, fundraisers, fundraisers; rallies and late-night phone calls and people whispering terrible things in my ear. I miss votes on the floor. No one cares. I am told I have star power. I am told I am the voice of a generation. I can only recall the past in the third person, as though I were watching a movie: my parents, my childhood, my first love—all storyboard concepts I am familiar with but don't know by heart.

I miss you and your mother but I have begun to spend less time at home because I am afraid; my behavior is growing so erratic, so unpredictable. I have lashed at your mother on several occasions—my mask of control is growing harder to sustain. There are periods where I black out for 10, 20 minutes; sometimes for up to an hour: I'll come to on the couch, in the shower, even on the kitchen floor, sobbing.

So I look for other ways to eclipse this growing darkness, the anxiety and unease that waits for me around every corner of every anonymous convention center or when I sit alone in my darkened hotel room, after the rallies and the flesh-pressing, the flashbulbs and fake smiles, staring out across the illuminated skylines of a thousand cities, every single one the same, glass after glass of scotch to wash down the fistfuls of pills I've started taking. I watch the people go home from work and the light slowly leak from the land. The neon lights roar to life and a new wave of people wash across the city streets and below me there is life: some good, some bad but it is all life and it is in these moments when my sense of alienation is most acute. There is a rhythm to the world but while I can apprehend this rhythm, which I can understand as a concept, as something I might learn from a textbook, it is forever beyond my grasp. I feel as though something crucial is missing, that I am somehow incomplete and therefore I can only sense this other; I can never experience it directly.

So instead, I sit here in the darkness, numbing myself until they come to get me. And when they do, I will turn on again, like a machine. I will stand before the very people I now watch and they will believe in me, despite the fact that I have come to believe in nothing.

Love,
Your Father

Chapter 12

Tiber City
Aug. 31, 2015
7:16 p.m.

Springwood Rest Home had always disturbed Dylan. It was not simply the fact that the woman who gave birth to him was essentially incarcerated here, doped up for the majority of her waking hours and dependant on an anonymous, revolving cadre of administrators. That was certainly part of his disgust but there was something more to Dylan's loathing of the hospital—a still-evolving philosophical revulsion.

Part of this loathing, Dylan considered as he approached the main building, the rain coming down hard and soaking his jacket, was generated by the phrase "rest home." Over the past few decades, a vast societal consensus had formed: By adding or subtracting a few syllables, man could put enough distance been himself and reality to make it through the day. Of course, reality wasn't altered; it was just enhanced.

In Dylan's opinion, this trend—the embrace of the euphemism—only made the inevitable breakdowns in civilized behavior all the more atrocious. It was as though when the stark realities of life finally slithered their way under, over, around, and through all the artificial constructs man threw up, the strain was too great and people just snapped. And not snapped like punching a hole in the wall, but snapped like shooting up your office then cannibalizing your boss. Or driving off a bridge with the family in the car because the kids were possessed and DCS frowned upon DIY exorcism—that kind of snapped.

One such solution devised to keep these existential demons at bay was the rest home. But unlike, say, substituting police action for genocide or vision clearance engineer for a fucking window washer, the name rest home was quite apropos; just not in the sense most people applied it. A rest home, Dylan had come to discover, was not designed to provide "rest" for its occupants. However, it did provide a great deal of rest for those on the outside, relieving the arbiters of sanity of any further responsibility. Keeping the undesirables under chemically induced lock and key was just another means of keeping reality at bay; no need to interrupt life.

Although Dylan assumed that there was such a thing as genuine, biological insanity, he also knew that, sometimes, people just broke. And when our fellow citizens shattered like porcelain dolls swept off an end table, society couldn't be bothered to put down the remote or log off the Internet long enough to consider why. Not that Dylan had been interested in playing existential investigator after his mother collapsed. He was as guilty as everyone else. When Dylan's mother broke, he never asked why. He simply accepted it, swallowing the medical jargon bandied about by the legions of shrinks whom the court-appointed guardians paraded through his parents' home just like he swallowed the drab off-blue pills pressed into his palm.

Over the past year, Dylan's visits to his mother—while still erratic—had at least begun to increase. Maybe it was his growing sense of guilt over his own culpability, his recognition that he should have pushed harder to learn why she broke, why his old man decided to redecorate a hotel suite with his frontal lobe. It was because of these reasons that, a week after his 24th birthday, he was standing in front of the entranceway to Springwood Rest Home.

From the exterior, Springwood was nondescript. No freaky ramparts with gnarled stone fingers clawing at the heavens. No electric fences ready to stop foaming escapees before they could contaminate the sane. In fact, Dylan still remembered the night before the first time he visited his mother at Springwood: He hadn't slept a wink, terrified by visions of a cruel warden, leather straps, and shock therapy. The real shock, however, came at how normal Springwood appeared. Dylan remembered initially finding comfort in the sanitized confines of Springwood. It was such an enormous relief to realize his childhood preconception of mental institutions was so divorced from reality that, departing after his first visit, he considered that Springwood might in fact be the best thing for his mother. But as time passed, and Dylan spent more time at Springwood, he began to dread the place, although not at all for any of the reasons that fueled his initial nightmares.

Rather, the horrors of Springwood were more subtle and thus, felt Dylan, much more sinister. For starters, the entire operation depended on a deluge of anti-psychotics and tranquilizers. And not just the shit Dylan would pop to come down off a coke binge, but hardcore stuff that left the residents subdued for days.

But it wasn't just the over-reliance on a one-size-fits-all doping scheme that freaked Dylan out: A distinctive heaviness mingled with the smell of antiseptics, suffocating the entire grounds, so while there was never any overt indication that anything was wrong at Springwood, everything felt wrong. The physical grounds were pretty, but in an absolutely typical fashion. The hospital's exterior was the same as its surrounding grounds: by no means an eyesore, but instantly forgettable. It was as though someone felt the use of color or architectural imagination would have sent the inmates into a frenzy, or at least wake them from their FDA-approved stupor.

The two glass doors serving as the entrance to Springwood were "automatic," or so a large yellow sticker proclaimed in bold black font, but as Dylan approached nothing happened. Dylan took a step back in case he had moved too quickly past the motion detector—nothing. Dylan could see through the doors, past the metal detector toward the front desk, which was deserted. The wind kicked up, a hot gust sweeping sheets of rain sideways, and Dylan was pounding on the glass, shouting. Finally the doors came to life with an electric whir, moving out toward Dylan in a slow, stuttering arc. He moved through the doorway and into the lobby of Springwood Rest Home.

After emptying his pockets—all he had was a Heffernan for Progress flyer, which on his way out of his building that morning someone had shoved into his hands, and, for some inexplicable reason, he had kept it—into a filthy plastic bin waiting on conveyor belt, Dylan took off his jacket, laid it next to the bin, and stepped through a metal detector while the conveyor belt carried his belongings past a security guard—mid-30s, obese, with a mess of red curly hair—who was so engrossed in whatever was showing on the television mounted on the other side of the room that he didn't even offer a perfunctory grunt as X-rays of

Dylan's iPhone and keys drifted past his monitor. On the other side of the metal detector, Dylan waited for the bin to emerge from the X-ray machine, shifting his weight from his right leg to his left leg then back to his right as he tapped his fingers against the end of the conveyor belt. Finally the machine spit out the bin and Dylan collected his belongings, threw his jacket on, signed into the visitors log and moved toward the door at the end of the lobby. A few seconds later, he was through the door and into Springwood's main wing.

As Dylan's footsteps echoed down the linoleum corridor, cries, not unlike the bleating of sheep, became audible, drifting out from several half-open doors along the stark white hallway. It was primitive noise—all other forms of meaningful communication were forsaken once one entered the residential wings of Springwood. After all, the rest home was not designed to cure. It was designed contain. Yet in this amorphous alien noise Dylan sensed an impulse of resistance to the heavy medication thrust upon Springwood residents. Physical resistance was unlikely; the heavy sanitized air of the hospital had strangled most of this dissidence long ago.

Now all that remained was these soft yet insistent moans, cries proclaiming that there was something sinister behind the well-manicured front gate and colorful foliage that greeted the residents as they stared out the windows during the daily recreational hour. Even after her break from reality—another euphemism for "fucking crazy"—Dylan's mother had continued to project an aura of defiance, some internal commitment to struggle against the shadow draining her identity. Yet, over the course of her stay at Springwood, Dylan's mother slipped even further into her insanity, slowly yielding ground to the madness.

Last time he had come to visit—three, maybe four months ago—his mother had not spoken a single world. Instead she sat next to Dylan, staring out the window, breathing heavily through her mouth. Dylan could still recall fighting the urge to shake her until the past and the Halcion tumbled out onto the cold linoleum floor. Her once striking blond hair had begun to give way to a washed-out gray and when he kissed her on the forehead as he got up to leave, she began to cry. When Dylan asked her what the matter was, her mouth opened, then shut. Then she turned away from him and resumed staring through the walls and into nothingness.

120. 121. 122. The room numbers seemed to rush by. Each time he went to visit his mother, things seemed too fast, out of control—like he was propelled down the hall, rather than moving under his own volition.123.

Dylan stopped in front of 123, staring at the stark white door to his mother's room. He used to bring decorations for her door—pictures of their family's old beach house, of his mother and her sisters at her college graduation, of his mother standing on the edge of a pier smiling as the sun set behind her, of the life she used to have and love—but the staff took them down. No more pictures, thank you, they said, with a practiced smile perfected by human resource directors and mid-level government bureaucrats over the course of the last century.

Dylan knocked softly on the door. There was no response. He knocked again. Still no response. Maybe she was sleeping. He pushed the door open a crack.

"Mom?"

His mother was sitting on the edge of a crisply made-up twin bed, her back turned to him as she stared out the window across the manicured lawn toward something. Toward nothing. This was how it had been since his father pussied out and pulled the trigger—she just turned off, unable to deal with what happened. Or, perhaps more likely, why it happened.

Dylan walked into the room, wincing as he placed his hand over her terry cloth covered back, protruding shoulder blades only hinting at the frailty Dylan could sense surrounding her.

"Mom," he said again, moving around the side of the bed before taking a seat on one of the wood and vinyl chairs provided for visitors, chairs Dylan swore were designed to minimize the length of Springwood visitations.

"How are you?"

When his mother turned to face him, turned away from wherever she was, whenever she was, he could see—clearer than he had seen anything for quite some time—the extent to which this place was destroying Elizabeth Fitzgerald. She had aged terribly: Gone was her *Vanity Fair* beauty, replaced by dry, tight skin pulled taut across her stooped frame. Drained of all color, her legendary blonde tresses were listless strands of gray, the same color as her skin, pulled backward into a bun.

"My God," she whispered. "You look so much like your father."

Dylan just nodded and smiled as he moved to embrace his mother. But she pulled back, raising her hand and pressing it against his check as she studied him. The room smelled like cleaning products and stale perfume—the glamour of his mother's old life strangled by the hyper-sanitary existence that replaced it. She was breathing hard through her mouth now, her warm breath wafting toward him in waves and he began drifting around her room, fingering the leaves on the fake plant resting on the wooden dresser in the corner of the room, telling her how good she looked, how healthy, asking about the food, the staff, if she made any new friends but when he noticed her wedding ring on a glass finger on her nightstand he fell silent.

"Why are you here," she asked, her voice a flat monotone.

"It's my birthday," Dylan replied. That it was days after the anniversary of his father's death went unspoken. "Actually, my birthday was a couple of days ago but..." he trailed off, tired of lying.

"But I just couldn't make it down any sooner." *Because I'm a piece of shit* he wanted to add but instead just looked away, out the window and into the rain still strafing the landscape. The air looked heavy and Dylan could see a fog forming along the perimeter of the grounds, pressing forward toward the institution, the natural world determined to asphyxiate the rest home.

"I'm never coming home, am I?" his mother asked, breaking the silence.

Dylan turned back toward his mother, who, now sitting in one of the broken down chairs provided for visitors, looked smaller than he could ever remember.

"No Mom. That's not true at all. You'll be home as soon as the doctors say you're well."

She snorted. "Well. What does that mean? They give me so many pills, how can they even tell? I..." she paused, her voice cracking, "I don't even remember what I felt like...before coming here. I can still recall everything. Sometimes...sometimes I dream about the past, about when you were a baby...but mostly about your father. But when I dream, I never feel anything. I simply observe. I have this one dream where I'm with your father in that hotel, on that night. And I'm watching him put on his suit, drain the bottle of whiskey, load the gun. But the whole time, I feel nothing. Even when he puts the barrel in his mouth."

"But Mom, that's good, right? Isn't that what you wanted," Dylan inquired. "To not be afraid? To be able to get past what Dad did to us?"

"Maybe once. I don't know anymore."

She paused, any remaining hint of color vanishing from hard, dry cheeks.

"What is that?" she asked.

"What is what?"

"Sticking out of your coat pocket. That flyer. What is that for?"

"Oh that," Dylan said, confused at the shift in the conversation, at his mother's sudden interest in the flyer. "When I was on my way here someone was passing them out by the subway...lotta people have been talking about this guy lately so I just took one. I meant to throw it out but..."

"Give it to me."

"What?"

"Dylan. Give me that flyer."

His face frozen in a quizzical half-smile, Dylan reached into his pocket and pulled free the still-damp, crumbled red and blue flyer, smoothing it against his chest as he studied his mother as she stood in front of him, her arm reaching out for the flyer, her hand opening and closing and then opening again in accordance with some internal rhythm.

"Yeah...sure thing, Mom...it's just a stupid flyer."

But before he could even finish his sentence his mother was ripping the flyer from his hand, holding it up toward the harsh LED lighting imbedded in the ceiling, and Jack Heffernan was staring back from the flyer at both of them, and it was in that moment—maybe it was the lighting or the angle of the shot or the way the rain made the ink run, blurring the details of the photo—the would-be president's resemblance to Dylan's father was uncanny.

And then his mother was screaming, ripping the flyer into pieces, her eyes reflecting a kind of intensity and anger that he hadn't seen from her in years, the kind of defiance he had last seen in the months before his father's death when his parents would argue about his father's health, about the constant campaigning, about the booze and the pills and everything else the old man had used to try and keep his demons at bay.

"Don't you understand," his mother was shouting. "He did this! He did this!"

"What? Who did what? Jack Heffernan, the guy running for president? What did he do?" Dylan asked, trying to speak softly as he took his mother's arm, tried to get her to sit down on the bed, a sense of helplessness pressing down on him. But she spun away from him, her hysteria growing as she continued to pace the room, tugging at her scalp, her cracked fingers coming away with small clumps of gray hair.

"You don't understand," she kept repeating. "You don't understand."

"Understand what, Mom? Just try and calm down and we can figure this out together," Dylan pleaded.

But his mother just continued screaming, her eyes growing larger as the focused anger that had flashed just a moment earlier was replaced by a directionless rage. In the hallway outside the room Dylan could hear movement and then someone was knocking on the door, asking if everything was all right, and although Dylan assured them it was, his mother's screams contradicted his claims. The knocking grew louder and his mother—now pressed into the corner of the room, looking impossibly small and frail, her bathrobe slipping off her shoulder—continued to rant about the Heffernan flyer.

"Those are your father's eyes," she was telling him as the orderlies finally forced open the door. "Don't you see that?"

And then Dylan was being asked to leave, being *told* to leave. It was suggested that maybe his visits weren't particularly helpful—that maybe he needed to reconsider any plans for visits in the near future.

Someone put a hand on his shoulder and he lost it. Wheeling around, Dylan took a swing, his fist flying blindly toward the source of the passionless drone—a pear-shaped bureaucrat in his early to mid-40s, not tall, not short; not skinny, not fat: simply there. But the blow missed its mark and Dylan was tumbling forward, the earth surging up to break his fall, a vision—or was it a hallucination—of his mother scrawling something onto the back of the Heffernan flyer before stuffing it back into his jacket pocket along with something else, something small and silver, was the last thing he remembered.

Over the course of her life, Elizabeth Fitzgerald had heard Death described in a variety of ways: grim reaper, pale rider, gentleman caller. But when Death came for her, it had a different name, albeit one she had heard before, one her husband used to cry out in his sleep: Malachi al- Salaam. Al-Salaam was an ambassador of the desert, a dark man who whispered of loneliness and alienation and the 21st century. He slipped into her room, materializing out of the darkness and speaking to her about her husband; her son. Al-Salaam told her some truths; he told her some lies, mixing and twisting the two. But mostly, Death asked her questions. Questions about her son: What had she told him, al-Salaam wanted to know. Even when her silence was greeted by physical pain, she said nothing.

Instead, she only found it curious Death was not omniscient after all.

It came sooner than she hoped, but no sooner than she expected. Her only regret was that she did not tell her son more; that she did not do enough to prepare him for the coming storm. That was a mother's job—to prepare her children. And as Death forced open her mouth, ramming pills down her throat, her only fear was that she had not done her job well enough.

The Journal of Senator Robert Fitzgerald
Excerpt # 4

To Dylan,

Riding in the back of a limo after a Progress Party fundraiser in Boston, something went wrong. This incident started off as just another panic attack, the kind where I feel untethered from this world. When these attacks strike, I feel like I have no boundaries, that I am the alpha and the omega, the beginning and the end. What's the problem, you're probably already thinking. Absolute freedom, defiance of limitations: These are the pinnacles of human existence, the things we strive for each day. A year or two ago, I would have agreed. But I've come to understand that when most men talk about absolute freedom, they are referring only to their ability to have limitless choices, limitless options; endless means of amusement, entertainment, and comfort. In reality, such an abundance of choices just allows man to wander for an even longer time, to be distracted and never find his place.

Every man has his place, and when he finds that place and learns to exist within its boundaries he is free to fully realize himself. These are not arbitrary boundaries—nor are they the product of any government, any bureaucratic scheme. Rather, they are the product of a natural order that I have come to know only because I exist outside of it; I doubt I would even notice this sensation were I able to commune with this order: I suspect the fact I recognize this separation is a direct result of my inability to make this connection.

This must sound insane! But my son I promise you there is something more to life than what we can see and touch every day: I know it is there but despite the fact that every privilege in the world is mine for the taking, I simply cannot ever know this other—and that is the price of this absolute freedom. I have tried going to church, I have tried going to temple. I sat down with Buddhist monks in a monastery outside Seattle and I saw fear in their eyes when they asked me to leave.

So what happened in Boston? I was in the limo and one of these attacks began: I poured myself a drink and stared out the window watching the lights of satellite towers blink red on the horizon, transmitting information into space; the pit of my stomach went cold and I was so afraid: There was something electric out there, something waiting for me to…respond. That's the best way I can describe it. I sense that, were I able to connect with this force on even the smallest, most insignificant level—perhaps even a subconscious level—I might have been OK. Instead my body went into some kind of frenzy: uncontrollable seizures that left me writhing on the floor of the limo, strange white foam pouring out of my mouth. And then, there was nothing.

When I awoke I was in a helicopter being lifted over the city, red and green and yellow wires connecting me to machines that, for the moment, were keeping me alive. All around me men were shouting over the roar of the blades; the wind blasting over, under, around the copter; the bleat of the machines. And then a man appeared by my side—I had seen him before; he was one of Morrison's security personnel—and as the helicopter continued to rise, he jammed a syringe into my vein and the world started to glow, the thump thump thump of the rotors soothing as I drifted back to sleep.

Love,
Your Father

Chapter 13

Tiber City
Aug. 31, 2015
10:10 p.m.

For almost two days, Campbell slept, his body exhausted and wracked with fever as the Treatment worked its way through his system. His dreams, like always, were filled with half-formed creatures pleading with him, begging for something he was supposed to know but could not remember. When Campbell woke, Sweeney had been dead for a little over 10 minutes.

It was not, however, the bartender's death that jolted him out of his drunken stupor. Piano wire around Sweeney's neck had sliced the man's jugular, turning the top of the bar into a crimson mess: The bartender's execution, while messy, was silent—a severed windpipe tends to have such an effect. Instead, Campbell was woken from his hibernation when Sweeney's killer's left boot crashed through the rotting stairwell leading from the main bar up to the loft.

He shot to his feet too quickly and a wave of nausea coursed through him, the Jameson still sloshing about in his stomach, the Treatment leaving his joints inflamed. Stumbling backward, Campbell caught his balance against the side of the wall just as the lock on his door sprung open. It shouldn't have been so easy to pick that lock, he thought, his hands grasping behind him for any type of offense—even the most rudimentary type of weapon would have done. But within seconds the door was ajar, a massive shadow eclipsing the entire doorway. Campbell had just enough time to steady himself, his hands closing around the base of one of the candles left burning beside his cot.

A man loomed in the doorway, tattooed and enormous, gold teeth glittering as the candlelight emanating from the bedroom rose and fell and rose again. Muscles, the work of serious tissue grafting, threatened to swallow the man's features whole. Seconds later the man was in the room, walking toward Campbell, a large syringe dangling from his right hand.

"Exodus needs you," the giant growled, holding up the syringe as though it was a warning. "You're rejoining the Project: The only question is what kind of condition you'll be in on your first day."

Campbell smiled, a response that seemed to confuse his assailant, causing the giant to pause. That split second of hesitation was all Campbell needed: He charged the invader, driving the flaming end of the candle into the man's right eye. The eyeball exploded from the heat, splattering all over Campbell's shirt. The intruder reeled backward, clawing at his face as the flame began to spread, his momentum carrying him back onto the rotting stairway. The force of his attack pulled Campbell forward as well and the combined weight of the two men was too great: The decrepit stairs groaned and then collapsed.

Smashing hard into the earth, Campbell felt his world go fuzzy, darkness bleeding into the corners of his peripheral vision. As he struggled to remain conscious, Campbell twisted his neck left, then right, looking for his assailant: The man lay in a heap 10 yards away, impaled on the broken edge of railing, his corpse consumed by the flame from the candle. Yet, fire was avaricious by nature and within seconds, the flame spread to the bar, devouring the ancient wood and spilled alcohol, flooding the room with smoke.

As high-proof bottles of alcohol began exploding around him, shards of glass raining down like razor–tipped hail, Campbell saw another figure cutting through the shadow and smoke—it was Jael moving across the bar with her gun drawn, swinging the barrel in an arc around the room as she called out to him. Campbell opened his mouth to reply but his lungs filled with smoke and he was gagging, hard. And then Jael was over him, pulling him to his feet. He was able to stagger a dozen feet toward the exit but the blaze continued to spread, greedy and unforgiving. Campbell's body faltered. The world began to spin and as Campbell crashed to the earth, he noticed Sweeney's corpse roasting behind the bar, the man's black tongue sizzling from the hellish temperatures.

And then there was only black.

Chapter 14

Tiber City: Glimmer District
Aug. 31, 2015
2 a.m.

Pressing up against the blackened steel rail that ran the perimeter of the open-air platform, Dylan stared down at the mass of flesh pressed together in celebration of The End of World—one of Tiber City's roving bacchanals. The End of the World was thrown at irregular intervals in different locations across the city: Information about the party was restricted to an exclusive guest list and disseminated via encrypted transmissions to would-be revelers' mobile device of choice.

Earlier that night, Dylan received his invitation and even though he should have stayed home and slept every time he closed his eyes, he saw his father's face, heard his mother's pleas—he needed to get out of his apartment, go somewhere, do something. Anything. His mother had scrawled an address and some numbers on the back of the Heffernan flyer before she slipped it back into his pocket—just more crazy shit—but instead of just throwing the thing away, it just sat on the nightstand next to Dylan's bed, Heffernan's eyes following him as he paced the apartment like an animal. But the flyer wasn't the only oddity: There was a key as well, a tiny silver thing with jagged teeth. He wanted to believe there was some method to his mother's madness, that she had created the whole scene so she could slip Dylan the key without the security cameras noticing—at least not noticing until he was on his way back downtown. But no matter how many times he replayed the events of that afternoon in his head, the truth remained elusive and now his brain was just spinning.

He tried calling Meghan but he got her voice mail and that only made the situation worse. Sure, they were going to take whatever was between them slow but his life wasn't exactly tailored to gradual revelation. Not only could a few key search engine terms reveal more facts about his life than he even remembered—in part because lots of information was embellished or straight up bullshit—but the issues he was struggling with were beyond his control: His demons had a life of their own, manifesting themselves when and where they chose. Dylan's emotions bled through whatever façade he tried to throw up, a trait that could wear on relationships, a trait that might explain why Meghan Morrison wasn't picking up her cell phone. Not that he could blame her; maybe that night at the bar had reminded her that the good old days weren't that good, they were just familiar, and in these days, in this city, that counted for a lot.

He finally gave up trying to get a hold of Meghan and fired off a series of texts to Chase and Mikey, explaining that the last few days had been pretty heavy and were they up for an End of the World party?

Tonight, the End of the World was being held in one of the Jungle's abandoned warehouses and by the time Dylan and his friends arrived, the party was well underway. A grated platform rising two or three stories in the middle of the space—a cube-shaped industrial artifact that once upon a time was used to store goods before they were shipped across the country, the continent, the world—now supported a massive stone altar. The surface of the altar was a jumble of video monitors and turntables, which a DJ—female, topless, and wearing a World War I style gasmask—used to create the electronic trance music blasting out across the party: sinister, androgynous vocals purring over relentless pulsing backbeats, the lyrics dark and terrifying. Occasionally this high priestess of the Tiber City underground would raise her hands as the music built to a crescendo, the crowd mimicking her movements, the beats moving faster as the vocals stretched endless before the DJ threw her hands down and the music crashed back into its rhythm, sending the crowd into a frenzy.

A fashion runway jutted out from behind a curtain covering the back wall of the massive warehouse, cleaving its way through the glitterati and gilded starfuckers gathered on either side. The ceiling above the runway looked like the nest of some mechanical monster: titanium girders running in every direction to form the foundation for a giant overhead conveyer system; clusters of black wires and steel chains filled the gaps between girders. At the end of several of these chains, giant meat hooks dangled above the assembled masses, carrying female fashion models, one after the other—naked, motionless and covered in bruises and blood that may or may not have been fake—the length of the runway before snapping to a halt at the end of the platform. The conveyor belt then let out a mechanical hiss that was audible even over the music and the hooks jerked the models right, then, immediately, left in a perfect re-creation of an end-of-the-runway pose, the girls, hands on hips, staring into the crowd with open, expressionless eyes but no one was paying attention even though it was difficult to tell how exactly the girls were attached to the hooks—the lighting rose and fell in rhythm with the music and each time Dylan tried to figure it out the room again plunged into darkness and the next model was rolling down the runway, her eyes perfect reflections of oblivion.

Exhausted, Dylan stumbled back from the edge of the platform, crumpling onto one of the many black leather couches that formed a loose square around several glass tables. Chase and Mikey were lost in the crowd and now Dylan found himself pressed next to several young looking Japanese girls all wearing tiny pink backpacks lined with white fur. One wearing too much eye shadow and purple lipstick, white knee socks and tiny pink ribbons in her jet black hair, offered Dylan a shy smile. On her spray-tanned wrist was a bracelet made of alternating pastel beads, the kind that look edible, the pattern broken only by a series of white beads in the middle, each with a letter, the combination of which was meant by the manufacturer to spell her name but instead read W-H-O-R-E. He wondered how old she was. Maybe 16? Maybe younger? He looked away, the dark, pulsing trance continuing to swirl around him.

There was a massive line of coke sitting on the table in front of him; he wasn't sure who had cut the line and he didn't really care—he just leaned over and, pressing his left nostril shut, snorted the entire thing. When Dylan pulled his head back, blood fell from his nose, crashing into the table in front of him, blurring his reflection. With a trembling finger, Dylan reached down and began to trace a picture, outlining his skull, then adding two eyes and a twisted smile. The blood was beginning to flow a little more freely now. He wondered if maybe he'd broken something. Several carefully wound hundred dollar bills lay scattered about the table. He wondered if he even cared. His heart was hammering his rib cage and one of the Japanese girls was saying something else to him but all he could think about were those eyes: Jack Heffernan's eyes. And not just the ones watching the entire city from skyscrapers and video monitors but the eyes captured by the news footage of the IDD riot, the ones that reflected the same nothingness staring back at him from the blood splattered glass table in front of him. He should have looked up that address, he thought. There's something wrong with the coke, he thought.

And then the Japanese girl was saying something to him. At first he thought she told him that there was an ancient belief that photographs could steal their subject's soul and that was why she tried to avoid paparazzi—at least when practical, she stressed, or at least he thought she stressed, but the music was loud; he could have misunderstood and she seemed to sense this, to sense his confusion and lean closer, and he could see her lip gloss glisten, light reflecting off the strobe from the dance floor, and then she was saying something about wanting to suck his cock but again he wasn't certain because his nose was really bleeding and the world was starting to turn a little fuzzy and that was not what good coke did: Good coke made everything clean and tight and shiny and bright—adjectives that in no way captured his present situation.

He tried again to get up but he couldn't and the Japanese girl kept turning to her friend and giggling. The sound grated on Dylan, and he was really sweating now, the world coming in and out and back into focus as the music in the warehouse began to rise toward another frenzied peak, strobe lights spinning through the dark and although he wasn't sure if the girls were giggling about the blood, or about sucking his cock, or even why they would giggle with the vacant outline of his face—the one traced with his own blood—staring back at the room he couldn't focus: At this point he was just trying not to pass out. His thoughts spiraled out of control: cocainebloodpaparazziwhorecelebrityvanishdesignersfatherlightsinformationmeghan.

It was at that moment Dylan realized he was overdosing, but as the lights from the club reflected off his blue eyes, making them glow ghostly silver, the music continuing to climb toward a moment—toward *the moment*—he simply did not give a fuck. He finally felt like he got his old man, finally understood why the motherfucker pulled the trigger. Staring straight ahead at nothing, he lurched to his feet, laughing a soft, sick laugh as he moved toward a glowing red sign he thought was an exit but then someone was calling out to him, warning him that it wasn't an exit and then he was falling forward, crashing through the glass table into utter nothingness.

He was his father's son.

Chapter 15

Tiber City: Jungle District
Sept. 3, 2015
2:27 a.m.

O nce upon a time, the motel bed on which Campbell now lay on had been stiff as the lid of a freshly cut coffin. However, after more than a decade of service, the mattress—a virtual Jackson Pollock of piss, blood, and semen—teetered on collapse. The springs and coils were shot; the passing years had seen too many dull-eyed whores moaning canned porno lines while cranked up johns railed away. The busted springs didn't bother Campbell; the hourly rates splashed across the neon sign out front led him to expect as much. No, what pissed him off was the junkie sag, the section of the mattress where smack heads must have lain for days, shooting up with the same dirty needle, into the same collapsed vein, before, during, and after pissing and shitting all over themselves. Such occupants only got out of bed for two reasons: Pizza guy was at the door or they were out of smack. And occasionally even such blessed events were not enough to rouse the junkies— overdoses made getting out of bed real tough. In such instances, they would just lay in the motel room for days, their rigor mortis ridden bodies sinking a little deeper into the flame retardant rayon, sunken eyes staring at reruns of *All In The Family* while the neighbors bitched through the crumbling concrete and plaster wall about the smell: These were the images dancing through Campbell's dreamscapes the past few evenings as he lay on a motel bed somewhere in the teeming, anonymous slums that were the Jungle, his own feverish body already reshaping the sheet-less, shattered mattress in his own ruined image.

On the third night, when Campbell came to a little after sunset, stripped to the waist and slick with sweat, he tried to take inventory of the situation. The last thing he recalled was the inferno engulfing Sweeney's bar, the ceiling beams collapsing around him as the whole universe seemed to bow before the flame. By any account, he should have been dead. Instead, there was just a lot of blood, a hell of a lot of blood, but, so far as Campbell could tell, nothing was broken and he almost certainly was not dead. Were he dead, his environ would be a lot hotter. Then again, maybe he was dead but someone had cut him some slack and this was only purgatory. Languishing in a seedy motel for a few millennia while the Big Bureaucracy upstairs reviewed his case? Not exactly paradise but given Campbell's previous predilection for the mortal variety of sin, such treatment wouldn't have come out of left field.

For the time being, however, Campbell was sticking with the assumption he was still a terrestrial being, attributing his survival to yet another side effect of the Treatment: abnormally resilient bone structure. This made sense: Living to 120 wouldn't do much good if your hips were brittle as a gingerbread house. So when he fell over the railing and onto the floor of Sweeney's bar—a tumble that would have killed most men his age—he walked away with only a few nasty bruises. Not that it didn't hurt like all hell; he just wouldn't die, which, at the moment, didn't feel like such a good trade-off.

But the pain wasn't even the worst part of the deal: Without somewhat regular injections of the Treatment, those pains would pale in comparison to the agony of withdrawal symptoms. And therein lay perhaps another problem: His last batch of the Treatment's black market approximation Jael had procured for him had been in his room above Sweeney's bar.

Groping over the edge of the filthy mattress, Campbell's sweaty, swollen fingers discovered a nightstand. A plastic whiskey bottle, streaked with condensation, lay on its side on the middle of the stand, right next to a compact cell phone that did not belong to Campbell. He wasn't sure how either the phone or bottle got there; hell, he didn't even know how he came to occupy a very used mattress in some anonymous fuck pad miles away from his last memory—Jael dragging his sorry ass out of Lazarus bar just before the whole thing collapsed in a massive inferno.

But Campbell felt way too fucked up to try and answer such questions; he was simply glad he—or maybe Jael—had the good sense to purchase plastic: Glass bottles and memory blackouts were a bitch. Eyes shut tight against the pain, Campbell yanked the mystery bottle off the table and raised it to his blood-caked lips. Cheap, piss-warm whiskey flooded his mouth, careening past his esophagus as smoothly as discarded motor oil. There was a gaping socket along Campbell's lower gum line that had once upon a time housed a molar or two. Now only the raw nerve endings remained, jutting out into his oral cavity, twitching furiously as the whiskey washed over them. Campbell gagged, but shoved the bottle further into his mouth. Not too much, he cautioned himself; just enough to get yourself together.

A bottle of pills, initially concealed by the whiskey bottle, was also on the nightstand—an ancient, "some assembly required" piece of shit covered in nicks and tattooed with knife grooves—next to the bed. Even as the whiskey slithered through his system, that warm familiar feeling extending its way from his gut to his extremities, announcing the alcohol's arrival, Campbell's pain continued to grow, until another blackout seemed inevitable.

Shooting up from the motel mattress like a reanimated corpse, Campbell grabbed the bottle and tore off the lid, the plastic seal still bound around its edges. He dumped several—maybe even a dozen (it was too dark to even bother counting)—colorful capsules into his right hand.

"Down you go," Campbell muttered to the darkness as he catapulted the painkillers into his mouth. A splash of whiskey sent the pills ricocheting off his pharynx before the mess of medicine and alcohol cascaded into his belly. If he didn't go into a coma, the pain would stop. The. Pain. Would. Stop.

For an instant, these words were all Campbell could focus on, lighting up his brain like the flickering neon lights outside his window. Somewhere in the distance, a chopper slung low across the city's grid, stalking Tiber City's Jungle district, its searchlight glued to the back alleys, the city's unseen arteries, its dying slums where government housing projects were begun and then forgotten and then begun again, concrete stacked on top of concrete, shantytowns built on top of shantytowns, buildings stacked like corpses in a concentration camp. The search beam cut through the blinds, bathing the room in a bright white light as the chopper wheeled around, preparing to make another pass, continuing its hunt for some motherfucker whose dog/car/

plasma screen television told him—downright *insisted* upon it if you wanted to know the truth—that he slaughter the teenage girl who lived next door after raping her for several agonizing hours. And this was the world Campbell had, once upon a time in the New Mexican desert, sought to save.

Vertigo set in and Campbell knew Yeats was right, that the center could not—would not—hold and that all was lost. That men like Michael Morrison, having flung the meek down several flights of the socio-economic stairwell, were now first in line to inherit the earth, whether God liked it or not.

Morrison. The name reverberated through Campbell's skull like the thunder of heavy artillery. How was he, lying half-naked, barely alive, and soaked in whiskey on the floor of a junkie flop pad, going to stop Michael Morrison? A leveraged buy-out? Perhaps Campbell would just place a call to his broker, try and buy up all outstanding shares of Morrison Biotech. Despite the pain in his jaw, Campbell could not help but laugh out loud at the idea of himself standing before the board of Morrison Biotech, looking sharp in a new three piece pinstripe suit and proclaiming himself the new CEO; he'd be dead before he got within 100 miles of that place. Or maybe not: At the moment Morrison seemed far more interested in dragging Campbell back to Exodus—literally; hell, there was a reason Morrison's thug at the bar was carrying a syringe rather than a semi.

The helicopter made another run over the industrial graveyard, the illumination from its searchlight, amplified by the neon of the Jungle night, again breaching the motel room's twisted Venetian blinds with ease. As the light raced across the room, Campbell caught a glimpse of the entire room as reflected in the cracked mirror hanging above the dresser where the television might once have been. That's when he saw it: Carved into the back of the door was the symbol of the Order: an asterisk in a circle. And in the middle of that sign, nailed like the Wittenberg theses, was a large manila envelope.

Lurching upright from the dilapidated motel bed and onto his knees, Campbell reached into the middle of the symbol and tore away the envelope, leaving the bare nail firmly ensconced in the cracked plaster. Inside the singed envelope was a stack of paper an inch thick: It was the research Morrison had given him. There was also a makeshift cover page, informing Campbell not to leave the room unless absolutely necessary.

Campbell collapsed back onto the broken bed, wondering about the strange silver cell phone resting on the nightstand next to him, the collection of papers tumbling to the floor next to the bed as the alcohol and pills washed over him in a great neurological tidal wave while outside his window the chopper continued to hunt its prey, the entire city laid out before it, endless and terrible.

Project Exodus Memorandum # 99-081-3382-x

Re: Mneme Group Status Report

Summary:

Ten years ago, the Mneme Group was formed to address one of Project Exodus' greatest challenges: human memory. Early on in the Exodus process, it was decided that adult males, not infants, would be the most efficient means of meeting the Project's primary goal—genetically engineering a new breed of American leader. As has been noted in various Exodus-related studies, even the strongest gene pool can be undermined by socio-environmental factors. Many negative adult tendencies are the result of negative childhood experiences and are capable of undermining even the most powerful of genetic codes.

In order to maximize the likelihood that the Project will succeed, the Exodus team must be capable of not only producing a genetically optimized human being, but a fully developed adult male with 18 to 20 years of artificial memory. These memories, however, must be the product of rigorous study and evaluation: Simply simulating a childhood, although necessarily part of the Project, is insufficient. Therefore the Mneme Group has worked to develop not only the method of simulating and then implanting human memory, but to also devise a series of artificial experiences that, when pieced together to form the product's "memory," will provide a psychological profile that will not undermine, but actually enhance, the product's genetic perfection.

In order to meet these objectives, Mneme worked along with the Project's human genome team to isolate the areas of the brain where "memories" are stored. It is important to note that, unlike a computer, the brain does not store all memories in a single location. Rather, the several components of the brain all contribute to the creation of long-term memory. Mneme was able to break the concept of "long-term memory" down into several subsections and, in turn, isolate the sections of the brain responsible for each section, a process aided by Exodus' groundbreaking work on the human genome.

By determining which sections of the brain were responsible for storing and accessing long-term memories, Mneme was able to produce a series of memories, which were then uploaded directly into the Exodus subjects. By relying on focus-group feedback, as well as input (presented as hypothetical scenarios) from leading psychologists and childhood development researchers, the Mneme Group was able to create a series of memories that would allow the Exodus subjects psychological and emotional profiles to match their tremendous physical capabilities.

Due to computational and logistical limitations, however, the subjects were unable to be fitted with concrete memories. Rather, the memories uploaded were vague and impressionistic; the subject is left with a series of images and associations that, when considered as a whole, seem (to the subject) to form a cohesive, extremely positive narration—one that, with the aid of modern media such as television and cinema, will come to resemble an American childhood. The images the subject draws upon will bear enough similarity to modern media archetypes that the subject will subconsciously begin to associate these popular culture images with those already uploaded into his memory banks, each reinforcing the other until Mneme's inability to create a complete narrative is neutralized. Furthermore, this process will be aided by the subject's own need to have some sort of "growing up" narrative; this need, combined with the sheer implausibility that an individual might not have such a narrative, will spark the Exodus subject to fill in any remaining gaps with an internally constructed narrative substitution.

Conclusion

There has been a great deal of internal debate regarding the childhood/family background narrative being created for Exodus product Robert Fitzgerald. For obvious reasons, Fitzgerald's family must be both unknown and transient—creating a "Kennedy-esque" family history is unnecessarily complex. Therefore, it is proposed that Fitzgerald be presented to the public as the ultimate rags-to-riches story; a self-made man whose parents died when he was young, and who has no extended family. Specific physical reminders, ranging from personal mementos to public records, will be in place to support the narratives created and implanted by the Mneme Group.

Chapter 16

Tiber City
Sept. 4, 2015
11:12 a.m.

The languid sky hung heavy overhead, pressing down on the mourners gathered for Elizabeth Fitzgerald's funeral. Dylan, dressed in a dark suit, sat in a chair a few feet from the newly dug grave, staring into the earth. It had been drizzling all morning and despite the crowd, the cemetery felt enormous and empty: Everything was washed out and fucked up—no colors, just variations of gray and black. Every now and again, the harsh cry of a crow would echo across the cemetery, its tidings of hunger, remorse, regret reverberating through Dylan's skull. He shut his eyes tight, trying to focus on the priest's eulogy for his mother, on Meghan's hand pressed into his.

Four days ago, after overdosing at an End of the World party, he had woken up in Meghan's apartment. Details were vague and the Internet was roiling with rumors, forcing his spotty, hazy recollection to compete with blogger bravado. This much was clear: The coke had been cut—maybe with a methamphetamine but there were also whispers of new strains of coke turning up on the streets, powerful designer models black market chemists came up with to counter the stream of stepped on baby-powder laxative shit coming in from Mexico. Maybe the whole situation was some enterprising dealer's decision to circulate a new strain at a party filled with Tiber City's wealthiest reprobates—a misguided attempt at product placement.

But whatever the cause, Dylan had managed to leave Meghan enough voice mails that she arrived at the party just as Chase and Mikey were dragging him, bleeding and unconscious, through an alleyway and into a cab. It remained unclear whether his friends were planning on accompanying him to the hospital or just tossing a wad of cash at the driver: Dylan's breathing had grown shallow and concerns over liability, potential police involvement, and drama over who would appear on which cable news show loomed large. So Meghan had intervened, taking Dylan back to her place where she forced several benzodiazepines down his throat, reducing the strain on his cardiovascular system. He passed out and slept for two days, his dreams formless and terrifying. When he finally woke up, Meghan told him the news: His mother was dead.

As his mother's casket was lowered into the raw earth, the steel chains that held it creaked and groaned against the strange warm air washing down from the hills, suffocating the city. The priest's words were hollow and empty, swept away by the wind as soon as they left his mouth. He made all the proper incantations, all the prescribed gestures and facial expressions and yet there was nothing. The eulogy was sheer self-indulgence, polished and pretty, and most of all, sound-bite ready. A pang of disgust shot up Dylan's spine, eluding the numbing effect of the two tranquilizers he had choked down immediately upon waking that morning and realizing that before he was 25 he would have buried both his mother and his father.

The priest was saying "ashes to ashes, dust to dust," and then his mother was in the earth and everyone was throwing flowers on the casket, filing past him, hugging him, touching him, telling him, "I'm so sorry."

Suicide: That was the official explanation.

His final visit: That was the insinuated motivation.

Bullshit, Dylan pronounced. He didn't buy suicide. Accidental OD? Maybe. Hospital fuck-up? Likely. But it didn't matter; she was dead and all other details were irrelevant. Lawyers and accountants were circling and the process would take on a life of its own: immortality through litigation.

"Let's go for a walk," he whispered to Meghan. She nodded and they began moving away from the plot, away from the crowd, weaving their way through the headstones together, his shoes and her heels—designed for boardrooms and ballrooms, not burial grounds—leaving imprints in the dead grass.

Dylan blinked and there were only sunspots and the distant, artificial supernovas of flash photography. Scanning the headstones, the gaudy mausoleums, he wondered about the plot's occupants, trying to reconstruct an entire life from the few sentences and dates that marked the graves. Dead grass. Dead men. Raw. Rotting. Lifeless. He stared at a marker for a child who never made it to his second birthday and the desperation in the raven's cry was immediate and unbearable and Dylan felt as though he could not go one step further, that he literally could not lift his left foot and place it in front of his right foot. He stopped.

He and Meghan were in the middle of the cemetery now, surrounded by massive stone testaments to the dead. The trees grew hunched, as though the weight of the sky was too great, and even through the low-hanging branches and pale, limp foliage, the city was visible: No matter which direction Dylan turned, the Tiber City skyline tattooed the horizon. Claustrophobia washed over him in a terrible wave and he staggered back against a moss-covered statute of an angel with its hands folded in prayer. The rain continued, maddening in its languid yet relentless consistency and somewhere in the distance he could hear sirens—that grating shriek of emergency vehicles that seemed always to accompany rain. Even though her face was a mask of cool and control, he could feel Meghan starting to tense up next to him. She sighed softly, shivering even through the air was warm, damp, dead.

He needed to get out of the city. They needed to get out of the city.

"I need to show you something," he said, turning toward Meghan, "something my mother gave to me the last time I visited her."

Meghan was looking at him, waiting, expectant, her face wet from the rain, strands of her dark hair pressed flat against her forehead.

"No, not here," he said. "We need to go back to my place."

"What about all these people?" Meghan asked, gesturing across the cemetery, toward the gates.

Dylan glanced back at the play actors gathered below, all rehearsed in the language of grief—at the cluster of men and women gathered around the 3-by-7 trench where his mother would spend the rest of eternity, at the paparazzi waiting patiently by the gates, as though remaining *quiet* while snapping photographs of, and setting up live video feeds from, a funeral somehow demonstrated an appropriate level of respect and decorum.

"The last time I went to visit my mother," he began, the back of his suit jacket flapping as another gust of wind whipped out of the north, not content to sneak under pant legs or collars but determined to penetrate all layers of fabric. "That last time, she wrote an address and a number on the back of a 'Heffernan for President' flyer. She also stuffed a key in my pocket, just before the guards placed her in restraints."

"Where's the address?"

"Near my family's house on the shore. It's probably just more crazy shit. But I dunno…I feel like I need to check it out. I could never help her in any other way, never reach her. And who knows—maybe it is meaningful after all…"

"And the number," Meghan asked, shoving her hands into the pocket of her black lightweight blazer. "Was it like a phone number?"

"No: Just a bunch of random numbers. Normally I'd just forget it but, Meg, she seemed so certain. I mean, it's almost like she knew that that night was her only chance to give this to me; like she had been waiting for the right moment and that was it."

Standing in the middle of the cemetery that now held the bodies of both his mother and his father, Dylan looked up toward the heavens, remembering the times when his mother used to ask him what kind of shapes he saw in the clouds and he could remember shrieking with laughter as dinosaurs and dump trucks paraded past—absolute proof that the world was a place of wonder and possibility. But now, staring into the palette pressing down on the living and the dead alike, Dylan could only make out amorphous colorless clumps drifting through the smog without purpose or identity.

Most of the mourners had begun to leave, shaking their heads and whispering about Dylan's troubles—some sympathetic, most with a wicked, hard-edged glee—departing in a line of expensive foreign luxury cars now snaking along the single road leading between the hills adorned with markers and monuments to the dead, variations in size and grandeur that belied the simple fact that under the well-manicured lawn the worms made no distinction when it was time to feed.

It was raining a little harder now and the priest, after casting one last look toward Dylan and Meghan shook his head before gesturing to the cemetery workers standing in the distance—there were schedules to keep, deadlines to meet—and then an engine was sputtering to life, the sound of backhoes and other earth-moving machinery stirring, echoing across the empty, sad afternoon—stage hands ready to clear the set.

"The flyer and the key," Meghan was saying. "Where are they?"

"Come on," Dylan said. "I'll show you."

Less than an hour later, Dylan and Meghan arrived outside his apartment door, damp from the endless drizzle and still dressed in mourning black. Emotionally drained and physically exhausted, his body still reeling from last week's overdose, Dylan leaned back against the hallway's brick interior, patting the various pockets lining his suit in search of his keys, wondering what purpose this building had originally served—in another era before the ad men and the money men arrived with the glitterati in tow: There were hints of an industrial, manufacturing past; maybe something was made here? Something useful? One of those items taken for granted by society but upon which the orderly functioning of society depended: washers, screws, buttons, bolts?

He found the keys and popped open the door, letting Meghan in first. The entrance opened into the kitchen, which was the same as every other high-end loft kitchen in Tiber City: stunning with zero functionality; track lighting installed over gleaming black granite and stainless steel appliances. Dylan didn't even know if they worked—he couldn't remember the last time he had used them, if he ever used them; they came with the place and he got take out or delivery every night. He didn't even own a dining room table; meals were a rushed, uneventful affair, a menagerie of ethnic foods— Chinese, Japanese, Thai, Indian, Vietnamese, Ethiopian, Mongolian—that eventually all tasted the same, most a Western approximation, an idea of how various cultural cuisines should—not did—taste; meats and noodles drenched in hot spices delivered by a smallish delivery man of indeterminate age and precise cultural heritage. Unlimited options for nourishment narrowed down to a single choice based on a vague determination of preference: Do you *feel* like Thai?

Before he had left for the funeral, Dylan had stuck the flyer to the sub-zero refrigerator like it was a child's drawing or a homework assignment that got an A—something that would have been unheard of in the Glimmer district of Tiber City: Almost no one had kids and the few who did sure as well weren't going to fuck up that stainless steel gleam with stick figure drawings or spelling tests.

His mother's handwriting was cartoonish: large fat letters scratched across Senator Heffernan's face. It dawned on him that maybe he should have put the flyer somewhere a little more private but slapping it on the fridge was an insurance policy against inaction: Every time he walked through his front door, Jack Heffernan, cosmetically enhanced via his mother's scribbling, would be staring back at him. If he hid the thing, the odds were much higher that he would be able to force himself to forget about it, to fabricate reasons why he should put off doing anything about it until tomorrow or next week. For this same reason, he left the key his mother slipped him on the counter adjacent to the fridge: the thing's awkward edges a sharp contrast to the kitchen's cool black granite and functionless design.

He grabbed the flyer off the fridge, holding it up for Meghan to see.

2720 Linmont Road, Westland. That was the address, and it was a familiar one; Westland was a small town on the coast, and he spent lots of time at the shore as a child: His family owned a beach house in Havenport, a few towns over.

061280091177. That was the number written underneath. The number was not familiar.

He pulled out his iPhone and typed the address into Google, the search engine's autumnal theme aggravating in its perkiness, its elementary school appreciation for minor Hallmark holidays and seasonal changes. A second later, the website offered him several options: Did he merely want to see a map? Or would he prefer directions to and/or from that address? There was also an option for an aerial view of the geographic area in question, but even after selecting a locale, there were still more choices: Did he want to see traffic patterns, terrain overview, or satellite imagery? Finally, there was the option to see video of the desired locale, prompting the question: How was this accomplished? Did the search engine have thousands and thousands of employees crisscrossing the country with video cameras, endlessly recording and uploading, recording and uploading? Or were there only a few intrepid explorers charged with filming every address in America? What drove these modern Magellans? Was corporate sponsorship involved? The idea of a small band of men and women roaming the country filming every square inch was both absurd and terrifying: What was the point? And what happened when, as was inevitable, buildings rose and fell and rose again? Or was the process endless? Did fathers pass on this task to sons, who, in turn, would pass it on to their own sons, like some medieval curse, a burden to be borne?

Finally the information he was waiting for popped up: According to Google, the address belonged to a bank in Westland, two hours east of Tiber City and less than 20 minutes from his family's beach house. Dylan tossed the phone onto the table, patting his pockets for a stray cigarette, while Meghan jotted down the directions. The bank was too close to the beach house to be a coincidence. He stared at the numbers: 061280091177. He considered the possibilities: Could be a bank account; could be some sort of deposit box. More important than what was *why*: Did his mother have an account there? Unlikely: The institutionalization process included a review of all personal assets.

He lit the cigarette and slumped back against the granite counter. He was exhausted: After overdosing and burying this mother in the same week—not to mention dealing with the anniversary of his father's death, a process that got harder as the years passed—to say that he could use a little downtime was an understatement. But no matter how exhausted he was—physically, mentally, emotionally—more than he needed rest, he needed answers.

"You OK?" Meghan asked, bringing her hand to the side of his head, running her fingers through his hair.

"Look, whatever this is, I'm going with you," she said, their faces now inches apart. And then she was kissing him, soft and searching at first, but then, as he started to kiss her back, more confident, her intensity increasing, the years falling away, and Dylan remembered a time when words like "future" "identity" "mystery" and "love" held any meaning for him at all.

"I missed you," she was saying, her head now on his shoulder and he was telling her the same thing over and over, terrified because he meant it.

They stumbled backward into the apartment, fumbling with each other's clothes, her taste familiar but still electric and then they were on the couch and he was inside of her, their bodies moving together and they were fucking but it wasn't just fucking, it was different and he was excited and terrified at the same time; she was on top of him, her hands on his chest, her hair falling forward over her face as she stared into his eyes and then he was coming, pushing himself deeper into her as the outside world faded away and there was only the sound of their breathing, rhythmic and free.

Chapter 17

In the week since the attack at the bar, Campbell had found shelter under the neon canopy of the Jungle's post-industrial sprawl. Moving constantly, he was changing motel rooms once, sometimes twice a day, sleeping no more than four hours at a clip, the mysterious cell phone that had been left on top of the motel nightstand now tucked into the one pant pocket without a hole in it. Campbell knew he could only blend in for so long; Morrison's men would find him and try to force him to return to Exodus. And if he refused, he knew that, this time, they wouldn't hesitate to torture him; eventually, they would execute. In the meantime, Jonathan Campbell sought redemption.

The days slipped into nights back into days, and all the while Campbell tried to absorb what had been left for him, spending most of his time sitting on grubby motel carpets, the singed pages of Morrison's karyotype report—the one showing the two extra pairs of chromosomes in Project Exodus experiments—spread around him in a sloppy, scattered circle. He had read through everything once, twice, three times and still his mind would not stop churning as he tried to make a connection between the failures of

Exodus and what Morrison had dubbed "the Omega gene," the only gene that the greatest scientists in the world could not reproduce.

He was drinking but not heavily—just enough to keep a buzz going and to take the edge off some of the speed he copped from the pregnant 20-year-old who was dealing out of a corner of an abandoned Arby's parking lot. The brawl at Sweeney's had done a number on him: He was covered in bruises and his whole body ached, the old wound in his leg flaring up in an orgy of pain and discomfort. A dose of the Treatment would have helped with all that but that option had been left behind somewhere in the smoldering ruins of Sweeney's bar. He would need to come up with a substitute soon, but how soon was tough to gauge.

It was going to have to be a delicate balance of Benzedrine and Jameson: Just enough booze, just enough speed and he might survive long enough to figure out the identity of the Omega gene and to—somehow—put an end to Project Exodus. After that, what happened next didn't matter.

Some nights, the speed and alcohol feeding off one another, his discipline over his chemical concoctions wavering, he waxed almost pornographic, fantasizing about running, just vanishing into the Jungle, fuck the Order and fuck Michael Morrison. He would spend a few months drifting further off the grid, shaking just enough to stay alive but not enough to draw any attention, and then taking off for Mexico, heading for the lawless border region where Exodus was born but ignoring the past and continuing down into South America; getting lost in any one of the shantytowns outside Sao Paulo would give him five, six more years on this earth. Five or six more years of guilt and neurological decay spent trying to scrap together enough black market chemicals to approximate the Treatment only to mistakenly shoot up rat poison, die seizing and foaming at the mouth in a stall behind some banana republic brothel. There were moments when, suffocating under the weight of his sins, such escapism felt almost erotic.

And then one night, the cell phone began to buzz. For a moment Campbell thought he was losing his mind; that the combination of too much Benzedrine, too little sleep, and no Treatment had sent him over the edge and the aural hallucinations were kicking in. Then he caught a glimpse of the phone resting atop one of the many miniature mountains of paper spread across the room, its tiny display screen flashing with an incoming call. With a strange mixture of relief and terror flooding his already overtaxed system, he flipped open the phone:

"Hello," he rasped.

"He is coming for you," a familiar voice warned. "Take only what you absolutely need and leave now. You know that megachurch on 111 and Phoenix?"

"Yeah, I think so."

"I'll meet you there. But go. Now."

"Wait—who is coming? ..." Campbell asked, staring into the receiver.

"There is no time," the caller said and then the phone went dead.

It was a little past 3 in the morning, and Campbell, having left the motel 15 minutes earlier, was cutting through the Jungle, the booze and speed pushing him past the death, decay, and neon of Phoenix Avenue. Helicopters circled above the city like vultures ready to pick the Jungle's steel skeleton bare, their spotlights zigzagging across the ocean of shattered lives and empty bus stops and underground clubs where people disappeared, where entire lives simply ceased to exist and all the while the dark energy of this digital era rushed through the city, harnessed by false prophets with expense accounts who encouraged the dead simply to reinvent themselves.

Campbell was no stranger to the Jungle. Having often sought chemical comfort down some of the district's darker rabbit holes in the past, he was able to work his way through the hordes of girls in fishnets and guys in leather, past *hey mister* pushers insisting they had exactly what he needed and junkie rent boys, who, shirtless under denim jackets, mistook him for another old faggot prowling while his wife was out of town. Campbell ignored them, ignored their sunken, sallow eyes, the HIV positive eyes of boys that couldn't afford the vaccine because their pimps ran a quick cost-benefit analysis and decided to let nature take its course, and kept moving, his face shifting from light to shadow to light as he passed underneath the overhang of the illuminated 24-hour convenience stores. Across the street, grimy police tape hung limp around the rim of a rust-red dumpster.

Campbell pushed ahead, glancing over his shoulder as he darted through the endless sprawl. Intersecting highways built over liquor stores, 24-hour video stores, motels, and nondescript industrial parks created massive cave-like underpasses where small wretched communities were strung together like burnt-out lights on a Christmas tree—displaced men, women, entire families trying to make sense of What Went Wrong, staring out over the shopping cart graveyard and dirty rainwater runoff that was their children's backyard and toward the giant, unblinking red eyes that marked the helicopter landing pads and satellite towers that rose above all else in the East.

The air sizzled with unnatural electricity and Campbell felt fear exerting a stranglehold across the land. He passed a scared looking white man in pleated Dockers, another Jungle tourist trying to make it back to the suburbs before the sun stumbled over the horizon. Campbell gave him a 50-50 shot of making it out of this place alive. Most likely scenario: The guy sticks his dick in the wrong glory hole and gets rolled by a couple of skinheads cranked to the gill—that was how things worked out here. All around Campbell the world appeared to shimmer and fade until it seemed as if the earth itself was laboring for breath and Campbell wondered how long this city, this whole country, could hold together before everything collapsed—a breaking point at which it was all too much: and after that, disintegration? Most people expected something cataclysmic: a nuclear blast or complete economic meltdown—endless lines outside of banks, riots in the streets, the collapse of world governments, mushroom clouds billowing under a blood red sky. But looking around the Jungle, Campbell realized this was a gradual decline; society was unraveling slowly enough that the corporations and world governments had the time to fill the resulting vacuum left by loosening of family, tribe, and empathy. Corporations like Morrison Biotech.

His head down, lost in thought and trying to blend in, Campbell would have overshot the CitiMart megachurch but a flare of light from a 16-foot cross attached to the side of a sprawling two-story building that looked more like a mall than a house of worship—dig the giant "CITIMART" sign casting light into the dark—snapped him back to the present.

It had been a long time since Campbell had seen the inside of a church. That's not to say he hadn't considered returning to the old continent faith of his parents, of his grandparents—he just had no business setting foot on holy ground. Besides, if he felt worthy to kneel before an altar of God, he sure as hell wouldn't have picked this place.

For starters, the glowing cross aside, Campbell would have never realized the building in front of which he now stood was meant to be holy ground. The building itself was made up of some sort of post-modern, gaudy white tile, giving the entire place an institutional, over-sanitized vibe. Slapped onto the face of the building was a digitalized news tracker—like the kind they have in airports or on Wall Street. Rather than displaying flight schedules or stock market fluctuations, however, this particular tracker displayed worship times and local advertisements, with random bits of "The Good News," the temperature, and stock quotes tossed in for good measure—abundance, after all, was a sign of His blessing.

In order to capitalize on the growing megachurch trend of the new century, several of the more prominent evangelical media superstars teamed up with various corporate conglomerates to move beyond the early megachurch model, which consisted of amphitheatre-sized churches, television broadcasts, satellite feeds, and book deals. Still reeling from the negative publicity brought on by the exorbitant executive bonuses, shareholder losses, and cozy bankruptcy agreements of the last decade, the suits were happy to help: In exchange for naming rights, the corporate coffers doled out enough cash to help several enterprising digi-evangelists create worship centers where churches melded with lifestyle centers to satisfy the needs of modern America. The most prominent evangelical preachers in the land were able to sign lucrative exclusivity deals with larger corporations or development groups— the CitiMart Church was a product of this movement.

When it was built, the CitiMart Church was meant to be the cornerstone of yet another Jungle revitalization project. That particular project, like so many other renewal schemes, failed, but the church attracted a decent congregation on weekends: There were still some men and women in the Jungle trying to make an honest living, immigrant families severed from nation and family, seeking anything resembling community—the fabric of American life was unraveling too quickly. There was also a smattering of junkies and winos searching for a different kind of fix, as well as the freaks that gobbled hallucinogens and sat at rapt attention through six services straight.

Squinting against the neon glare, Campbell walked toward the two reinforced, bulletproof glass doors, which swung open automatically as he approached. He moved through a series of metal detectors, those ubiquitous metallic butlers of modern America, and into the lobby, where he was greeted by the smiling visage of a youthful but not exactly young man looking down at him from a giant high-definition plasma television mounted over another set of double glass doors perhaps two-dozen feet from the main entrance.

To Campbell's surprise, the man on the television began to speak.

"Welcome friend, to the CitiMart Church of Christ. We know that when it comes to your all-in-one worship needs, you've got a lot of choices. So thanks for choosing CitiMart. I'm Pastor Rick, and I hope you'll let me share just a few moments of your time to help explain to you just why we're Tiber City's most successful faith-based lifestyle center."

Campbell stood motionless in front of the massive, digitalized talking head, staring at the man's perfectly styled hair as the honey-smooth voice rolled over him. Clearly, it had been a long time since Pastor Rick had set foot in the CitiMart faith center. Not that Campbell was surprised: Most of these digi-evangelists recorded from a central location and then franchised the rights, making personal appearances at only the most deserving, i.e., most lucrative, congregations. From the looks of things, the Tiber City CitiMart Church was not such a congregation.

Two additional concourses ran from either side of the lobby, and signs on both sides of the monitor listed which concourse led to which shop or restaurant. Thing was, the entrance to concourse A had been boarded up a long time ago, a "Please Bear With Us, We're Undergoing Renovations" sign, complete with a picture of a smiling bear pleading for patience, plastered over the sheetrock and plywood, framed by exposed wiring. And it didn't look like construction had ever even begun on concourse B: The pathway leading from the lobby toward the signs for concourse B went for 20 or 30 feet before running into a solid concrete wall.

"Hallelujah," Campbell muttered as he walked through the lobby doors and into the church, while behind him Pastor Rick continued to preach, spreading the good news about a sale in the phantom concourse B.

The inside of the church was deserted. Deserted, at least, of any human presence. Other than that, the joint was jumping. Stadium lighting lined the sides of the ceiling, illuminating the gigantic flat screen video attached to the walls on both sides of the pulpit with a harsh cold light. Despite the absence of parishioners, the monitors continued to pump out the same messages Campbell had seen on the smaller ticker outside the church. The left monitor was offering an inspirational message—a reading from the Gospel of John—while the monitor on the right extolled the Christian virtues of life insurance from Homeland Insurance Co. The monitors' messages were also competing with the building's PA system, which was bleating out Christian pop—the end result being a cacophony of noise that made Campbell wince. Yet, the oddest thing, thought Campbell, was what seemed to be an ATM, complete with neon Jesus screensaver, installed in the back corner of the church.

Scanning the pews, Campbell realized he had been mistaken: He wasn't alone after all. At the front of the church, kneeling in the front row, was Jael.

He walked down the center aisle toward her but before he could reach her pew she was already on her feet, looking over his shoulder, at the entrance to the church.

"What took you so long?" Jael asked.

"It's nice to see you too," Campbell said, sliding into the plastic pew next to Jael. "Considering that a couple of days ago I woke up half dead in some motel and can barely walk, I thought I made decent time."

"Yeah, you're welcome for that," Jael replied, still standing, her eyes locked on the door at the back of the church. "Were you followed?"

"Don't think so. But like I said, I'm in rough shape so I was moving slow."

"No shit: I can smell the fucking booze from here, Campbell. I didn't drag your ass out of that fire just to let you finish the job yourself," she said, traces of an accent—maybe South American, maybe Mexican—surfacing as it often did when she got angry.

"That's not what I meant. Is this why you saved me? Buy yourself a few more years of giving me shit?"

"Let me tell you something, Campbell," she said, her voice going up an octave as she turned to face him. "If I had any say in the matter, you'd have been a dead man long before that fire, but lucky for you I don't, so..."

Some people might have been offended by Jael's revelation, Campbell considered; it was always difficult to accept that a fellow human being not only actively wished death upon you, but would happily do the deed. But Campbell couldn't blame Jael. After all, he knew about the experiments in the urban slums. The black SUVs. The vaccines and the tests. The men who came out of the desert and slaughtered Jael's people. Campbell knew it all. Sure, he didn't know anything at the time, but he was the father of Project Exodus—Morrison's crimes were his cross to bear.

A noise echoed in the back of the church, cutting Jael off mid-sentence. She brought a single finger, crowed by a painted nail, to her burgundy lips in the signal for silence. With her other hand, she reached behind her back and pulled a Magnum out of her waistband, training the sight in the direction of the echo.

Campbell sat motionless in the pew, his neck craned toward the church entrance as he stared past the endless, tumbling labyrinth of pews and lights and monitors. Seconds turned into minutes as he imagined the church operating for infinity, independent of man or God, a shrine not to the Yahweh of Moses and Abraham but to automation and bloodless process.

And then Jael was moving out of the pew and, her gun still drawn, toward the very front of the church, where, traditionally, there would have been an altar but now sat a massive pulpit flanked on either side by massive JumboTron video monitors. Campbell followed her, glancing once, then again, toward the entrance to the church,

Jael knelt next to the video monitor to the right of the plastic pulpit, gesturing for Campbell to take the other side. Together they began to exert pressure—he pulled, she pushed—and the monitor began to slide to the side; there was a set of wheels attached to the bottom of it. Campbell maintained his grip on the other side of the video screen and together they managed to move the screen about three feet to the right before his bad leg gave way, forcing him to let go and stumble back against the podium.

Over the course of his life, so many unusual things had happened to Campbell that when Jael slammed her boot through the rotting wooden door concealed behind the monitor, Campbell barely raised an eyebrow.

Chapter 18

Tiber City: Jungle District
Sept. 5, 2015
5:42 a.m.

After tugging the monitor back over the hole in the wall, Campbell turned around and took in his new surroundings. At first glance, the room under the CitiMart Church appeared to be some sort of forgotten storage area: Wooden shelves lined the walls, filled with forgotten icons and other relics that once upon a time had been sacred. One shelf was devoted entirely to Ziploc bags filled with communion wafers—competing with the cobwebs, forever waiting consecration.

Blinking hard against the dark, Campbell stumbled forward, knocking into one of the shelves. A two-foot tall statue of the Virgin Mary—reds and blues and a hand raised in benediction—was jarred loose by the impact and tore free of the Sunday comics and spider webs it was wrapped in, pitching forward off the shelf before crashing to the earth, the noise of shattering ceramic echoing over and over until it faded into the darkness.

"Careful," Jael hissed, appearing by his side, flashlight in one hand, Magnum in the other.

"Where the hell are we?" Campbell whispered.

"Technically speaking? The basement of a Catholic church. But it's not on any map; just another one of Tiber's forgotten spaces. I mean, I'm sure it's on a blueprint or something in some office downtown, but that's about it. When the city tore down the original building, they couldn't spare the time to finish the job; they just threw the new one—CitiMart or whatever the fuck they are calling it these days—up on the original foundation. It was faster and cheaper to just bury everything else. I swear—the city has collective ADD. The only time anyone ever gives a fuck about the past is when it gets in the way of something new."

Jael paused, waving the flashlight around, the bright yellow beam sending cockroaches scurrying into the cracks in the wall as it crisscrossed the room. The swirling streams of light triggered a strange rush of memory and emotion, reminding Campbell of the opening night of new research centers, of gala fundraisers, of the way a city looked from the cabin of a private jet, beams of light dipping and diving in exaltation of celebrity. A cockroach raced across Campbell's boot; the past faded.

At the far end of the room, a wall had collapsed, revealing a tunnel into the darkness.

"And this place," Jael continued "Isn't getting in the way of anything."

"So we're safe here?" Campbell asked, running his fingers along the wall, tracing cracks in the cool concrete.

"For a little while anyways; it won't take Morrison too long to track us down. There is a passage ahead that will take us back to Ramoth."

"Back to Ramoth?"

"For some reason, the Order wants to keep you alive," Jael said, spitting the words out as she began to make her way through the storage room, pushing aside old chests and crates, her flashlight trained on the opening in the wall.

"At least somebody does. Thing is, I have no idea why," Campbell muttered as he fell in step behind Jael, climbing over chunks of concrete and into the tunnel. He trudged forward, following the arc of Jael's flashlight. He was aware of the sound of dripping water, of insects, of Jael's leather jacket, of the crunch of stone under his boots.

"Trust me, Campbell, there's a good reason," Jael laughed, her voice a low rasp.

"So enlighten me," Campbell said.

"What do you know about the field of neurotheology?" Jael asked.

"The whole proving-God-through-science thing?"

"Crude, but essentially correct."

"What about it?"

"Neurotheology is the method the Order uses to pursue its primary goal: mapping and cultivating the human soul," Jael said.

"The soul?" Campbell asked, skeptical, his words echoing off the decaying walls and into the darkness ahead.

"The soul," Jael affirmed. "And not some abstract philosophical concept, but the real deal; an actual, physical thing. Hell Campbell—you've seen the backroom at Ramoth, all that equipment. That's what it's for: mapping the soul."

In spite of everything—the fact that he was stumbling through a dark, dank tunnel that smelled like decades' old sewage, choking on air so thick he felt like he might suffocate, every joint in his body feeling like it was on fire—Campbell had to laugh.

"Sweeney laid a similar story on me when I first arrived," Campbell said. "I'm not saying I thought it was bullshit, but I wasn't really in any position to argue. The Order had just saved my life..."

"It sounds insane at first; I had the same reaction. But the Order makes one hell of a case," Jael said, the beam from her flashlight still dipping, darting as the terrain continued to shift.

"Try me," Campbell said as he pressed into the darkness, trying to keep his balance, the stone under his feet smooth, hard, and increasingly slick. He could hear water in the distance, the drip-drip-drip of leaky pipes occasionally interrupted by a loud splash that sounded too big to be made by a rat but not big enough to be made by a human. Campbell attempted to focus on maintaining his footing, on following Jael's story.

"The Order's studies rely solely on one very specific component of neurotheology: brain imaging. They've got a tomography camera that can detect a radioactive tracer injected into the brain—it basically performs a high-tech PET scan that creates three-dimensional images that can show what's going on in the brain."

"But why brain images?" Campbell interrupted.

"When the Order began its search for the soul, it measured the brain activity of volunteers."

"Volunteers," Campbell repeated.

"Yeah—volunteers," Jael said. "The members of the Order don't just all live underground and sleep in coffins. They're monks, sure. But they have ties to the academic community, to research facilities. Especially in the beginning, before we found you. And we're not the only ones to have run these kinds of experiments either. We just had a more specific approach."

"So what kind of results did these brain images produce?"

"Initially, in every test, the Order found unusual and unexplained activity in a tiny section of the brain called the Orientation Association Area, or the OAA. This section of the brain is always active: There are varying levels of activity, different people have different levels—but always *some activity.* When the tracer goes through this part of the brain, it registers the activity in this area but usually that's all it picks up: constant, low-level activity, like a computer in sleep mode. In fact, this activity seems so unremarkable that most scientists dismiss it as an evolutionary vestige, like the tailbone. Something humans used to need but don't anymore."

Campbell felt a chill race down his spine; dismissing unusual biological phenomena as vestigial or inconsequential: That was one of the flaws of Project Exodus.

"But contrary to popular scientific belief," Jael continued, "the activity in this part of the brain does not always remain constant. There are studies that have shown that some people—Buddhist monks and Franciscan nuns for example—have the ability to push this mundane, low-level OAA function into a level of activity so frenzied that it eclipses the rest of the brain scan. These explosions of OAA activity almost always occurred during religious services or when the subject was meditating or praying. And each of these experiences was accompanied by the subjects reporting incredible feelings of a connection with something greater than themselves, something transcendent."

Jael's voice grew more intense, more passionate as she continued to explain the Order's experiments, her trademark air of lethal, detached cool fading. The tunnel began to narrow and twist, the turns coming more suddenly, and at harsher angles and Campbell found himself struggling to match Jael's pace.

"But that's not even the most interesting part," said Jael, her voice drifting out of the darkness toward Campbell. "Some of these experiments revealed similar, unusual OAA activity in regular people. And by that I mean people with no specific religious background or training: not people who spent hours meditating but construction workers, teachers, lawyers, guys stuck working 9-to-5 in tiny white plastic cubicles—anyone. Some of these regular people reported feeling only a tiny surge of emotion—perhaps just a momentary elation; certainly nothing they would consider spiritual or religious—but *something* nonetheless. Each of these moments occurred at random intervals and across a wide spectrum of experiences: For some, it was a particular piece of music; for others, a moment when they found themselves alone under a sea of stars. Some of the others though…They were described—and bear with me here because this sounds like mumbo-jumbo bullshit at first—as experiencing a fleeting apprehension that there was something 'more to life,' and something 'ancient and fundamental and bigger than themselves.' These descriptions were vaguer than those offered by the mystics and clergymen who comprised the original study. But this discrepancy made perfect sense, as the OAA activity in these laypeople was nowhere near as intense as the explosion of activity in the monks and clergymen. But each and every person tested was found to have some constant level of inexplicable OAA activity."

Campbell's head was spinning, trying to make a connection between the Order's brain scans and the Project Exodus data stuffed in his jacket pocket. Fortunately, Jael made the logical leap for him.

"At least," she said, "that was until the Order ran the OAA test on some creatures recovered from landfills in the New Mexican desert, as well as the ones recovered from the shantytowns, the ones a certain biotech company 'imbedded' with the transit populations living on the outskirts of major cities." Jael paused, and Campbell could hear the anger in her voice rising like a slow boil.

"The rumor was the company wanted to see if these creatures could handle social interaction. Even the most *normal* of these creatures—they were definitely not human—would last a few weeks, maybe a month—before the mutations began to manifest themselves. Until that point, these poor fuckers looked like everyone else. And that's when the men would come and either take the creatures away or, if there had been too much interaction with the population, kill everybody—humans, creatures, everyone—then burn the bodies and make it look like a gang-land thing. But it didn't even matter—no one was paying any attention. No one ever pays attention. That's one of the reasons they picked the Southwest. All those transient populations living along the borders, along the outskirts of major cities—these were expendable people." Jael seemed to snarl rather than speak this last sentence, the venom tangible and terrifying.

Campbell opened his mouth to protest but Jael cut him off.

"Yeah, yeah. You didn't know. I get it."

"Are you telling me the Order rescued those creatures, the ones from Morrison's lab, only to run more experiments on them?" Campbell asked.

"Hardly. The Order has always been interested in the soul's progression. As part of this interest, this belief in the human soul, its members are called to service. This service has always been one of the cornerstones of their belief system. Let me put it this way: These guys are walking the fucking walk. So at first, they were just doing what they do—taking care of society's refuse, the discarded, the forsaken and forgotten. The Order is committed to the idea that looking for the soul is futile unless the searcher's own ego has been subjected through meditation and through service to the suffering. But it became apparent that while these creatures' physical deformities were the source of tremendous agony and suffering, there was something else going on, some kind of medical anomaly—many of the monks were skilled physicians and medical researchers and yet, these deformities and diseases defied all explanation. Something else was killing your brood. Something the Order had never seen before and couldn't stop. And given that most of these creatures were being found in the shantytowns and slums near Morrison Biotech, they started to get suspicious."

Your brood. The words echoed off the tunnel walls, repeating the accusation over and over until it reached the darkness sprawled out in front of them. Campbell realized his feet were wet; that a pool of water had collected in the middle of the tunnel and he was standing in the middle of it.

"The Order spent years trying to figure out what was killing these poor creatures. As a last resort, they started looking at brain scans," Jael said. "Their brain scans revealed zero OAA activity. At no point did the monsters you helped create in the laboratory ever demonstrate any OAA activity."

"And you think this is what killed them? Lack of OAA activity?" Campbell asked, his tone aggressive, skeptical, as if disproving this one assertion might somehow absolve him of everything else.

"Actually," said Jael, turning away from Campbell and resuming her march down the tunnel, "I do. But it's not that simple; it's not just the lack of OAA activity in the brain that's killing these creatures—that's just the symptom. No, there's something else, something that's missing."

In that instant, it was suddenly so clear that Campbell could barely get the words out.

"And the Order thinks it's Project Exodus' missing gene. The Omega gene?"

"They used to. Only they don't refer to it as the Omega gene. They call it by its more traditional name: the soul. This was only a theory at first: That these creatures were dying because as close as he, or anyone, might get, Morrison will never be able to exactly replicate the human genetic code. But we can still fight him; the Order can still work to lessen the impact he has on this world. And that's why you're still alive."

Campbell had lost track of time. How long had he and Jael been weaving their way through the maze of tunnels that would lead them back to Ramoth? It could have been minutes; it could have been hours: Each tunnel fed into a seemingly identical tunnel, the only indication they had made any progress was the fact that the isolated pools of water had now congealed into a steady stream, a miniature river of ancient, polluted rain water and raw sewage running down the middle of the cracked stone floor.

As they pushed deeper into the tunnels, Campbell began to notice giant holes in the walls and, once, when the beam from Jael's flashlight cut across the collapsed concrete, he saw a mattress and a pile of books and what he swore was a dollhouse and he remembered stories he had once heard about men and women, about entire families, who lived in abandoned subway lines or sewage systems under Tiber City. Most of these people, Campbell had been told, were junkies and drifters, hustlers who would work the streets above, then retreat down below. But then there were others, the families who had drifted across an America they no longer recognized, chasing phantom jobs for hundreds, sometimes thousands, of miles, all the way to Tiber City. And then there were those for whom life—modern existence—had become too terrifying, too enormous; individuals for whom the city was a beast of steel and neon and noise noise noise, a ravenous wild creature so far beyond their control or comprehension that they fled underground, finding solace in the basic art of survival. These were the whispers Campbell heard in the bars at night; these were the messages Campbell had seen scrawled in subway stations and posted on Internet forums—missives that, until now, he had dismissed as urban legend.

But there was no time to investigate and Campbell pressed forward, following the sound of Jael's footsteps, the frantic yellow beam from her flashlight. His brain returned to Jael's stunning revelation: The Order not only believed that there was an actual human soul but that the soul was Project Exodus' final missing genetic puzzle piece. He was intrigued, but he was also skeptical—after all he was still a scientist and old habits died hard.

"Jael," Campbell said, calling ahead into the darkness. "Let's say for a minute that this gene is the soul. Even if that's the case, why can't Morrison replicate it?"

"Can't say for sure," Jael replied, "But the Order has a theory. Forget about the cheesy popular notion of the soul: This has nothing to do with the afterlife or what happens when we die. Instead, think of the soul, your Omega gene, as a biological radio transmitter that, despite varying levels of reception and static, is always working to receive a signal—a divine transmission. And when I say divine, I am not talking about any specific religion. As far as I am concerned, religion is irrelevant: Buddhist monks, Franciscan nuns...as OAA brain scans indicate, a particular religious belief isn't even necessary to obtain elevated OAA activity levels. But individuals capable of not merely reaching, but maintaining, these elevated activity levels for a sustained period of time are the outliers, mystics who are way ahead of the evolutionary curve with regard to their ability to access and process this divine transmission."

Campbell's mind was racing, but his limbs felt heavy and his mouth was dry. The Benzedrine buzz was wearing off and he needed something else. He patted down his pockets in the dark: nothing.

"The most important thing about this transmission," Jael continued, "is that it requires a receiver tuned to the same frequency. Whatever happens when man recreates this gene, you lose that ability, you somehow tune it internally to a different station. That's not to say this gene is entirely divine. Think of it more as a middleman, a way of mediating the strictly natural with the supernatural. The gene does it through a process that cannot be manufactured in a laboratory."

"Let's say this is all true. Every last word—right on the money. What is this transmission? Why does it matter? Why do people without this gene unravel?" Campbell asked.

"This gene is the thing that keeps us connected to one another," explained Jael. "It allows us to taste those sweet moments when the world feels as though it's aligned and everything else around us fades away and we are aware that there is something more, something we cannot express, something even the most talented wordsmiths and poets have trouble describing. But it's undeniably there. You know these moments I am talking about: You're walking alone late at night and you look up into the heavens and the wind sweeps over you and at that moment you apprehend IT; I have no idea what IT is…it's something divine, something that's larger than you or me or Michael Morrison or anyone. But it's also something that forms a common thread between all mankind; it's accessible to anyone, except those poor bastards you helped Morrison create. And that's why these meltdowns occur: These creatures are forever severed—utterly and completely—from their fellow man.

"What message is this divine transmission sending?"

"It's not a message—it's just an apprehension that there is something else. It's a connection, or at least a reminder of the original connection between God and mankind. And this taste, this teaser, does marvelous things to the human brain, things science is only just beginning to understand. That's why, when the signal starts to fade a bit, you can feel that something is wrong, that something is missing—that there's a void you can't quite put your finger on even if, superficially anyway, you've got all your fucking ducks in a row. So you try and fill that void right? Pop some pills, go shopping, shoot up in bathroom stalls, work 19 hours a day; these are all variations on the same theme: trying to fill that strange void. Most of the time, these substitutes, while inflicting long-term damage to the soul, to the ability of this genetic radio receptor to apprehend the divine signal, work well in the short term. Just think about MDMA; synthetically, it produces the same sensations reported in many of these transcendent encounters. Same thing with peyote and other hallucinogens. However, when you're experiencing these emotions, that OAA section of the brain never lights up like it does for the mystics and monks when they're having a religious experience. And the next day you feel like shit because you tasted a cheap approximation of the divine and now your soul is even hungrier than before for the real thing."

Campbell fell silent, listening to Jael as the terrain continued to dip and rise, the cracked, broken concrete crunching in the dark. Sometimes Campbell could hear the city above them, nothing specific just a dull, distant roar that faded in and out as the tunnel pushed ahead. The noise a reminder of a city on the brink of something terrible, or, even worse, nothing—just endless expansion, the past buried under the shiny bright promise of an impossible future.

"When people lose the signal for too long, and all the substitutes aren't cutting it—that's usually when shit starts going wrong. Sometimes people just commit suicide. But others...when that link is severed for too long, people can freak out in a different way. You've read about it on the Web—those moments when people just snap, normal men and women freaking out and eating their neighbor after frying their kid in the microwave. So why do otherwise normal people, who are capable of functioning at a socially acceptable level, cannibalize the nice lady next door? They've lost the signal for too long, that's why."

"That's pretty extreme," Campbell remarked.

"No shit," Jael said. "But it's the most vivid manifestation. And I'm not saying that every homicide out there is the product of this soulless disconnection; there are mental illnesses, things like that. But society is sick Campbell; you don't need me to tell you that. And so many of the things destroying us, the things that allow us to be swallowed by greed and indifference and violence—they are the product of this lost connection.

"Now, consider what life must be like for someone who hasn't lost that connection but was never even able to make that connection in the first place. Think about what life must be like for your Exodus experiments."

They had done brain scans as part of Exodus, the same scans Jael was now describing. But when Exodus conducted these scans and saw that the activity had vanished, Campbell assumed he had helped take man one step further; that he had pushed evolution forward at his pace. The idea that this brain activity was communing with something else, something that could not be replicated in his laboratory; that thought had never crossed Campbell's mind. He was a scientist—had been a scientist. The scientific method his catechism. The notion that there was something else, something unverifiable, would have been heresy. But Campbell the scientist had died in the swirling, radioactive sands of the Chihuahuan desert, only to be resurrected as Campbell the servant. And Campbell the servant, he *believed*.

He opened his mouth, his brain struggling to bring order and form to the thoughts racing through his skull, but before he could say a word Jael stopped, raising her right hand, the one holding the gun—an indication Campbell should do the same. The beam from the flashlight quivered then steadied, the pale light trained on a metal door with no handle, the center of which was marked with a dark red stencil: the asterisk symbol. Jael put her hand down; Campbell heard the safety from her gun click off. He felt her tense; something was wrong. Jael shifted the flashlight and Campbell saw the metal door was open. There was a two-, maybe three-foot gap between the wall and the door.

Jael pulled a cell phone out of her pocket and punched a series of numbers into the glowing handset. She held the phone to her ear; Campbell could hear the number ringing on the other end. It rang over two dozen times before she slammed the phone shut. That's when he noticed it: the smell of rotting meat, faint but unmistakable. He heard Jael swear under her breath and then she took off, shooting through the narrow opening into Camp Ramoth. Campbell took a deep breath, and then plunged into the dark after her.

Something was very wrong.

Campbell had followed Jael through the back entrance to Ramoth, the entrance that was supposed to be secret, the entrance that was left wide-open like some suburban screen door. They passed down several poorly lit hallways, his fear growing with every step. He had never entered Ramoth through this route, but he knew that nothing was as it should be: No one appeared to greet them; the doors were all unlocked, even the rudimentary security systems were offline or disengaged. The only sign of life was the blinking security cameras mounted on the wall. Campbell shivered as memories of New Mexico and Morrison's underground laboratory dragged him into the past; the smell of rotting flesh smacked him back into the present.

He and Jael passed through another doorway—no security, no locks—and into a round room that was empty save for a series of gamma cameras—the imaging devices capable of recording brain activity—arranged in a loose circle around a single mat laid out in the center of the room. The cameras looked like props out of some cheap '70s sci-fi flick—the sensitive equipment hidden under a beat-up-looking hard-plastic shell the size of an old pillbox hat and mounted on a two-legged steel gantry. Thick black wires ran from the cameras into the wall where fiber optic cables would carry the data to computers located in other rooms somewhere in the underground warren that was Camp Ramoth. Instantly Campbell realized where he was: This was one of the rooms where the Order did its research; where, according to Jael and Sweeney, the monks would spend hours, days, weeks losing themselves in prayer and meditation while others watched the data as it projected in 3-D across massive computer monitors.

Campbell wanted to pause, investigate the equipment, the data from the brain scans, but Jael kept moving, not even acknowledging the instruments and monitors, stalking the corridors without a sound, never looking back, using hand signals to beckon Campbell forward, back, left, right, hurry the fuck up. So Campbell kept moving, propelled by an awkward half-jog half-stagger as he tied to keep up, dodging through the camp's hallways and storage areas, past the kitchen and monks' barracks. The place was empty, but the smell was growing more intense.

Finally he hit the entrance to the camp's main room. The lock wasn't just broken—the entire door was gone, the hinges smashed and useless, a gaping black hole left in its wake. Campbell leaned back against the side of the hallway and dry heaved. The smell had become almost unbearable. But Jael plunged forward into the darkened room, leaving Campbell with little choice but to follow.

The room was dark save for a single florescent ceiling panel flickering on and off, the room vibrating with an electric hum as it labored to fulfill its single reason for existence, but like everything else it was damaged so the lighting was inconstant and weak: shadow followed by rapid bursts of illumination followed by shadow. And it was through one of these sudden bursts that Campbell saw the source of the stench: human corpses, at least a dozen, probably more, all wearing the tattered remnants of pale green surgical scrubs, laid stacked in the middle of the room.

Jael was standing over the pile, her face frozen in horror as she sunk to her knees. The lighting continued to flash on and off, the massacre revealing itself in bursts of weak light as Campbell stumbled into the room. He had witnessed his share of human cruelty and slaughter: He had seen terrible things in the labs of Morrison Biotechnology; he had spent years drifting through the American underground. He had watched dozens of children suffer and die in Camp Ramoth. But this was different—each of the dead gurney men had been expertly tortured. Large swaths of skin had been peeled away from each of the bodies, the exposed muscles and bone dosed with chemicals; limbs had been severed, the wounds cauterized to prevent the victims from dying too quickly. Worst of all, however, was the sound of thousands of white maggots feeding on the mangled, mutilated flesh that once constituted human beings. The sound of mindless insects swarming over one another—like someone churning a vat of cottage cheese—seemed to amplify by the second, growing louder and louder in Campbell's mind as he staggered toward Jael, who was still kneeling beside the pile of bodies. One burst of light showed her lips moving in prayer.

There were other bodies as well: A row of cots lined each wall and while some were empty, others still held their occupants—all children—each of whom seemed to have been executed by a single bullet to the brain. Although they bore no signs of torture, the children in these beds had suffered—their bodies riddled with deformities and puss-cakes lesions. IVs and surgical carts stood like silent sentries over the dead.

From somewhere behind him, Campbell heard Jael scream: not in fear but anger, a rage so sharp and clear it sent a chill down his spine. He turned in the direction of the scream and that's when he saw it—past the pile of bodies and maggots, past the corpses in their hospital beds, toward the back of the room. A man, also wearing the tattered green hospital rags, had been crucified against the far wall.

Crossing the room, every step accompanied by a sickening splash, the bottom of his pants soaked crimson, Campbell approached the crucified man, the sloshing of maggots seemingly synched to the hum of electricity as the lights continued to cut in and out.

The man—well into his 60s with longish gray hair, thin but not fragile—was pinned to the concrete wall by three steel spikes: one driven through his right heel, another through the left heel, the last entering through the palm of his left hand at an angle, exiting through the wrist and into the wall. Although there had been a fourth spike driven through the palm of the right hand, it had torn loose, bone and sinew sliding forward, over the head of the spike and away from the wall, and now the man's right arm dangled awkwardly at his side, blood still running from the entry and exit wounds.

Campbell stood motionless in front of the crucified man, frozen by a combination of terror and helplessness. The man was still alive. His breathing was shallow and ragged, punctured every few seconds by an agonized gurgle as his hyper-extended lungs filled with blood. Given the amount blood on the floor, on the wall, soaking the man's body, it was a miracle he was still drawing breath.

The man's eyes rolled back in his head and his entire body began to spasm: his chest pressing forward as his one free arm reached toward Campbell. The nail had smashed through muscle and tendon, leaving a hole in his palm the size of nickel framed by the jagged edges of shattered bone. His other three limbs strained against the nails pinning him to the wall, every muscle in his body jerking and twitching as his mouth began to open and close, each time slamming shut with a violence that reminded Campbell of a malfunctioning hydraulic press. As the man's jaws burst apart yet again, his face contorted as he tried to generate the strength to communicate, Campbell realized the man's tongue was gone—gone as in had been ripped out of his mouth; a thrashing pink nub, loose strands of muscle dangling in the back of his mouth, the only evidence this man had ever been able to taste, to speak, to communicate.

Campbell took a step closer, now standing only centimeters from the trembling fingertips of the man's ruined right hand that continued to reach toward Campbell, straining to convey what his mouth could not. The cruci- fied man's eyes reflected a physical agony unlike any Campbell had ever seen, a pain that seemed to be amplified beyond any natural limits by his inability to cry out, to express this suffering. And then the man began shaking as another violent seizure ripped through his body, his ribs pressing so hard against his flesh that, one by one, they began to crack with a sad, defeated crunch. His mouth was still pumping open and shut, trying to speak, the fact that his tongue had been removed lost somewhere in neurological trans- lation.

The man finally lost any control he had over his broken body: His head began snapping back and forth as his bowels emptied onto the hard con- crete. The trickle of blood dribbling out of the man's mouth became a steady stream and, like a man electrocuted, his entire body began convulsing in a final massive spasm, so violent Campbell was convinced that the nails pin- ning the man to the wall would not withstand the pressure.

A single shot rang out and the man's chest exploded, spraying Campbell with a crimson mist, small bits of flesh and bone flying into his open mouth as he tried to scream. He whipped around just in time to see Jael squeeze off another shot—he felt the heat from the bullet as it whizzed past his ear; he heard the sound the bullet made when it hit its target: the center of the man's forehead. Gore exploded, splattering across the wall behind the man; spraying out across Campbell's face.

Jael was screaming, emptying the rest of the clip into the ceiling, squeez- ing the trigger over and over even after the last round was gone, the empty chamber clicking uselessly. Neither she nor Campbell saw al-Salaam slip out from the shadows in the corner of the room; by the time they realized they were no longer alone, al-Salaam's blade was sliding across Jael's throat, severing her carotid artery with a single movement. Jael went down in a hail of crimson, dropping to her knees first, her face twisted with rage as she brought he hands to her throat before collapsing face down on the concrete, gurgling and grunting as her heart stopped beating.

Al-Salaam turned toward Campbell, smiling as he stepped over Jael's still-twitching body.

And then the cell phone tucked in Campbell's pocket began to ring.

"Well, what are you waiting for?" al-Salaam asked, gesturing at Campbell's pocket with his bloody blade. "Answer it."

Wiping the blood off his face with one hand, Campbell flipped open the cell phone with the other, and raised the handset to his ear.

"Hello Jonathan. Its Michael," the caller said. "I think you and I need to talk."

Chapter 19

Tiber City–Havenport
Sept. 5, 2015
7:22 p.m.

Borne by his father's old Harley Davidson XL50 1200, Dylan sped through Tiber City's industrial sprawl. Meghan was sitting behind him, her arms wrapped around his waist, her hair flying loose as dusk fell across the burnt-out landscape.

As they swung away from the city's core, towering skyscrapers gave way to a mixture of nondescript midsized office buildings that in turn yielded to empty lots and dead factories left to rot in abandoned industrial parks where, one time or another, there had been a plan, an idea, but now there was only cracked concrete and ragged weeds fertilized by glittering broken glass. It had been years since Dylan visited his family's beach house and the path out of the city had changed: His father used to lead the family through the labyrinth of on-ramps and off-ramps and mergers and lane closures and massive eighteen-wheelers blasting down the highway. Now Dylan was trying to remember the way; Meghan's grip around his waist tightening every time he had to cut across several lanes to make an exit, horns blaring. He remembered his old man guiding the family SUV by memory; Dylan had to switch on the bike's GPS system but even that was useless: The streets and alleyways were forever shifting, mutating in accordance with the dying city's erratic rhythm; buildings melting into one another in a frenzy of underground mergers, acquisitions, hostile takeovers, outsourcing, and corporate restructuring. Collapsed buildings swallowed up entire avenues; whole industries would explode on Monday only to vanish by the following Sunday, fortunes won and lost in a matter of hours, a matter of keystrokes, random fragments of data on a server in Bonn the only evidence this vanished wealth ever existed. No matter how many of their steel suns cluttered the sky, these satellite-mapping services couldn't keep up. Eventually, the GPS tracker crashed, leaving Dylan with no choice but to aim the bike east, away from the fading sunlight and toward the coast.

Located a few miles off Havenport's boarded-up main drag, the Fitzgeralds' beach house had been his father's sanctuary from the pressures of public life, a place for the family to regroup before the grueling campaign seasons. The Fitzgerald retreat, as the press liked to call it, was sealed off from the outside world by a 15-foot, ivy-coated brick wall, complete with two wrought-iron gates that locked in the middle and were controlled by a password-protected guard box at the foot of the quarter-mile-long gravel driveway.

It had been at least five years since Dylan had been to the beach house, maybe more. There were the promises around Christmas: next summer, *that* would be the summer that he and his mother would invite their extended family down to the house for a long weekend but those long weekends never materialized because when the next summer rolled around there was always one other party Dylan had to be at, always some other girl, some other group of people doing something—summer weddings upstate, lost weekends in Vegas; it didn't matter what, there was always something, and Dylan was just drifting.

Gazing up at his father's house from just outside the main gate, his motorcycle idling, a flood of images came rushing over those brick walls, threatening to overwhelm him with the emotions they triggered. Memories Dylan thought he had sealed away years ago now ripped free from their chemically constructed confines; his father showing him how to break in a baseball glove with oil and twine, his mother teaching him how to read under the brilliant canopy that seemed to form a green halo over the entire property. Dylan shut his eyes, trying to recall some of the prayers his mother had taught him when he was younger—any of the prayers—but the words just swirled about in his brain, lost to the amnesia of adulthood. The God that once seemed so real to the little boy growing up behind the walls of the Fitzgerald estate had long since given way to the more easily accessible and—for a socially conscious East Coast scion—more acceptable gods of whiskey, cocaine, and 19-year-old pussy.

It took Meghan's hand on his shoulder to jar him back to the present.

"You all right?" she asked over the noise of the engine. "Look, even if the numbers and the address on the Heffernan flyer are bullshit, it's good we're out of the city. You need some rest. And it'd be nice to spend some time together without all the bullshit."

Dylan nodded. He knew she was right but rest was the last thing on his mind. There were too many questions, too many uncertainties. He leaned over and punched the access code into the black security box outside the gate. The tiny digital display flashed red. Dylan frowned and re-entered the code, this time with greater force, as if extra emphasis was what had been missing in the first place. The display flashed red again and Dylan slapped the side of the box.

"The caretaker must have changed the code. He's supposed to let us know when he does…" Dylan's voice trailed off as he looked up at the security cameras mounted along the wall, staring down at the land below like gargoyles—passive sentinels of steel, wire, and glass. Dylan waited for a few seconds, expecting the cameras to do something, anything, but a stillness was settling over the land and there was only the sound of the ocean competing with the low growl of Dylan's bike, waves crashing against the rocky beach like they had for centuries, for millennia; a constant, violent rhythm, terrifying in its permanence. The cameras remained motionless, their darkened lenses indifferent.

And then, without warning, the two gates controlling entry to the driveway popped open, each gate swinging out in opposite directions, revealing a clear path to the house.

❧

Run-down and washed-out, the place was in desperate need of a paint job, and the gutters were still overflowing with dead leaves from previous autumns. As a result, gutter water had spilled out, leaving muddy streaks all down the sides of the old colonial. A few of the black shutters were crooked, battered by the storms that would assail the coastline.

The landscape wasn't in much better condition. The garden on the side of the house where Dylan's mother had once spent much of her time now lay barren, the flowers and vegetation she had spent the past two decades cultivating had vanished, either choked out by weeds or chased underground by the now-rocky soil. Throughout the backyard, the once-majestic oaks looked bent and sick, their foliage a pale, timid green, as if the trees recognized the futility of entering into a full bloom.

As he wandered the property's perimeter, his fingers trembling as he tried to light a cigarette, Dylan felt a pang of guilt, knowing that, to some extent, the property's disarray was his fault, that he should have taken responsibility for the place, at least checked in on it a few times.

"It's not your fault," Meghan said with a sad, sympathetic smile.

"Wait till you see the inside," Dylan replied.

The house was big but not too big: five bedrooms—three upstairs, two downstairs. Two bathrooms. There was a fairly modern kitchen on the first floor that had an island stove in the middle and opened up into a living room. The TV was ancient but that was OK; it was mainly used for ball-games or DVDs on rainy Sundays—no high definition required. Besides, there were books stacked all over the house; that random accumulation of books that seemed to always inhabit beach houses: German philosophy and books about sailing mixed with fat, dog-eared paperbacks—Chandler and King and O'Connell; the autobiographies of businessmen wedged next to Danielle Steel and books from freshman year in college that Dylan never read, their covers still glossy, some even still in their plastic shrink wrap; a half-dozen Bibles in various editions, the Word of God hotly disputed and lost in translation. These were the books pulled off the shelf in the rush to get to the beach that ended up keeping you up until dawn, these were books that had, more often than not, been dragged out to serve a purely decorative function—no bookshelves looked bad; empty ones looked worse—and instead wound up an integral part of summer vacations.

The rest of the house was a blur of long hallways, liquor cabinets, and nautical décor; of cedar chests, sleeper sofas, and white tile. Dylan gave Meghan the tour—the living room was the worst: All the wallpaper was peel-

ing; the ceiling was warped and waterlogged. Remnants of the family's final
trip to the beach—almost a decade old—were still scattered throughout
the house: gas station receipts, glasses stashed behind overstuffed chairs, an
old bathing suit hung out to dry; the fireplace still filled with ash. A panic
washed over him and he was convinced he made the wrong decision; they
should have stayed in Tiber City. He wasn't thinking straight; the overdose
at the End of the World and his mother's death were triggering weakness and
bad decisions. He jammed his hand into the pocket of his jeans and felt the
flyer: Fuck the bank and fuck Heffernan—he should burn the thing.

But Meghan was opening bay windows and lighting candles, driving the
dead air and decade-old silence out into the dusk, replacing it with the smell
of the ocean and the sound of waves crashing over the rocky beach. Exhaustion smashed into Dylan and he staggered back onto one of the couches in
the living room, his eyes slamming shut.

He opened his eyes 12 hours later: There were some bagels with cream
cheese on a plate next to the couch and a note from Meghan:
At the beach. Come down when you wake up?

Dylan pulled himself up off the couch. At some point in the night he
had taken off his leather jacket and balled it up into a makeshift pillow,
which was fortunate because he had sweat through his T-shirt—the nightmares had been terrifying and senseless. He had dreamed of the earth before
creation: dark water and swirling, formless matter.

He pulled on a pair of shorts and stumbled into the bathroom, chewing
on one of the bagels despite the fact that his jaw was sore from grinding his
teeth. There was a mouth guard he was supposed to wear but there were a
lot of things he was supposed to do; remembering to shove a cumbersome
hard-plastic object into his mouth before sleep wasn't high on his list of
priorities—he'd rather the nightmares just stop. He took a piss and tossed
some cold water on his face, catching a quick glimpse of himself in the mirror. He looked a little older, a little more like his father. The ancient central
air system kicked in, rattling the vents and Dylan felt a blast of cold on his
skin—the house seemed emptier, quieter than it ever had. A familiar anxiety
began to creep up from the pit of his stomach and Dylan didn't want to be

alone in his dead parents' house for another second. He ran out of the bathroom and didn't stop until he was halfway down the path that led from the
backyard to the beach; until he was far enough away from the peeling, faded
wallpaper and the water-stained ceilings and the smell of decay and neglect
that seemed to smother the entire house no matter how many windows were
opened, no matter how many candles were lit.

By the time he hit the beach the sun had dipped behind the clouds,
pushing the temperature into the 60s. A wind kicked up out of the west,
strafing the dunes and blasting sand in every direction. Meghan was standing
at the water's edge in shorts and a bikini top, the surf washing over her bare
feet, her painted toes, her arms wrapped around herself as she stared at the
horizon. Dylan hung back along the edge of the dunes, watching the wind
whip her hair and wondering what was going to happen to them, to him; the
address his mother had given him looping through his brain over and over
like a cable news crawler in fast forward.

Dark clouds were gathering on the horizon and it was getting difficult
to distinguish the sea from the sky, and then he was running toward Meghan, tearing off his shirt with a war whoop as he tackled her into the surf.
They both tumbled forward, crashing into a wave and the world went silent:
Stereo surround sound cut off in favor of underwater mono. Dylan opened
his eyes and saw nothing but murky grays and browns, swirling sand, and
the outline of Meghan's thighs. He popped his head back up, the salt water
stinging tiny scrapes and cuts he hadn't even realized he had and for a second
Meghan looked pissed but then she started laughing, telling him he was an
asshole, but slipping off her top as she said it; her nipples hard against his
bare chest. When she kissed him it tasted like salt and sun block, her arms
draped around his shoulders as waves broke over them, around them, the rip
tide tugging at their feet.

They spoke of the past.

"I'm sorry," Dylan said.

"I know," said Meghan.

Dylan laughed. "You realize how fucked up things are in my life right
now? Why do you want to be a part of this?"

Meghan flipped her hair back, spraying water everywhere. "It's not like I
really have a choice in this," she said. "Of course it's fucking crazy. I've spent
the last five years trying to tell myself that. I just knew if I didn't come to
the bar that night, the next time I would have seen you was at your funeral."

Dylan groaned: "Bullshit." The protest was half-hearted at best. He knew it; she knew it. No one had to say anything.

They did not talk about the future; the address his mother had scrawled on the back of the Heffernan for President flyer; the oil tankers cluttering the horizon, massive gray vessels en route to the other side of the world.

Waves continued to crash around them. Dylan waxed nostalgic:

"My dad used to take me out in the chop, show me how to body surf: It would drive my mother crazy."

Meghan said: "Show me."

"Yeah?"

"Yeah, come on."

"All right. It's not too hard: Just wait until the right size wave comes, and try to get out in front of it. The swell will pick you up and then, when it breaks, you'll just ride the crest. Keep your hands out in front of your face and you'll be fine. Otherwise you'll lose a tooth."

"That's it?"

"That's it."

Dylan crouched low in the water, gesturing for Meghan to do the same. A few medium-sized waves came, but the breaks weren't right and Dylan dove under the swell; Meghan bobbed over the top. Finally a bigger wave rose up, building at first, gaining speed as it headed toward shore; Dylan started to paddle out in front of it but in seconds the swell picked him up and he was on top of the wave. Then the wave broke hard, throwing him down into the water but he stayed with it, his arms outstretched, streamlined as he surged forward with the crest so quickly that his shorts slipped off, lost in the wake. And then he was twisting to his side, trying to shield his stomach and balls from the rocky shore but the wave was still going strong and he flipped head over heels, crashing onto the beach in a blur of sand and surf and seaweed.

He heard Meghan laughing and when he looked up, he saw her sprinting off the beach, towel pressed to her chest with one hand, waving his shorts like a captured flag with the other.

Dylan sat on the shore for a minute, naked, catching his breath as he watched her go. Then he rose to his feet, shaking himself dry before sprinting up the path after her. Halfway to the house, he heard the outdoor shower kick on, the pipes rumbling and groaning, years of rust falling away, their purpose restored. And then he was opening the door to the shower, his cock growing hard at the sight of Meghan, naked, her back turned to him, running her fingers through her hair as the dual shower heads blasted away the salt and sand. He started kissing her neck, his hands reaching around, squeezing her tits. With one hand, she braced herself against the stained cedar walls; with the other, she reached between her legs and, grabbing his cock, guided him inside of her, her breath catching as he pushed deeper, steam rising out of the shower like an offering to the fading afternoon sun.

For the next week, Dylan and Meghan stayed at the house: They went for runs along the water in the morning, swam in the afternoon, sat out on the beach until long after the sun had vanished in a flare of red. They read some of the old books stashed throughout the house; watched old movies when thunderstorms rolled through: *Ghostbusters, Caddyshack, Top Gun*. They found a case of Veuve Clicquot in the basement next to the washer and dryer and drank entire bottles at night, making love on the living room floor, on the dining room table, in Dylan's old bed. They got sunburned. They left the door to the master bedroom shut.

Meghan brought the kitchen back to life, dusting off pots and pans that had been dormant for the last decade. They bought groceries in town and cooking smells—bread baking in the oven, steak on the grill—began gradually to replace mildew and decay. When Meghan cooked, Dylan would landscape, raiding the garage for equipment that, despite the cobwebs and rust, was still in decent shape. Someone had arranged for a service to tend the property, but the effort was half-assed at best: It probably didn't take the landscapers very long to figure out nobody was paying attention. So Dylan laid siege to the overgrown oak trees and the branches scraping the side of his father's house, to the weeds choking his mother's garden, ripping them out until his fingers bled. He even found a ladder and, with Meghan holding the base steady, he climbed onto the roof, tossing off clumps of rotting leaves, plunging his hands into the gutters, cold murky water up to his wrists as he scooped out the black sludge that, when it rained, would spill down the side of the house, leaving black streaks in its wake.

Dylan felt his body mending, growing stronger by the day, the damage from the overdose fading like his sunburn.

Dylan said, "I feel good."

Meghan said, "You look better."

"Better than what?" he asked.

"Just better," she said.

Neither one of them mentioned his nightmares, or the fact that when they let go of one another he would lay awake for hours, sweating as he listened to the house shift and groan, his mind racing, wondering why his father killed himself—not the reason he was given but the real reason, the truth he knew was out there—and considering the dozens of things he was convinced he could have done to prevent his mother's death, the past pressing down on him with such intensity that his chest would constrict and he would shoot upright in bed, gasping for breath and scaring the shit out of Meghan.

"I've got some issues," Dylan said.

"You buried your mom a few weeks ago. Give it time," Meghan replied.

But the champagne was running low and a cold front swept up the coast: It rained for three days straight and Dylan began to feel restless. He started wandering the halls of the house at night, after Meghan fell asleep, talking to himself, to his father's ghost. One morning, Meghan found him passed out on the floor of the master bedroom: The lock had been smashed but he couldn't remember if he had done it—let alone how or why.

"You must have done it," Meghan said. "How else did you get in?"

Dylan frowned. He could feel the house coming back to life: pipes and wiring resurrected; wood and stone and steel reborn. Maybe he had spoken to his father last night; maybe it was just another nightmare.

The next morning it had stopped raining but the beach remained raw and damp. Gulls wheeled through the sky, their cries echoing off the empty beach. As they sat atop one of the dunes, staring toward the horizon, the last bottle of champagne wedged in the sand between them, Dylan turned to Meghan and said, "It's time."

The Journal of Senator Robert Fitzgerald
Excerpt # 5

To Dylan,

My relationship with Michael Morrison is unusual to say the least. He was the force behind my decision to enter politics; he and his company, Morrison Biotechnology, have funneled millions of dollars to my campaign over the years. He has legions of consultants, spin doctors, and security personnel, all of whom have played a massive role not only in my success, but in the rise of the Progress Party as well.

But Morrison also plays another role. In my previous letter I mentioned that, after the incident in the limo, once I was aboard the helicopter, I received an injection from one of Morrison's security personnel. This wasn't a mere sedative—for years now, Morrison and his team have been working to help me control these attacks, these meltdowns. I routinely travel to New Mexico, to Morrison Biotech HQ where Morrison runs extensive tests on me—I am unique, he tells me. I ask him for specifics but all he will say is that more tests are needed. I've sought other opinions, but other doctors just advise me to get a little more rest; I'm just working too hard they tell me. But otherwise, the consensus is unanimous: I am the model of physical health. And yet, I feel like every fiber of my being is unraveling, disintegrating. And so I will continue to work with Morrison, continue to allow him to run his tests. The injections he provides seem capable of warding off madness at least temporarily, so I will continue with those as well.

Why am I burdening you with this knowledge? My blood runs through your veins and I fear that whatever it is that has left me so isolated from my fellow man, from my wife and child, may come to torment you as well. I want you to be aware that there is something else out there—something beyond the immediate physical world, something I can apprehend but cannot ever truly experience. This is my condition. It has no name and I can only pray it has not passed on to you.

Love,
Your Father

Chapter 20

Tiber City
Sept. 11, 2015
11:29 a.m.

Sitting in the backseat of a idling Mercedes SX in an alley next to Tiber City's Museum of Modern Art, Morrison could feel the entire city humming with anticipation—an expectancy fueled by days of Internet rumors, rampant message board speculation, and the ever-amorphous "industry buzz." Such expectations, for Morrison, were only natural: The last time Morrison Biotechnology held a similar black tie gala for investors, senior researchers, and management, its CEO announced the development of an AIDS vaccine.

The Tiber City Museum of Modern Art was a monument to Bauhaus architectural egoism. Devoid of any decorative details like cornices or eaves, the eight-story building was a concrete maze of smooth, hyper-hygienic facades and nondescript cubic shapes. The color scheme was a blur of whites and grays, beiges and blacks, blending each room into the next, the parade of monotones interrupted only by the occasional red splashed across a canvas. The décor's purism appealed to something at the center of Morrison's being: The emphasis on straight edges; smooth, slim forms; and uber-functional shining steel furniture sprinkled between exhibits seemed the architectural embodiment of the city's present drift into numbing, anesthetized nothing. It was, in Morrison's opinion, the perfect setting for tonight's presentation.

Yet, Morrison had chosen the Tiber City MOMA not only for its aesthetic but also for its penthouse-level ballroom, which was home to the world's largest collection of Zero Movement art. It was in this ballroom, surrounded by the Zero collection, where Morrison would make his announcement.

Stepping out of the car's climate-controlled interior onto the concrete, the door held open for him by a giant piece of muscle stuffed into an expensive black suit, Morrison was enveloped by four additional security guards who escorted him the two dozen or so feet from the idling car to the back entrance of the museum. Morrison's security team had swept the immediate area several times over the past two hours, purging the blocks surrounding the museum of its tiny homeless population.

The rest of the neighborhood—expensive brownstone co-ops inhabited by yuppie trustafarians; an overpriced organic market whose profits were driven by "herbal supplements" produced by a subsidiary of Morrison Biotech; a bank that despite having changed names three times since its construction in 1998 sought to convey a sense of timeless dependability with its entrance framed by two massive stone columns—seemed to pose little threat, but snipers lined the roof just the same. Plainclothes operatives, armed to the teeth, roamed the storefronts and coffee shops, studying the population for any potential problems. While annoying, such draconian security measures had become necessary—the number of credible death threats against Morrison continued to spike. And although Morrison had enough men on the ground to neutralize any assassination attempts by rival corporations—Japan's Optika Group, for example, seemed to consider such tactics a necessary component of the mergers and acquisitions process—given the importance of this evening's proceedings, the extra precautions seemed prudent.

Taking one final glance over his shoulder, his eyes seeking out the horizon where the sun had begun its final descent and the skyscrapers and spotlights were already bursting to life, Morrison felt like the air was a living thing—as though there was so much information coursing through the atmosphere it had coagulated and taken on a texture, a weight, an *identity* of its own. And as this weight pressed down on the city, driving its inhabitants mad, Michael Morrison couldn't help but smile: This was his kingdom. And then he was gone, disappearing into the back of the museum as his security agents continued to swarm, preparing for the arrival of yet another VIP.

Standing alone in the museum's control room, Morrison watched as footage from a series of security cameras played back across several large monitors—his guests had begun to arrive. He had invited most of his top-level staff: the dozen or so vice presidents and directors of various corporate subdivisions, his senior research staff, and, most important, his communications people—those masters of media and spin who, each time the company's research facilities shattered another natural barrier, convinced the world there was nothing to fear. It was rare for Morrison to gather his people together like this: He only did so on special occasions. And tonight was a very special occasion indeed.

The footage continued to stream across the monitors, transmitting video of Morrison's employees filtering from the reception in the lobby, up the elevators, and into the penthouse-level ballroom. The room was huge, with vast stretches of shiny hardwood flooring running from end to end, interrupted only by a series of sculptures, collections of metal, fiber optics, and circuit boards twisted together and scattered seemingly at random across the floor. Waiters in tuxedos carried trays of hors d'oeuvres—salmon, foie gras, fatty tuna sushi—all shaped to resemble DNA helixes, as electronic lounge music pulsed low in the background, snaking its way across the room, its only competition the sound of heels echoing off the hardwood, the clinking of champagne flutes, and the subdued roar of human social interaction: greetings, introductions, acknowledgements, pleasantries, speculation on the purpose of the evening. All of these details, however, were mere footnotes compared to the ballroom's walls.

The walls of the MOMA's Zero wing were digitalized, and displayed a real-time image of the data flowing throughout various cities across the globe. The walls were divided into sections by a series of stainless steel girders, and each Zero artist controlled a section of the wall—an individual terminal where he was free to remotely manipulate this data using various computer-imaging techniques.

Most artists were content to use 3-D "hyperbolic geometry" programs, thereby transforming the data, which, in its raw form, appeared as an unintelligible stream of letters, 1s, and 0s, into a series of more traditional images—circles, squares, triangles—that would rotate in every direction—growing in size, then decreasing, then growing once again—in an attempt to convey the very rhythm of human life.

Holding the biotech gala in the MOMA was unusual in and of itself; in general, Morrison hated art. Chunky Madonnas and comically haloed Christs comprised the bulk of his early impressions of the medium; useless, mythical figures who offered no insight into the relentless chaos of the modern world. But the Zero Movement—originally part of a market-research program born in the high-tech towers in the heart of Tiber City's financial core—had managed to present a worldview that reflected what Morrison deemed to be essential truths: mutability, truth through reason alone, and defiance of old gods long dead. Over a dozen artist terminals lined the walls of the ballroom, each section alive with Zeros—the artists awake for 24, 36, 48 hours in a cramped studio somewhere, anywhere, in the world, fingers flying across multiple sets of keyboards, forgetting to eat, some sipping mushroom tea, others gobbling speed by the fistful—all trying to create an image that communicated the reality of modern life. Occasionally a monitor went dark: Even the most devoted Zero sometimes slept—although, as Morrison understood it, most collapsed, only to jack back in to his terminal upon regaining consciousness; after all, there were lots of other hungry Zeros on the make who would do anything for a terminal in the Tiber City MOMA. But, no matter how good, how talented, or how devoted these kids were, they had nothing on Morrison's personal favorite: Tiber City's own Cording Jax.

Jax was the "leader" of Tiber City's Zero Movement. Yet, whereas his peers sought to use the modern world's massive and varied communication networks as a canvas, its data as paint, Jax retained this data in its raw form, the streaming alphanumerics that constituted the physical manifestation of digital information. But Jax didn't preserve just any data: He specialized in capturing, or, if the event were unexpected, recovering, the raw transmission of data at the exact instant some epoch-defining event occurred—the first shot of a revolution, the assassination of a president, the detonation of a dirty bomb, a tsunami triggering hundreds of thousands of deaths. And then Jax would take several of these images and make a collage, as though he were putting together a jigsaw puzzle—the superficial suggestion being that there was some underlying connection between these occurrences, if only society would look more closely. Many believed that Jax had discovered something, that there was a message, a truth, perhaps even a prophecy, hidden in his collages. For his part, Jax remained silent, allowing the buzz associated with his name and his work to grow.

Morrison, however, knew the truth: While there was indeed a connection between these data extractions, it was not the one most people, even some of the other Zeros, believed. What Jax sought to convey was the ultimate reality: There was no order, no truth, no explanation for life's cruel, senseless tragedies, just numbers, data, information repeating into infinity. But even while acknowledging the chaotic condition of human existence, Jax's work remained defiant, refusing to retreat into religious fairytales or false philosophical constructs.

Instead, Jax brought order to the chaos of life, creating his own meaning where, inherently, there is none. When man shouts into the whirlwind, demanding answers for his condition, and is answered only by silence, he has no choice but to shape the world in his own image—that was the realization that had led to the founding of Morrison Biotech, to the creation of Project Exodus. And so Morrison considered it only fitting that the digitalized walls of the Zero wing should serve as the backdrop for tonight's proceedings.

At the end of the ballroom, a giant stage had been erected, flanked on either side by floor-to-ceiling video monitors, which, at the moment, displayed the Morrison Biotech logo, spinning and twisting, disappearing and reappearing with wild, expectant energy. And in the middle of the stage, a black podium, also adorned with the red corporate logo, awaited the evening's keynote speaker.

Without warning, the lights dimmed, then went dark, eliciting a low gasp from the crowd. The Morrison Biotech logo vanished from the two screens on the side of the stage, replaced by a stunning high-definition, first-person video shot by a camera racing across the surface of a vast ocean, churning under an ashen sky. As the camera moved over the surface of the water, a disembodied voice—female with an electronic, anesthetized tinge—began to narrate:

Since the beginning of time, life on planet Earth has been subject to inherent limitations. Although the evolutionary process has allowed for certain, arbitrary transformations, these changes have occurred in accordance with these natural limitations.

As the voice spoke, the oceans on the monitors began to morph into a massive map of the human genome.

Morrison Biotechnology, since its inception, has struggled to free man from this tyranny of the natural world. While it has allowed for considerable evolution, the human genetic code is, as we here at Morrison Biotech are all aware, inherently flawed.

Slowly the video's perspective began to pull back as if it were moving through a human cell, and then from the cell into tissue until it became obvious that the camera was traveling through a human body—up from the stomach through the esophagus, passing the tongue as it pushed toward the daylight waiting beyond a series of small, crooked teeth.

Bursting into the light, the camera surveyed a world very different from the roiling seas seen at the beginning: There was no water in sight, only dry, broken plains stretching endlessly under a cloudless, indifferent sky. Twenty feet off the ground, the camera came to a stop, shifting its perspective back toward the earth, back toward the human being whose body it had just left: a tiny, malnourished child, his lips cracked and covered in dust, who had been left to die under the unforgiving sub-Saharan sun.

By 2009, AIDS had killed nearly 30 million people in Africa alone. Another 35 million were living with AIDS. It was Morrison Biotech's unflagging belief that man can defy genetic limitations that made this stunning scientific breakthrough possible.

Still observing the presentation from the control room, Morrison smiled: The video omitted how Morrison's financial demands had bankrupted several African governments, a story that, in the aftermath of the vaccine, received scant coverage. And then there was the story that received no coverage at all: the one where several of the most impoverished African nations had provided Morrison with hundreds of research "volunteers." In a land where human life was perhaps the cheapest and most available of all commodities, it was, conceded more than one despot, a small price to pay, to control the distribution of the AIDS vaccine—one of the most powerful political tools ever known. Wielding the power of the vaccine, more than one warlord was able to topple democratically elected governments. These were all details scrubbed from the official reports, details Morrison savored in private.

By developing the world's first HIV vaccine, Morrison Biotech again defied the limitations imposed by the natural world and, as a result, saved millions of lives. Manipulation of the human genetic code—the primary objective of Morrison Biotech—has come at considerable cost. The rewards, however, have been staggering.

The video of the dying African child vanished, replaced by a montage of the same boy, now healthy and nourished, playing with friends in a grassy field, celebrating a birthday with family, graduating from a university, getting married, and then, finally, having a child of his own, the video freezing as the boy—now a man—held his child for the first time.

And now, ladies and gentlemen, please welcome the man whose vision has driven so many of this company's triumphs—Michael Morrison.

During the final moments of the video presentation, Morrison had left the control room, taking a private elevator to the penthouse level. With perfect timing, he hit the stage right on cue.

The audience burst into applause, cheers echoing off the ballroom walls as Morrison strode toward the podium. It was rare that the CEO addressed his employees so directly and the excitement in the room was palpable. There was a nervousness as well—many of the researchers had never met their boss, never even seen him in person. Morrison waved to the hundred or so of his employees gathered before him but his eyes were looking past them, drawn to the never-ending stream of alphanumerics cascading down the walls of the ballroom, and in that instant, he had never felt more certain in his vision for the human race.

"Ladies and gentlemen," he began, "thank you for joining me for what, I believe, will be a very special occasion. I have two announcements to share with you this evening, although both relate directly to the video presentation you just saw: Morrison Biotechnology's vision for the future of the human race. Now, over the years I've gotten into some trouble—with the media, with some politicians, with various religious activists—because we here at Morrison Biotech refuse to accept the fact that the pace of human evolution should be dictated by nature or a God or any external factor."

A cheer rippled through the crowd as Morrison paused, adjusting a black cuff link and smiling back at some of the best and brightest minds of a generation.

"Perhaps one of the greatest lies ever propagated is the notion all men are created equal. Deserving of equal rights, sure. But *created* equal? Now that is bullshit. The only thing equal about human beings is our potential: Each and every one of us has the same genetic base; we all start from the same foundation. After that, it's a roll of the dice. Some hit the genetic jackpot—just take a look around this room. Others are born with crippling defects, psychological disorders, mental retardation. Or perhaps even worse, some are average, destined to plod through life and then die. Why should this be? Why should some suffer while others thrive? Because nature or a God mandates it? Enough! Just as this company refused to accept that millions should suffer and die from AIDS, we reject the notion that mankind should be subject to the genetic roulette wheel: some born strong, others disease-ridden and subjected to a lifetime of misery."

Morrison paused, taking a sip of water as his words reverberated across the room.

"To that end," Morrison continued, "I am pleased to announce that Morrison Biotechnology is introducing a new product line, one that will position our company at the forefront of the next generation of biotechnology. No longer will our company work primarily with governments or massive health care providers. We are moving aggressively into a direct relationship with the American public—and, soon, the rest of the world—through a new line of services called TruLife—a series of embryonic genetic modifications that will allow future generations to experience life free of the natural limitations, be they disease or defects or even just general mediocrity. A 'truer' life, if you will."

The monitors on both sides of the podium again flared to life, this time displaying the details of a series of "TruLife" packages: the academic package, the sports package, the Hollywood package; there was even Morrison's favorite, the golden embryo special, which combined all other packages into a single spectacular creation. There was even a buy-three- modifications-get-a-fourth-free "Holiday Special," which would be out just in time for Christmas.

For a brief moment, the assembled employees were silent. And then, they all began talking at once, cries of amazed disbelief filling the ballroom. Morrison stood back from the podium, watching with amusement as it finally dawned on his researchers what it was that their work of the past decade had been building toward. Granted, TruLife was only part of a much larger picture. But for the employees who assumed tonight's announcement was going to be about another vaccine, the TruLife package was something of a shock. And that was nothing compared to what was coming next.

With one hand gripping each side of the podium, Morrison leaned forward, unable to control the smile that stretched across his ageless visage, revealing his perfect teeth.

"Our company is going to be facing a lot of challenges in the coming months. Fortunately, we're going to have a little more help. Please join me in welcoming back to Morrison Biotechnology, one of this company's founding fathers, Jonathan Campbell."

For a moment, the entire room, which was still buzzing over the Tru-Life announcement, again plunged into silence. Then the unimaginable happened—Jonathan Campbell appeared on the side of the stage. Thunderous applause filled the ballroom, and Campbell made his way slowly across the stage, shaking hands with his former protégée as the crowd continued to cheer, the walls of the ballroom glowing with the endless streams of data that were now considered art, the very lifeblood of a city, a country, a people.

Morrison squeezed Campbell's hand, grinning as he looked into his former mentor's eyes, before turning to the crowd, holding Campbell's hand in the air like a victorious prizefighter.

Chapter 21

Havenport
Sept. 12, 2015
1:15 p.m.

Dylan sat alone in the tidy office, staring at the pictures arranged on the far wall: a mixture of canned family portraits, vacation photos, and a child's scribbling. The pictures consisted of Mike Beasley, the manager for Capital Bank's Westland branch, whom Dylan had just met and was currently looking up information on the safety deposit box that corresponded to the numbers on the back of the Heffernan flyer; a fading blonde in her late 30s-early 40s, a woman who was still pretty but the years and the pounds were piling up, a transformation documented by the collection of pictures which seemed front-loaded with memories of a younger Mrs. Beasley, all tits and white teeth, big hair and no crow's-feet; and then there were the kids: By Dylan's count there were four. He didn't know anyone that had four kids. He wasn't even sure if he knew anyone with three.

A wooden ceiling fan rotated overhead, pushing the same stale air in circles around the room as seconds stretched into minutes and Dylan grew restless. He and Meghan had entered the bank just over 20 minutes ago, moving in stops and starts through the line created by a nylon strap attached to a series of plastic pillars. When it was their turn, Dylan approached the only open teller's window and asked for information on account number 061280091177. Although it was possible his mother hallucinated the whole thing, that she pulled these numbers off a television bar code, his gut told him otherwise.

The teller—a girl in her mid-20s, not much older than Dylan but wearing a wedding band and too much makeup—punched something into her computer: maybe the numbers Dylan had given her, maybe something else. She tapped her bright blue nails on the mouse, she snapped her gum, she frowned.

"I'm going to need to get the manager," she told him.

The bank manager had taken his license, along with social security number, and gone off to verify that Dylan was authorized to open the safety deposit box. Was he authorized? Dylan had no idea.

Fighting the urge to pick things up off Mike Beasley's desk, he took out his iPhone instead because he needed to do something, to be entertained or amused or at least distracted in some way. He called up the Web browser, punching in a few random websites, mostly Tiber City news or gossip blogs—scrolling, scanning but not absorbing; information for information's sake, something terrible yet soothing and familiar in the blur of banner headlines, graphics, hyperlink stacked on top of hyperlink, a continual flow of raw data: heroin for the 21st-century boy.

And then Beasley was back, shuffling a stack of papers as he re-entered the room, flakes of dandruff shaking free from his hair gel's iron grip, floating down toward his shoulders as he spoke.

"Mr. Fitzgerald, you are indeed one of the authorized account holders for safety deposit box 061280091177. One of our oldest and most valued accounts."

Despite his rising anxiety, Dylan laughed.

"I'm a valued account holder?" he asked.

"No," Beasley said, his face expressionless. "But your father was."

As he approached Capital Bank Westland's safety deposit box vault, Dylan was simultaneously underwhelmed and terrified. A lifetime of Hollywood movies had conditioned him to expect military-grade levels of security: retina scans and thumbprints, beefy men with automatic weapons. Instead, the security guard was old age personified. Pick a stereotype and this guy fit it: He moved slowly, he talked slowly, he shuffled, and stuttered, and shambled. His uniform fit his frail frame like a tent, loose and billowing as he stood to greet Dylan.

The old man nodded at Dylan; the bank manager had called ahead and the ancient guard was already opening the round vault door. His heart pounding, Dylan stepped past the guard and into the vault.

The inside of the vault was filled with a terrible stillness—a patience at odds with the modern compulsion toward perpetual motion. Hundreds of black rectangles of various sizes lined the walls, each with a single keyhole and a silver plate mounted dead center. And on each of these silver plates was a series of 12 numbers.

Dylan looked down at the papers in his hand, nodded, and made his way across the vault, stopping in front of box number 061280091177. He paused, looking around the vault, half-expecting someone—the bank manager, the old guard, anyone—to appear and explain how to proceed. Instead, there was only the silence of the vault.

Struggling against a creeping sense of claustrophobia, Dylan remembered the gnarled key in his back pocket. He took the key out, turning it over in his palm a few times. The metal was cool and hard and with trembling fingers, Dylan pushed the key into the lock, twisting it until he heard a mechanical click. The safety deposit box popped open, and Dylan reached inside.

An hour later, Dylan was pushing his way through the revolving glass at the front of the bank, staggering out into the parking lot, tears forming at the corner of his eyes, rage twisting his stomach into knots. A hot wind swept through the parking lot; plastic shopping bags, empty beer cans, and sand cascaded in between the cars, under the cars and somewhere in the distance Dylan could hear sirens. When he was little and an ambulance sped past, he used to cross himself. But that was a long time ago, before sirens took his father's lifeless body to the hospital; these days he just watched, irritated that someone else's crisis—the misfortune and suffering of a stranger—made it more difficult to hear his iPod. But at that moment he was overcome by such a monumental wave of empathy that it almost drove him to his knees.

In middle of the parking lot he saw Meghan, standing by the bike, two cups of coffee from the local chain resting on the sidewalk, her sunglasses down, shielding her eyes from the debris, which continued to spray the parking lot like buckshot.

She reached for him but Dylan pushed past her, the tears streaming freely now.

"What is it? What did you find?" she was asking.

But he just shook his head and pulled himself onto the bike, the roar of the engine drowning out Meghan's pleas for an explanation. Seconds later he was blasting out of the parking lot, the woman he loved receding in the distance, the two items he found in Capital Bank Westland's safety deposit box 061280091177 stuffed in his jacket pocket: a thick, beat-up black journal filled with letters from his father, and a flash drive marked with a strange symbol.

The Journal of Senator Robert Fitzgerald
Excerpt # 6

To Dylan,

Bad night last night. There were pills and booze, there was a woman but the details are hazy. I remember she spoke with a Hispanic accent and had a tattoo of an asterisk inside a circle on her lower back. But when I woke up this morning the woman was gone and in her place was a flash drive bearing the same symbol.

Project Exodus_231.avi—That was the name of the only file on the drive, a video I wish to God I never opened.

The footage was mostly dark—but I could hear grunting and groveling and anguished braying.

Then whoever was behind the lens hit the infrared button.

Creatures—monstrous, misshapen beasts—filled the screen.

And every one had my face.

Love,
Your Father

Chapter 22

Tiber City
Sept. 12, 2015
2:30 p.m.

Guarded on either side by jet-black Hummer H5s, the stretch limo raced down the highway toward the Tiber City airport, broken street-lights observing the caravan's progress like burnt-out angels on high. The TruLife unveiling had ended less than 24 hours ago; Campbell and Morrison would be at the airport in 20 minutes, where a private jet was waiting to take them back to Morrison Biotech. It had been a long time since Campbell had been to New Mexico, since he had been to the desert. Sitting in the back of the limo, staring out into the starless, moonless night, Campbell wondered if agreeing to rejoin Project Exodus was the right decision. But what choice did he have?

Return to Project Exodus or what happens to the rest of the Order's camps makes Ramoth look like a tea party: That had been Morrison's ulti-matum. Campbell had to buy enough time to warn the Order, to clear out the camps—only then could he make his move. But how to warn the Order? It wasn't like he could just drop the gurney men a text. And so, under the guise of assisting the TruLife product launch, Campbell was returning to Exodus.

"Tell me Jonathan, is it bullshit?" Morrison asked, shattering Campbell's train of thought.

Campbell looked across the limo at Morrison, who was sitting with his legs crossed, a drink in one hand; his face, neither young nor old, shifting from shadow to light, light to shadow, the artificial illumination pouring out from Tiber City's skyscrapers momentarily eclipsed by concrete each time the car passed under an overpass. The back of the limo consisted of two leather seats capable of accommodating four people, two on each side. Morrison sat with his back to the tinted glass partition; Campbell faced forward.

"Is what bullshit, Michael?" Campbell replied.

"The story that crucified monk told Lieutenant al-Salaam. He seemed convinced that the Omega gene is..." Morrison paused and took a sip of his drink, a smirk dancing around the corners of his mouth. "The human soul?" he finished, his voice dripping with mock reverence.

The car entered a tunnel—one of the dozens of two-lane, claustrophobia-inducing concrete tubes that ferried traffic under Tiber City—and the inside of the limo went dark. Campbell blinked, his eyes trying to adjust to the sudden change. He was exhausted but still running on adrenaline, on fear, on rage—each time he shut his eyes he saw the Ramoth massacre: monks dismembered; the bodies of children slain while they slept. He had accepted an injection of the Treatment at the MOMA just before Morrison announced his return to Exodus; having used a synthetic substitute for so many years, the initial rush almost killed him. But now he felt the familiar warmth flowing through his veins, revitalizing each of his body's 11 systems. It was rather ironic, Campbell considered: The Treatment, designed to ensure the founders of Exodus remained physically and mentally sharp well into old age, was now providing Campbell with the endurance he needed to destroy the Project.

"No Michael, it's not bullshit," Campbell said. "Is it the human soul? That depends on what you think the soul is. It has nothing to do with an afterlife. But there is another component of human existence, something beyond the physical, beyond the material—I'm convinced of that and this gene is the key to that *something*. A radio tuned to the divine: That's the way the monks explained it to me. This gene is what holds people together, what makes them whole. Without it, people are cut off—not only from one another but from...God."

The words felt strange coming out, but right—he believed. Campbell paused, waiting for Morrison to ridicule him. To his surprise, Morrison smiled.

"What would you say if I told you I agree?" Morrison replied.

"I'd say that since you're already blackmailing me, lying seems a little excessive," Campbell said, studying Morrison's face for any physical sign his former pupil was mocking him. But Morrison gave away nothing.

The limo burst out of the tunnel, sunlight flooding the backseat of the car and Campbell watched as Morrison finished his drink and poured two more, one of which he handed to Campbell.

"Perhaps you've forgotten, but I've never denied the existence of a God. Project Exodus was, and still is, a direct response to God—to his indifference, to his sadism. God has abandoned man, left him to wander through this life alone, to suffer alone. Exodus is about creating new men who are gods unto themselves—beholden to nothing."

"Maybe he hasn't abandoned them after all," Campbell said. "If this gene really is the human soul, if it really offers a connection between mankind and the divine, then perhaps the connections have gotten a little fuzzy on our end, the terrestrial end."

Morrison rolled his eyes. "It's just a failsafe; a control mechanism. A means to deter competition." He paused, then lowered his voice and snarled, "a fucking trademark."

"Jesus, Michael," Campbell said, looking away, out the window as the limo began crossing the massive, four-lane bridge that traversed the Acheron River. Massive steel girders were twisted in a webbed arc over the bridge, which rose sharply at first, then leveled out for a mile or two before an abrupt decline. There were guardrails on either side of the bridge but they struck Campbell as the mere fulfillment of some bureaucratic mandate, measured to meet the minimum standard necessary to prevail in a lawsuit—no way those rails were stopping anything bigger than a scooter.

"Besides," Morrison continued, "one gene defeating the greatest minds of the 21st century? How can I not accept the possibility it is somehow… supernatural."

"Let's pretend for a moment that I buy any of this," Campbell replied, taking a sip of his drink—whiskey, neat. "What about Heffernan? You've got a U.S. senator, who you're trying to put in the White House, on the verge of a complete physical meltdown. How the fuck do you remedy that one?"

"What time is it?" Morrison asked.

"What does that matter?"

"You asked how I'm going to remedy Exodus' current woes, and I'm going to show you. But first, I need to know what time it is."

Campbell reached into his pocket and pulled out his cell phone. He glanced at the external display: 2:58 p.m.

"Two minutes to 3," Campbell told Morrison.

"Very good," Morrison said, before producing a tiny remote control from the pocket of his suit jacket. He pointed the remote at Campbell as he pressed one of the remote's two red buttons. The classical music cut off and a small video screen began to descend from the ceiling, glowing with that pale, expectant light given off by televisions and computer monitors tuned to a dead feed. But then Morrison pressed another button and the screen flared to life: CNN was broadcasting a Jack Heffernan rally live from Santa Fe.

Heffernan was standing behind a pulpit on a massive stage in the middle of a town green, delivering the final lines of his stump speech, slight variations of which Campbell had caught in a hundred different sound bites scattered across dozens of different mediums. Just as the speech began to build toward its crescendo—the candidate's voice booming and feverish; the images from American mythology displayed on video monitors behind the senator changing until they were almost indistinguishable from one another: pilgrims morphing into the Apollo moon landing morphing into Iwo Jima into Washington crossing the Delaware—two gun shots rang out, followed by a third, and Heffernan lurched forward, crashing into the podium. Secret Service tried to form a protective circle around Heffernan but cameramen were everywhere, jostling for position, for that perfect shot that would distill an American tragedy down to a single picture, the image that would become the collective reference point for an entire generation. Then the screen went blank.

"Turn it back on," Campbell shouted to Morrison. Morrison just smiled and shook his head as he put the remote back in his pocket.

"There's nothing more to see," Morrison said. "Why bother with mere speculation and 'unconfirmed reports' when I can tell you exactly what's going to happen?"

Campbell was too stunned to speak. He finished his drink, the whiskey burn the only assurance he had that this wasn't some terrible nightmare.

And then, even though Campbell couldn't remember Morrison using the remote again, somehow the television had turned back on, scenes from another American tragedy playing out in high definition; mourning in Dolby

Digital. A blonde reporter holding the microphone a little too close to her mouth—her suit proclaiming professionalism, her glistening lip gloss hinting at something else—verified what Campbell had just seen: Jack Heffernan had been assassinated. As the reporter spoke, video showing Heffernan reacting to the shot—hands to the chest, crashing into the podium—looped over and over, interrupted only by shots from a helicopter that provided an aerial shot of the crime scene that, ostensibly, would provide new insight on the tragedy but were little more than a clusterfuck of yellow police tape, emergency vehicles, people standing around, and news trucks jockeying for satellite position. And yet, this useful footage shot from the helicopter would be run several times an hour throughout coverage of the assassination—content was king.

Campbell shut his eyes for a moment, trying to process everything that had just happened. When he opened them, the assassination coverage had cut to commercial: a 50-something man and woman defying erectile dysfunction in Vegas, on a cruise ship; tumbling dice on green felt, dancing on the upper deck under a starlit sky.

"Why me?" Campbell asked.

Morrison laughed, metallic-tinged taunt that made Campbell think of giant industrial freezers; of too-bright hospital wards at 2 o'clock in the morning.

"You are the father of Project Exodus. You know the workings of the human genome better than any man on this planet, including myself. It pains me to admit that, but we both know it's true.

"The things your monk friends told me...Well, let's just say they gave me a new perspective. If Exodus can't replicate this soul gene, so be it. It's not like I can fault God for trying to protect his monopoly on creation—it's a smart business move. But if the human soul is a gene that functions as—how did you describe it? A radio receiver?—then some people will naturally have better, stronger receivers than others. As your monks made clear, the function of this gene can be cultivated, enhanced—they told me about the OAA differentiation—but never artificially replicated. If an attempt is made to replicate it...well, I think the failures of Exodus have, so far, made that rather clear."

Still reeling from the footage of the assassination, Campbell tried to focus on the implications of what Morrison was saying.

"But why now?" Campbell asked.

"Until very recently," Morrison replied, "I was convinced that our team could break the secret of this gene. I wanted Exodus to be self-contained: man made entirely by man. But there's more: Jack Heffernan's genetic makeup is so perfectly balanced, so finely tuned, that the introduction of a foreign gene might disrupt the genetic mix we spent so many years trying to perfect."

"But the alternative..." Campbell began.

"Correct," Morrison snapped, adjusting one of this onyx cuff links, a look of frustration flashing across his face, gone as quickly as it came. "The alternative is the meltdowns that destroyed Senator Fitzgerald, the meltdowns that were beginning to consume Jack Heffernan as well. Should I have considered this approach sooner? Perhaps. But the past is irrelevant. There is only the future. And Jonathan, let me show you what the future looks like."

Morrison gestured at the television monitor. The live broadcast had vanished, replaced by a single image of a young man in his mid-to-late 20s with longish brown hair, blue eyes, and a few days worth of stubble. Campbell had no idea who the kid was, but the eyes—he knew those eyes.

"Allow me to introduce Dylan Fitzgerald," Morrison said.

"Shut it off," Campbell whispered.

"You might remember his late father, Robert, a former U.S. senator with a rather distinguished gene pool."

"Off," Campbell said.

"Dylan's recently deceased mother, Elizabeth, on the other hand, while quite striking, has a slightly more mundane genetic composition."

"Off," Campbell roared but Morrison continued, his voice steady and seductive.

"It seems like one of the best decisions I ever made was to allow you to leave Exodus alive. You brought me to the people who managed to do the one thing Exodus never could: figure out the purpose of the Omega gene. Now, I guess the only question left is: Does Dylan Fitzgerald have a soul? If he does, then Exodus is back in business."

Leaning forward and looking down at his drink, Campbell struggled against the urge to smash the glass into Morrison's face and if that didn't kill the motherfucker, to slit his throat with the shards. But he knew Morrison was trying to goad him and there was too much at stake: Campbell closed his eyes and saw the aftermath of the massacre at Camp Ramoth. How many more would die if Morrison's men moved on the remaining camps? He sat back, forcing his body to relax and for an instant his former pupil looked disappointed, as if Morrison had been relishing the prospect of violence.

"And how do you propose we answer that question?" Campbell asked.

Smiling, Morrison began to explain.

Chapter 23

Havenport–Tiber City
Sept. 13, 2015
7:38 a.m.

Dawn collapsed into day, the light limping across the horizon before being caught and devoured by night, and all the while, Dylan rode north, away from the shore, away from the Jungle, away from Meghan Morrison. He ate little, slept less; He had been on the road for hours, yet was making little progress: Severe thunderstorms throttled the land and rain was coming down in slanted sheets, driven by 50 mph wind gusts and sudden thunderclaps. Accidents slowed the interstate to a crawl so he tried the back roads, but those were worse, ferrying him from one burnt-out industrial valley to the next, a series of small manufacturing towns that hadn't manufactured anything of value since the 1950s, rising brown rivers slowly taking back what the mills had stolen. Although these roads were almost empty, the elements remained steadfast in their opposition to human progress and despite almost burning through an entire tank of gasoline, by nightfall Dylan had only made it as far as the lands that ran like a tattered police line around the perimeter of these northern industrial valleys, the Jungle's neon lights still visible on the horizon like a million atomic stars.

His cell phone rang a dozen times—11 calls from Meghan, one from an unlisted number. Dylan fought the urge to answer. He needed to think first, to digest the journal he discovered in the safety deposit, the story that the journal told: that his father had been something less (or was it more?) than human; that his father's death had likely come at the hands of Michael Morrison, rather than his own.

These suggestions were breathtaking in their audacity and yet Dylan couldn't dismiss them—his father had been many things, but delusional was never one of them. It was tempting to write the whole thing off as a bad trip: Somebody slips the old man some new designer shit and voilà, clones and laboratories. But the fact that his father had sealed a flash drive, the one with the Ω symbol, on the inside of the front cover made his case a little more compelling. Dylan needed to find a place where he could read the letters again; a place where he could explore the flash drive and see if it contained the footage about which his father wrote.

But the night was barreling down upon him now, hungry and expectant, and he realized how tired he was: He decided he'd stop at the next decent-looking motel—maybe one with an ancient business center where he could plug in the flash drive. But the highway seemed to stretch eternal in each direction, and the weather was getting worse. Hail, frozen yet still sizzling from its rapid descent through the murky atmosphere, now accompanied the thunderclaps and hot, driving rain; a sulfuric stench announced its arrival, a reminder of the diseased skies from which it came.

The hail was coming hard and fast, slicing into Dylan's four-day-old beard and bouncing off the side of his skull. He could taste a tiny trickle of blood from where the hail cut him and he stood straight up on the bike and began to scream, not in pain, but defiance. A strawberry-size piece of hail whizzed past his ear and Dylan felt a rush of exhilaration; the exhaustion receded and he was loose and alive, consumed by dread and fear but at least it was an honest dread rather than the kind that manifested itself when his Internet connection dropped or he paid too much for slightly lower quality coke. And then he heard a loud POP as his rear tire blew, sending his bike into a fishtail. He struggled for control of the vehicle, but the road was too slick and the bike crashed to one side, shooting across the concrete in a burst of sparks and screeching metal. Dylan tried to control the slide but he had been going too fast and then the world went black.

The scene played over and over in his head, low-grade video with static-y audio, like some YouTube clip stuck on repeat: His father was in an enormous hyper-modern hotel suite—lots of hideous paintings and muted tones, aesthetic forever divorced from function. But that was all on the periphery and vaguely out of focus: Whoever was directing this clip seemed most interested in Dylan's father, who was slumped in some overly formal black stuffed chair and gripping a glass of scotch and melting ice cubes so tightly that Dylan wondered why it hadn't shattered, cutting his father and sending the watered-down scotch to the cold black tile. His dad appeared older than Dylan had ever remembered him looking: huge black circles, cracked skin, and a five- or six-day-old beard—the old man never had stubble. He was wearing suit pants with dark socks and a white undershirt, which wouldn't have been that unusual except Dylan could count on one hand the times he had seen his father in an undershirt. It was his father and it wasn't: This man was only a shadow, an approximation of Senator Robert Fitzgerald. But that was how it had been in those last weeks. And that was something Dylan would never forget.

His father wasn't alone in the hotel room; there was someone else, someone off camera at the moment. This person was speaking; Dylan could make out pitch and tone: muffled, garbled snippets of speech but no actual words. Dylan wanted to fast-forward the scene, to get to the end—he was getting very cold—but the director was insisting on pacing. And then his father was struggling out of the chair, pointing to the person off camera, raw hatred radiating through the old man's bloodshot eyes. The senator was on his feet—unsteady, but standing nonetheless, his nose starting to bleed—and then the glass of scotch was flying across the room, shattering against some unseen wall, object, person, mirror—it didn't matter because seconds later Dylan knew what would happen: His old man would pull out a gun, suck on the barrel, pull the trigger. He'd been watching this rerun for years. But then something was changed: There had been a last-second rewrite and instead of reaching for a gun under the chair, his father just stared off screen, a profound sadness settling across the man before Michael Morrison walked into the shot, pumped a single bullet into his father's head, wiped the handle for prints, and then placed the gun in his father's hand.

Dylan came to on the side of the road soaked and screaming, tangled in the machine that used to be his father's motorcycle, huge chunks of hail still blasting from the sky. It was pouring rain and his right leg was ripped up, but nothing felt broken. Still, the bike was ruined and he needed to wrap up his leg—not to mention the fact that the hail seemed to be getting bigger, sharper, and one direct hit might send him back into unconsciousness. He dragged himself to his feet, his weight shifted onto his left leg. He tried to take the bike but it was too much and so, still trembling from the crash, Dylan left it along the side of the road as he began to scan the area for shelter, the image of Michael Morrison executing his father looping through his frontal lobe as he staggered north.

Ten minutes later, Dylan saw it: a solitary structure coming into view on the side of the empty highway. The place looked closed but he'd have to take a chance: The storm was showing no signs of letting up and his iPhone wasn't getting any reception, let alone email, texts, or Internet—even if he wanted to contact someone, he couldn't get through. His leg was bleeding badly and tonight wasn't the night to find out how much blood loss was too much.

A jagged streak of lightening slashed the clouds overhead, throwing a momentary burst of light across the land and through this light Dylan could make out a series of gas pumps and the vague outline of a service station. He was moving as fast as he could but it wasn't fast enough—the hail was coming harder, the rain falling faster and for a moment Dylan was sure he wouldn't make it, that this is where his life would end: no resolution, no purpose, no meaning. He lifted his head back and felt the hail bouncing off his face; he tasted the rain's acid tinge, that strange battery flavor that reminded him of elementary school calculators and discarded circuit boards, of the color brown, and Dylan just let the pain course through him: no barriers, either physical or chemical. In between thunderclaps, Dylan heard an ominous, metallic ding. He looked up and, to his surprise, he was standing in the parking lot of a service station.

Rising a little more than 10 feet off the ground, a steel totem pole offered all the information a potential consumer might require: On the top of the pole was a dented aluminum sign, maybe 8 by 10, informing Dylan that he had arrived at Joe's Gas-n-Go; further down the totem were four smaller signs, each proclaiming the price of a different grade of gasoline. The one on the bottom, diesel, had been gnawed away by something or someone so only the number nine was discernable. But the strange teeth marks were the least of Dylan's concerns; it had been a very long time since this service station had been in operation—unleaded gas hadn't cost $3.50 a gallon in at least five years.

Dylan made his way across the desolate filling station parking lot, past a series of pumps, each identified by a number, one through 13. Several of the pumps had been stripped: all the parts gone—steel, aluminum, copper—removed with something less than technological acumen, an operation performed quickly under chemical duress—the onset of methamphetamine withdrawal didn't lend itself to mechanical precision. Most of the parts were probably in some Tiber City pawn shop but that wasn't Dylan's concern so he kept on moving, past the pumps until he reached the glass door that served as the main entrance to Joe's Gas-n-Go.

Knocking on the glass door would be pointless: The lights were off and likely had been for a while. So Dylan grabbed the curled silver handle and pulled, his flesh sticking to the frozen steel, wondering if maybe he might catch a break—that whoever had closed the store last had forgotten to lock it, had maybe been so preoccupied with some pussy waiting in an idling pickup in the parking lot that they just dashed out, allowing the door to swing shut on its own. Or maybe it was some sort of genuine political preoccupation—not that pussy waiting in an idling pickup wasn't a valid distraction—with rumors of wars and pending global economic collapse whispered across anonymous Internet message boards and late-night talk radio. But regardless of the cause, the end result would have been the same: an unlocked door that no one ever returned to secure. But when he pulled on the handle the door held firm—someone had locked the door on the way out—and while he had expected this, Dylan felt a stab of anxiety. Why lock the door if you weren't coming back?

Whoever ran this place, this tiny outpost for refugees from the Jungle, long-haul truckers, and 24/7 tweakers—what happened to that person? Death? Disease? Disinterest? Just another lost soul swallowed whole by the blur of modern life? Then again, thought Dylan, what did it matter? He could ponder every existential question ever posed and the door would still be fucking locked; hail stinging his exposed skin; his father still slain. Excessive rumination at the expense of action was the primary source of his current predicament: If he had acted sooner, if he had just refused to accept the lull of Tiber City life, maybe he could have at least saved his mother.

"There's gotta be another way inside," Dylan murmured as he limped away from the door, working his way around the side of the building toward the back, ignoring the lights winking at him from the horizon—lights that promised high-speed connections, endless streams of data, fresh content, on-demand everything; need, desire, want, want, want; yeah there's an app for that; all sustaining the illusion that your opinion mattered, that your personal preferences were unique to the point of being revolutionary, that these huge towers of titanium and steel and fiber optics were monuments to you.

He turned the corner and discovered a series of double-doors lining the rear of the service station but these were also locked, as was the triple-bay garage behind the station. To the right of the garage, Dylan spotted another sign that this service station had been abandoned for a very long time: A decaying red dumpster adorning the rear of the property was overflowing with corroded scraps of metal and mortar. A gust of wind exploded across the landscape, propelling hail and rain like buckshot. The large sign in front of the gas station was moving in a strange, arrhythmic jerk, creaking and moaning as the wind blasted past. There was another noise as well: a strange crunching sound that at first Dylan thought was the hail hammering the earth, ricocheting off the bits of metal punching up out of the dumpster and toward the sky, but the noise began to grow louder and Dylan realized it wasn't hail—it was something else, a desperate, frenzied clawing coming from inside the steel dumpster, the sound of a rat, or maybe something bigger, maybe the thing that had taken the chunk out of the diesel gas sign, trying to work its way up through the labyrinth of forgotten scrap, its nest of manganese and iridium under siege from the hail. As the air from the Jungle drifted up into these old mill towns, even Nature began turning against her own, lashing out with indiscriminate fury.

A wave of anxiety swept over Dylan and he pulled out his iPhone, ready to call Meghan or Mikey or Chase or even a fucking taxi to take him to the hospital, let someone else take care of him, and after he got out, book a flight to Mykonos or Malta; somewhere, anywhere warm, maybe develop a hip little heroin addiction, try to forget everything—he felt himself beginning to crumble under the weight of the questions swirling around him, of the decisive action his father's journal commanded. And so Dylan began moving his finger across the phone's touch screen but before he could decide whom to call the tiny bars in the corner of the screen that indicated reception strength vanished.

"Motherfucker," Dylan screamed, slamming the phone back into his pocket: eight gigs of music, two hours of high-definition digital video, a personal GPS, and a 24/7 concierge—fucking useless. Exhaling as the pain in his right leg mushroomed, Dylan tried to focus: He needed shelter and he needed it now. Locked or not, his only option was the gas-and-go; he was going to have to find a way inside.

There were several pieces of corroded metal jutting out of the dumpster, some intersecting others horizontally, like makeshift metal crosses. Dylan took hold of one of the horizontal pieces of metal and after shifting all his weight to his left leg, pulled hard. It didn't budge. Dylan pulled again and again, trying to wiggle the piece free, cursing and shaking the metal as he tried to balance on his one good leg.

Slamming his palm down on the side of the dumpster, Dylan howled in frustration. If he could only get one of the pieces free, he could use it to pry the door to the service station open. But the metal held firm and Dylan's body ached in ways he never imagined it could—he was exhausted; the pain in his left leg was increasing with every movement, and his brain felt like an overheated circuit board, sparking and smoldering as the CPU demanded more than which it was capable. Tilting his head toward the sky, Dylan felt the sting of the hail as tears began to stream down his face. He opened his mouth to scream again but this time no sound came out. Instead, Dylan felt the world recede, the mundane replaced by hyper-real awareness of the glow of Tiber City in the distance, of the dark sky above, of the rain, of the hail, but he wasn't just aware of these things—they weren't just set pieces in a play: There was some connection, some reason that seemed so close that if he just focused, just concentrated a little harder, he might be able to comprehend. He wondered if he was dying, if he had survived the overdose and the motorcycle crash just to drop dead next to some rancid dumpster behind an abandoned gas station.

The air felt electric, almost alive, bursting with possibility and mystery and the insistence that there was something *more* waiting under the surface of things, something forgotten, some necessary truth. There was no active thought process; no reasoning involved. Dylan simply understood and at that moment, he was aware of *something else*—something other than himself—and his body responded: He felt a surge of emotion, as if something buried deep inside of him was not only awake, but straining to connect with that *something else* that had somehow not just surrounded him, but overwhelmed. And as quickly as it had begun, the experience was over, the feeling and emotion gone and a new sense of clarity and purpose settled across his beaten body and beleaguered brain. Seconds later, Dylan turned back to the dumpster and, with barely any effort, slid his scrap metal Excalibur from its shit-hole sheath.

And as soon as the broken piece of metal fell away from the garbage dump, the world rushed back into focus. By tearing away that single piece,

Dylan had disrupted some sort of détente between the various elements of the scrap heap and piece after piece began to collapse onto one another, the remaining scrap metal crosses sinking down into the snow-covered mountain of filth. A terrible stench assailed Dylan's nostrils and in a moment of awful realization it struck him that perhaps this wasn't just a huge scrap heap after all, that maybe this place was abandoned for a reason, but now he was moving away from the dumpster, back around toward the front of the building, his numb fingers wrapped around the thin-but-solid piece of scrap metal. Moments later, he was wedging the piece of scrap metal through the tiny space between the door and the front of the service station. Having spent most of his teenage years trying to sneak out of various boarding school dormitories, Dylan had grown quite adept at bypassing locked doors and Joe's Gas-n-Go proved to be no exception: The door popped open with a simple click and for the first time in several years a human being entered Joe's Gas-n-Go.

Ambushed by darkness, cobwebs, and the overpowering stench of ammonia, Dylan groped the side of the wall until his still-numb fingers found and flicked the light switch. When nothing happened the first time, he began to flip the switch up and down, as if he could somehow transform his frustration into fusion and get the joint jumping again. Just as he was about to break the switch off, a single florescent ceiling light at the far end of the room sputtered to life, flooding Joe's Gas-n-Go with a weak white light.

Whereas most gas stations were now mini-supermarkets complete with gourmet coffee and Wi-Fi, Joe's had been an old school service station. There was no brand-name coffee kiosk welcoming travelers weary from the trials and tribulations of SUV ownership: just a chipped glass coffeepot with a plastic orange handle left out amidst a sea of cups and stirrers and white packets of real sugar, not the synthetic shit that, although rife with carcinogenic properties, might help keep an extra quarter of an inch off one's waistline. Air fresheners, although not enough to dispel the odd odor, which Dylan could only liken to cat piss, and discarded plastic motor oil containers tipped on their side littered the aluminum stocking shelves that cut down the middle of the room while an ancient cash register sat expectant on a dusty countertop, guarding the cigarettes and chewing tobacco stored inside the off-green Newport Lights sign hanging overhead. Behind the counter, plastic phone cards dangled from the back wall: The flags grouped together told Dylan that once upon a time someone tried to organize the cards by continent; the grouping of Angola and Israel and Spain told Dylan someone wasn't a geography wiz. Underneath the phone cards was a near-empty magazine rack; a few plastic sheathed copies of *Swank* drooping over the edges were the only selections still in stock.

Dylan pulled a cigarette and a lighter out of his jacket pocket. Although he was soaking wet, the pack—in addition to surviving the crash—managed to stay dry. It took the lighter a few clicks to catch, but flame finally burst forth and, as he limped down the aisle, Dylan took a long drag, his mind returning to the experience he had moments ago behind the store.

The Connection—that was the only way Dylan could describe what he experienced. Something within him had leapt at something out there—something unseen yet absolutely present. *I'm describing something supernatural,* he admitted to himself. *And it sounds insane.* But for the first time in his entire life, Dylan felt like he was part of the world, as opposed to separate from it. And perhaps the most compelling part of the experience was that he felt like he was only apprehending the very surface of things, that there were unseen depths to the world that he was not capable of touching, at least not at that moment—of that he was certain.

There was no rational way to explain what happened: If he had been back in Tiber, moving through the parties and the clubs, snorting or smoking whatever anyone put in front of him, he could have just written the whole thing off as some drug-induced hallucination. But he knew that wasn't it—it was different, somehow. When he did bump lines and the evening dissolved into a blur of coke chat and overconfidence, there was always some part of him that knew the experience was just chemically induced bullshit. But what happened in front of that dumpster felt authentic in a way drugs never did. And sure, it could just have been a product of physical and mental exhaustion; maybe the pain from his leg played some role in the experience. Whatever the source, the experience, this Connection, had quieted his mind and allowed a sense of calm to spread through his being.

He finished his smoke and began limping toward the other side of the store, his mind filled with a sense of clarity and purpose he hadn't known in a very long time. He passed an unplugged power cord, which was coiled around the side of a machine like a tail. Although the sliding-glass top was caked with a flaky black mold, part of the covering had collapsed and Dylan saw the freezer was filled with rib bones and discarded ice-cream containers. The rib bones were big, too big, thought Dylan and there were still some resilient bits of meat hanging off the bone. But he just pressed forward, trying to stay focused on finding a first-aid kit and a working telephone.

To the right of the freezer, a low, narrow doorway led into an even narrower room: 10 by 10, at best, with wooden walls plastered from end to end, top to bottom—even the ceiling was covered—with pictures ripped from porno magazines, some glued on top of others, all ripped from their stapled bindings in some sort of frenzy and slapped onto the walls without any discernable pattern. The room was awash in a dirty yellow light—a sickly illumination that Dylan associated with band-aids and the 1970s. In the center of the room was an ancient mattress—no frame, no box spring, no sheets—stuffing spilling out of several tears in the scratchy gray surface.

Surrounding the mattress was a mess of broken glass beakers, hot plates, empty lantern fuel cans, duct tape, red-stained coffee filters, and a blowtorch lighter—meth-lab garbage. Joe's Gas-n-Go: putting a new spin on the term "full-service station."

Dylan lowered himself onto the mattress, dust exploding up into the air like a miniature mushroom cloud before the fallout fluttered back to the filthy rayon. Next to the makeshift bed was a metal container, maybe the size of a shoebox. Like everything else in the place, the padlock was rusted and busted, dangling uselessly. Dylan knocked it to the floor and lifted the metal lid. Jackpot: Underneath a ton of pictures, faded, dog-eared memories with names and dates written on the backs in smudged ink, was a large bandage, a wad of cash—mostly fives and ones, a few 20s—some matchbooks, an old AM/FM radio, and some antibiotic cream. And underneath all that was a silver snub-nosed .45: all the crank chef essentials.

After taking off his shredded jeans, picking the shards of highway and glass out of his leg, and spreading ointment over the wound, Dylan leaned back on the mattress and began wrapping his leg with the bandage. He tried to lay back but his head knocked against something hard hidden beneath the tattered rayon pillow. Reaching under the pillow, Dylan felt the familiar plastic case of a laptop computer. He pulled the laptop out from under his head and held it up into the light. The case was black, scrubbed of all brand names or trademarks, and covered in gray scuffmarks. A power cord was still attached to the back of the computer, running from the laptop to a socket in the wall behind the bed. He popped open the laptop. Aside from a small crack in the screen's upper right corner and a missing "E" key, the machine was in pretty good condition—there were even two USB ports along its side, the kind that would read the flash drive Dylan found in his father's journal.

"No way," Dylan muttered to himself as he pressed the power button. To his surprise, the power button flashed green and, after several seconds, the screen burst to life, an obsolete Windows operating system logo floating in front of a black background. It took the system a few minutes to boot up but eventually a desktop appeared. A quick tour of the computer's hard drive told Dylan nothing about the service station or where its owner had gone: It was loaded with various tutorials on optimal meth-cooking methods, a collection of decade-old MP3s, and tons of pornography—with names like ass2mouthsluts_6, myanalsummervacation, and DPCougars_9, it wasn't too hard to guess at the files' content.

Balancing the laptop on the mattress, Dylan slid the flash drive into the USB port: There was a single video file, titled "Exodus." Dylan dragged the cursor over the file and double-clicked.

The footage was shot with a night vision lens, greens and grays mixed with black. In the bottom left-hand corner, a single sentence appeared: Project Exodus recovereds.

The camera operator's hands were shaking and for the first few seconds the footage was third-person schizophrenic, jumping from blurry object to blurry object. There was audio as well—an inhuman wailing that persisted over the steady drone of electronic equipment. Finally, the camera steadied and the picture began to clear, revealing a large room, lined with two rows of beds.

The camera panned the room, offering a panoramic view of a primitive medical facility—the place looked like a World War II field hospital. Men in green masks moved between the beds but the camera ignored them, choosing instead to begin moving down the center aisle toward the back of the room. Reaching the end of the room, the camera stopped before turning to the right and then down toward the last bed in the row. For a moment the lens was out of focus but only for a moment: The picture came back into focus, revealing a pair of feet, covered in sores and puss-caked lesions, protruding from under a single sheet. One foot had seven toes, each with long, black nails curling toward the ceiling; both ankles turned at impossible angles.

The camera lingered for a moment before panning up the cot. Dylan could see the outline of a pair of legs and a lower torso visible under a stained, rumpled sheet and he wanted to look away; he wanted to take the laptop and slam it against the wall but he couldn't—the camera was moving and through the thin sheet he could see a man's chest covered with what appeared to be six or seven crusty eyes, each blinking madly, the eyeballs themselves darting in every direction, rolling back under the infected lids to escape the light of the camera. Dylan leaned over the edge of the bed and threw up.

The video seemed to anticipate such a reaction, lingering for a few moments on this creature's ruined chest before resuming its march up the length of the cot, past a jagged, jutting collarbone and a bloated neck, swollen with throbbing veins. Dylan had no explanation for what came next. At first, he was certain he was hallucinating. He closed his eyes for a moment, listening to the sounds of ragged, agonized breathing coming from the laptop competing with the sounds of the wind whipping against the gas station walls and the faint roar of an airplane overhead.

Then Dylan opened his eyes and screamed.

The video had ended and the screen was frozen on the final frame: the face of the creature on the cot. Only, it wasn't just the creature's face. It was his father's face; his father's eyes, the eyes that watched the city from a hundred Jack Heffernan billboards—the same eyes that stared back at Dylan every time he looked in a mirror.

Chapter 24

Tiber City
Oct. 2, 2015

Dylan had crashed at the abandoned Gas-n-Go for the past few weeks, spending his nights reading his father's journal, the collection of letters, over and over, trying to make sense of the story they seemed to be telling: that his father had been, somehow, not entirely human, that Michael Morrison bore responsibility for his dad's condition, and that Morrison had most likely murdered his father. There were too many moving pieces, too many facts still obscured, but Morrison wasn't exactly an auto mechanic or anything—if anyone had the ability to do the things his father was suggesting, it was the world's preeminent geneticist.

It was breathtaking in its audacity and yet Dylan believed. Part of his belief was, of course, the footage: He had watched the video on the flash drive at least a dozen times and when the camera zoomed in on the broken, deformed cot-creature's eyes, Dylan not only saw his father, but he saw himself as well. Whatever had broken his old man, it was alive inside of him too.

But it wasn't just the video that consumed him; it was the other things his father had written about: about the alienation he felt, about the incident in Boston—and how something had reached out to his father, something his father needed but couldn't respond to, an inability to experience that *some-*

thing had driven the man insane. Had Dylan read those words months, even weeks ago, he would have been skeptical. But how was he able to reach out and make that connection that forever eluded his father?

On more than one occasion he considered heading back to Tiber City, or at least checking into a motel somewhere further down the highway. But he needed some time alone first and while crashing in an abandoned service station that more likely than not moonlighted as a tweaker pad hardly constituted a monastic retreat, it was what Dylan needed: no television, no cell reception, no Wi-Fi, no way of anyone tracking him down. He even made a trip back to the scene of the motorcycle crash and retrieved his ruined bike, which he stashed in one of the garages behind the service station—he didn't need rescue workers looking for him or, even worse, celebrity bloggers speculating about his death.

His leg was still in bad shape, but the infection had faded and nothing was broken—just a deep gash that would produce an ugly, crooked scar. The accident had left him weak, so in the mornings he would leave the service station, wearing a pair of jeans he had found tucked under the mattress, a torn T-shirt, and his old leather jacket, which had survived the accident, minus a chunk out of the right shoulder. He walked north, testing his leg as he drifted toward the old industrial towns—a blur of brick buildings and barbed wire; of dried-up riverbeds that once served as tributaries to Tiber City's mighty Acheron River but were now little more than glorified garbage cans, a sad trickle of brown rainwater struggling to circumvent abandoned shopping carts, ancient automobiles, and mounds of unidentifiable plastic and metal.

These towns were home to dozens of abandoned factories and early-20th-century mills, and Dylan spent entire days wandering through these structures—squatters had broken the locks a long time ago and no one had bothered to replace them. These were foreign places to him, stranger than the Jungle district's darkest rabbit holes and filled with the tools of industry, none of which he could identify, let alone operate. Dylan knew words—drill press, lathe, four-slide, injection-molding machines, boring mills, radial drills—but he couldn't connect these names with any specific machine. This realization disappointed him and he would spend hours in these manufacturing graveyards, limping across the shop floors and loading docks, wiping away the massive cobwebs that now linked many of the machines. He imagined that each morning these machines waited for their masters to return, for that first jolt of electricity, unaware that their time had passed and that the world had moved on.

He couldn't remember when he last spent this much time alone and unplugged but as he limped across the empty manufacturing plants Dylan learned to welcome the solitude—his mind remained clear and quiet as his limp faded and his body healed. He brought his father's journal with him and as he sat among these ancient industrial tombs he read sentences, paragraphs, entire letters aloud over and over until his own voice faded and his father's began to emerge from the prose. The old man asked his son for understanding, forgiveness, vengeance. The son understood; the son forgave. Vengeance would come.

As darkness fell, strange clusters of men would appear on the fringes of these towns, materializing from the gathering dark before sweeping through the old factories and junkie pads—flashlights and hard whispers and the crackle of radio static heralded their approach—and so when dusk began to creep across the horizon Dylan would return to the service station, stopping only to purchase food from one of the anonymous vending stalls littering the landscape—tiny wooden frames that served as docking stations for lunch cards: no names, no menus, no seats, cash only. Gnarled old men with windblasted skin and heavy accents would back their carts into these stalls and throw together two or three dishes, which they then displayed on a rack over the counter; noodles, stew, hot dogs: The menu selections broke down into one of those three categories. A few offered a single beer selection as well but it was a bitter, foul-smelling brew and Dylan usually passed, selecting only a carton of noodles, which he would devour as he walked down the access roads and alleyways that led back to the service station. And as he walked, he tried to make sense of everything that had happened.

What was the truth about his father?

What was this *experience* that he had felt, and that his father had so desperately sought?

He was nearly certain that, whatever the truth was about his old man, Michael Morrison was responsible for his death.

And if his father was something other than human, what was Dylan?

Each night as he walked back to the gas station he would think about these questions, his brain turning each issue over, seeking connections he might have missed, details ignored—perhaps some alternative means of resolution. But time and time again, he reached the same conclusion: He would confront, and then kill, Michael Morrison. What surprised Dylan the most was not the ease with which his mind settled on killing a man, but that this decision sparked no anxiety within him, no urge to gobble a fistful of pills; gone was the nagging dread that cast a shadow across life in the 21st century.

Some nights it was too hot to sleep inside the service station. Dylan would position the radio he found in the trunk on the windowsill and sit outside, smoking, watching the satellite towers and Tiber City skyscrapers twinkling in the distance as the tuner struggled to pick up signals from the surrounding countryside—keyed-up late-night talk show hosts ranted about strange flashes in the sky and a vampire coven operating out of a warehouse in the Glimmer district. Listening to the scratchy AM signal as the world lay dark around him reminded Dylan of when he was young, when his father was away and he couldn't sleep and he would turn on the radio—the one his old man bought him for his seventh birthday so he could listen to the Tiber City Black Sox, even when they were on a West Coast swing and Dylan's mother made him go to bed before the first pitch—and lay in the darkness by himself but not alone.

On more than one occasion he found himself standing in front of the dumpster behind the service station, his hand resting on the cool, sticky aluminum as though merely touching this glorified garbage can would somehow trigger the Experience, the Connection he had felt when he first arrived at the gas station. But of course it didn't and Dylan would wind up smoking an entire pack of cigarettes, waiting for the sun to come up as he watched a solitary police boat make slow, sad loops across a small section of the Acheron, trawling for a body it would never recover.

The next day, he turned his phone back on; there was still no reception. But he carried it with him as he once again headed back up the highway, snub-nose revolver tucked in his waistband, toward the crumbling mill towns. Dark clouds were swarming overhead, devouring what little blue sky and sunlight were left—the air was stifling, working on suffocating, and although it was only mid-afternoon, he could feel the thunderstorm building.

A mile away from the gas station, he heard his phone beep: Dozens of backlogged messages flooded his screen—digital coverage restored. But he ignored the messages; scrolling past them until he found the number he was looking for and pressed send.

Meghan answered on the third ring.

"I need to meet with your father," Dylan said. The reception was weak—static danced across the connection and he could hear noises in the background. The wind kicked up—a hot, dry burst that sent dust and highway garbage cartwheeling through the thick summer air. In the distance Dylan could hear the groan of cables, of ancient power lines struggling against nature's sudden surge.

"Where are you?" Meghan asked.

Dylan gave her the address.

"You'd better have one hell of an explanation," Meghan replied.

Dylan looked down at his phone and saw she had hung up. He lit a cigarette and began to make his way back toward his roadside sanctuary, wondering how you break it to the woman you love that you're probably going to have to kill her old man.

Two hours later, with Meghan by his side, Dylan watched the video for a final time. It was funny: Each time he viewed the clip, he expected it to be somehow different, that the footage would be revealed as a hoax, or end differently—maybe with some contrite resolution that would clear everything up, that would provide some sort of explanation for why a creature that looked very much like his father, very much like *Dylan*, was locked up in what appeared to be the Morrison Biotech laboratories. Of course the ending didn't change and when the clip concluded Meghan was crying. He showed her the journal and while she read it the wind rattled the front door so hard Dylan was certain it would shatter. But the door held and when Meghan finished reading she stood up, dropped the book, and kissed him hard; her face was wet, still streaked with tears and mascara and she whispered into his ear: "I'm sorry."

"It's not your fault," Dylan told her but she was already pulling away, shaking her head, telling him he didn't understand.

"Understand what?" Dylan asked as she turned and started toward the front of the Gas-n-Go market, toward the exit.

"I just need a few minutes," she called back to him as she pushed open the door and stepped out into the twilight.

Dylan thought about going after her but considering everything he just laid on her, he was lucky that she asked for a few minutes—and not a restraining order. So instead, he picked his father's journal up off the floor and began to rip out each entry, page by page, before tossing them into the unplugged freezer sitting in the middle of the store. He then began grabbing anything else left on the store shelves that looked flammable: old maps detailing countries that no longer existed, coffee filters, and discarded motor oil containers. He retreated into the back room, tearing some of the porno pictures off the wood-panel walls and crumbling them into a ball, just like he used to watch his father do with newspapers to start a fire on Christmas morning; he popped open the metal footlocker and grabbed the pictures, the cash, and the matchbooks—all of which he tossed into the freezer.

Standing over his makeshift pyre, Dylan lit a cigarette and studied his work. It would end here: No matter what happened next, there would be no record of his father's transgressions and there would be no media circus. He didn't need the journal to confront Morrison—Dylan himself was living proof. Taking the cigarette out of his mouth, he held it above the pyre, pausing for a moment to watch the smoke curl toward the ceiling before flicking it into the freezer.

He heard the door rattle behind him and he swung around, expecting to see Meghan standing in the entranceway. But there was no one; just empty shelves and a decade-old cigarette ad hanging over the checkout counter—the actors' once smug and satisfied expressions now faded and blank. Dylan shook his head and turned back to the pyre, back to the flame that was licking and clawing the side of the freezer, fed by the pages of his father's journal. He closed his eyes, focusing on the warm glow thrown off by the fire. And then he felt a sharp prick on the back of his neck. His legs went rubbery and he was falling forward, toward the burning pyre but at the last second a pair of hands grabbed the back of his shirt, and he hung suspended inches above the flame. And then the world went black.

The Journal of Senator Robert Fitzgerald
Excerpt # 7

To Dylan,

Disintegration seems imminent. I haven't sleep well in months; every time I close my eyes I see scenes from that video. Even when I take three, five, seven Ambien and fall asleep, the nightmares are relentless: ruined, forsaken monsters reaching out for me, calling my name as their faces morph into mine until I am standing in that underground hospital, surrounded by dozens of deformed versions of myself. They reach for me and I wake up screaming, the sheets soaked and bunched up around me, ripped from where I tore at them in my sleep.

Tomorrow night, I will confront Morrison. I want to know everything: about the videotape, about the injections, about "Project Exodus." But no matter what Morrison tells me, one thing is clear: Effective immediately I am leaving politics; I do not want to run for president. I no longer want the kingdom Morrison offered me so many years ago. I'm coming home.

Love,
Your Father

Chapter 25

The American Southwest
September–October 2015

For the past month, Jonathan Campbell had been unable to sleep—images of the massacre at Ramoth seeped into the darkness of his dreams and he would snap out of semi-slumbers with a jerk. He'd lie awake in the darkness, trying to catch his breath, shivering as the air conditioning blasted his sweat-soaked skin. Once his limbs stopped shaking—or at least steadied enough that he could hold a bottle—Campbell would exit the suite, drifting through the gleaming, sterile corridors of Morrison Biotechnology. Even though the hallways were empty he could hear the echo of hard-soled shoes, snippets of muffled conversation, the constant chime of arriving elevators, as he traversed entire wings that all seemed to pulse with the same garish fluorescent light—a constant glow that made it difficult to remember if it was night or day and on more than one occasion Campbell had gotten lost.

Sometimes he found himself standing alone on the 18th-floor observation deck, watching as lightning bolts slashed the horizon. The sky was always the color of a bad bruise and on most nights Campbell would swear he could hear voices crying up from the desert. He tried to convince himself it was just satellite dishes being battered by the wind but there were shapes in the darkness below, long black shadows that slipped into the desert whenever a security drone appeared overhead, its searchlights swirling across the sand.

Campbell would stand alone on the sweltering deck, pressed up against the railing, smoking, and taking pulls from the flask he kept tucked in his back pocket, and stare at the fires burning in the distance; at the strange lights that would sometimes appear in the sky over the arcology, glowing orbs that flashed through the poisoned atmosphere, diving toward the cities far in the distance, at the edge of the desert. On some nights, he would stare down at the rocky terrain and consider flinging himself over the rail, imagining his own death as if he were a director; he'd pull the camera back, imbuing his soundless, pre-dawn plunge with an eerie, almost cinematic grace. But on other nights, he would watch the sky, the whiskey a temporary talisman against the cold; but eventually the alcohol wasn't enough and Campbell's leg would begin to ache—the cold seemed to seek out the old scar tissue, clawing the tendons and tissue that never quite healed, driving Campbell back into the arcology.

Once inside, there was only one thing left for Campbell to do: ride the elevator down into the Exodus laboratories, to where Dylan Fitzgerald was being held.

The Exodus laboratories had changed since Campbell's initial work on the Project. Gone were the deformed infants and murky vats, replaced by neuroimaging equipment: PET scanners, SPECT machines, and legions of mainframe computers and network servers, monitors stacked on top of monitors, gray plastic sentinels that kept vigil through a blur of red blinking lights and the hum of computer fans clicking on to cool off overheated hard drives, giant memory vaults that stored the Exodus data, evidence of Campbell's sins preserved in ones and zeros for all eternity.

The most significant addition, however, was the young man whose brain activity these legions of machines had been designed to monitor: Dylan Fitzgerald, son of Robert Fitzgerald, the original Exodus man and the only reason Campbell was still alive. Each night for the past few weeks, Campbell had run tests on Fitzgerald, working with the dozen or so machines positioned around Dylan—Morrison's charge to Campbell had been both straightforward and impossibly complex: *Tell me if Fitzgerald has a functioning Omega gene; tell me if he has a soul.*

Campbell did as he was told; reporting to the laboratories when Morrison summoned, waiting for his opportunity. And as he ran the various brain scans and neurological feedback tests, Campbell spoke to the dead senator's son. The kid was semiconscious but that didn't matter; Campbell poured whiskey from his flask into a glass he kept in the laboratory and raised a toast to the kid's old man. Closing his eyes, Campbell would drain his glass and tell Dylan about Exodus, about Morrison, about his father, Robert. His eyes burning from exhaustion and the whiskey and the harsh lights lining the ceiling, Campbell told Dylan everything he knew about the Order and about the human soul. He poured another drink, lowered his voice, and spoke about his time lost in the desert.

There were nights when Campbell was convinced he could take Dylan with him, that they might be able to slip out of Morrison Biotech together, undetected, and head south, searching for signs of the Order along the chaos of the Rio de Janeiro-Sao Paulo-Buenos Aires mega-sprawl; Campbell would find work in the Uruguayan clinics, help the kid keep a low profile and hope that the Order found them before Morrison did. There were other fantasies as well, darker visions of wrapping his gray, weathered hands around young Fitzgerald's throat and squeezing and ending Exodus in the same place it started, deep under the Chihuahuan desert.

But sitting alone in the laboratory, talking to the dead senator's unconscious son, Campbell came to understand something: He might still find redemption, and Exodus might crumble, but the two weren't related. He had seen the road to his salvation and it was through the work he had performed in the Order's camps, tending to the dying and discarded, the forgotten. Any actions he took to destroy Exodus, to sabotage Morrison's plans to revive the program with Dylan—even if he somehow succeeded—came with a price he was unwilling to pay: slaughter. He would save the Order; that would be his redemption. And as the plan began to take form, for the first time in a long time, Campbell smiled.

Chapter 26

The American Southwest
Halloween 2015
2:19 a.m.

The suite was anonymous and over-sanitized, more laboratory than residence. Morrison made sure Campbell had the tools he needed to continue Exodus' pursuit of Dylan Fitzgerald's soul; as for Campbell's own soul, the suite's décor reminded him it was expendable. He had a killer view of the desert, but he kept his blinds closed; he saw too many lights in the sky, too many things he couldn't explain.

Since returning to Exodus, Morrison had insisted he accept a more rigorous Treatment schedule; every two weeks, Morrison's doctors appeared outside Campbell's suite: black suitcases, white gloves, clear syringes, murky liquid. After the needle delivered its payload, the men left Campbell prone on his bed, his skin on fire as his body struggled to remake itself. Normally, Campbell would be incapacitated for 36, maybe 42 hours after an injection of the Treatment. During that time, no one would be looking for him; his absence from the labs, from the security cameras would be expected. It would be explainable.

And so, in the dead of night, Campbell waited, eerily calm as he sat at his desk, ignoring the glowing red light on his phone, the flashing envelope at the bottom of his screen telling him he had unread email, the webpage that kept refreshing even though he didn't click the refresh button—as though the software couldn't wait to deliver more content; the browser could no longer hold the data back—there was too much. It just forced its way through the fiber optic cables that wove like veins behind the gleaming, stainless steel walls of Morrison Biotechnology, so many updates that stories were buried in minutes, sometimes even seconds, the new being the only measure of worth or quality or necessity.

Campbell sat at the desk only to ensure that, when the doctors arrived, everything would appear normal: He worked nights, stripped to the waist, sweating even though the air conditioning kept the room cool, whiskey bottle by his side, no glass, the passage of time measurable by how much of the bottle had vanished; by the warmth in Campbell's stomach.

Tonight, however, there would be two important differences: Campbell usually didn't keep a six-inch scalpel tucked in his waistband. And he usually didn't commit murder. But none of that mattered. By the time Morrison's men discovered just how different tonight was going to be, it would be too late.

The intercom on his desk buzzed sometime later that night, announcing the doctors' arrival. There was no need for Campbell to go to the door; Morrison's men all had access to his suite, including the doctors who administered the Treatment.

"Come in," Campbell rasped, as he rose from his desk. The door to his suite popped open and to Campbell's surprise, a single doctor strode into the room. Usually the doctors came in pairs; tonight there was only one—nondescript with thinning gray hair and wire frame glasses. Campbell smiled.

"I'm Doctor Miles Lynch," the man said as he laid an aluminum briefcase across the too-bright powder coat finish of an empty steel workbench. Lynch was still wearing his operating room scrubs; a surgical mask was dangling around his neck; and his hands were covered by white plastic gloves, the kind that left skin smelling like rubber for days.

Campbell stood up from his desk, his left arm extended forward in a gesture of compliance, his sleeve rolled up.

"Good man," Lynch said with a smile. "You're my last stop of the night, so I appreciate the cooperation."

Campbell stood motionless in front of the doctor, his left arm still extended as Lynch turned his attention to the briefcase.

"Biometric security system," the doctor was telling Campbell as he pressed his finger to the top of the briefcase. "Takes a few seconds...There," Lynch said as the briefcase emitted a low, electronic groan, an affirmation, a signal of some sort that the security system had been deactivated. Lynch reached into the suitcase, taking out a single clear syringe filled with a brown liquid. Campbell felt his heart skip a beat as Lynch held the syringe up to the light, sliding the cover off the needle and checking the dosage level. Satisfied, the doctor began to turn back toward Campbell.

"Now," the doctor began. "As far as the actual injection goes, this won't hurt a bit..."

You're right, Campbell thought as he snaked his right arm behind his back, feeling a grim pleasure as his fingers closed around the scalpel tucked into his waistband. *It won't.*

And then Campbell was lunging forward, his attack nowhere as graceful or fluid as he had spent the past few weeks imagining but he still caught the doctor by surprise, and before the man could react Campbell drove the knife-end of the instrument into his trachea, piercing Lynch's windpipe. The syringe holding the Treatment tumbled from his fingers as the force of the blow sent the doctor staggering backward, his arms reaching out toward Campbell, a look of disbelief plastered across his face. He was trying to speak, his lips moving, but no words came out—just a strange, slow hiss, like the air being let out of a balloon, that Campbell realized was coming from the wound. The doctor began twitching, his arms and legs seizing as he struggled against Campbell but it was too late. Campbell's left arm shot forward, grabbing a fistful of blood-soaked suit, trying to hold the dying man steady as he jerked the blade down, steel ripping apart tissue and muscle, crimson spraying in every direction as life drained from the man's body.

A wave of remorse washed over Campbell and he felt his knees buckle, his stomach tighten, as vomit rose in his throat. He swallowed hard and slumped back into his desk chair, quickly finishing the bottle of whiskey as he stared at Lynch's lifeless body—blood was still bubbling from the massive neck wound, running over the body and out onto the cool white tile, where it washed over the broken syringe, collecting in the grout where it pooled together with the Treatment. Campbell was breathing hard, vaguely aware there was blood on his hands, on his clothes, in his mouth. He shifted his gaze over the body, training his focus on the door to his suite, which he expected Morrison's men to burst through at any second.

Yet seconds morphed into minutes and no one came for him. Campbell sat still, listening, waiting. He could hear the soft hum of the air conditioner, the vents vibrating as cool air struggled against the heat that seemed to permeate every inch of the arcology. There were other noises as well: the desert wind had kicked into a frenzy and the individual panes were rattling so hard Campbell was convinced the blast resistant glass would shatter. But the whiskey felt warm and even though he felt older than he ever remembered feeling, he pulled himself to his feet, the realization that Morrison's men were not, at least yet, coming for him reverberating through his skull as he made his way toward the corpse. It would be dawn soon, and Campbell had a great deal of work left to do.

A few hours later, a security camera watched as Miles Lynch, suitcase in hand and still wearing his surgical scrubs, as well as a surgical mask, exited Jonathan Campbell's 15th-floor laboratory suite and headed down the hall toward the elevators. Although the camera's facial recognition software was unable to verify Lynch's identity—the surgical mask made an accurate scan impossible—satisfactory identification was presented at each of the floor's two automated security checkpoints: The individual in question produced Lynch's ID card as well as his laboratory clearance chip. And given that Lynch had the top-level clearance necessary to access the 15th floor, no alarms were triggered and Lynch was allowed to continue.

Another camera then picked up Lynch at the end of the hallway, slipping into an elevator, still clutching the black suitcase, still wearing his surgical mask. According to the elevator logs, he got off on the third floor and then there was more video of him moving toward one of the shipping bays and then he was gone.

It wouldn't be until three days later that Morrison's security would discover Lynch's bloated corpse, rotting in Campbell's bed. By then, Campbell was over a thousand miles away.

Campbell moved quickly, cutting his way toward the end of the continent. He passed shantytowns thrown up along the perimeter of great, dying

American cities and remembered his time wandering in the desert, before the Order, wondering if redemption would ever come. He had been afraid then; he wasn't afraid now. These were the lands where Exodus was born; these were the lands where Campbell would die. But first, he would be redeemed.

Morrison's assassin—al-Salaam—was hunting him, but it was too late. Campbell spoke the language of the new America that was emerging in violent fits and starts from the rotting carcass of a dying nation-state—the America of those who lived in the shadows of great failed cities, but who were determined to forge something out of the nothing they were given. Al-Salaam knew only the desert. As Campbell made his way through the sprawl that sprang up along the Rio Grande, he followed. Al-Salaam believed Campbell was going toward the two other camps operated by the Order: Golan and Bosor. Al-Salaam was wrong.

Billion dollar satellites aided in the hunt, attempting to track Campbell's movements from space; hackers who had gone corporate monitored pay phones, cell phones, email, websites, VOIP, text messages. Every modern method of communication was covered; Morrison's men assured him that any attempt to warn the Order through these methods would fail. They were right.

But there were other ways of communicating, of telling a story, of sending a message, that were forever beyond the reach of the thousand metal moons orbiting the earth: These were the means through which Campbell would warn the Order.

And so Campbell continued across the heart of the fading American empire, using whatever means of transportation was available to carry him from city to city; there was an increasing number of cars left at the edge of the desert by their owners as if they were some kind of sacrifice, an offering to the gods of unsustainable financing terms. Or perhaps some people just gave up and melted away into the desert nothingness. Campbell pressed forward, weaving in and out of immigrant slums and homeless encampments, stopping only to sleep, eat, or visit a church—not the iridescent megachurches but the older structures left to rot in abandoned neighborhoods. So much graffiti covered the walls of these forgotten structures that when Campbell added a new symbol to the mosaic of urban artwork—just like the Order had taught him—*almost* no one noticed. There would be a few watching, a

few who would see the asterisk drawn inside of a circle and know: Evacuate
the camps.

On the seventh day, al-Salaam caught up with Campbell. In the cities
that twisted and bent around the deserts of the American Southwest, men
lived in fear. And al-Salaam, the desert emissary, understood this fear, he
knew how to manipulate it, how to amplify it—men were eager to tell him
their secrets and so learning of the old gringo limping through the sprawl,
drawing on the walls of abandoned churches, was simple.

Kill the old man before he could warn the camps: that was al-Salaam's
order. But it was no longer clear that Campbell was going to the camps.
Campbell's fixation on abandoned religious structures amused him, so al-
Salaam was content to shadow him for a little while, a predator toying with
his prey, pleased that the old man had gone mad; pleased that fear drove him
to old gods long dead—their inability to save Campbell only reinforced their
impotence, their irrelevance.

Yet, on this last day, Campbell did not visit a church. Instead, he spent
most of the day wandering through one of the slums pressed between Los
Angeles and the desert. He spoke to no one: He moved silently, watching
the people—the displaced, the transient, the ones who went off the grid, the
ones for whom the American dream never quite clicked—before stopping at
a tiny cemetery at the center of the slum. There were no marble mausoleums,
no massive monuments to mortality: just rows of makeshift memorials—
chunks of jagged scrap metal strung together with barbed wire to approximate a cross.

Campbell moved from grave to grave, repeating the prayers Jael had
taught him. He spoke to her mother; her grandfather, her sisters, to the
anonymous crosses and the broken, ruined children whose lives had been
given in the name of Project Exodus; he explained that tonight there would
be redemption. And as the sun began to dip below the horizon, Campbell
smiled and, before turning toward the desert, told Jael's people he'd be joining them soon.

As darkness stole across the land, al-Salaam continued to shadow Campbell, following him as he moved from the slums to one of the dozens of industrial zones that stretched out into the Chihuahuan desert. The red lights of the Morrison Biotech arcology were visible on the distant horizon, stretching so far into the heavens that, from the desert floor, they were almost indistinguishable from the other celestial bodies and strange lights visible in the dying summer sky.

Campbell stopped in front of a multistoried brick building accented only by a huge red neon sign stating "Heritage Industries," but the H and S, the beginning and the end, had burnt out and no one bothered to replace them. This was it, al-Salaam decided. This is where he would confront Campbell. The old man would suffer and then the old man would die.

Campbell entered the factory through a backdoor and al-Salaam followed, moving like a ghost. The only source of light was a faint glow emerging from a giant cylindrical tower jutting out from atop the factory, pouring smoke up toward the heavens, and it was through this half-light that Morrison's lieutenant followed the old man, taking an elevator that went down instead of up, pushing further into the earth's crust, creaking and groaning as it struggled down an ancient shaft. Several times during the descent the elevator paused, as though it were hesitant to go much further into the earth. And each time it paused al-Salaam waited, the temperature rising, and this patience elicited an odd metallic groan from the machine, the gears yielding before the assassin's will, shuddering back to life and pushing further down into the darkness.

When the freight elevator lurched to a stop and its doors retracted into the sides of the wall, al-Salaam slid out onto a steel ramp, savoring the smell of sulfur and burning metal that strangled all life from the atmosphere. It was a fitting place to confront the man who betrayed Michael Morrison.

The ramp leading away from the elevator ushered him into the belly of a dark, sweltering foundry. Rusted hooks and pulleys crisscrossed overhead, carrying the tools of industry back and forth, up and down. To al-Salaam's left and right, conveyor belts descended from the ceiling, forming a giant V as they funneled garbage and other disregarded scrap toward the center of the room, where they were dumped into a enormous cylinder- shaped vat of bubbling molten steel held aloft by two mammoth titanium prongs. Beneath the prongs, the nothingness stretched out toward infinity and al-Salaam was pleased: He had indeed chosen the right place to confront Campbell.

For each piece of forsaken scrap that tumbled out of the darkness and into the liquefied steel, steam belched into the atmosphere before drifting up toward the rudimentary filtering system installed in the ceiling above. Eventually, these noxious fumes wound their way through the filtering system, primitive as it was, and into the plant's primary smokestack. This main smokestack served as a marker for the tomb these lands had become, blasting out deadly chemicals into an iridescent sky. And it was miles below this poisoned sky that al-Salaam reached the main walkway, finally falling on his prey: Campbell was standing a ten yards or so away at the edge of the platform staring down into the swirling, expectant molten steel.

"It is time," al-Salaam explained, as he reached Campbell, placing his black-gloved hand on the old man's bony, jagged shoulder. Al-Salaam waited; this was the moment when they begged, when they pleaded with the death dealer for one more day, one more chance. It almost made him sad, the feverish hope he sometimes encountered. Why didn't they understand? Such decisions were not the assassin's to make; he brought death and dust and that was all. There was no negotiating with death.

The temperatures were soaring now and al-Salaam squeezed Campbell's shoulder, spinning the old man around so that he would know who bestowed oblivion upon him and why. He heard some of the old man's brittle bones crack, a noise that echoed out across the molten steel, reverberating off the steel and titanium and al-Salaam was pleased. But then something went wrong: Al-Salaam was facing Campbell, staring into the old man's bloodshot, wild eyes, but what the assassin saw in those eyes filled him with a great unease: There was no fear, not even resignation; only acceptance. Acceptance and triumph; those were the only emotions that stared back at al-Salaam, emotions that had long been absent from these lands.

Smiling, Campbell took a step backward, away from al-Salaam and toward the edge of the platform. With the light from the molten steel glowing red against the side of the old man's face, he took another step backward and al-Salaam realized what was happening. He let out a howl of frustration and lunged forward, grabbing at Campbell as the old man moved toward the edge of the platform. This was not how it was supposed to be; this was not the betrayer's decision to make.

And then it happened: Just before Campbell plunged over the edge, he surged forward, and grabbed his would-be assassin's leg; a second later gravity took Campbell but he had caught Morrison's lieutenant by surprise and now al-Salamm too was tumbling over the side of the platform, the steel under his feet vanishing and there was only the hot dead air between him and the fire. He was falling and so was Campbell; they were now bound together and as they fell the old man put his arms around Morrison's lieutenant, embraced him, and began whispering in his ear, whispering words he had not heard in ages, words the old man had learned somewhere else, in his time away from the desert, prayers and truths that made every inch of the assassin's body quiver with fury, and al-Salaam was screaming, a terrible, vengeful cry but still the old man continued to whisper in his ear as they plunged toward the liquefied steel, joining the stream of industrial by-products that fell like rain from the giant ceiling chute.

And then, al-Salaam screeched in agony. But it was not the physical pain, or even the fact that he, the great deceiver, the death-dealer, had been tricked, that caused al-Salaam the greatest torment in these last few seconds of his life. Rather, it was the look of serenity on the old man's face as he hit the molten steel and his physical form melted away that caused Morrison's assassin such despair. Even as the fire consumed Campbell, there was something in the old man's expression that, in an instant, made manifest a terrible truth: It was al-Salaam who had been deceived, not by this old man but by his master. There was some fundamental truth this Campbell knew, a truth that al-Salaam had somehow been denied, one that now he would never know.

As he died, the assassin's body seemed to shimmer on the surface for a moment, refusing to acknowledge the inevitable. And then, in an instant, he was gone, just another sacrifice on the altar of industry. The spot where his body had landed was filled by other pieces of falling garbage and scrap, which were in turn replaced as soon as they faded away. And then it was over, al-Salaam's remains indistinguishable from Campbell's as they drifted up the smokestack together before filtering out into the sickly pre-dawn sky.

Chapter 27

Tiber City
Nov. 8, 2015
1:19 a.m.

For the past three nights, Michael Morrison had sat alone in his Tiber City office, watching the Jungle burn.

The riots were inevitable: Food shortages, rolling blackouts, and watching the Prince of Progress get his head blown off on national television had brought the city's denizens to the brink; the recent heat wave had blasted them over the edge.

Bureaucrats stood before the cameras and promised that the violence was contained, but the constant wail of sirens and the thump-thump-thump of military helicopters and bursts of automatic rifle fire echoing across empty streets told a very different story, one of a city at war, fueled by fear and need and a gnawing dread that crept over the land like a slow poison; of a heat wave so unbearable that the elderly were cooked alive in their living rooms, their saggy gray skin stuck to the plastic-covered furniture, television still blaring when their eyeballs burst; of digi-evangelists pushing End of Days theory complete with warmed over Book of Revelation imagery; of a Zero artist underground alive with whispers of strange data spikes, of new prophecies appearing deep within the codes, of ghosts in the subway pleading to

travelers with icy, metallic moans, of dreams where data streamed over abandoned, burnt-out cities, twisting and slicing across the neon and the gold and
the light—there was always artificial light, pale and weak but jacked up to
impossible wattage so there was never any rest, just nervous systems with-
ering under the 24/7 assault of content, the brain bouncing in a thousand
different directions, enslaved by artifice, jacked in but shut off, turned away
from the heavens, chained to the earth—of a city without a soul, the desert
reborn. Of Morrison's kingdom, come.

Morrison poured a glass of scotch—neat, aged 18 years—slid open the
office's glass door, and stepped out onto a large, white-tiled balcony. The air
was an oppressive—lifeless heat mingled with the rank smell of burning
plastics and even from this great height, dozens of stories above the city,
Morrison could perceive the fear and tension; it was there, clear as the fires
burning on the horizon, and in the distance there was the roll of thunder as
if nature was readying a violent response to the city's turmoil. Morrison took
a long, slow slip from his glass and, his eyes still locked on the city, allowed
himself a moment to savor his triumphs.

Exodus had taken an unexpected turn. The Omega gene proved to be a
divine failsafe, a jealous Creator's means of guarding the ultimate intellectual
property secret. The Order, like most of mankind, wanted to believe the soul
was some sort of divine conduit, a link between man and God that could
carry on after death; Morrison knew that was bullshit. The Omega gene
was the ultimate poison pill, a way of ensuring man could never break free
from the divine; it fostered some sense of connection, of community—but to
proclaim those emotions were positive things was absurd; as far as Morrison
was concerned, taking such a position was like arguing that heroin addiction
was good because shooting smack made people feel good and once they were
addicted, withdrawal was a bitch. Hooked on the divine; Yahweh as the alpha
and omega of the dope game.

Not that Morrison could begrudge the God responsible for the Omega
gene's design; in fact, he was impressed. And now, instead of trying to reproduce Omega, Exodus was going to do the next best thing: co-opt it.

For the last month, they had been holding Dylan Fitzgerald at the biotech arcology in New Mexico in order to run a series of tests. The purpose
of these tests was simple: to discern whether Dylan had a functioning soul.
The results of the tests were unanimous: Dylan Fitzgerald had the unique
genetic composition of his father but, unlike the old man, Dylan inherited a

functioning Omega gene. There was no question as to the source of Dylan's Omega gene, of his soul: Given the fact that Omega was excluded from his father's genetic code, Dylan must have inherited his soul from his mother. In fact, considered Morrison, the word "functioning" wasn't even fair; during some of the tests, the brain activity associated with Dylan's Omega gene was off the fucking charts.

Fitzgerald, not Heffernan, would be the one. Morrison would position Fitzgerald as the heir to the Exodus throne. And even if the Progress Party never captured the White House, did that matter? While an organic Omega gene was non-transferrable, and an artificial soul was unsustainable, perhaps a combination of the two, Morrison thought, could be both. And judging from Dylan's brain activity, breeding the Exodus genetic code with organic DNA could produce explosive "soul" activity in the brain. Customizable human souls, coming soon to a CitiMart near you. Morrison took another sip of his scotch and smiled.

True, Campbell had escaped, but al-Salaam had been dispatched to follow the old man to the Order's remaining camps, where Morrison's death dealer would kill Campbell and every last monk before vanishing, without a trace, into the desert. Indeed, Campbell's actions were expected, and now, the old man was no longer necessary; the final act was set to begin: Young Fitzgerald was en route to Tiber City. Morrison would meet with him and explain everything. He would show him the kingdom; the young man would not refuse—how could he?

Back in his darkened office, the phone was ringing and Morrison took one final look at the fires burning along the horizon before turning back inside. The computer monitor on his desk was glowing with a notice of an incoming call from the arcology. Morrison frowned before pressing the screen to accept the call.

"Go ahead," he growled.

One of his security teams' captains delivered the news: Al-Salaam was dead.

Morrison roared, squeezing his glass so hard it shattered, slicing into his palm. For a moment he fell silent, watching the blood first pool in his palm before it began spilling over the edge of his hand, splashing onto the shards of glass now scattered across the floor.

"Kill them. Kill them all," Morrison snarled, before snapping off the monitor and turning back to the window, back to the night on fire, blood still trickling down his right hand, the crimson pool on the floor growing larger as the call and response of automatic gunfire crackled somewhere in the night.

Two helicopters—gleaming beasts of steel and metal and war—carried four eight-man teams from the arcology into the border slums, blasting low across the desert toward the festering sprawl on the horizon. There were lights in the southwestern sky, strange swirling colors and shooting stars that maybe weren't stars. Hard men in black Kevlar sat on the edge of the helicopters, staring straight ahead, focused on the digital read-out glowing green in the corner of their goggles, their boots dangling loose over the sand and dying brush and hard red rock, lights from inside the copters reflecting off automatic weapons into the darkness.

A drone strike had been discussed but dismissed—Morrison demanded this mission be conducted with a personal touch. And so the men strapped high-carbon steel bayonets to their automatic rifles and waited as satellites transmitted detailed schematics of the target: an abandoned mission on the edge of the desert, several miles past an old train yard. And although the satellite photos showed no surface activity, there were tunnels that twisted under the mission, and it was in these tunnels that Morrison's men would find the enemy.

When the copters set down outside the mission it became clear that the information received from the satellite was inaccurate; many of the access points and entryways had vanished—if they had even existed. Instead, there was a single, arching entranceway, 10 or 12 feet high, carved out of the stone and governed by a heavy wooden door divided into halves. The bad intel set off some bad vibes, and Morrison's men went in hot, ramming down the door to the mission, the lights from their rifle scopes crisscrossing as they cut through the darkened building, moving in teams of two down into the tunnels, night vision on, safeties off. There was no sign of life, just claustrophobia and boots scraping over crumbling stone and the frescos carved into the walls: Crudely etched images of dead men resurrected and archangels with burning swords watched the mercenaries pass through the pitch black tunnels.

At the end of the tunnels there was a heavy metal door, locked and reinforced from the inside, but three thunderous booms from a twelve-gauge loaded with M-1030 breaching rounds shattered the bolt mechanism. *Masks on* someone roared as the door popped open and one of the mercenaries heaved a flash-bang grenade through the breach. There was a violent, split-second burst of light followed by a high-pitched ringing and then the door was gone, knocked aside as Morrison's men stormed into the camp.

It only took a few seconds for the mercenaries to realize the camp was empty—bayonets jammed into the mounds of blankets piled on top of cots spilled cheap yellow stuffing.

It would take the men another 10 minutes to realize that the paint on the symbol—an asterisk in a circle drawn across the ceiling—was still wet.

Chapter 28

Tiber City
November 2015

The last thing Dylan could remember was being with Meghan at the Gas-n-Go, ripping out the pages of his father's journal and tossing them into the flame. Everything after that was a series of half-conscious sensations: grays and blacks and there might have been a helicopter; there might have been larger aircraft, engines firing up and the shake and rattle as a jet blasted down a runway—there was transportation, movement of some kind, but Dylan was drifting in and out of consciousness so observational precision was out of the question.

And then the machines came—monsters of steel and industrial plastics and sightless scanners that hovered over him, inches from his face, moving across his body with inhuman patience. Conveyor belts fed him into claustrophobia-inducing plastic tubes that shook and whirred; he woke up screaming on more than one occasion, with thick black wires running from the back of his skull that he was too afraid to pull out.

He was in some kind of research facility, maybe a hospital, maybe something military—there were guards with guns and the sounds of boots echoing down hallways.

At some point an old man began to appear, sitting beside Dylan while the machines swirled around them, robotic arms hovering, grasping, whirling through the over-conditioned air, the sensation of automated movement always present on Dylan's peripheral. The old man, who said his name was Campbell, was accompanied by the smell of whiskey that would slice through the hallucinations. And then the old man would talk, his voice hoarse yet urgent, telling Dylan impossible things, crazy things—secret monastic orders and the truth about the human soul, about Dylan's own soul, about the desert: the same things that were in his father's journal. He saw the old man's back, the tattoo that marked his flesh—the same symbol on the memory stick. Dylan didn't respond, couldn't respond; he could only squeeze his eyes shut, calling out for Meghan, rage consuming the pain, the fear, fueled by the realization that whatever was happening to him now, his father had suffered worse. In his lucid moments, he was even able to put a name to his tormentor: Morrison.

Then as suddenly as it began, it was over: the machines, the old man, the hallucinations—then nothing.

For the first time in a long time, there was light—real light—and even before he opened his eyes Dylan could feel it falling across his skin, across his face, disrupting the darkness. For a moment, Dylan lay motionless, his eyes pressed shut. He was naked under crisp, freshly laundered linen sheets; the air smelled clean but not fresh and there was a lingering hint of antiseptic. Mouthing the words he counted to 10, praying that when he opened his eyes he would be back in his own bed, in his own apartment; that somehow the past month would be nothing more than a very intense dream. When he reached 10, he said the number out loud, as if he were casting a spell. He listened to his heartbeat once, twice, before opening his eyes.

The world snapped into focus. Dylan screamed and shot out of the bed, stumbling across the pale, distressed wood floor, squinting as he took in his surroundings. He was standing in the middle of a large, sparsely decorated hotel suite: sharp, minimalist décor; high contrast whites, blacks, tans, browns; clean lines; 90-degree angles; a vague but undeniable vibe of transience, of flux, of suitcases and phone chargers and promises. The bed was pressed against the far wall and there was a bathroom a few paces from the bed, a behemoth of cold black marble sinks and floors and a transparent glass shower with a stainless steel showerhead. But there was no nightstand, no dresser; just a mounted flat screen television, a thin nonfunctional desk, a single sliding-door closet, and a few open-face cubes attached to the wall: minimal storage space for the minimalist man.

The light that had woken him was filtering through the thin bamboo blinds pulled down over a massive sliding glass window, which consumed most of the wall behind the bed. The blinds looked sexy, they looked edgy; they helped advance the chic aesthetic sought by the designer. The blinds did not, however, block out the light and so Dylan was squinting as he searched for an opening in the blinds. His fingers wrapped around the smooth edge of the hyper-processed bamboo, but before he could yank open the blinds he was overcome with a strange certainty that beyond the window there would only be a massive desert. The hotel room seemed to recede, the walls and window dissolving, and for a single terrifying moment there was only a desert, one that seemed to stretch from the hotel window to infinity, miles of nothing—just rock and sand and a red sky and Dylan could even hear the crunch of earth under his boots, could feel the chill as the sun fell and the moon rose and predators began to stir. Then as quickly as the sensation had come, it was gone and Dylan was pulling aside the blinds and where the desert had been, the Tiber City skyline now loomed.

"The fuck," Dylan muttered, stepping back from the window. Tiber City was a big place, and although the landscape indicated he was in the Glimmer district, maybe somewhere near Chiba Street, there were over two dozen hotels in that part of the city and after awhile, they all looked the same. His frustration and fear were building, twisting around one another and he was reaching for the phone on the desk but it was dead. He ripped it off the desk and fired it at the window, hoping the glass would shatter and that someone in the street below would notice the shards raining down and come investigate. But the window held, and the phone crashed to the floor.

And that's when he saw it: There was something hanging in the closet. His eyes were still adjusting to the light and as he moved toward the closet he was convinced that a body was hanging from the ceiling; in the low light anything was possible and he saw a swollen rotting corpse, festering with flies, but as he inched closer, unable to swallow, his heart heaving in his chest, he realized that was no body: just a suit dangling from a hanger. And at first Dylan was relieved, more than relieved, actually, because now he wouldn't have to wander around naked asking for help, a scenario that seemed likely to end up with him being put in a hospital, maybe a rest home like Springwood. In fact, whoever left the suit had also been kind enough to leave matching shoes and a menagerie of toiletries—a lovely added bonus because the inside of his mouth tasted like someone had mistaken his throat for a garbage chute and every time he swallowed he tasted hospital. He had a beard and there were little gray sticky patches all over his body, as if something had been attached and removed, attached and removed, over and over. The vein inside his right arm was swollen; the skin around it littered with track marks.

The idea of showering, of cleaning himself and getting dressed, was so appealing that at first, Dylan didn't pay much attention to the suit itself; it wasn't until he was laying the suit out on the rumpled bed that he realized it was the same suit he had recently worn to his birthday party—his father's old suit. After that, things went a little fuzzy: He remembered shaving, remembered the hot water blasting his skin until it radiated pink, as if enough pressure and heat could wash away the past, uncover the future; putting on his father's old suit in front of a full-length mirror, his fingers trembling as he fumbled with buttons and zippers; hallways and elevators and smiling staff. There was an address written on a piece of paper that Dylan found in the jacket pocket, an empty book of matches. At some point he realized he was standing in the lobby of the Hotel Yorick. And that's when he started to scream.

Dylan was sitting in the back of what he thought was an H4, or maybe an H5—whatever the model or year a basic truth remained: This was a military weapon, a vehicle designed for urban combat and now it was being used to ferry Dylan across Tiber City. The idea was so absurd he just had to laugh and even though it was the fall, and it would soon be night—most of the sun had slunk below the horizon—the city was suffering through a massive heat wave and there was a voice on the radio whispering about animals being driven mad by the heat, tearing up their nests and devouring their young, and although there were conflicting reports on the matter, there were two things for certain: These beasts were coming to Tiber City and they were coming soon.

"Hey," Dylan shouted at the driver, banging on the bulletproof partition dividing the front of the vehicle from the back. "You gonna tell me where we're going?"

The driver didn't reply but the voice on the radio seemed to get louder, the host's voice rising, growing hysterical, addressing rumors of an underground network of alchemists responsible for a banking crash, of a res-taurant that had added human flesh to its menu, that entire streets in the Jungle district had begun to vanish, and it was all due to the heat wave but maybe there were other explanations and we can get to those after the break, the voice on the radio assured Dylan before the show cut out, replaced by an ad for gold coins, and Dylan was hitting the partition again, begging the driver to at least turn the fucking radio down but the guy just ignored him. Dylan couldn't even remember what the driver looked like: After having slamming down two shots of whiskey in the bar of the Hotel Yorick, Dylan's hands stopped trembling long enough to call the number on the card and whoever answered the phone—male voice, clipped, gruff, very official—had also ignored Dylan's questions, cutting him off mid-spiel and announcing a Hummer would be parked outside the Yorick in seven to nine minutes and that if Dylan ever wanted to see Meghan Morrison alive again, he'd keep his mouth shut and get in the fucking car. That had gotten his attention.

Seven and a half minutes later, the car arrived. Dylan climbed in and that's how he came to be in the back of an urban assault vehicle dressed in his dead father's favorite suit, with no idea where he was being taken. All he knew was they were blasting down Chiba Street, the four-lane artery that pumped life, and death, into Tiber City's Glimmer district and its mix of clubs and bars, bleeding-edge fashion boutiques and high-end electronics dealers, unmarked warehouses and sex clubs; all of which operated in the shadow of towering skyscrapers, home to multinational giants whose build-ings often went nameless, identified only by a logo.

Outside the car, the very streets themselves seemed to be wilting under the heat; the lines outside the Chiba Street clubs listless, languid, and Dylan leaned back against the leather seats, the lights of the city still visi-ble even after he closed his eyes. He thought about Meghan and he thought about his father; he thought about love and fear and the human soul. He tried not to think about beasts driven mad by the heat, rampaging across abandoned city streets. He replayed the video his father left for him on the flash drive over and over and over in his head; he could cite the old man's journal entries word for word. He tried to piece together any memories he had between the Gas-n-Go and the Hotel Yorick but before he could give order to the disjointed images and sensations rattling around in his skull, the car stopped, the locks popped up, and the door closest to Dylan swung open.

By the time the Humvee rumbled away from the curb, it had started to rain but Dylan was already moving, past a series of guards—Kevlar Knights rocking military-grade automatic weapons—through revolving glass doors and a battery of metal detectors, and into the main lobby of Morrison Biotech's Tiber City headquarters. Security didn't even blink. Neither did Dylan—as soon as he realized the Humvee had stopped in front of the Morrison Biotech building, things seemed a little clearer.

"Use the private elevator down the hall to your left," someone barked at him. "Penthouse level. You're expected."

Aside from the guards, the lobby was empty and Dylan hurried toward the elevator, weaving his way around enormous wrought iron statues—huge abstract beasts that loomed above the lobby like the skeleton of some prehistoric monster. There were televisions mounted on the wall next to the elevators, all tuned to continuing Jack Heffernan retrospectives and remembrances—the same footage that had looped over and over since the assassination: the horrified bystanders, the state funeral, the patsy fingered for the shooting being led in and out of courtrooms wearing shackles and a bulletproof vest on top of an orange prison jumpsuit, every last detail presented in gorgeous hyper-definition video. Allegedly the country was still in mourning and even as a smorgasbord of "religious leaders" mugged for the cameras, touting a "time of healing," the news ticker running under the video testified to the contrary: a gunman holed up in an elementary school outside of Albuquerque, a celebrity overdose in the Hollywood hills—life rolled on.

Dylan stepped onto the elevator and the doors snapped shut behind him, soundless, and then he was moving up and the walls of the building fell away: The elevator continued its ascent behind one-way, rain-streaked glass, rising 10, 20, 30 stories above the Tiber City streets.

As the elevator moved up through the darkness, the city followed him, a monster of steel and neon, pushing through the sizzling rain. Plumes of smoke and smog and gas drifted up from the city's maze of streets and alleyways, desperate offerings to an indifferent deity. As the elevator continued to rise, the city seemed to glow radioactive, the lights from the individual multinationals melting together, glowing with a menace that might, at any second, break loose and spill out across the entire city, country, world. Maybe that was why the entire city seemed to climb vertical—it was a desperate attempt to escape the terrestrial, like a starving rat, determined to gnaw its way into the celestial.

"Penthouse level," a vaguely female voice informed Dylan as the elevator glided to a stop. The doors slid open, revealing an office that might have been any other executive suite in Tiber City—if every other executive suite came with walls adorned with Zero Movement data feeds, a fireplace surrounded by black leather chrome-base coconut chairs, floor-to-ceiling windows offering a panoramic view of Tiber City. Michael Morrison was standing in front of the glass, dressed immaculately in a dark Armani suit, white shirt, and a deep crimson tie, his hands clasped behind his back as he stared out into the Tiber City night.

"Welcome, Mr. Fitzgerald." Morrison said as he turned away from the window, smiling. "Nice suit."

"You motherfucker," Dylan growled, as he moved toward Morrison, each step deliberate, cautious. He scanned the room for a potential weapon but there was only a desk with a computer, the flickering of the Zero art, and the glow of the city outside the window. "Why did you bring me here?"

Raising a bandaged right hand, Morrison made a sweeping gesture toward the fireplace at the back of the office. Dylan spun around, his stomach dropping when he saw the strands of dark hair spilling over the back of one of the chairs facing the lifeless hearth.

Dylan shot across the room, calling Meghan's name but she didn't respond. Kneeling beside the chair, he took her pulse—it was strong. He stroked her cheek with his fingers, whispering to her, trying to wake her—he couldn't.

Standing up, he turned back toward Morrison, his fists clenched, his face twisted with rage.

"Meghan's fine," Morrison said, although his tone was even, his smile was cold and the hint of menace was unmistakable. "She is simply my means of ensuring your undivided attention. So I wouldn't worry about her right now. Instead, I'd worry about myself. I'd worry that because some crazy old man's been whispering in my ear, or because I read some scribblings my dead daddy left behind, I was going to do something stupid. "

Dylan felt the surprise register across his face.

"Oh yes," Morrison continued, "I know all about Campbell and the things he told you. I know more than you could possibly imagine. In fact, I know a great deal of things, particularly about your daddy, that you might not know."

"Like how it felt to watch him die," Dylan said, his anger growing, radiating from his belly to his limbs in white-hot bursts.

"Do you want to know the truth about your father," Morrison asked.

Dylan held Morrison's gaze for a moment and then nodded.

"Then shut the fuck up and listen," Morrison snarled. The sound of rain pelting the outside of the tower filled the room and Morrison lit a cigarette.

"Toward the end of the Cold War," Morrison began, "the U.S. government decided a new generation of leaders was needed to lead our lost nation back to greatness. God's design was no longer good enough; there were too many mistakes, too many limitations. Project Exodus was launched in response to these limitations. This was before Morrison Biotech even existed; it was just Campbell and myself and a handful of other researchers. Only Campbell and I knew the truth. And even then, Campbell lacked the vision, the drive, to grasp what Exodus was truly capable of—the birth of a new man, one who would stand outside the limitations of God and the natural world. That man was your father."

Dylan was shaking his head; he wanted Morrison to stop, but he needed him to continue.

"I created your father in the Exodus laboratories miles under the Chihuahuan desert," Morrison continued, his words slithering out across the room, swirling around Dylan. "The only womb he ever knew was made of silicon and microprocessors. He represented the first great success of Exodus: An 18-year-old man, born fully developed with a set of implanted memories. The first man ever made by man."

Outside the rain began to fall harder and the wind picked up, rattling the windows and for a moment it felt like the entire tower was swaying and the power flickered once, twice, but held.

"There was only a single human gene Project Exodus failed to identify," Morrison said. "A gene that seemed to have no function; to serve no purpose. So we went ahead and created your father without this gene, which we dubbed 'the Omega Gene.' At first, it appeared Omega was indeed superfluous. I believe your father's…suicide proved just how wrong we were.

"So we tried again, this time with Jack Heffernan. Only in Heffernan's case, we actually replicated the Omega gene and included it in his genetic code. Yet, even with this artificial Omega gene, Heffernan still suffered the same meltdowns as your father.

"It wasn't until recently that I learned the truth behind the Omega gene—that it is the gene responsible for connecting man with his Creator, with God. You see Mr. Fitzgerald, the Omega gene is the human soul."

Dylan flashed back to the strange hospital, to the sensation of nodes being attached to his forehead, to the whirl of machines, and the stories an old man whispered into his ear: of the desert, of his father, of the human soul. Another explosion boomed somewhere outside the tower and the lights flickered in response, the grid overloaded and unlikely to hold.

"But deducing the identity of the Omega gene did nothing to advance the goals of Exodus," Morrison continued. "No, there was still one final question I needed to answer: Does Dylan Fitzgerald have a soul? The Omega gene manifests itself in a certain type of activity in the human brain. Your father's brain never experienced this type of activity; neither did Heffernan's. In fact, none of the prototypes we created before your father did. But the tests we ran on you revealed you not only have a soul, but that your soul is particularly sensitive to whatever external, possibly divine, stimuli engages with the Omega gene. Yet, curiously enough, there are times when your Omega activity drops to abnormally low levels as well. If you could find a way to harness that activity, to control and direct it…you could be the one to accomplish everything your father could not."

From every side of the office, Zero art flashed and swirled, shapes appearing on the digital canvas then vanishing back into the void, only to be replaced, seconds later, by another explosion of information given shape by a someone somewhere across the globe, maybe across the street, and as Morrison spoke and the screens roiled Dylan waited for the perfect moment to strike out and destroy the man who destroyed his father.

"Come with me," Morrison said and Dylan followed him out onto the balcony, waiting for his opportunity. Tiber City spread out before them, beautiful and terrible.

"This is yours for the taking," Morrison was telling Dylan, his voice low and seductive. "Not just Tiber City, but all the cities of the world. Power. Women. Treasure. Men will call you lord and master and crawl on their bellies before you. From every end of the earth, they will proclaim your glory and herald the dawn of a new age for mankind."

Dylan said nothing, he only nodded: If he squinted, the lights on the horizon bled together until there was no distinction between anything, just the profane uniformity of 21st-century America. A dark fantasy flashed across his mind: He saw himself in the desert, standing atop the tallest mountain, and all around him people were gathered, crying out exaltations and lamentations, flesh pressed together, arms and hands outstretched; he was ruler and he was lord but Meghan was nowhere to be seen and artifice and fear were the only currencies in this strange land. He would never know the Connection again; he would exist forever on the surface of things, separate from God and his fellow man, utterly alone. But he would be king.

Morrison was right—it was his kingdom for the taking, just as it was his father's. But like his father, Dylan just didn't want it.

"Listen to them," Morrison whispered, "they call your name..."

"It's not real," Dylan growled, cutting Morrison off. The vision vanished.

"But it can be," Morrison was assuring him. "Everything you want, you can have. There are no limits..."

"Did you kill my father?" Dylan asked.

His tone was low but steady and a look of surprise flashed across Morrison's tan, tight face but then it passed and Morrison seemed to be considering the question. Thunder rumbled in the distance, and the wind was blasting so hard the rain was blowing sideways, pelting the two men facing each other on a balcony dozens of stories above Tiber City.

"Did you kill my father?" Dylan repeated, raising his voice and taking a step toward Morrison.

"What does that even matter," Morrison snarled, raising his voice over the sound of the rain, "when I am offering to make you into a god?"

"Did. You. Kill. My. Father," Dylan demanded, again, his voice little more than a whisper, barely audible over the rain and the thunder. Lighting cracked over the city, a hard, jagged strike capable of splitting the earth in half.

"Yes, yes," Morrison was shouting, his tie gone, torn off and flung over the balcony. "I killed your old man. Just like I killed your cunt of a mother. And just like I'll slit my whore of a daughter's throat if you don't join me."

Morrison paused and then, lowering his voice, added:

"Of course, I'll wait to do that one until after your son is born. After all, if you won't join Exodus, perhaps your child will."

Dylan's mouth opened but no sound came out, his eyes wide in disbelief. Morrison began to laugh—a mean, bemused chuckle.

"Oh, you didn't know?" Morrison was asking as Dylan's world slowed, blurred, wobbled. "I thought she had told you. I guess she wanted it to be a surprise...Well, surprise."

Morrison was laughing as the world snapped back into focus and then Dylan was charging through the rain, swinging at Morrison. He connected with a wild right haymaker, flesh and bone slamming into flesh and bone and Morrison reeled backward, landing against the glass partition with an audible thud. But the glass didn't break and although his lower lip was busted wide-open, blood teeming onto his oxford button-down shirt, he was still on his feet.

Morrison wiped his lip with the back of his hand and spit blood onto the tile before starting back across the balcony toward Dylan, his eyes radiating hatred. He could feel the Treatment surging through his blood, accelerating his nervous system, the pain inflicted by Dylan's blows already receding.

"You stupid, stupid boy," Morrison was shouting as he moved toward Dylan. "I'll raise your son as my own. Everything I've offered to you, he will inherit."

Morrison lunged at Dylan, and Dylan twisted to the right, toward the railing, and although he moved fast he didn't move fast enough: Morrison's fist smashed into his ribs with an audible crack and then Morrison was on him, the old man's arms like pistons, pounding Dylan's body with an inhuman fury.

Lightening flashed overhead and there was an explosion in the distance, the sound of a massive transformer blowing, followed seconds later by the frantic moan of sirens. All across Tiber City, the lights began to falter, fade, and Morrison paused, allowing Dylan an opportunity to roll away, across the balcony, but there was nowhere to go and Dylan could only brace himself as Morrison came at him again, grinning like a madman, as he unleashed a fury of jabs.

But the balcony was slick with rain and sweat and before Morrison could land another punch he slipped and a second after Morrison hit the floor Dylan was on top of him, straddling his chest as he rained blows down on the man's face, pummeling it with a grim determination. He felt Morrison's nose break—the cartilage bent sideways as Morrison howled with rage, his face a crimson mask.

And then Dylan was wrapping his hands around Morrison's throat, squeezing so hard he thought he might pass out, the rain and wind strafing the balcony with such fury that Dylan could barely see; his world was a narrow window of blood and rain and the feeling of Michael Morrison's neck between his hands—slippery with soft mushy veins and a windpipe that felt impossibly fragile—and Dylan kept squeezing, watching Morrison's face contort, waiting for the end but the end didn't come: Morrison's hand shot up, his fist driving into Dylan's ruined ribcage.

Dylan yelped in agony, his grip on Morrison's neck broken. Staggering away from the old man, Dylan's momentum drove him backward until he crashed into the railing. The pain exploded through his entire body, and so when he first saw Meghan appear in the doorway to the office, he thought he was hallucinating. But then Meghan was stepping out onto the balcony, moving through the rain, toward him, her hair getting wet, sticking to her forehead, his blood staining her shirt as he crashed into her arms before collapsing to his knees. Looking up at her, he reached out and put his hand on her stomach, wondering if he would survive this night, wondering if he would ever meet his son—a son! He was going to be a father, and this realization drove him past the pain and back onto his feet just as Morrison was pulling himself off the tile, lunging for Meghan, the man's face a wreck of crimson and snot and sinew.

Morrison managed a single step toward Meghan before Dylan was on him, hammering him back against the balcony; Morrison's fingers clawing the wet concrete, seeking traction because he could hear the horrible roar of the city below; he could feel Tiber swell in anticipation; an impatient god, greedy for sacrifice.

Then Dylan hit him again—a direct blow right above the old man's heart—and then Morrison was tumbling over the edge of the balcony, slicing through the darkness, and as he fell toward the earth, Michael Morrison wondered if he had a soul.

Epilogue

Central America
Spring 2016

On the first day of spring, three men set out across the desert. They crossed the southern border and continued to push south, scouring the shantytowns for news of the young couple. Most turned away; others just shook their heads and stared at the earth. There were some, however, who took the men aside and offered what information they could—the older denizens of these desert lands knew these men; they remembered when things were different and so they spoke of the girl and the boy: how the girl had long black hair and was clutching her swollen belly; how the boy walked with a limp and held the girl's hand.

The men asked which way the couple had gone.

The ones willing to help could only point south.

These were not young men and their bones ached from the constant travel, the constant searching; from the wind and the relentless blast of desert sand and stone. But there was no time to rest; other men were hunting the couple as well; dark men who covered their faces and brought tidings of war and famine and civil unrest to these desert lands.

The radio crackled with news of Tiber City burning; of martial law and tanks in the street. The men turned the radio off and pressed ahead.

As they moved through the desert, sightings of the couple intensified; new signs of life were appearing where before, there had been only death. A shadow still lingered in these lands, however, and the men feared they would be too late.

One month after they had set out, the three men found the couple. The child had been born two days earlier in a tiny motel room on the edge of the desert. The girl had insisted on no doctors; on no help: The danger was too great.

The boy answered the door but he was no longer a boy; he was a man and the girl was a woman; their faces hardened by the sand and the wind and the sleepless nights: Months had aged them years but the man's eyes were still a deep blue, the same blue that was in his child's eyes, and he held the door open with his left hand; there was gun clenched in his right.

The three men rolled up their sleeves to reveal an identical tattoo etched across each man's forearm: an asterisk inside of a circle—the symbol of the Order.

"It's time," the first man said.

Acknowledgements

I would like to thank:
My wife, Whitney, for her love, support, and refusal to accept my bullshit;
Jack O'Connell, for his patience, friendship, and the guidance that made this book possible;
My mother and father, who believed in me;
Robert Cording, for the discussions that sparked this book;
Colin Heffernan, for always listening and reading;
John Heffernan, for his insights and early support;
Karina Rollins, for her killer early edits;
Sean Moran, for the early read and great music;
Rebecca Smith, for helping bring this story to life; and
My son Lochlain, for giving me a reason.

Made in the USA
Lexington, KY
20 August 2013